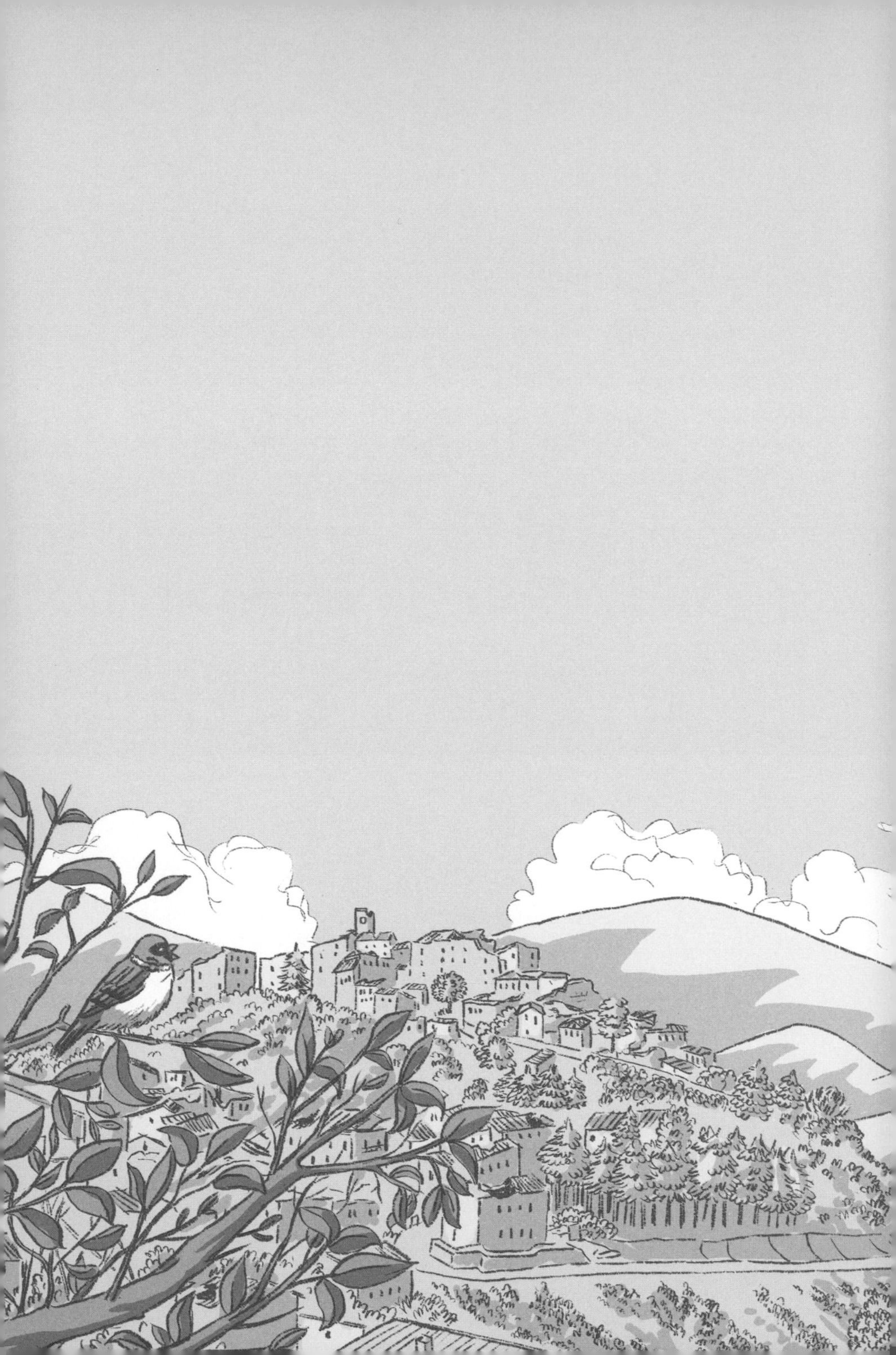

Silvia Vecchini • Sualzo

THE RED ZONE
AN EARTHQUAKE STORY

AMULET BOOKS • NEW YORK

Cataloging-in-Publication Data has been applied for and may be obtained from the Library of Congress.

ISBN 978-1-4197-3368-0

Text and illustrations copyright © 2019 Editrice Il Castoro Srl
Originally published in 2017 under the title *La Zona Rossa* by Editrice Il Castoro viale Andrea Doria 7, Milano, Italy.
Written and Illustrated by Silvia Vecchini and Sualzo
Color by Claudia Giuliani
English translation by Anna Barton

The poem cited on p. 105 is "Un papavero" by Walter Cremonte, published in *Con amore e squallore*, Associazione Culturale La Luna, 2016.

Printed and bound in China
10 9 8 7 6 5 4 3 2 1

Amulet Books are available at special discounts when purchased in quantity for premiums and promotions as well as fundraising or educational use. Special editions can also be created to specification. For details, contact specialsales@abramsbooks.com or the address below.

Amulet Books® is a registered trademark of Harry N. Abrams, Inc.

ABRAMS The Art of Books
195 Broadway, New York, NY 10007
abramsbooks.com

for all who have lost someone
for all who have lost their own home
for all who have felt the giant turtle move
for all who have known fear
for all who are still hurt whatever the reason
for all who despite everything still look at a poppy
as something lasting
for all who pull themselves together each day
and don't forget the gold.

– S.V. and S.

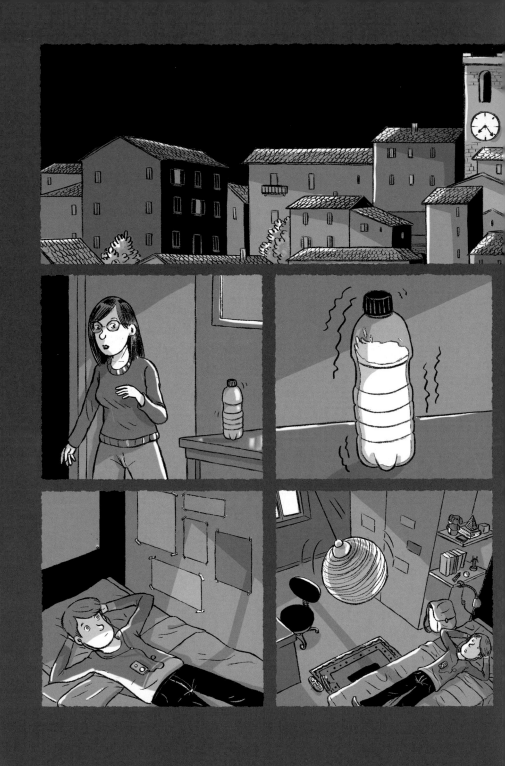

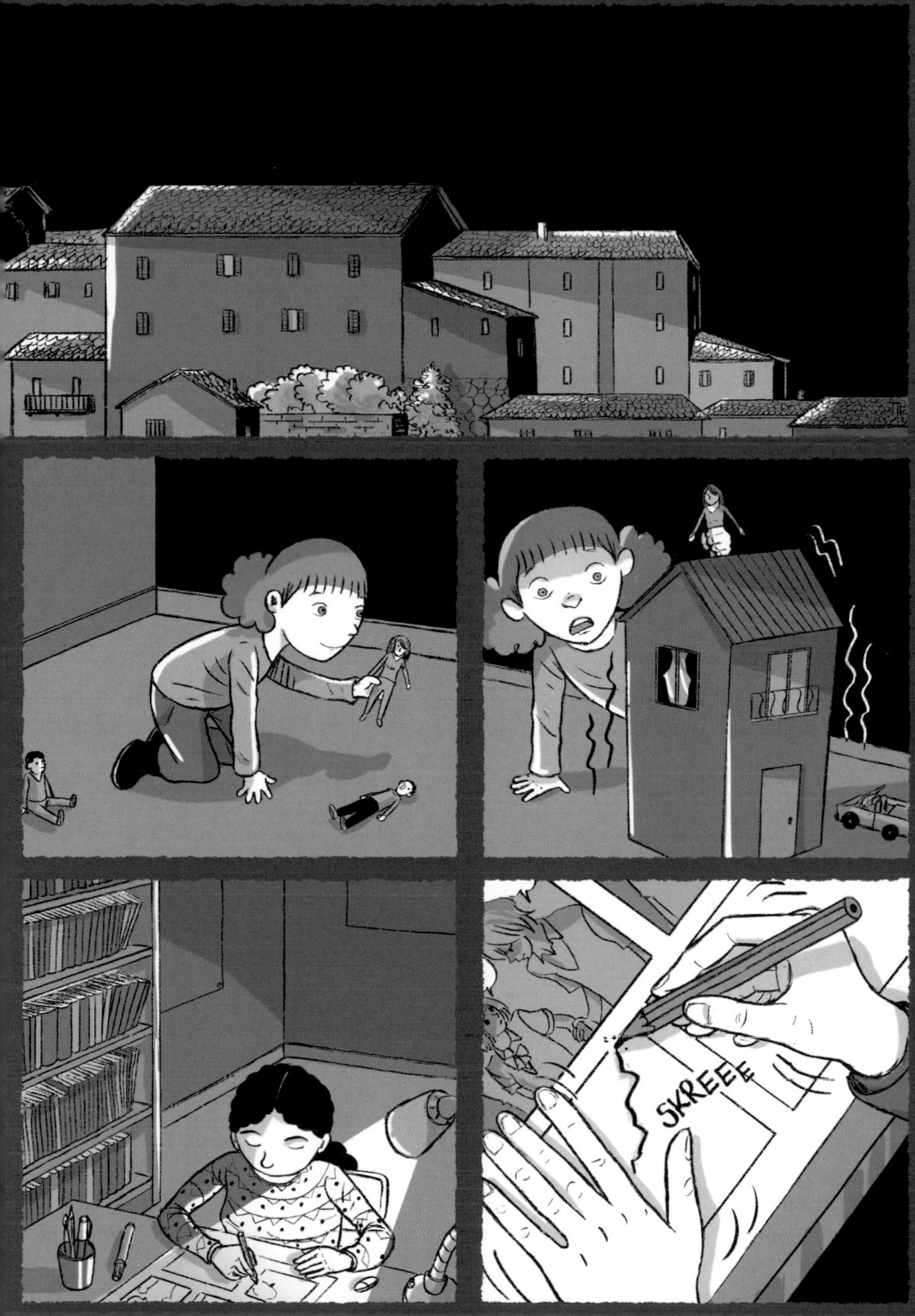
SKREEE

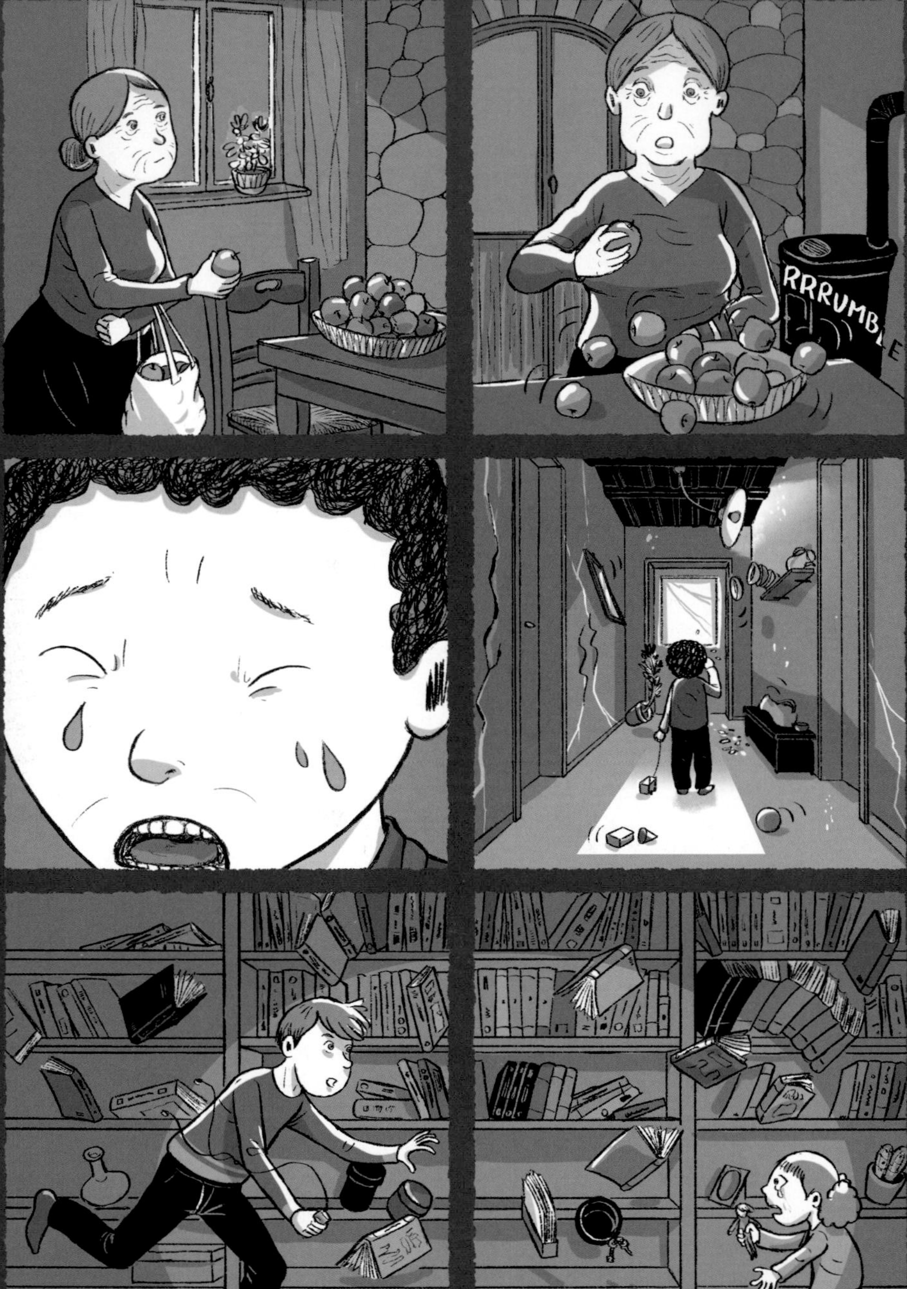
RRRUMBLE

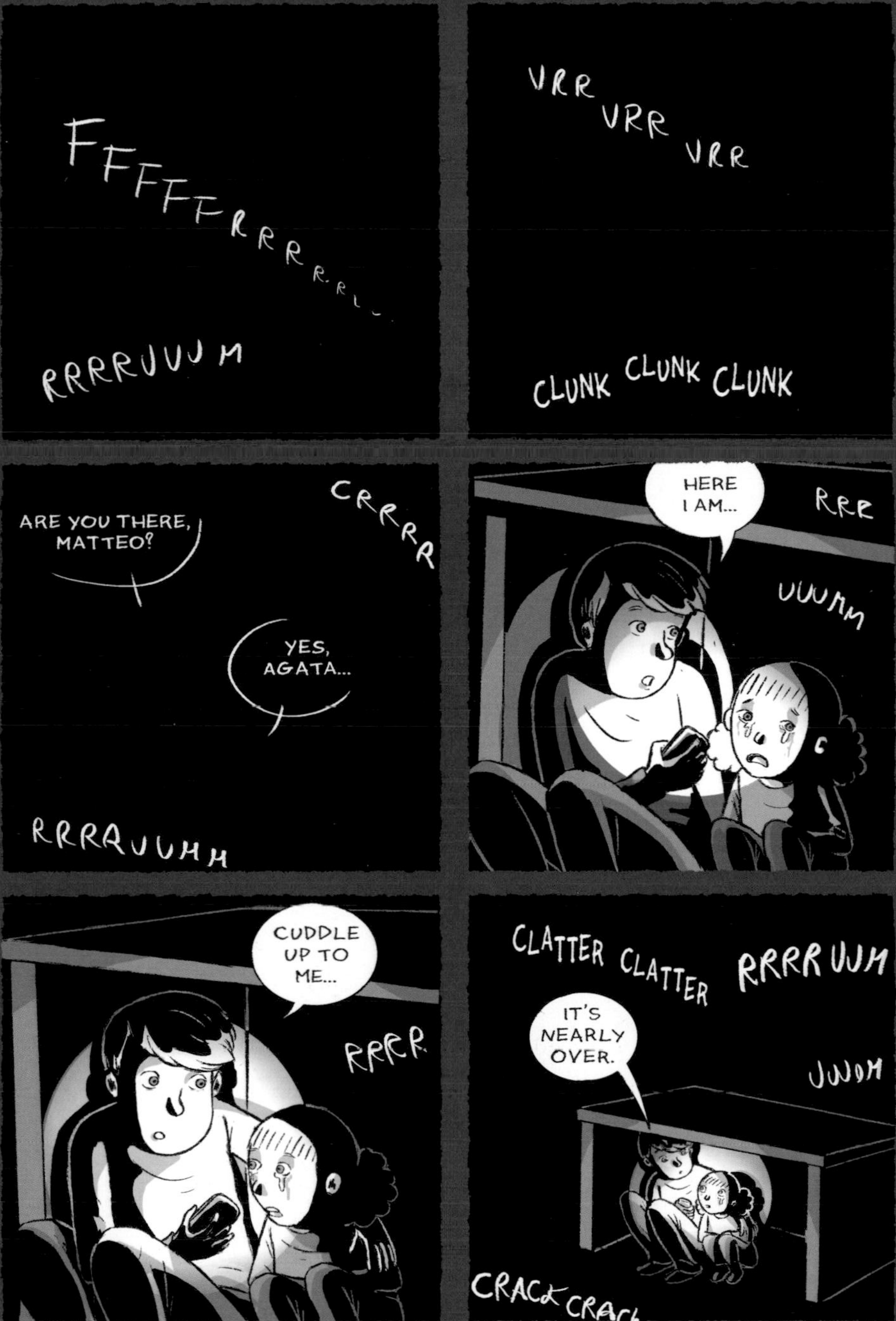
FFFFFRRRRRRLL
RRRRUUUM
VRR VRR VRR
CLUNK CLUNK CLUNK
CRRRRR
ARE YOU THERE, MATTEO?
YES, AGATA...
RRRRUUMM
HERE I AM...
RRR
UUUMM
CUDDLE UP TO ME...
RRRR
CLATTER CLATTER
RRRRUUM
IT'S NEARLY OVER.
UUOM
CRACK CRACK

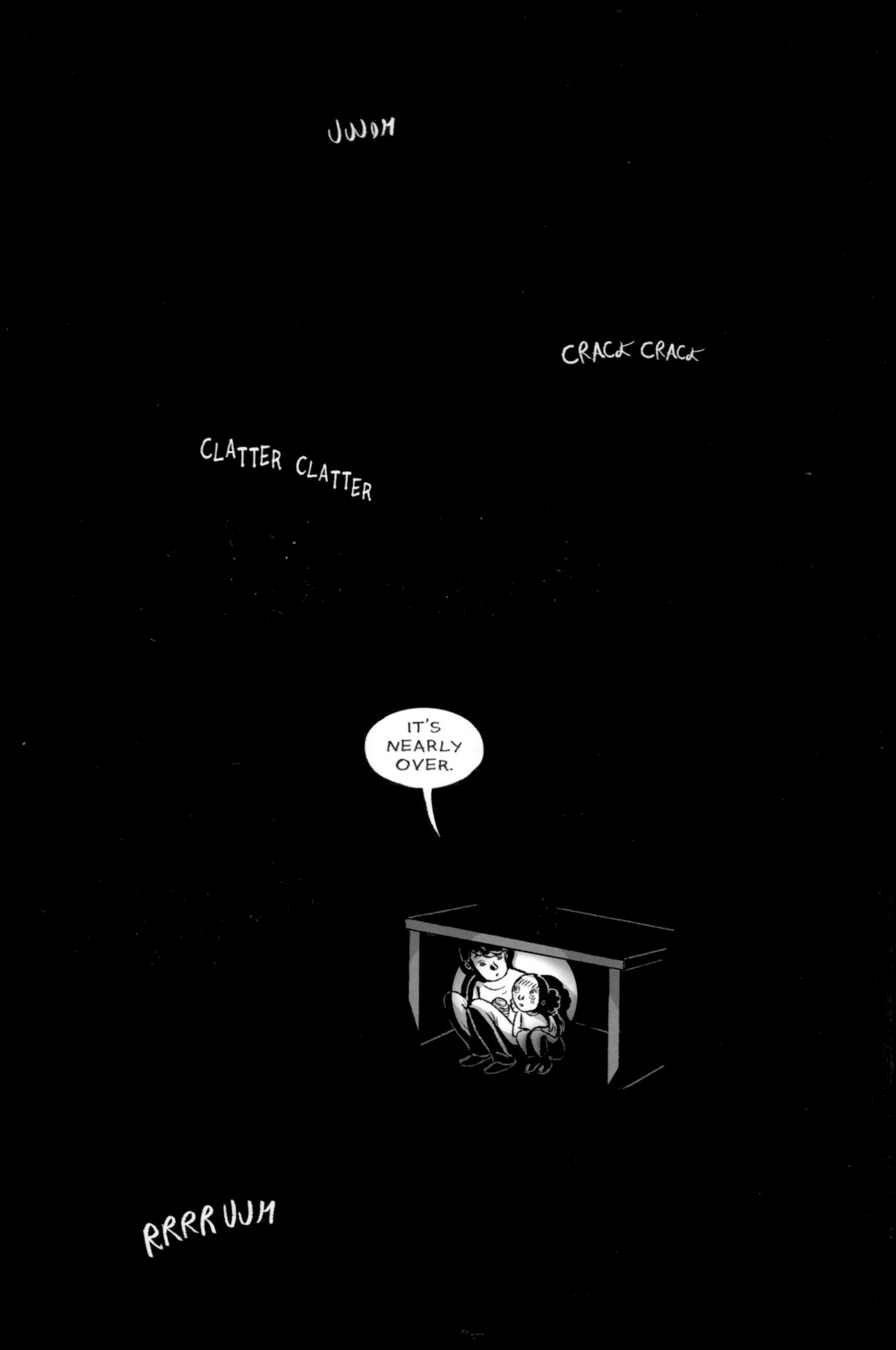
UWOM
CRACK CRACK
CLATTER CLATTER
IT'S NEARLY OVER.
RRRRUUM

1.

In which the sheep don't go to the sea.

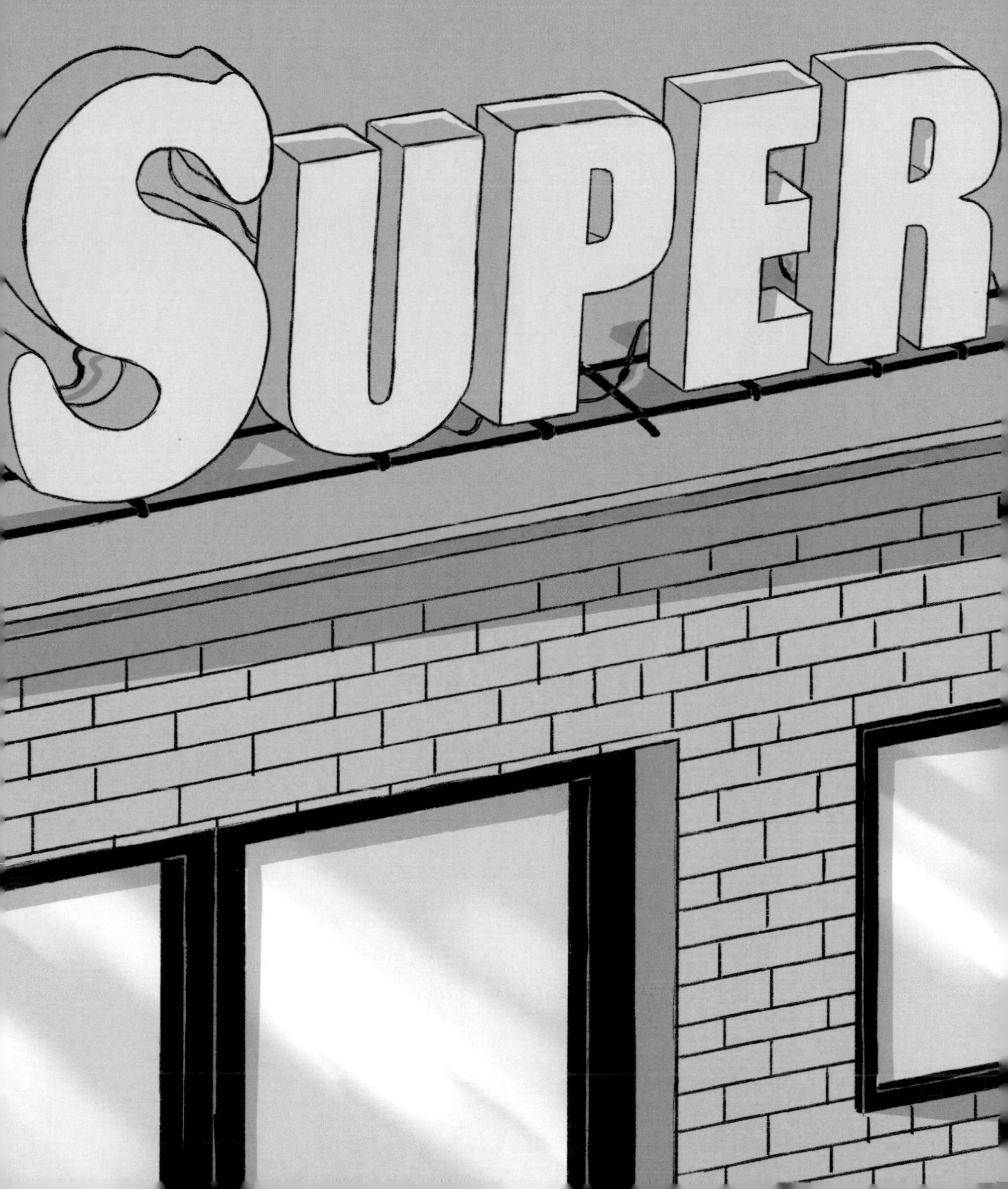
SUPER

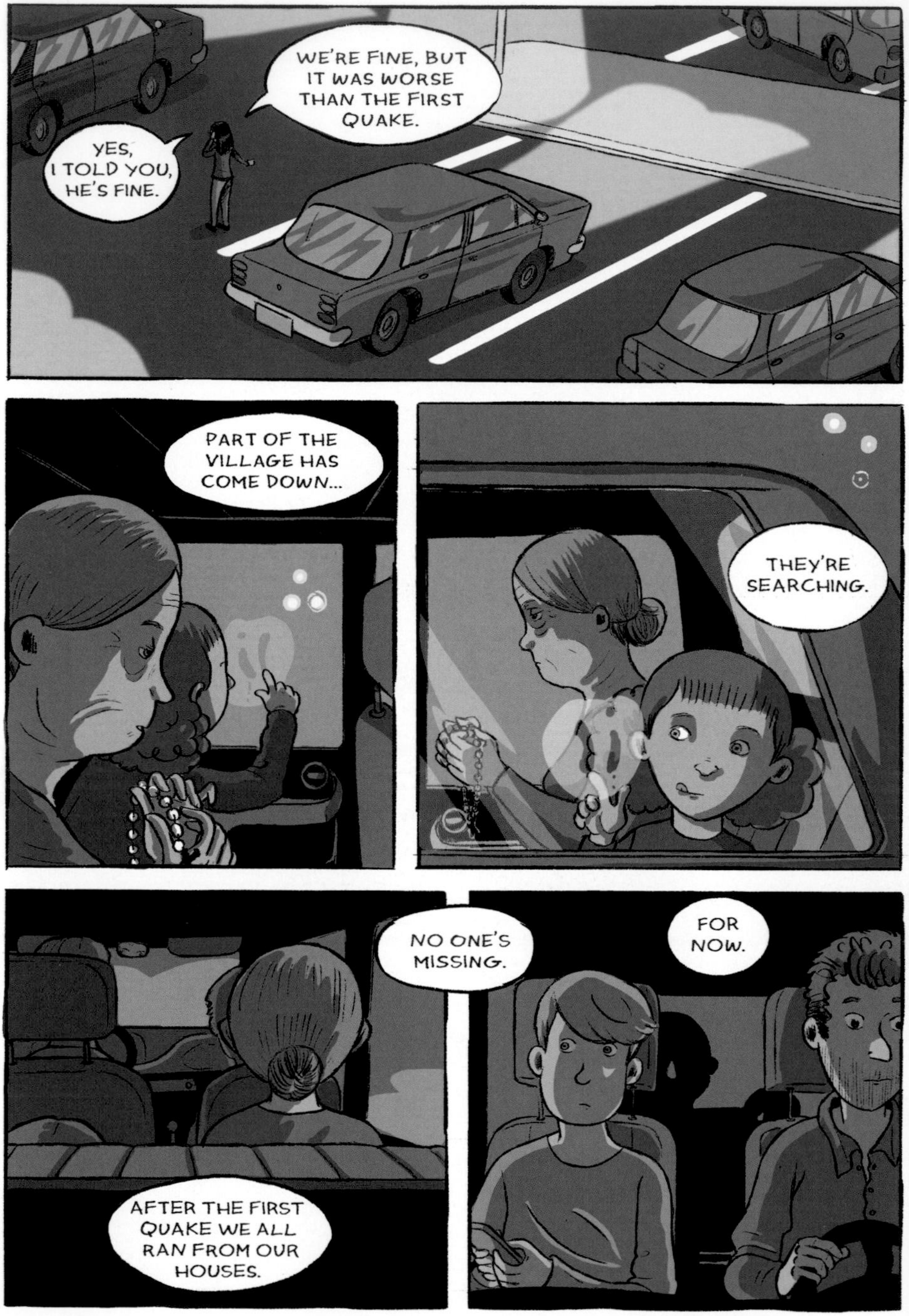
WE'RE FINE, BUT IT WAS WORSE THAN THE FIRST QUAKE.
YES, I TOLD YOU, HE'S FINE.
PART OF THE VILLAGE HAS COME DOWN...
THEY'RE SEARCHING.
NO ONE'S MISSING.
AFTER THE FIRST QUAKE WE ALL RAN FROM OUR HOUSES.
FOR NOW.

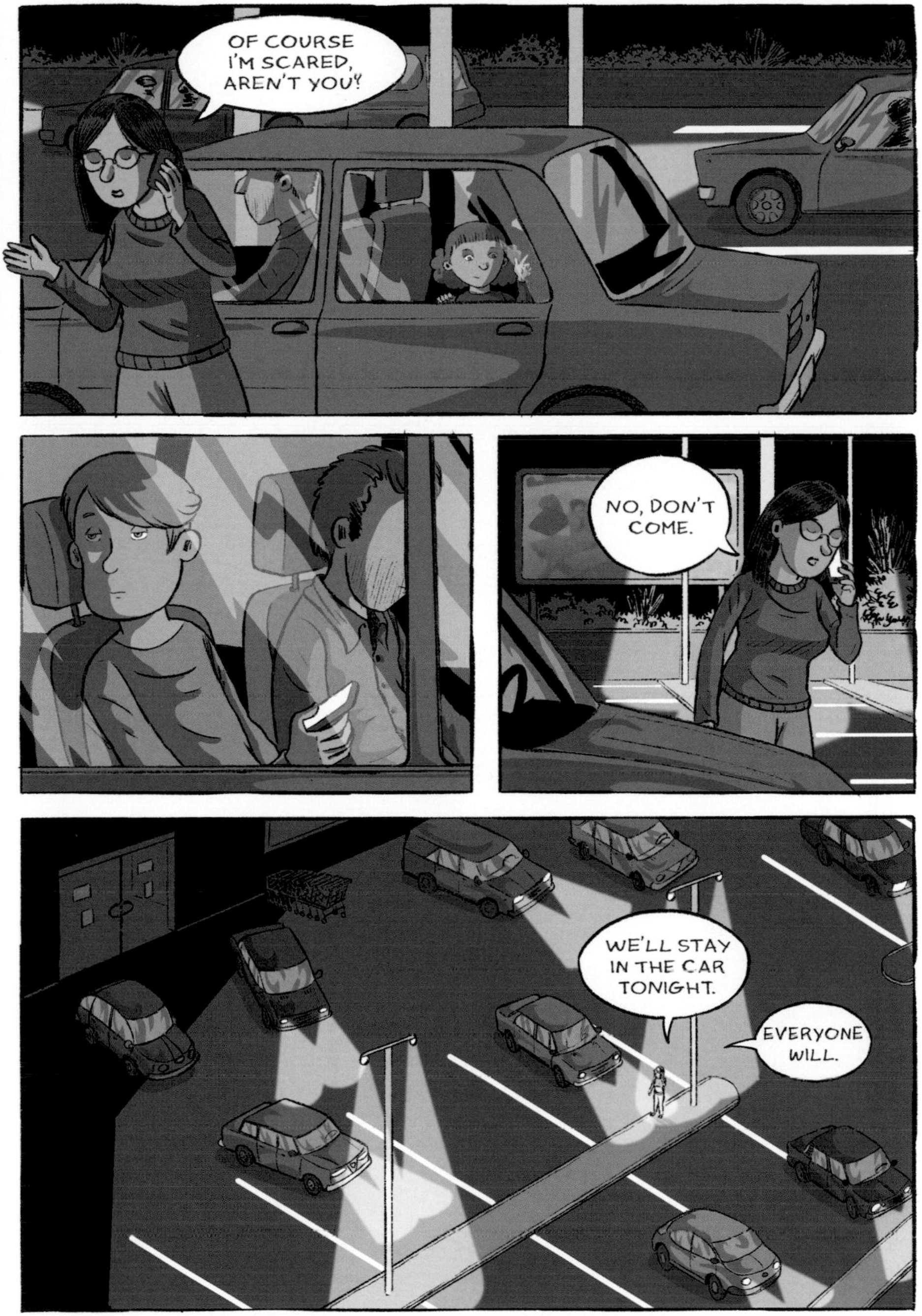
OF COURSE I'M SCARED, AREN'T YOU?
NO, DON'T COME.
WE'LL STAY IN THE CAR TONIGHT.
EVERYONE WILL.

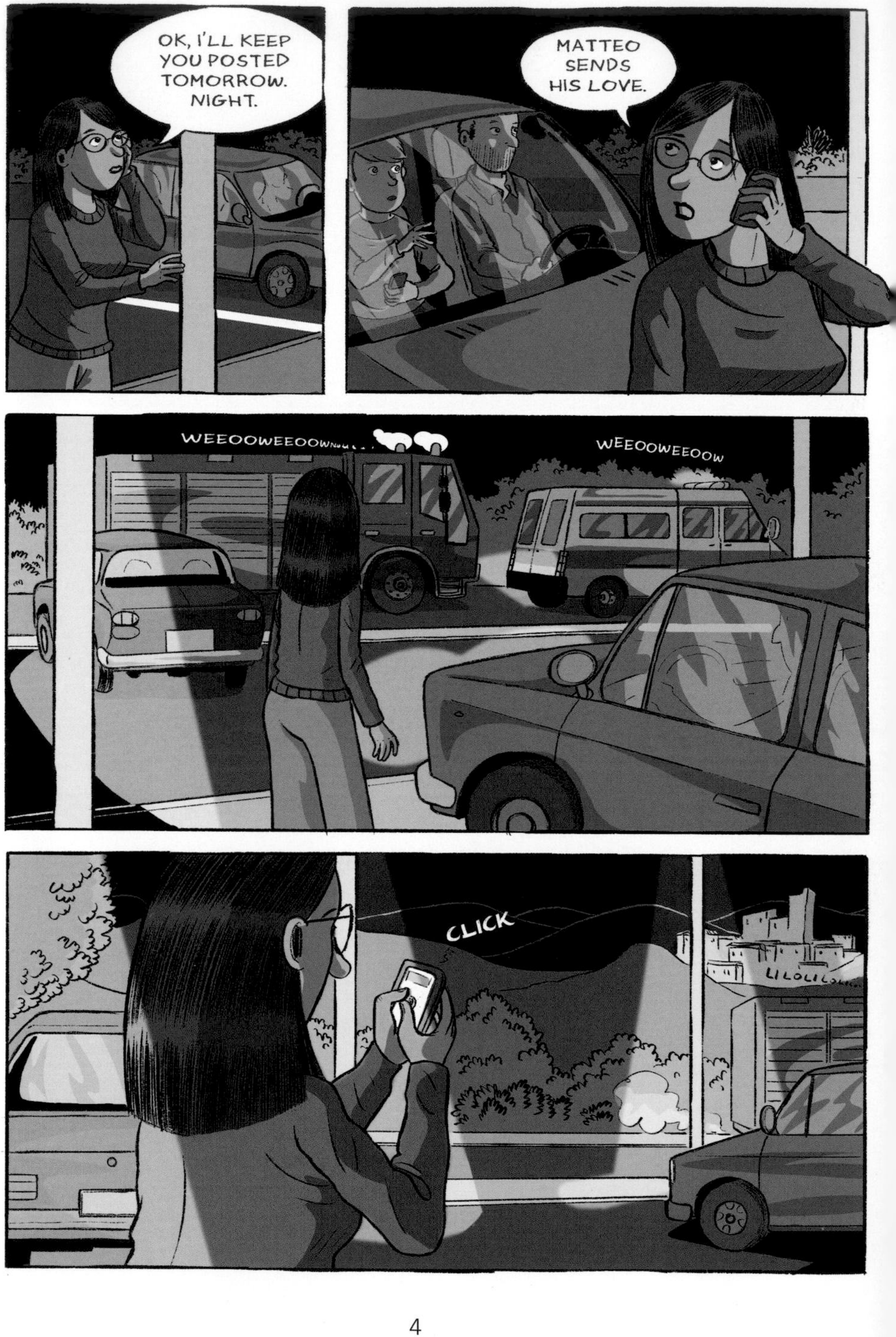
OK, I'LL KEEP YOU POSTED TOMORROW. NIGHT.
MATTEO SENDS HIS LOVE.
WEEOOWEEOOW
WEEOOWEEOOW
CLICK
LILOLILO

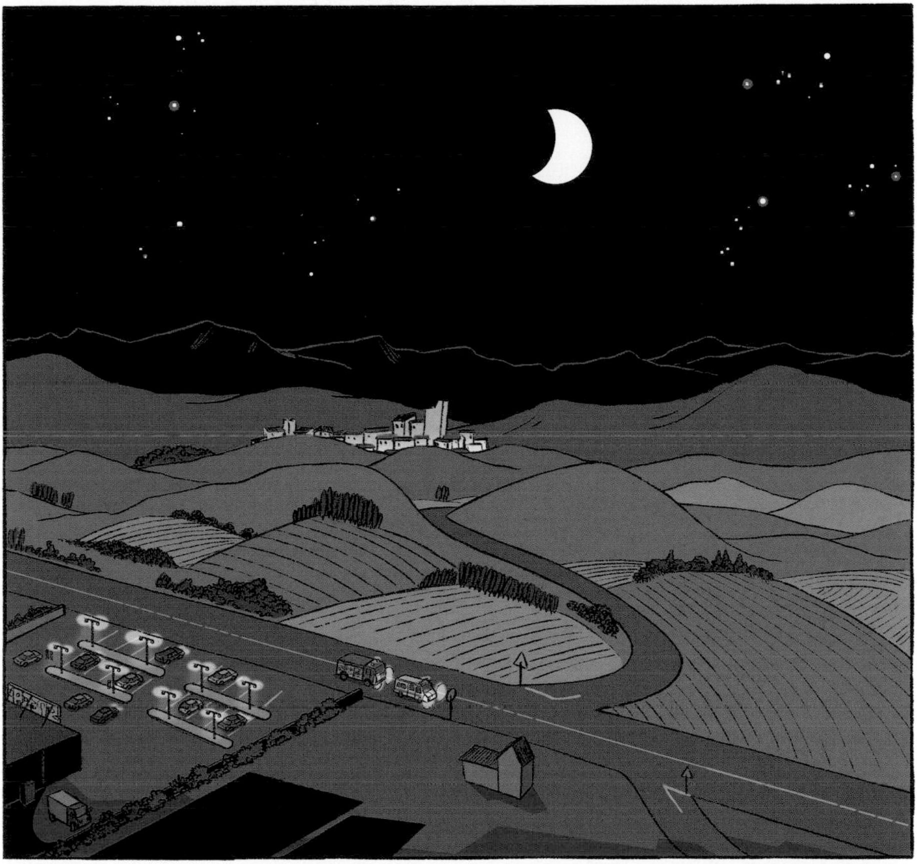

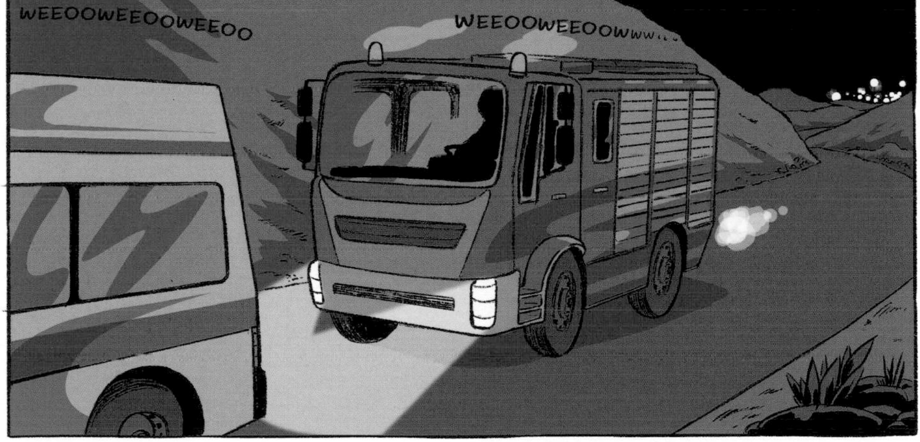
WEEOOWEEOOWEEOO
WEEOOWEEOOWWW...

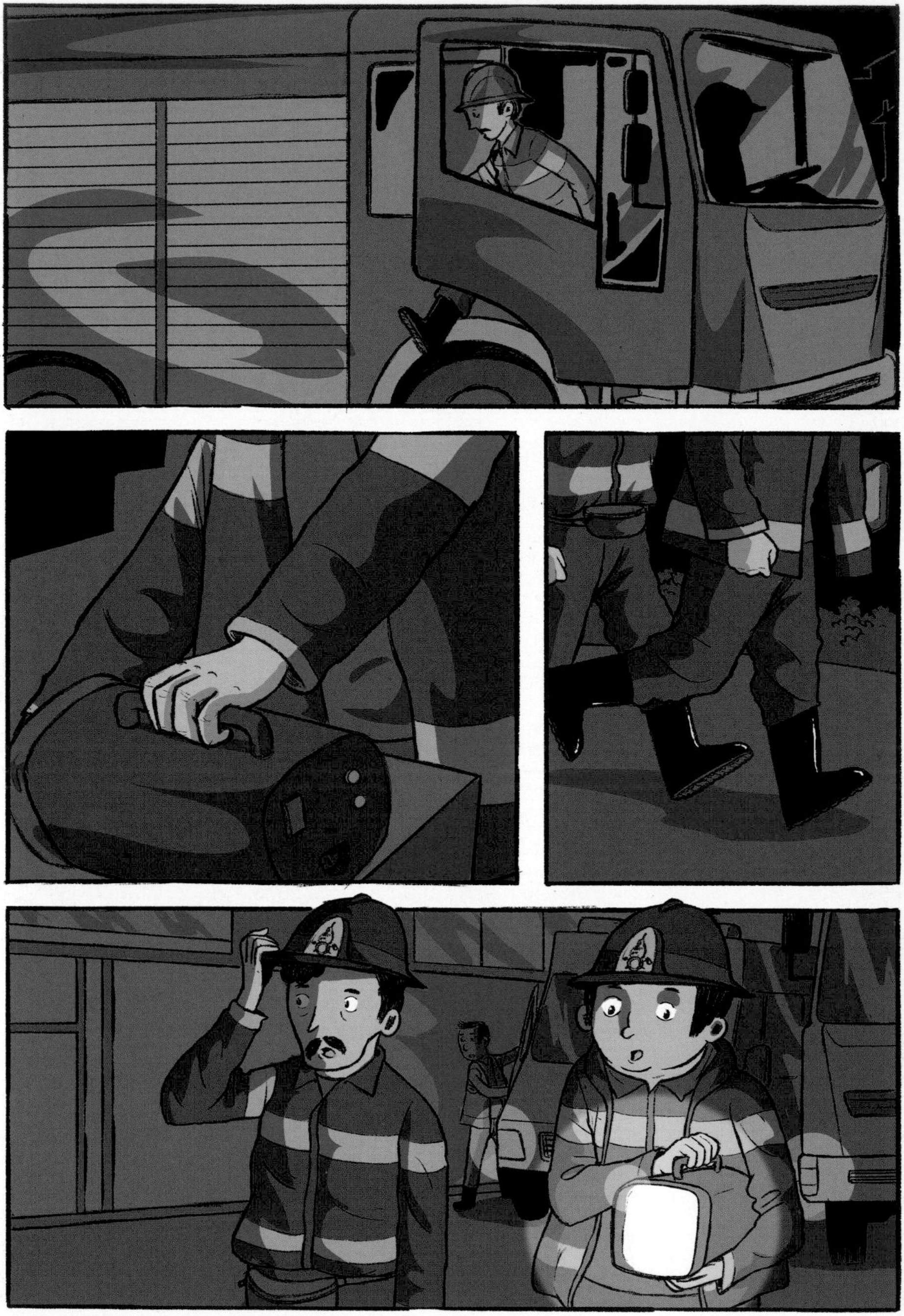

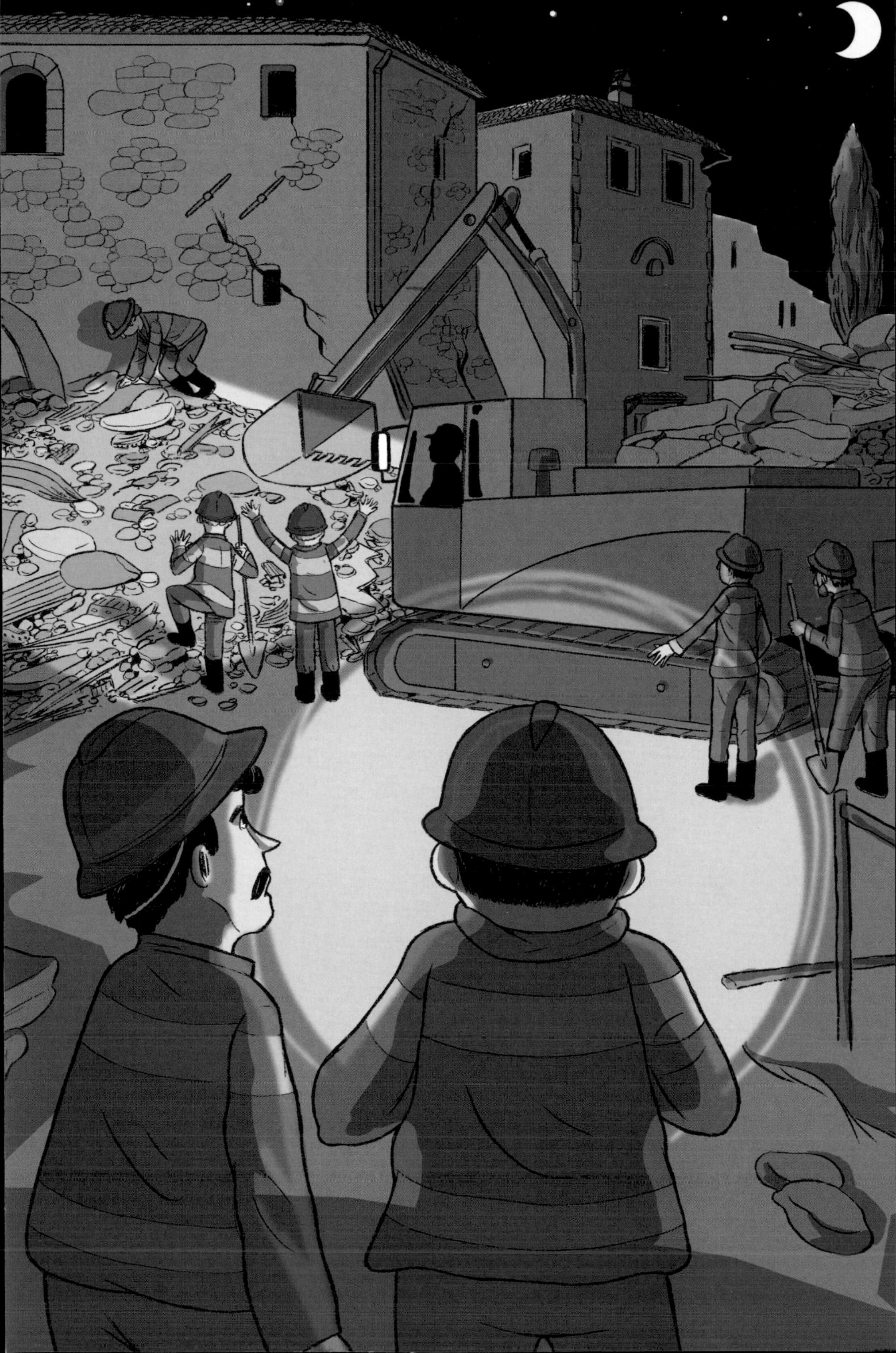

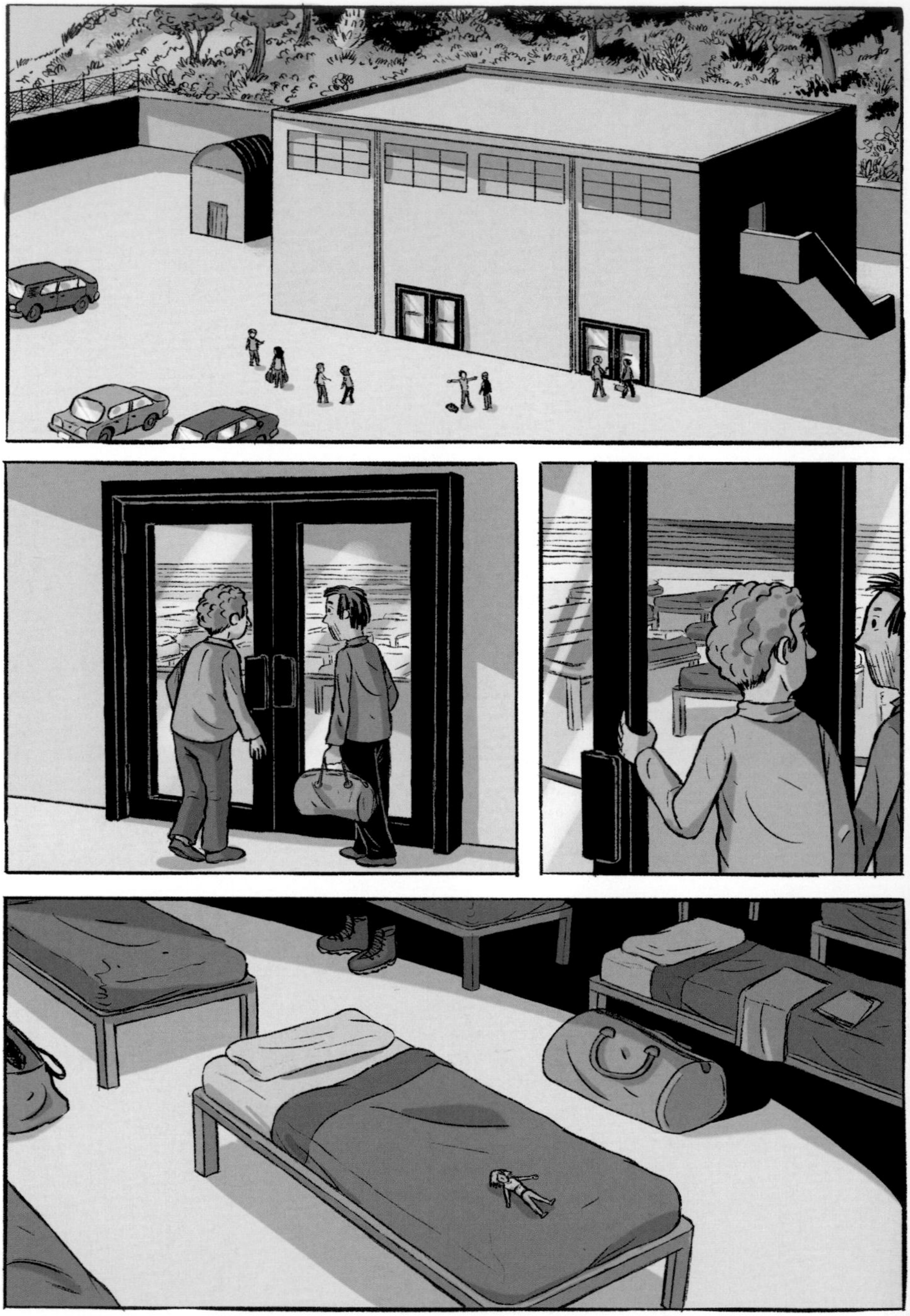

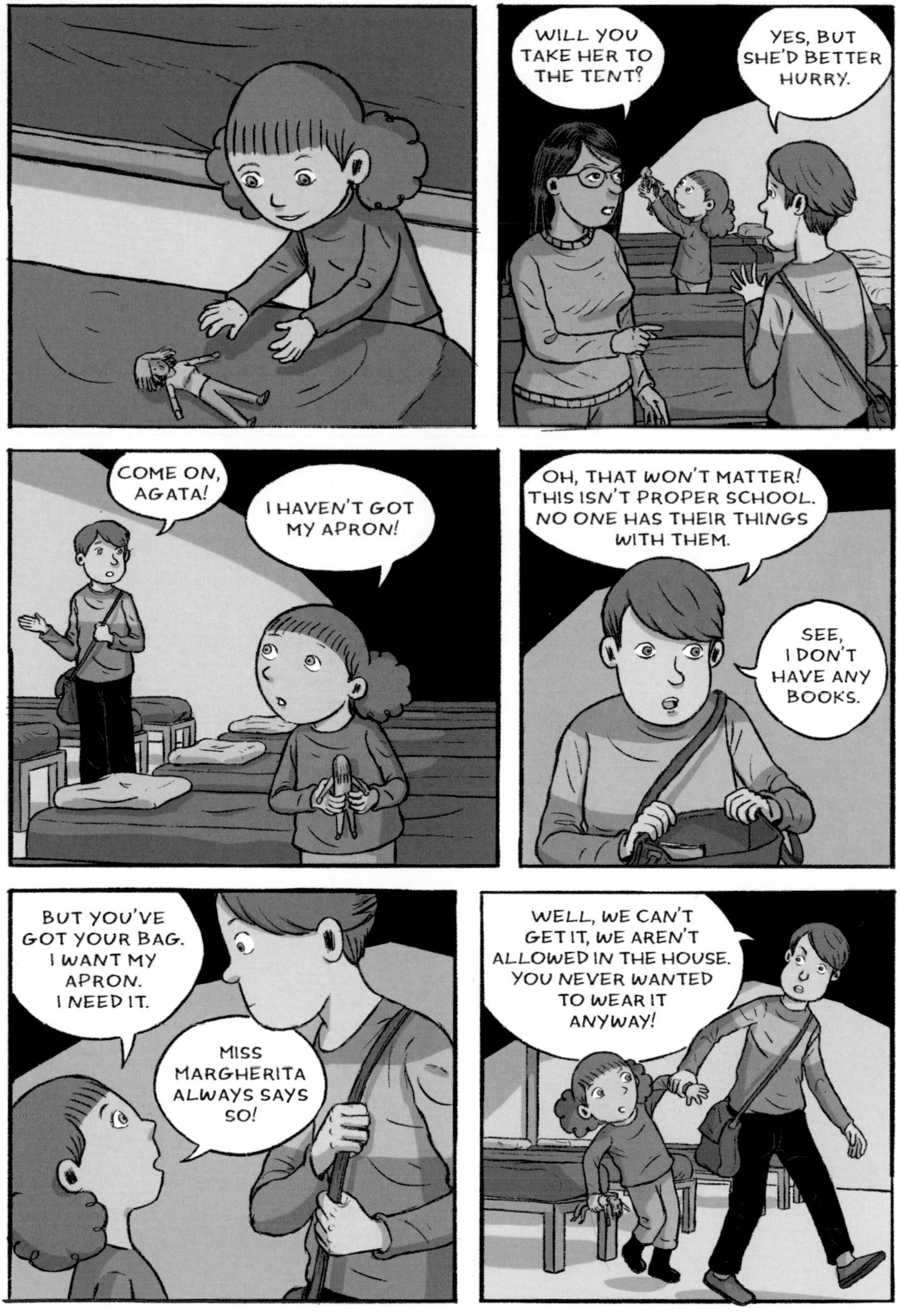
WILL YOU TAKE HER TO THE TENT?
YES, BUT SHE'D BETTER HURRY.
COME ON, AGATA!
I HAVEN'T GOT MY APRON!
OH, THAT WON'T MATTER! THIS ISN'T PROPER SCHOOL. NO ONE HAS THEIR THINGS WITH THEM.
SEE, I DON'T HAVE ANY BOOKS.
BUT YOU'VE GOT YOUR BAG. I WANT MY APRON. I NEED IT.
MISS MARGHERITA ALWAYS SAYS SO!
WELL, WE CAN'T GET IT, WE AREN'T ALLOWED IN THE HOUSE. YOU NEVER WANTED TO WEAR IT ANYWAY!

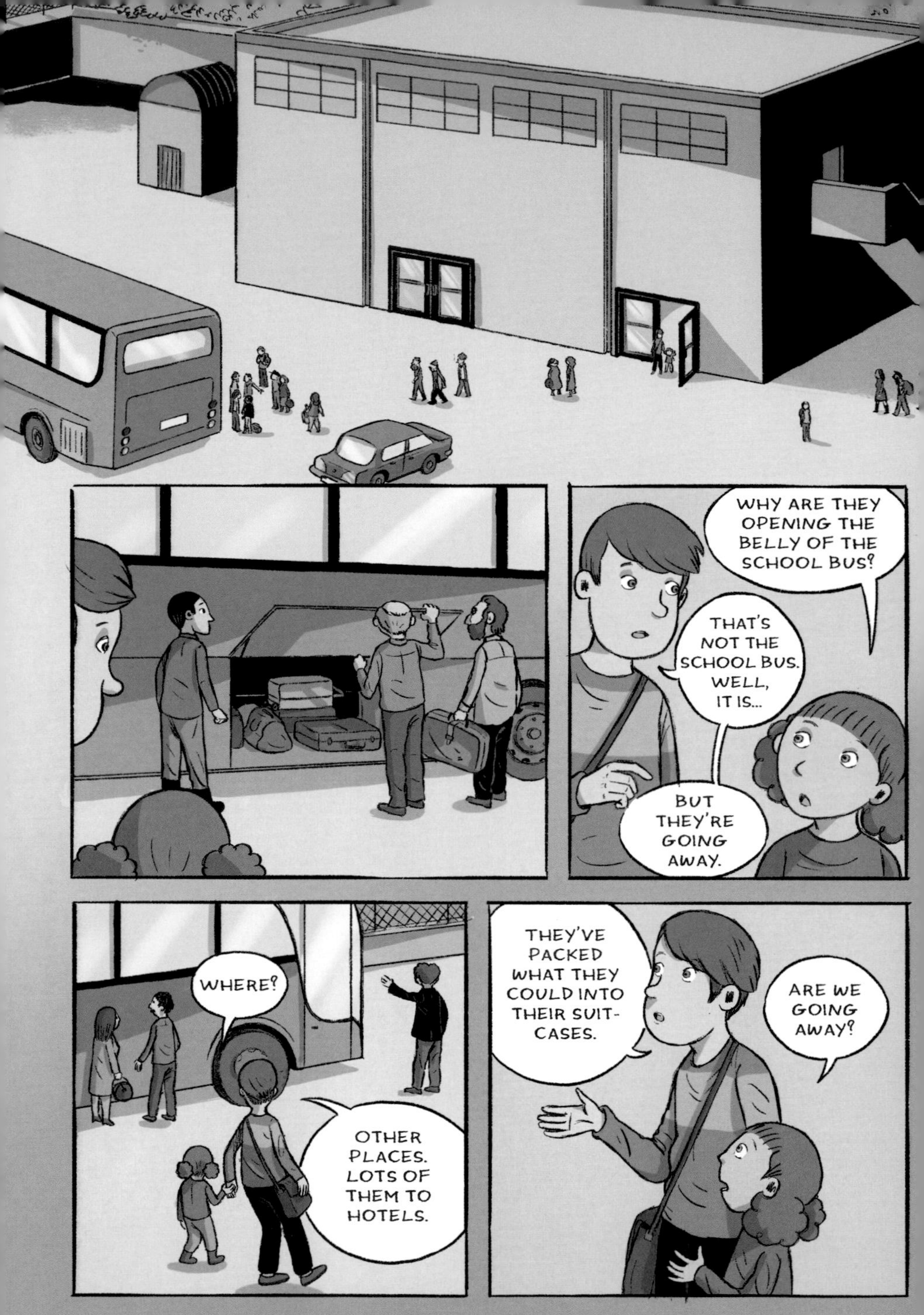
WHY ARE THEY OPENING THE BELLY OF THE SCHOOL BUS?
THAT'S NOT THE SCHOOL BUS. WELL, IT IS...
BUT THEY'RE GOING AWAY.
WHERE?
OTHER PLACES. LOTS OF THEM TO HOTELS.
THEY'VE PACKED WHAT THEY COULD INTO THEIR SUIT-CASES.
ARE WE GOING AWAY?

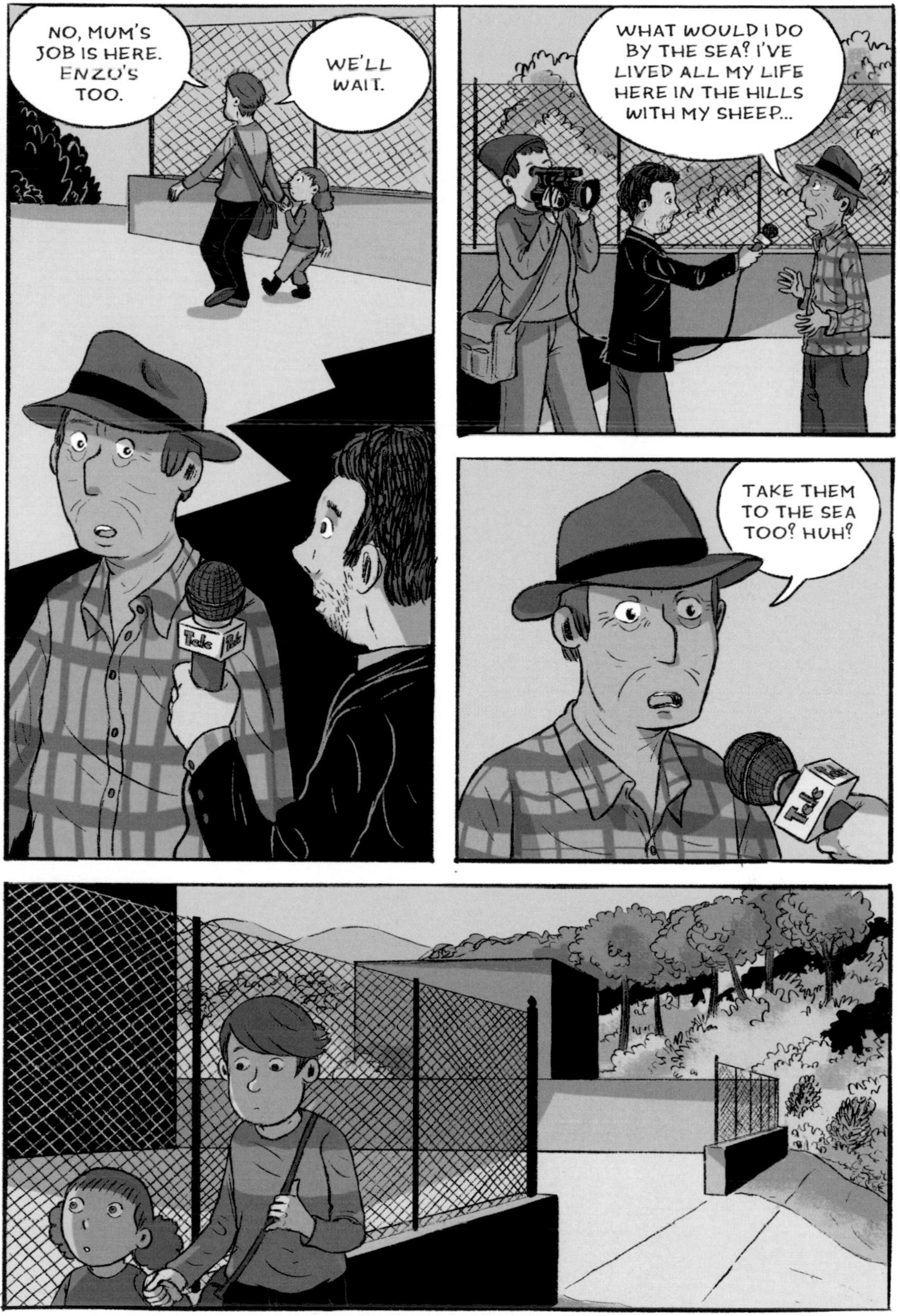
NO, MUM'S JOB IS HERE. ENZO'S TOO.
WE'LL WAIT.
WHAT WOULD I DO BY THE SEA? I'VE LIVED ALL MY LIFE HERE IN THE HILLS WITH MY SHEEP...
TAKE THEM TO THE SEA TOO? HUH?

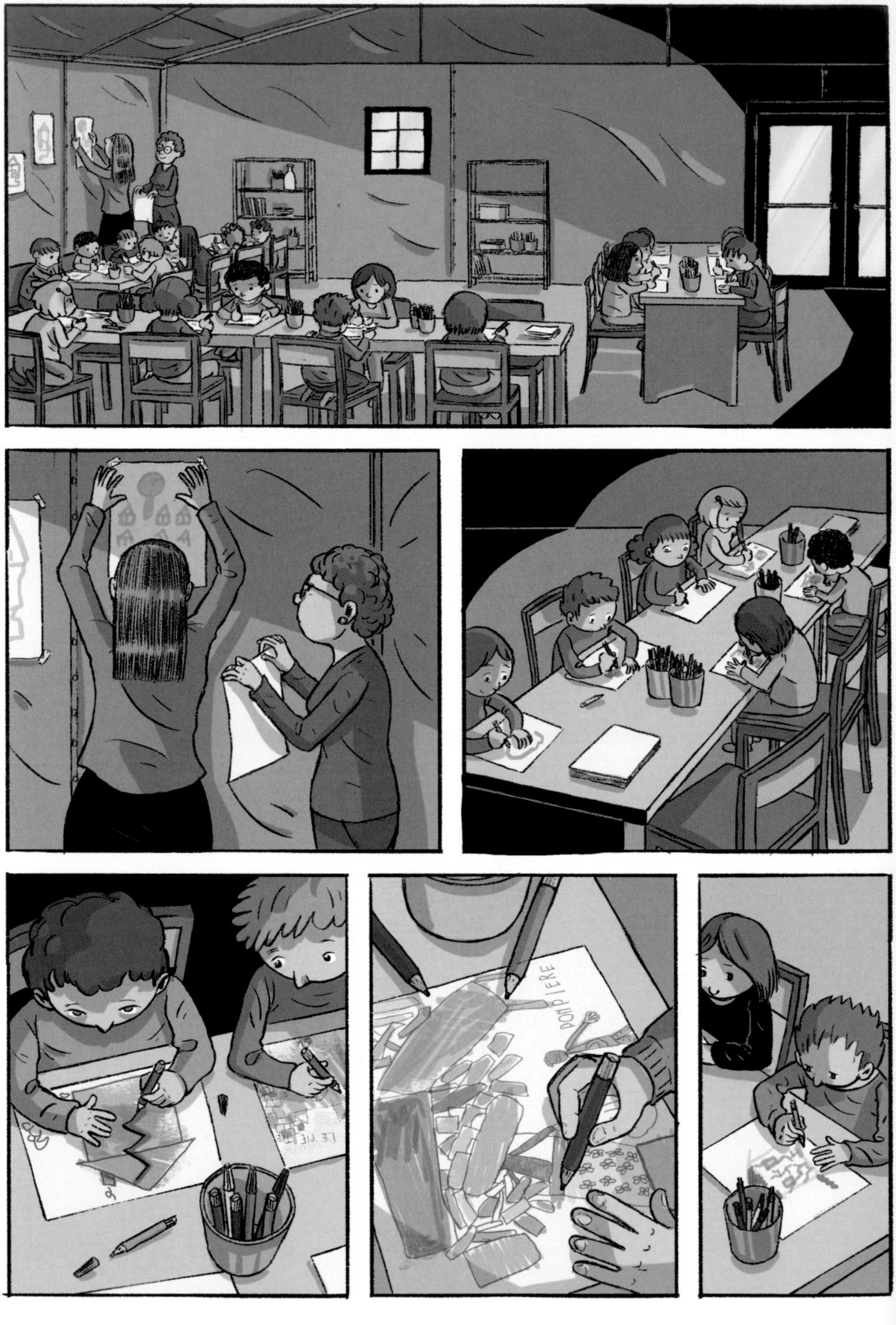
POMPIERE

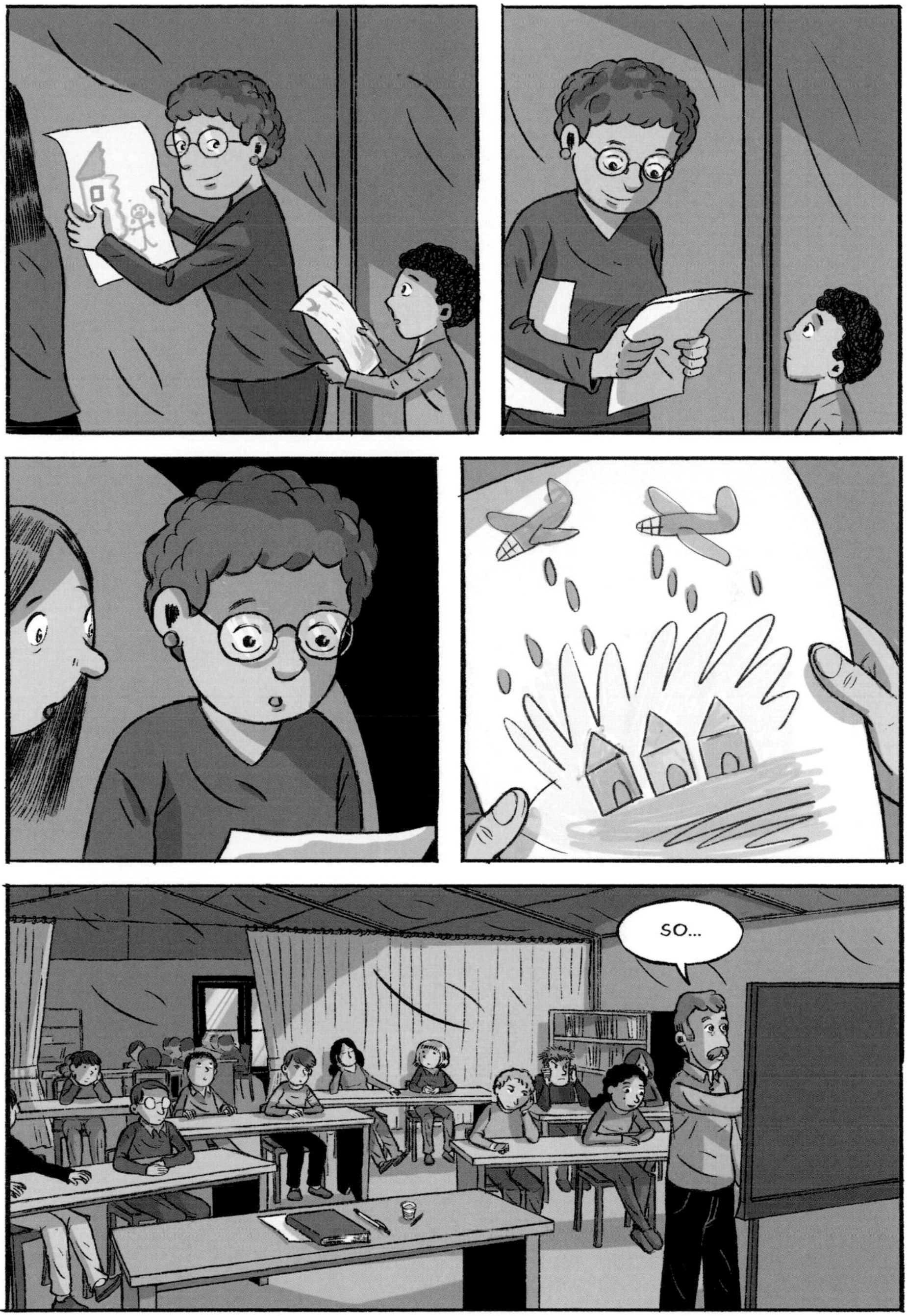
SO...

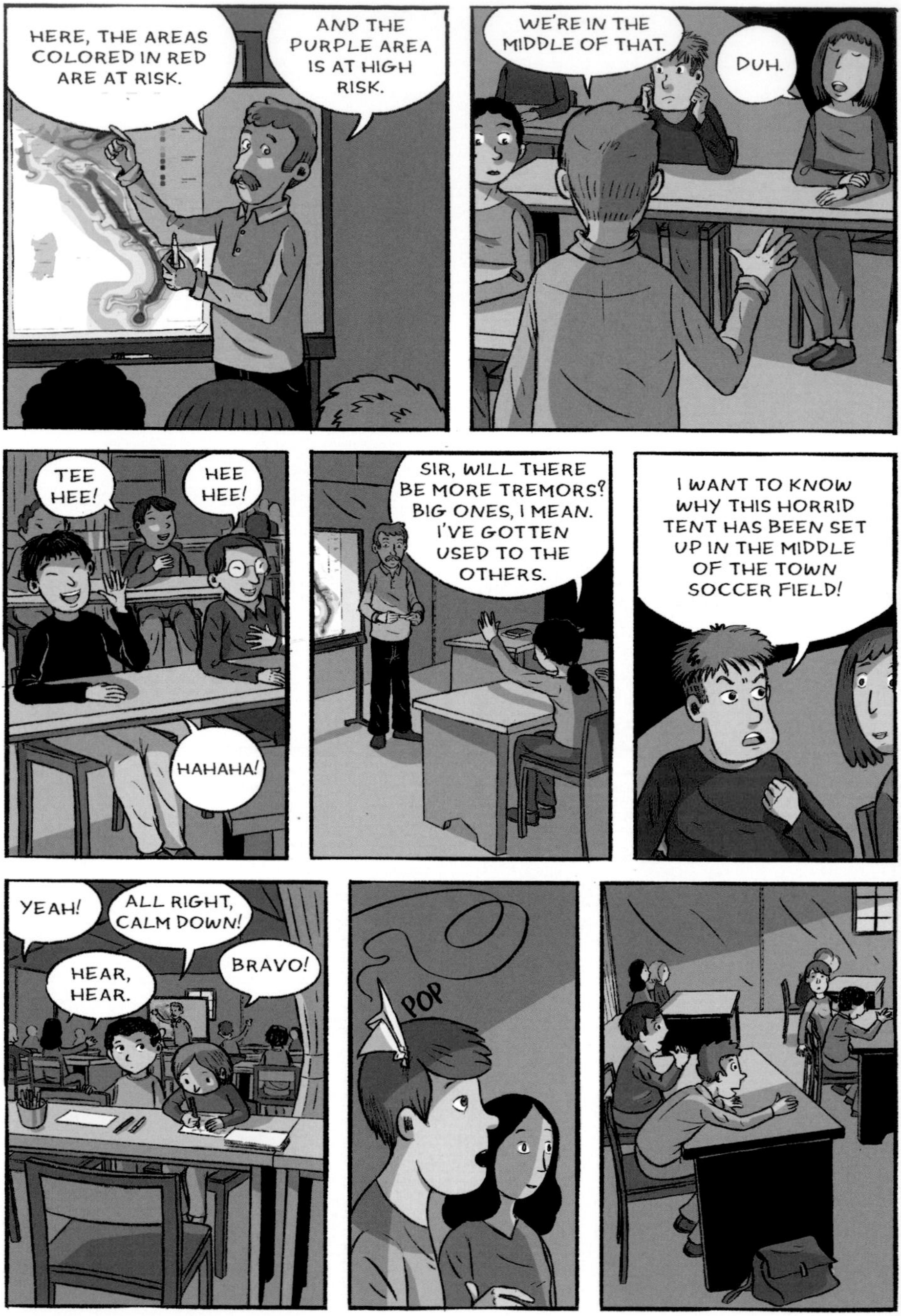
HERE, THE AREAS COLORED IN RED ARE AT RISK.
AND THE PURPLE AREA IS AT HIGH RISK.
WE'RE IN THE MIDDLE OF THAT.
DUH.
TEE HEE!
HEE HEE!
HAHAHA!
SIR, WILL THERE BE MORE TREMORS? BIG ONES, I MEAN. I'VE GOTTEN USED TO THE OTHERS.
I WANT TO KNOW WHY THIS HORRID TENT HAS BEEN SET UP IN THE MIDDLE OF THE TOWN SOCCER FIELD!
YEAH!
ALL RIGHT, CALM DOWN!
HEAR, HEAR.
BRAVO!
POP

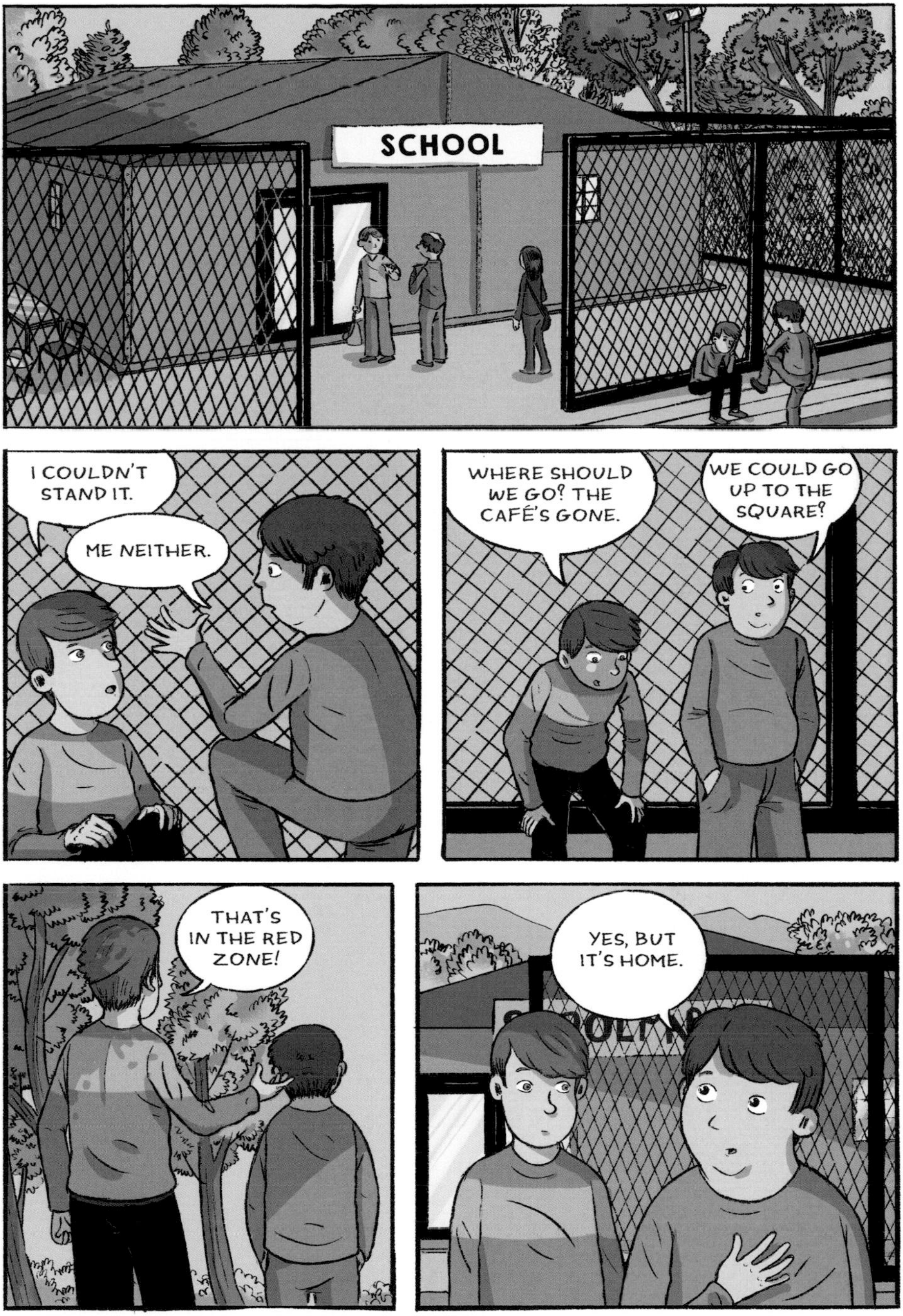
SCHOOL
I COULDN'T STAND IT.
ME NEITHER.
WHERE SHOULD WE GO? THE CAFÉ'S GONE.
WE COULD GO UP TO THE SQUARE?
THAT'S IN THE RED ZONE!
YES, BUT IT'S HOME.

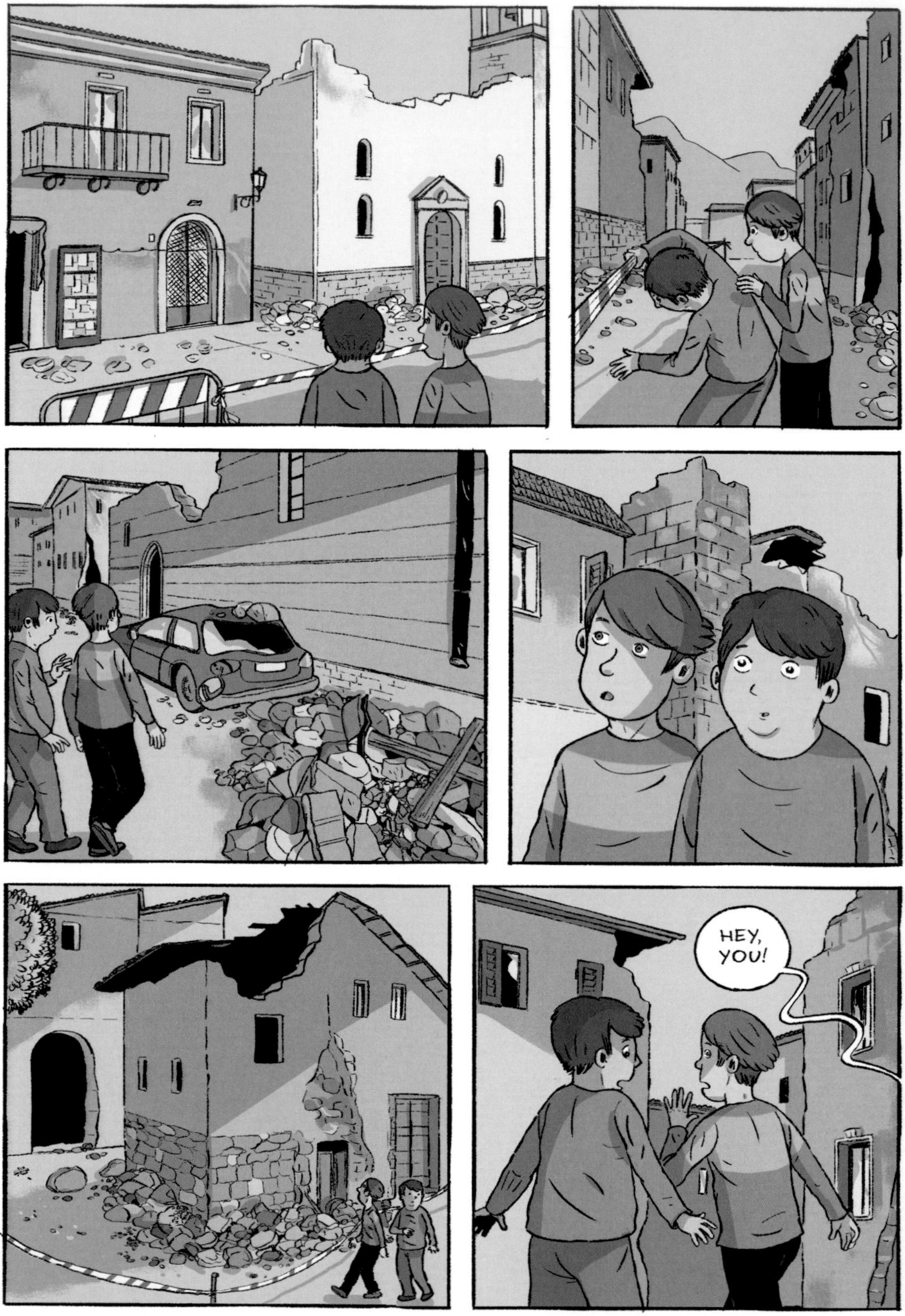
HEY, YOU!

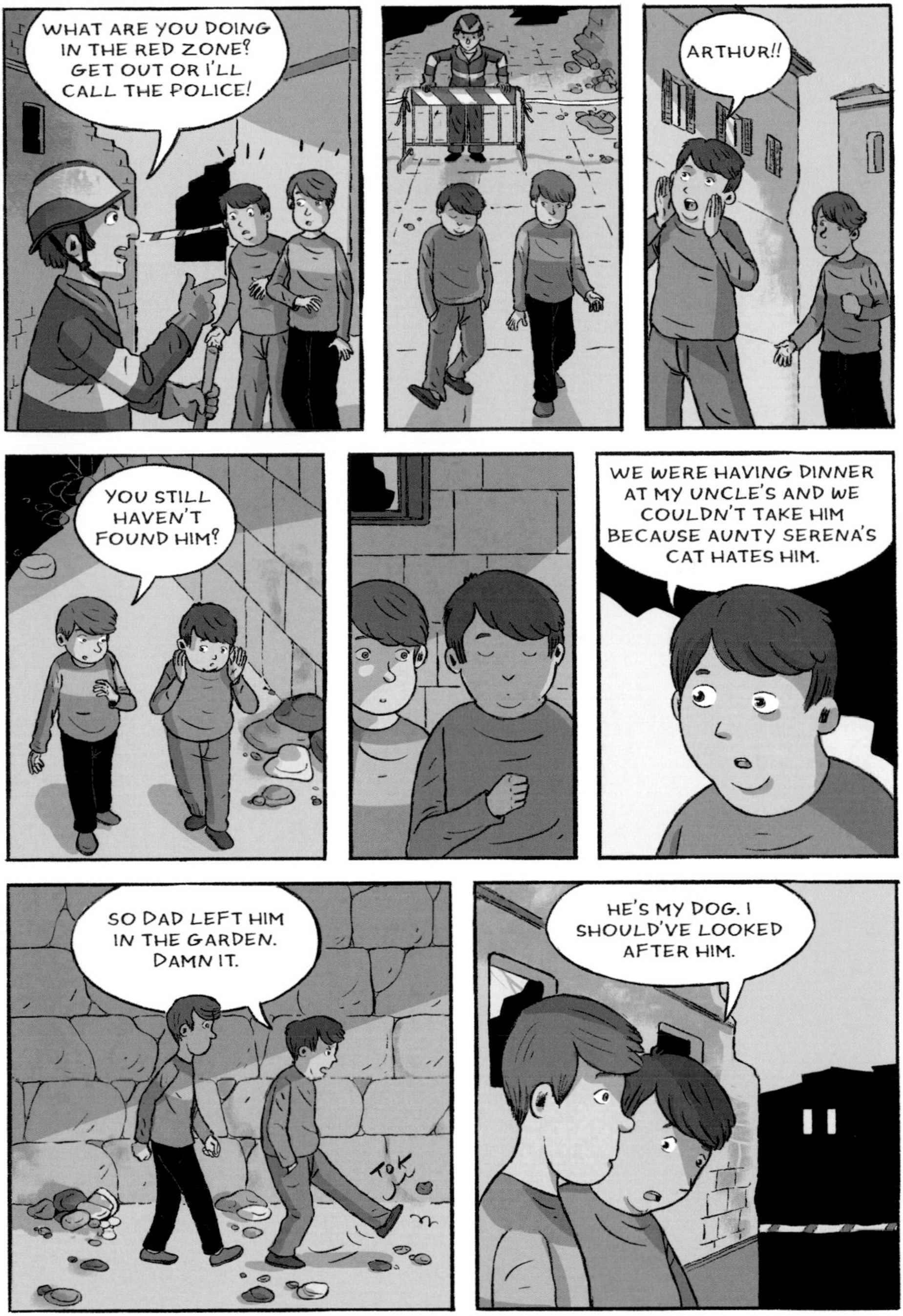
WHAT ARE YOU DOING IN THE RED ZONE? GET OUT OR I'LL CALL THE POLICE!
ARTHUR!!
YOU STILL HAVEN'T FOUND HIM?
WE WERE HAVING DINNER AT MY UNCLE'S AND WE COULDN'T TAKE HIM BECAUSE AUNTY SERENA'S CAT HATES HIM.
SO DAD LEFT HIM IN THE GARDEN. DAMN IT.
TOK
HE'S MY DOG. I SHOULD'VE LOOKED AFTER HIM.

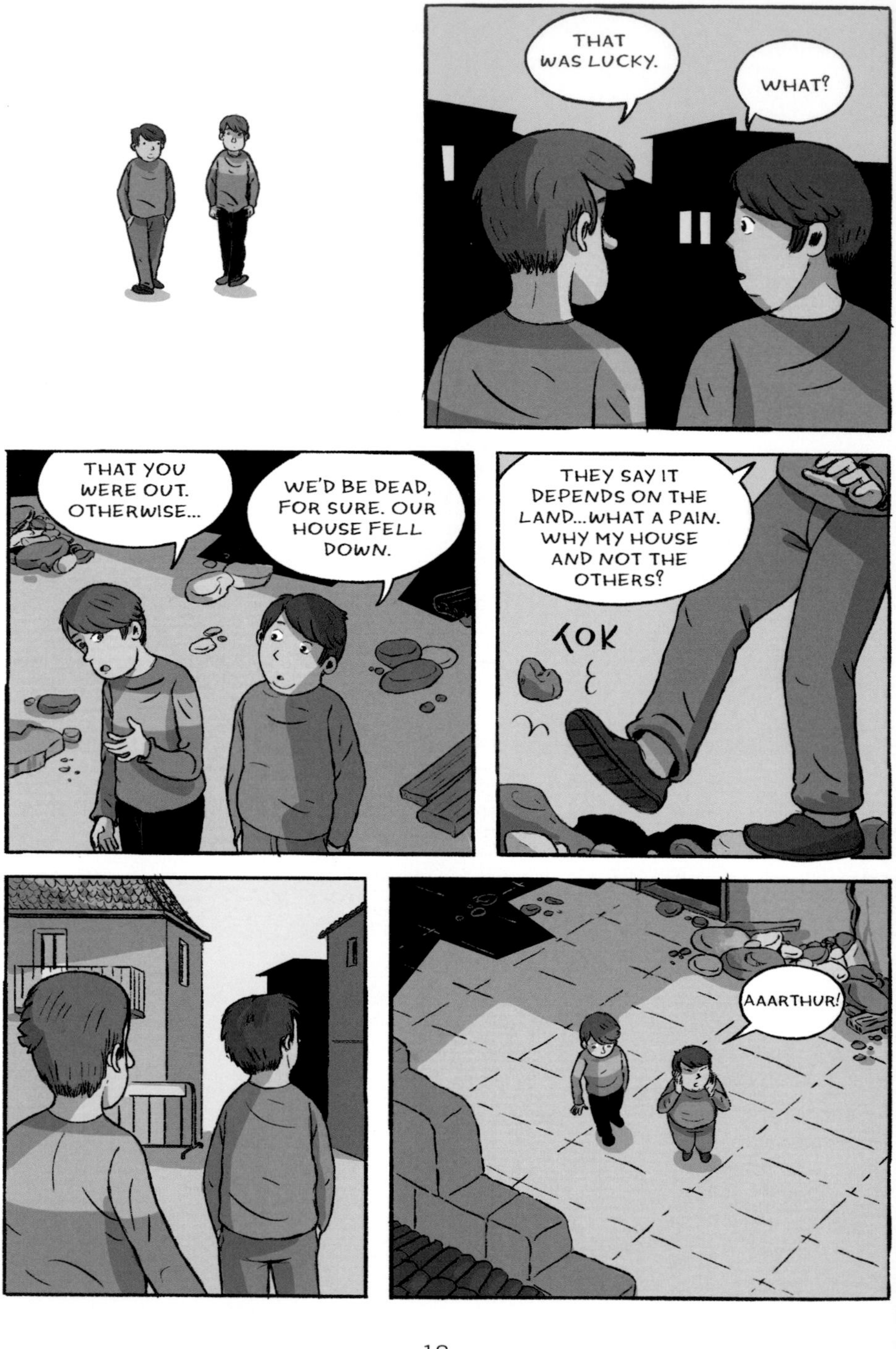
THAT WAS LUCKY.
WHAT?
THAT YOU WERE OUT. OTHERWISE...
WE'D BE DEAD, FOR SURE. OUR HOUSE FELL DOWN.
THEY SAY IT DEPENDS ON THE LAND...WHAT A PAIN. WHY MY HOUSE AND NOT THE OTHERS?
TOK
AAARTHUR!

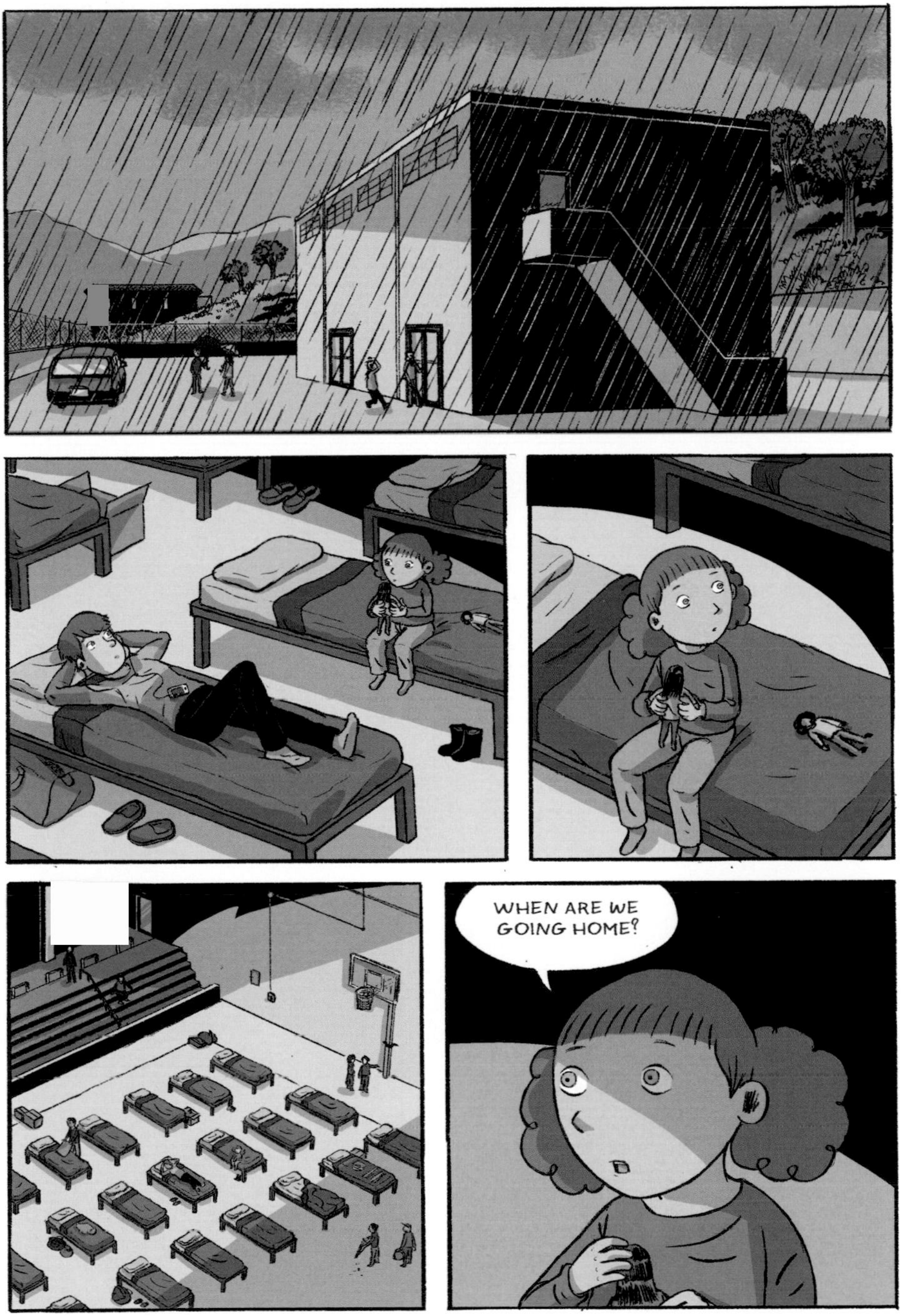
WHEN ARE WE GOING HOME?

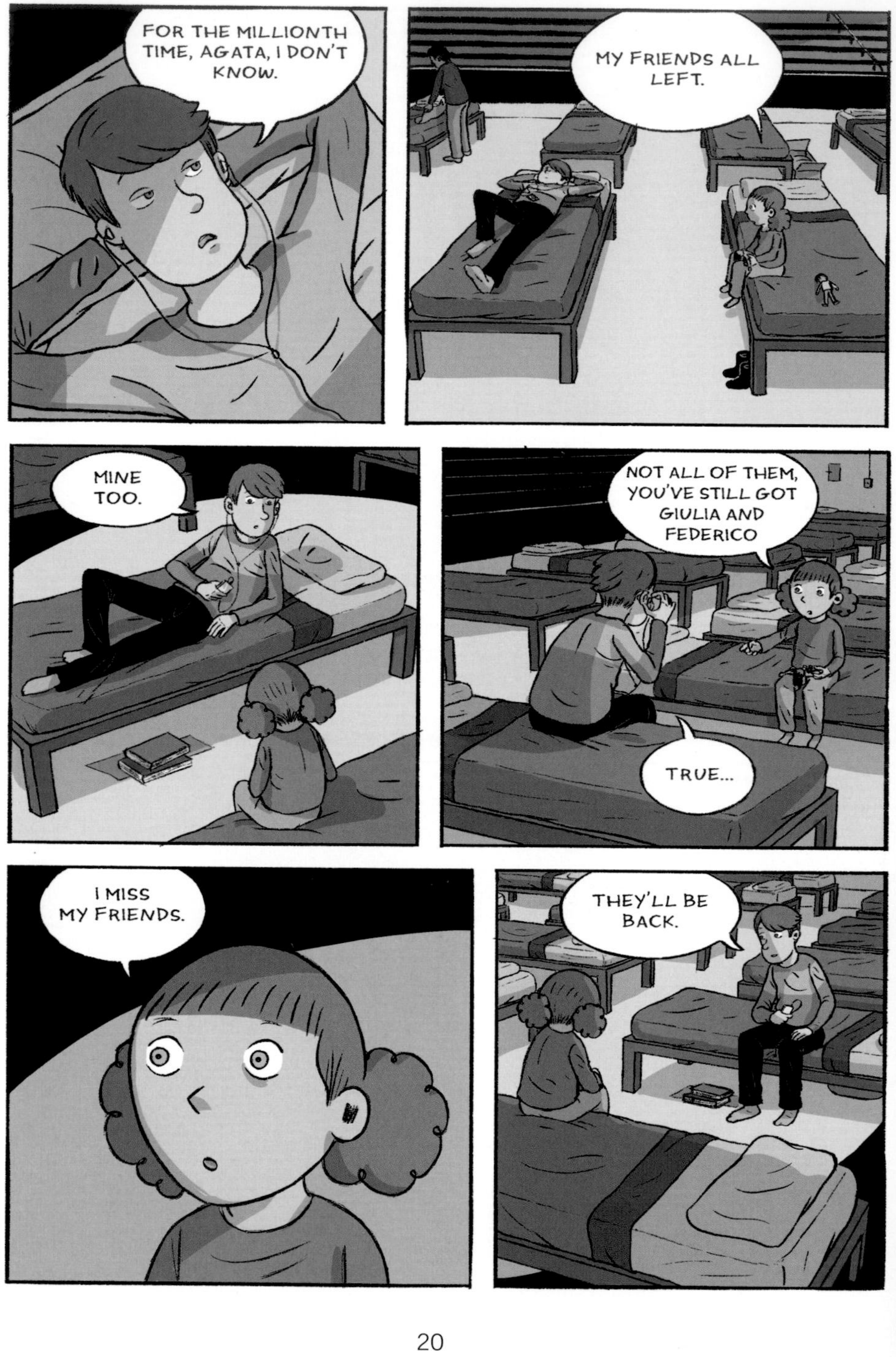
FOR THE MILLIONTH TIME, AGATA, I DON'T KNOW.
MY FRIENDS ALL LEFT.
MINE TOO.
NOT ALL OF THEM, YOU'VE STILL GOT GIULIA AND FEDERICO
TRUE...
I MISS MY FRIENDS.
THEY'LL BE BACK.

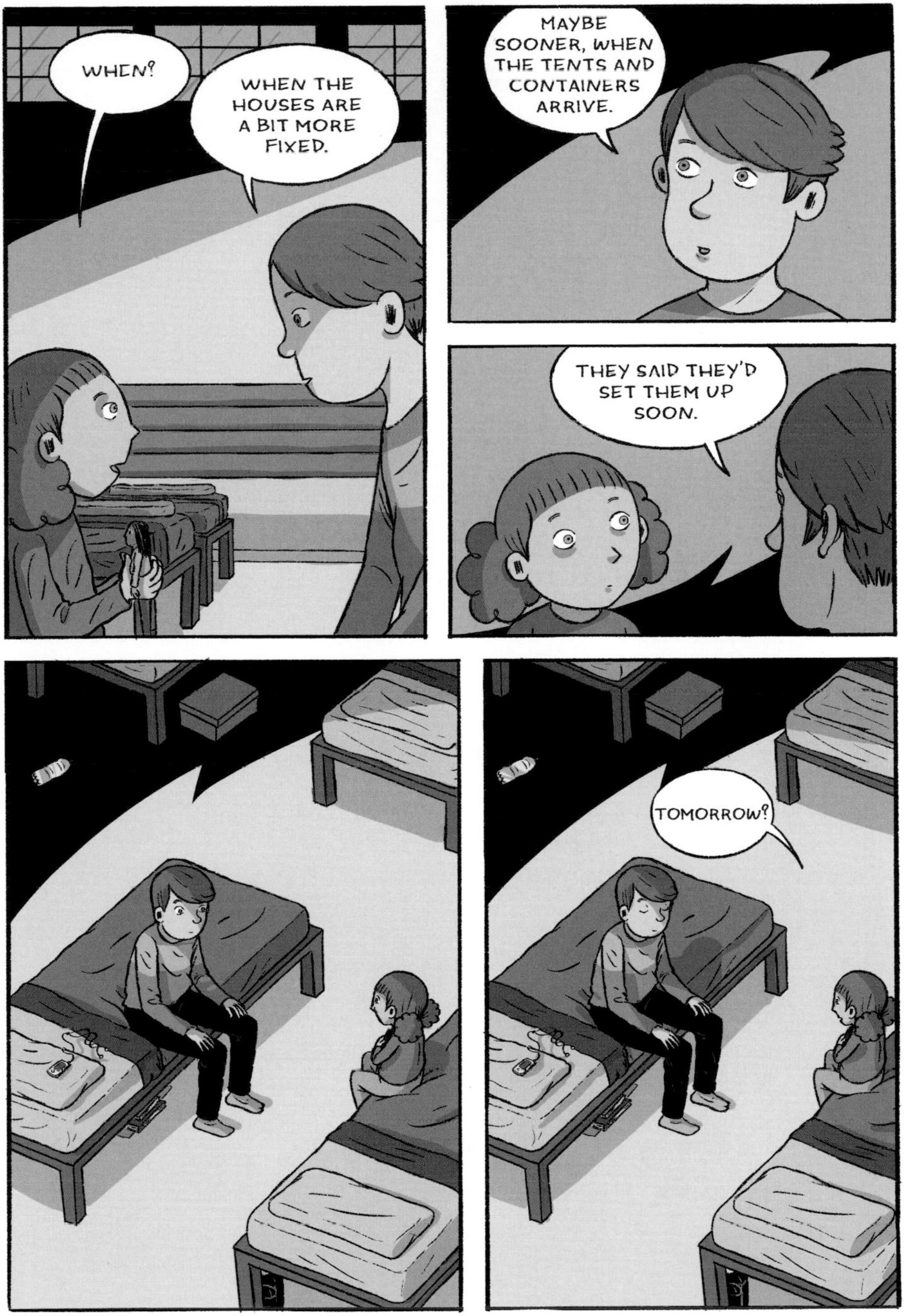
WHEN?
WHEN THE HOUSES ARE A BIT MORE FIXED.
MAYBE SOONER, WHEN THE TENTS AND CONTAINERS ARRIVE.
THEY SAID THEY'D SET THEM UP SOON.
TOMORROW?

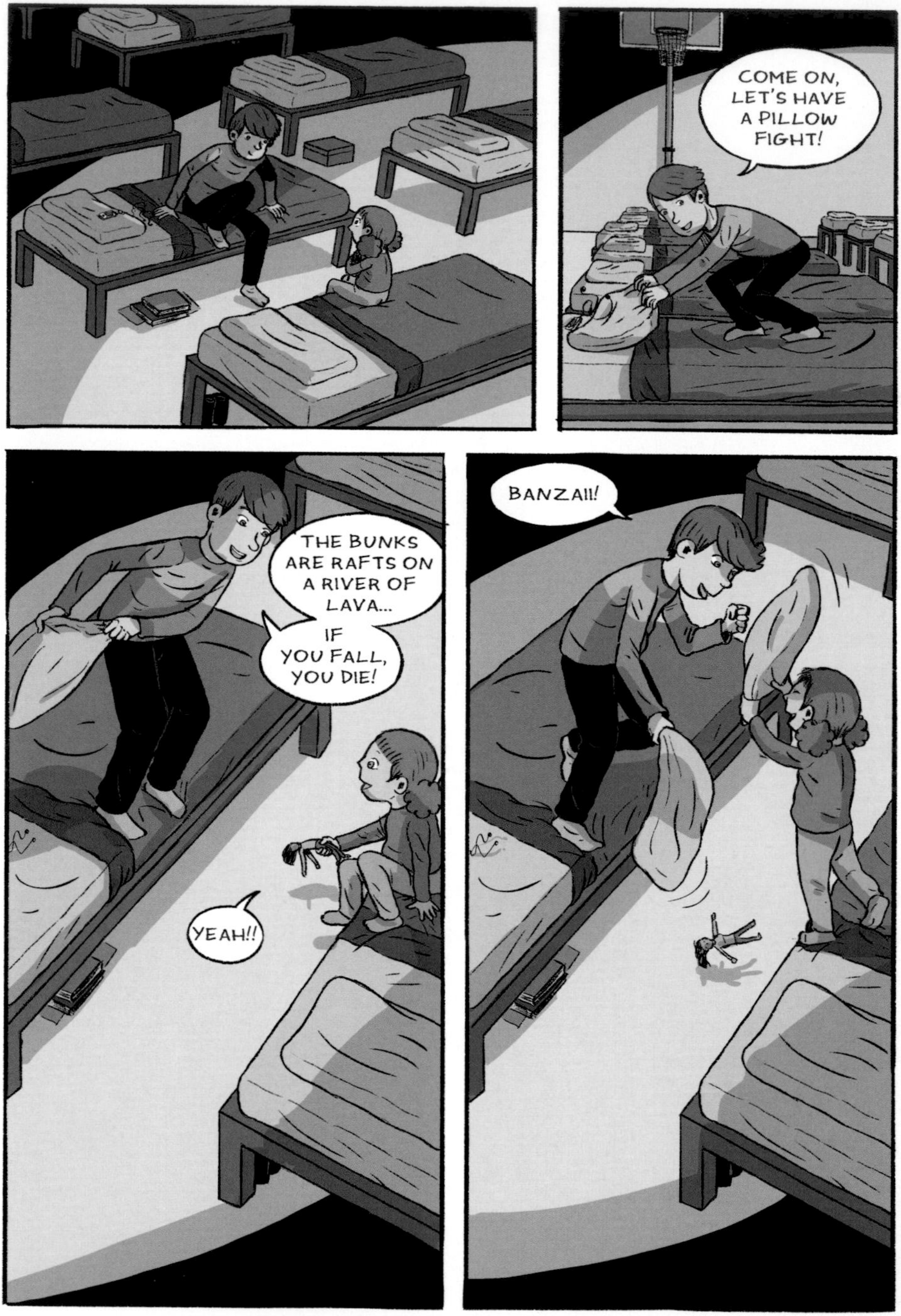
COME ON, LET'S HAVE A PILLOW FIGHT!
THE BUNKS ARE RAFTS ON A RIVER OF LAVA...
IF YOU FALL, YOU DIE!
YEAH!!
BANZAI!!

2.
In which we try to stand on our own two feet.

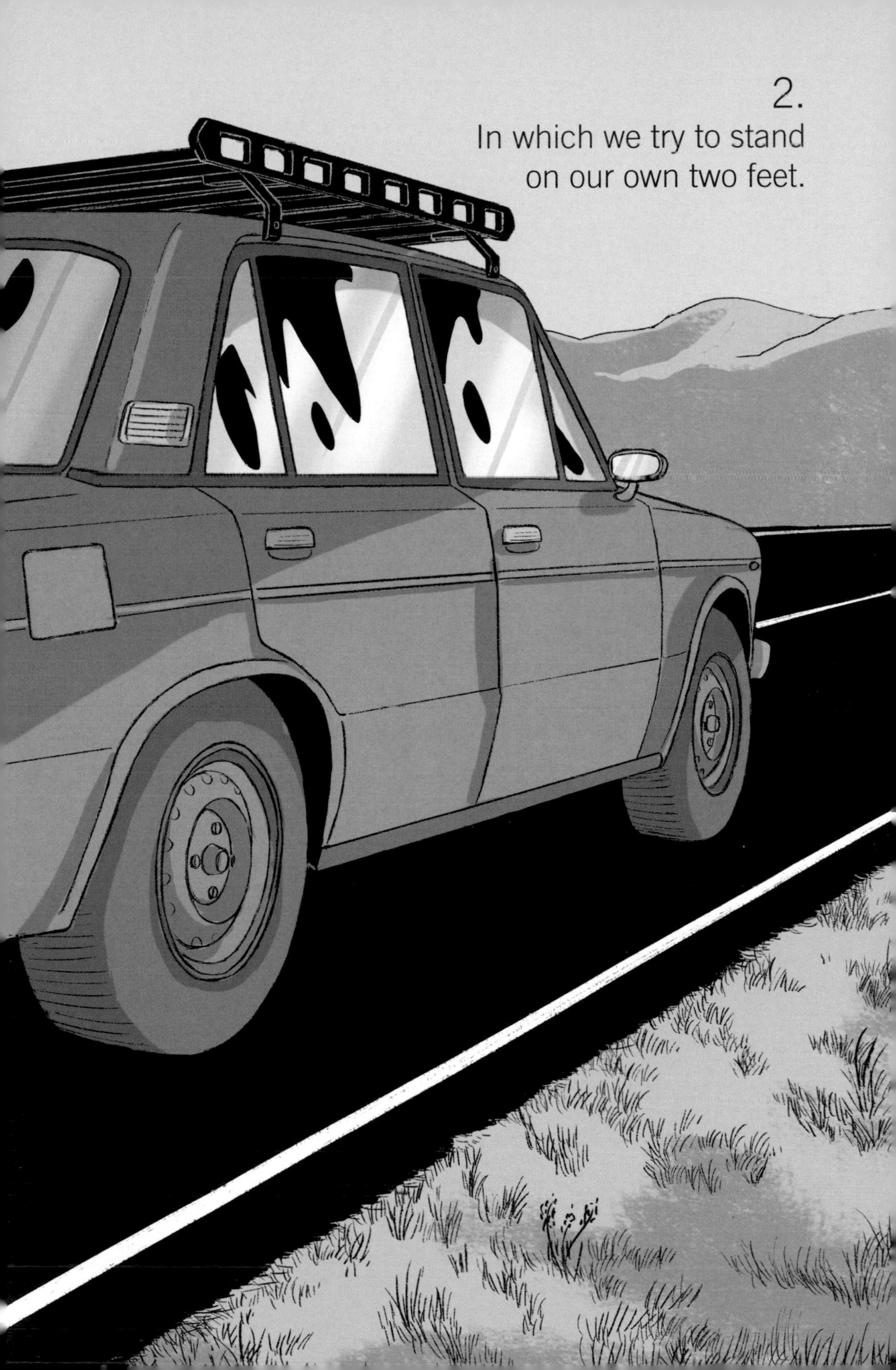

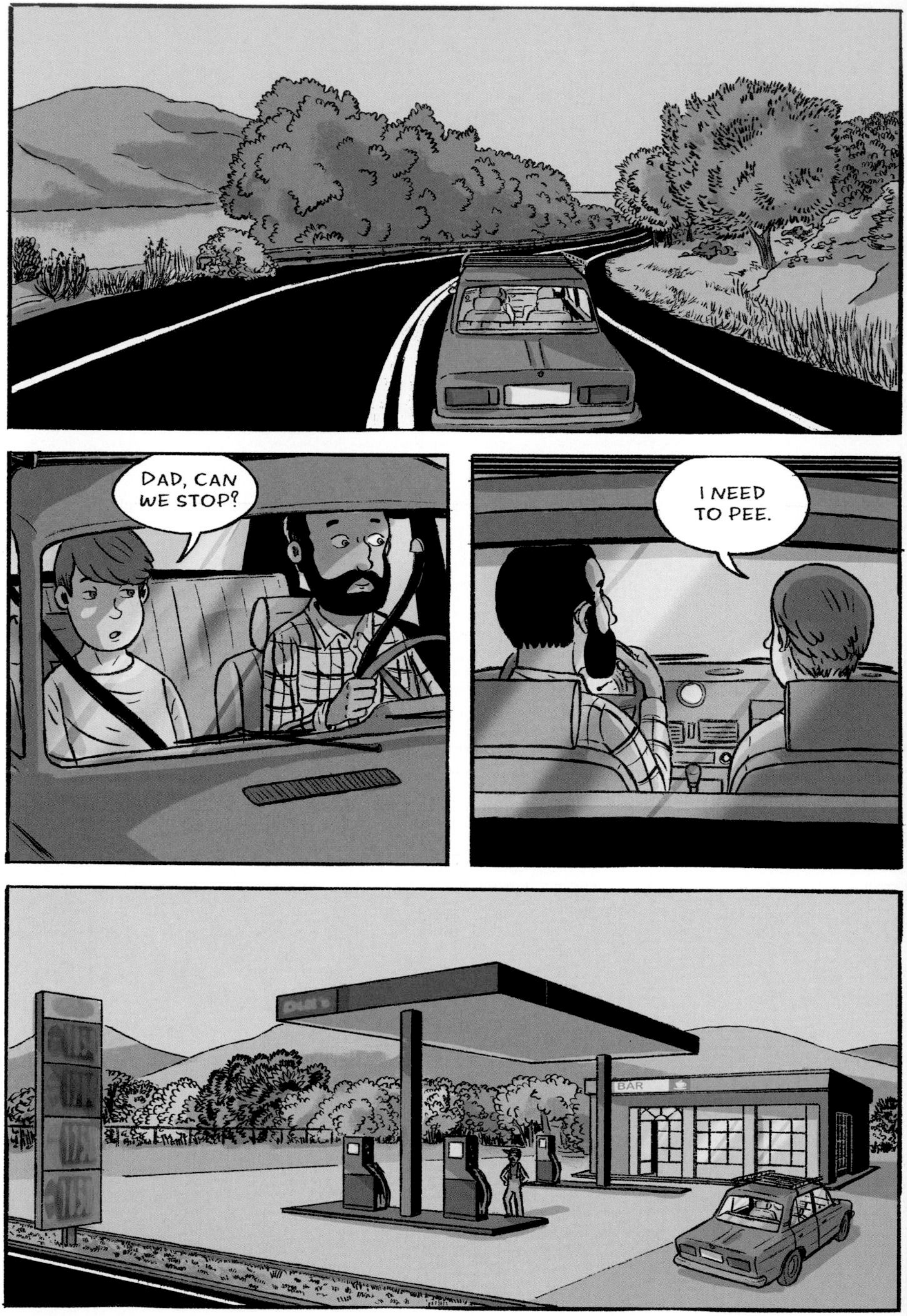
DAD, CAN WE STOP?
I NEED TO PEE.
BAR

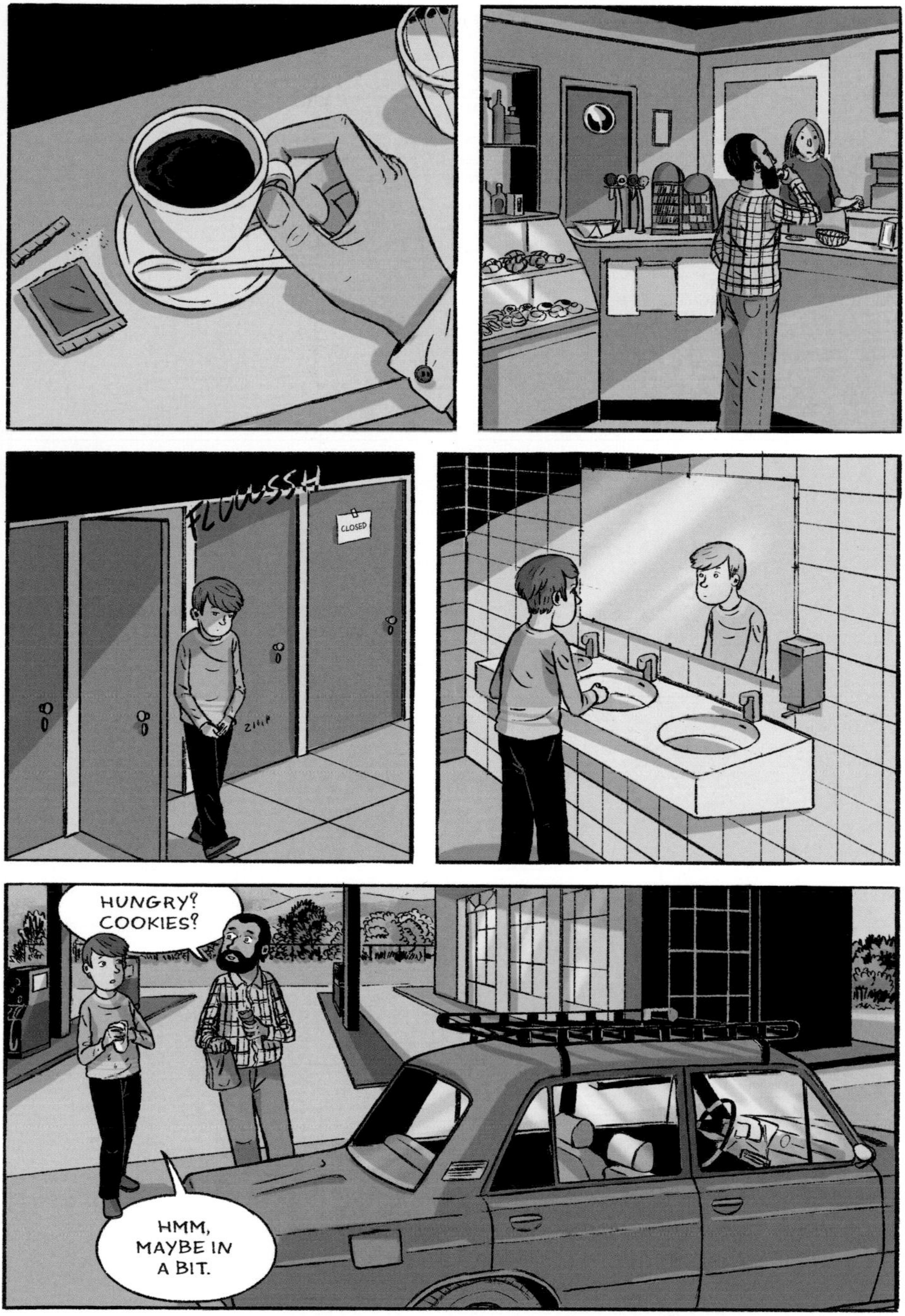
FLUUSSH
CLOSED
ZIIIP
HUNGRY? COOKIES?
HMM, MAYBE IN A BIT.

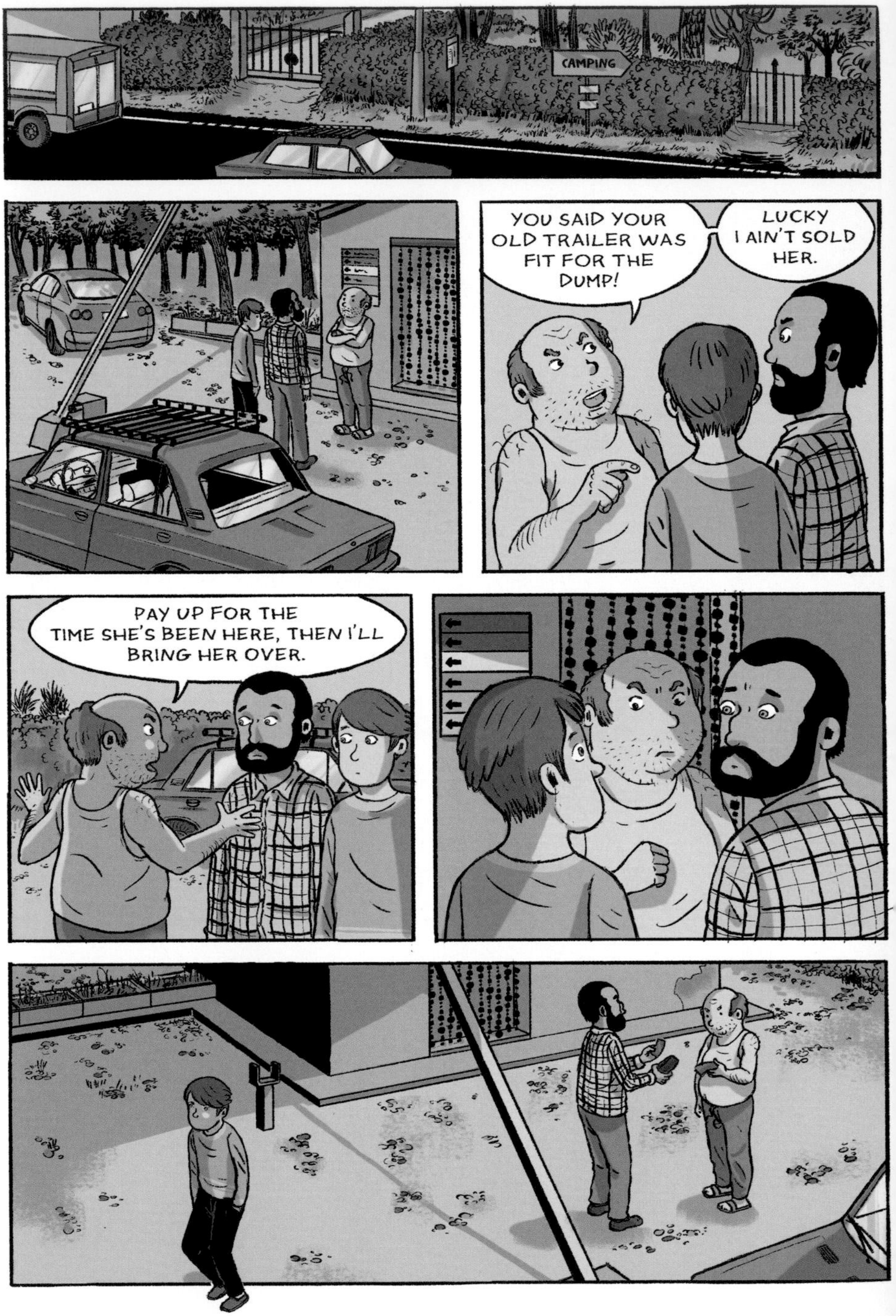
CAMPING
YOU SAID YOUR OLD TRAILER WAS FIT FOR THE DUMP!
LUCKY I AIN'T SOLD HER.
PAY UP FOR THE TIME SHE'S BEEN HERE, THEN I'LL BRING HER OVER.

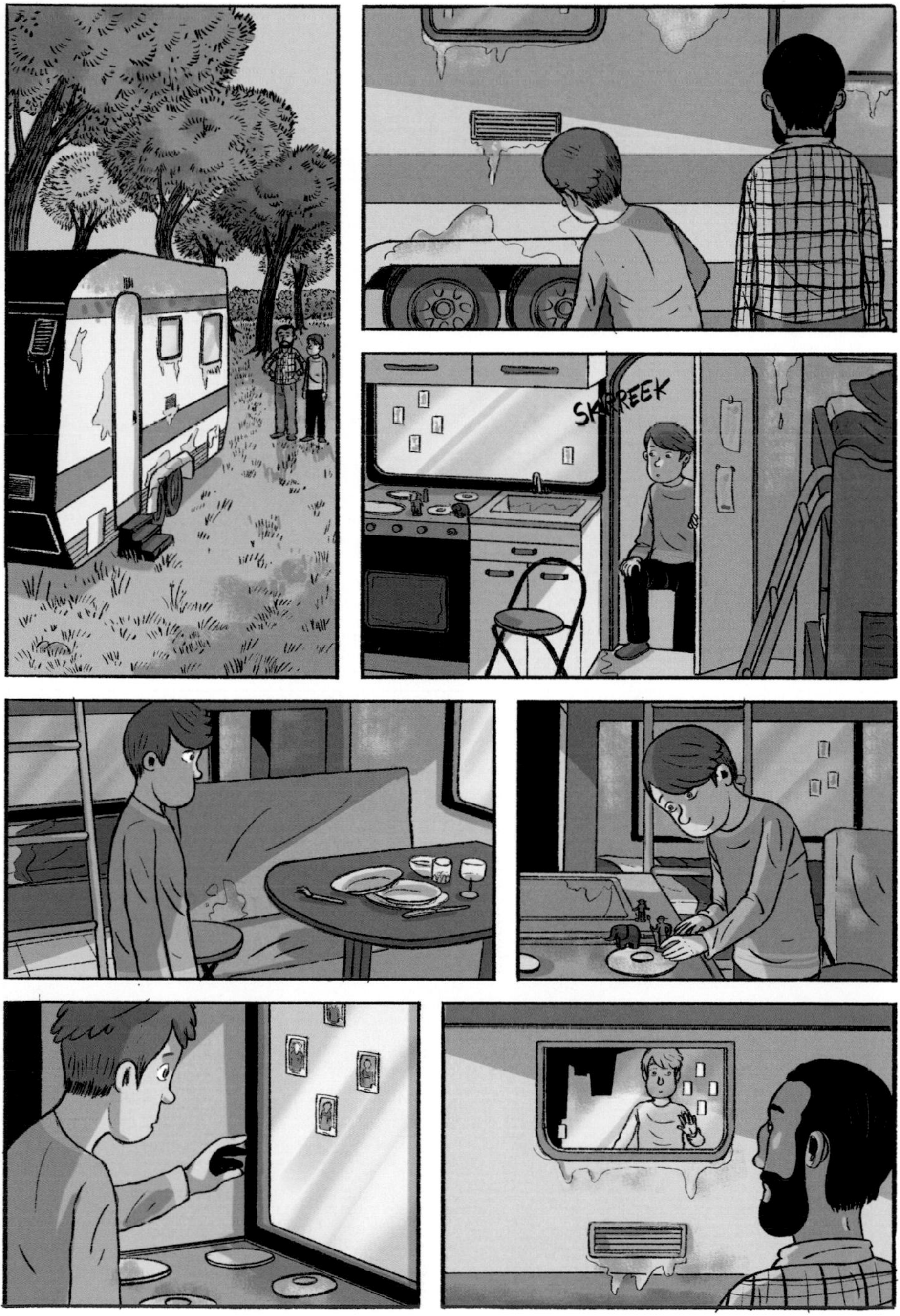
SKRREEK

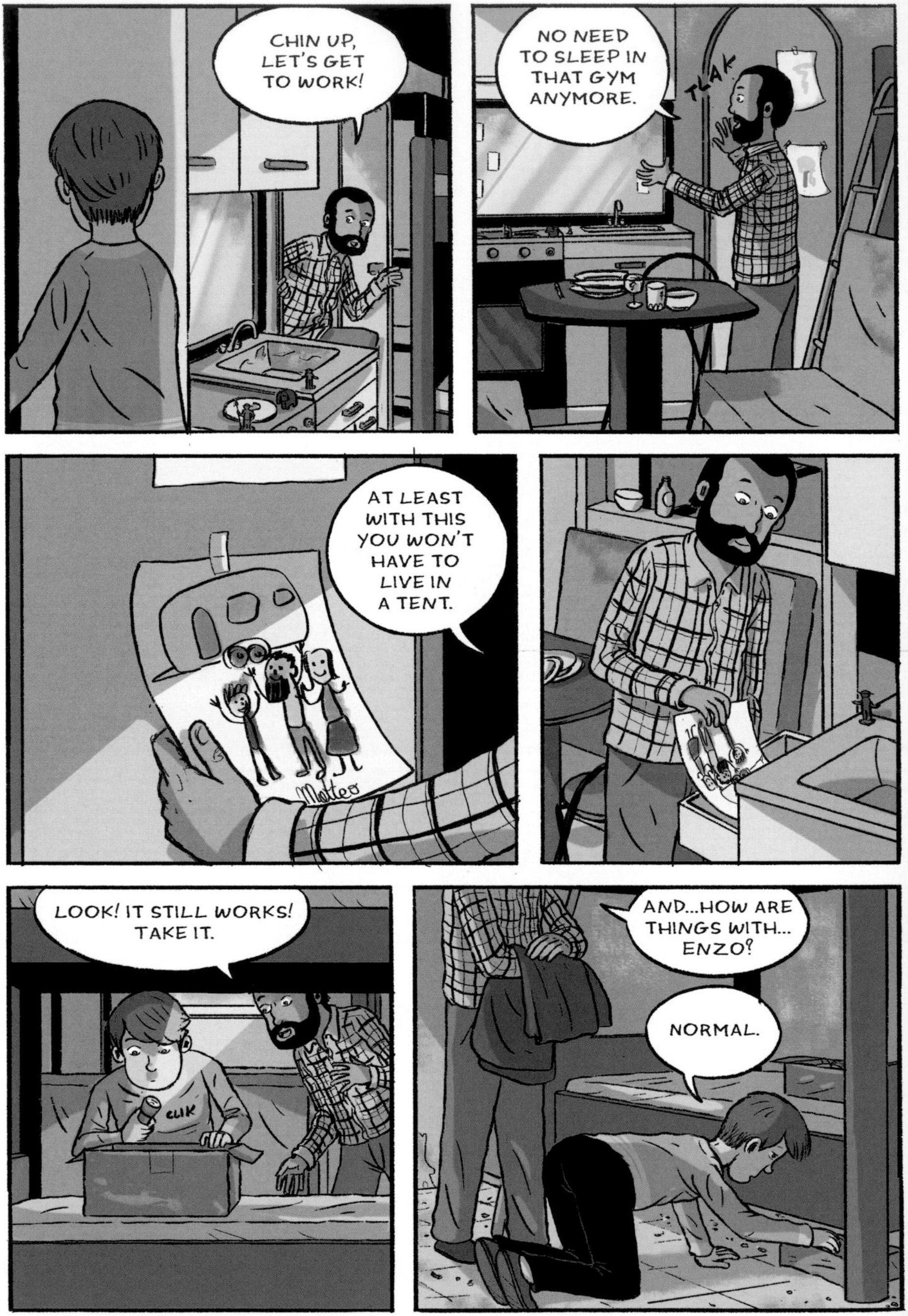
CHIN UP, LET'S GET TO WORK!
NO NEED TO SLEEP IN THAT GYM ANYMORE.
TLAK
AT LEAST WITH THIS YOU WON'T HAVE TO LIVE IN A TENT.
Matteo
LOOK! IT STILL WORKS! TAKE IT.
CLIK
AND...HOW ARE THINGS WITH... ENZO?
NORMAL.

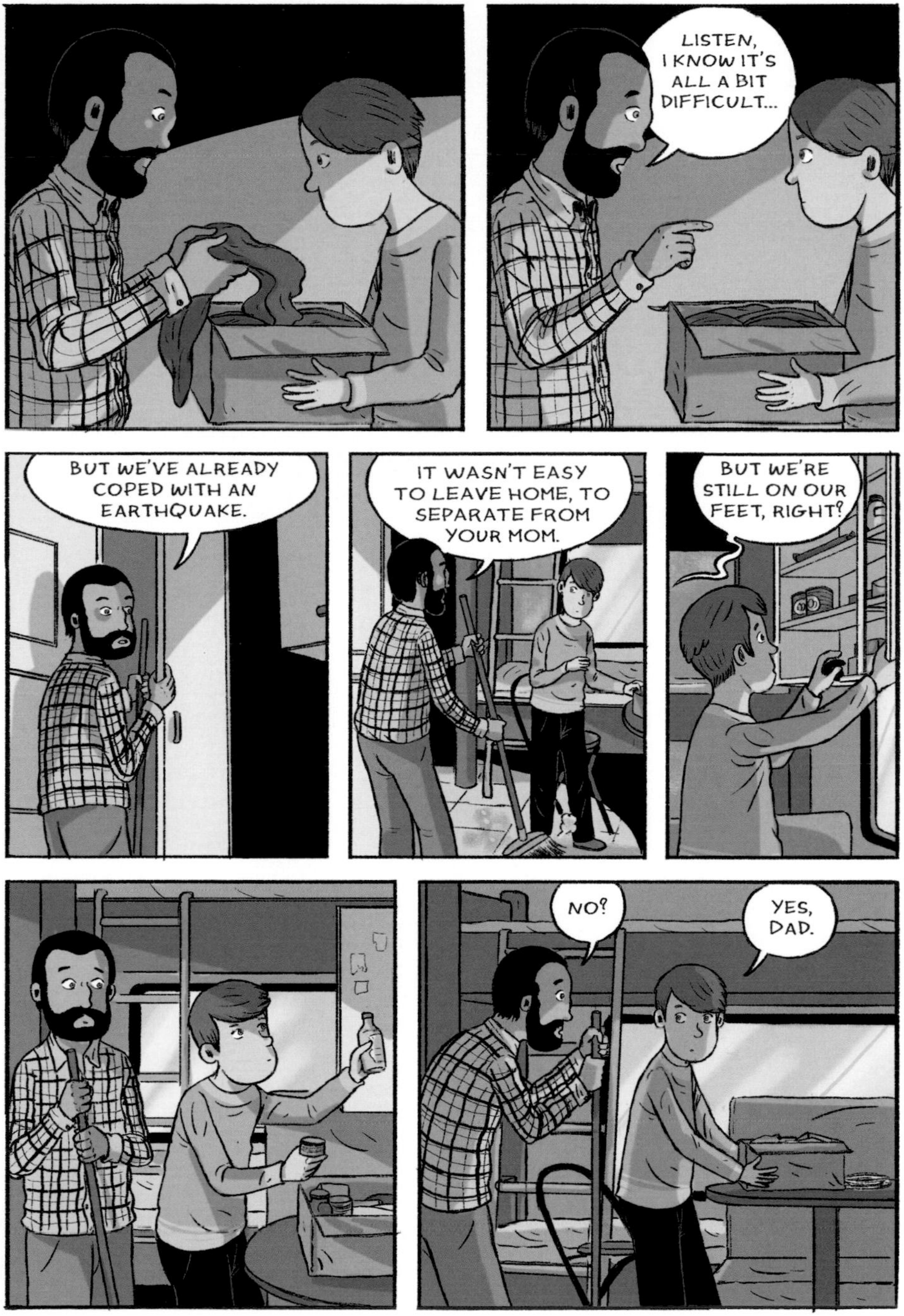
LISTEN, I KNOW IT'S ALL A BIT DIFFICULT...
BUT WE'VE ALREADY COPED WITH AN EARTHQUAKE.
IT WASN'T EASY TO LEAVE HOME, TO SEPARATE FROM YOUR MOM.
BUT WE'RE STILL ON OUR FEET, RIGHT?
NO?
YES, DAD.

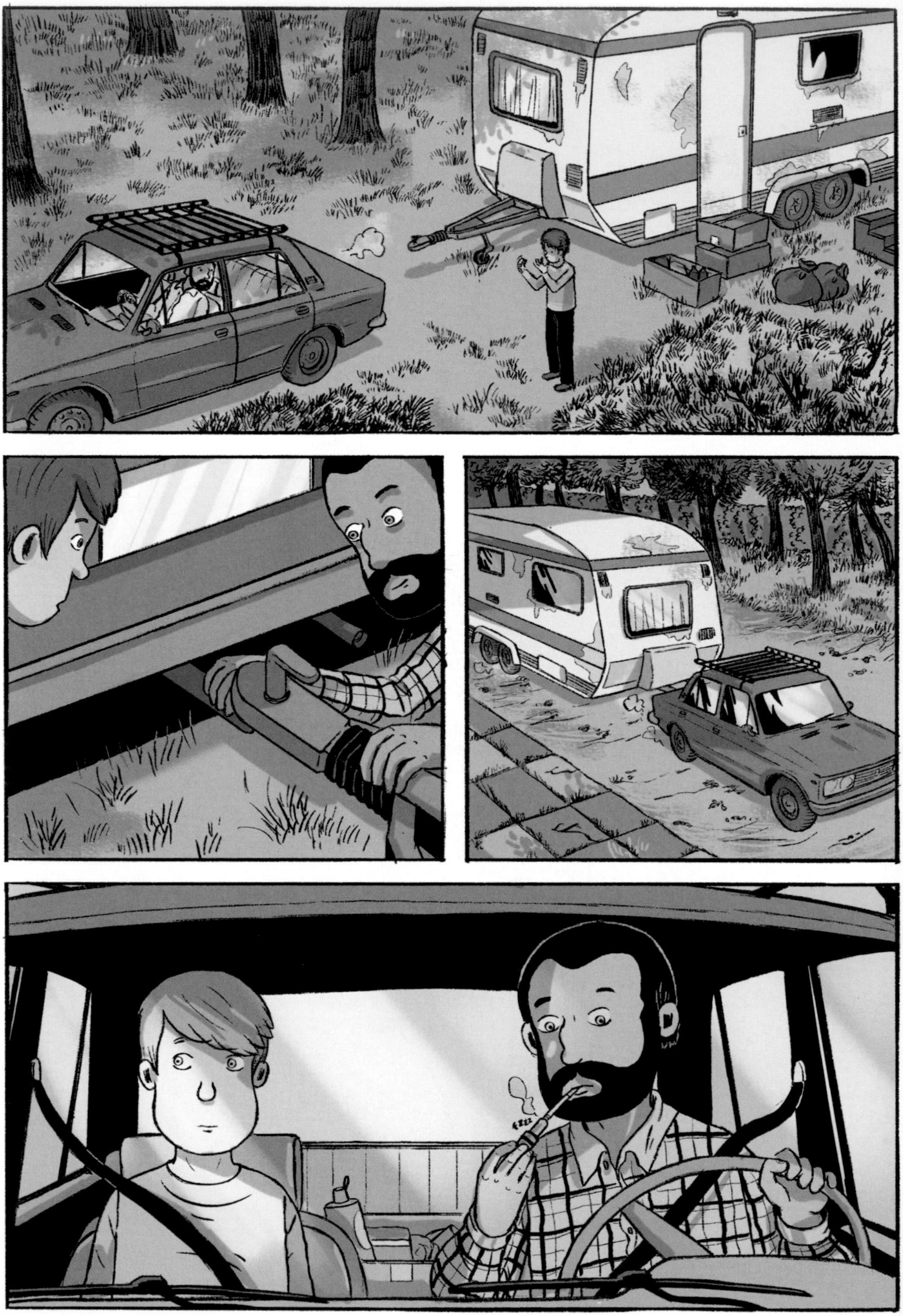

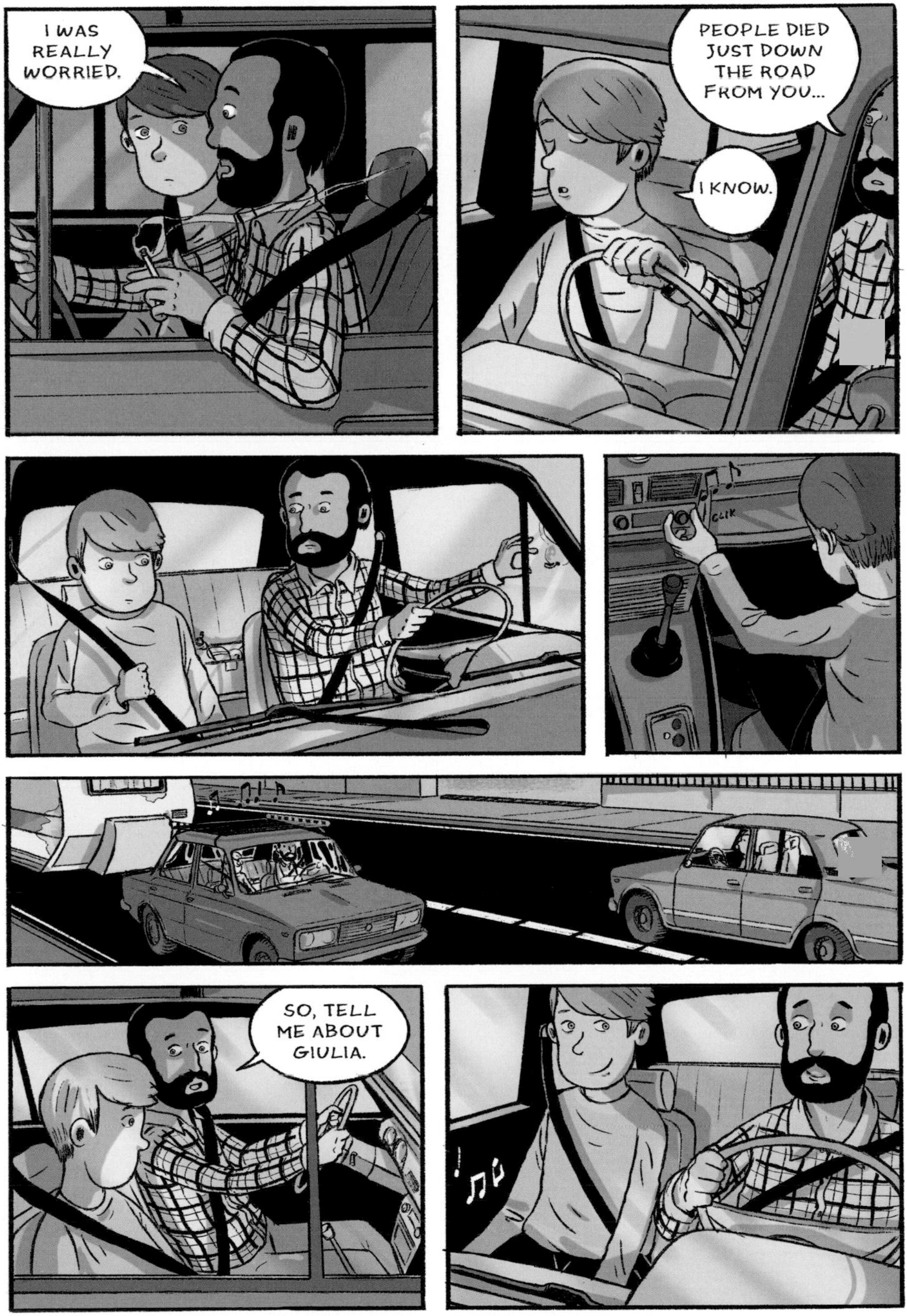
I WAS REALLY WORRIED.
PEOPLE DIED JUST DOWN THE ROAD FROM YOU...
I KNOW.
CLIK
SO, TELL ME ABOUT GIULIA.

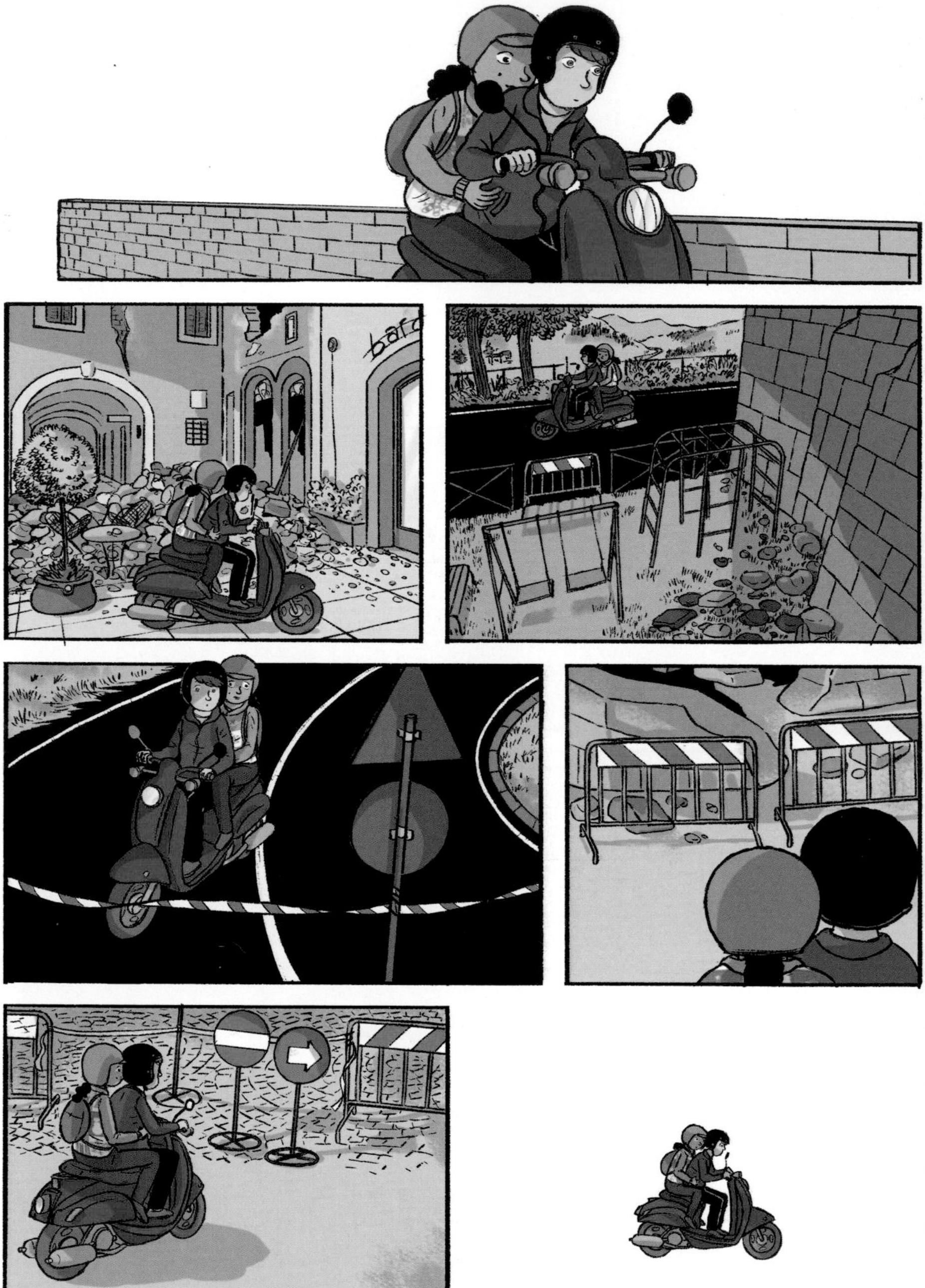

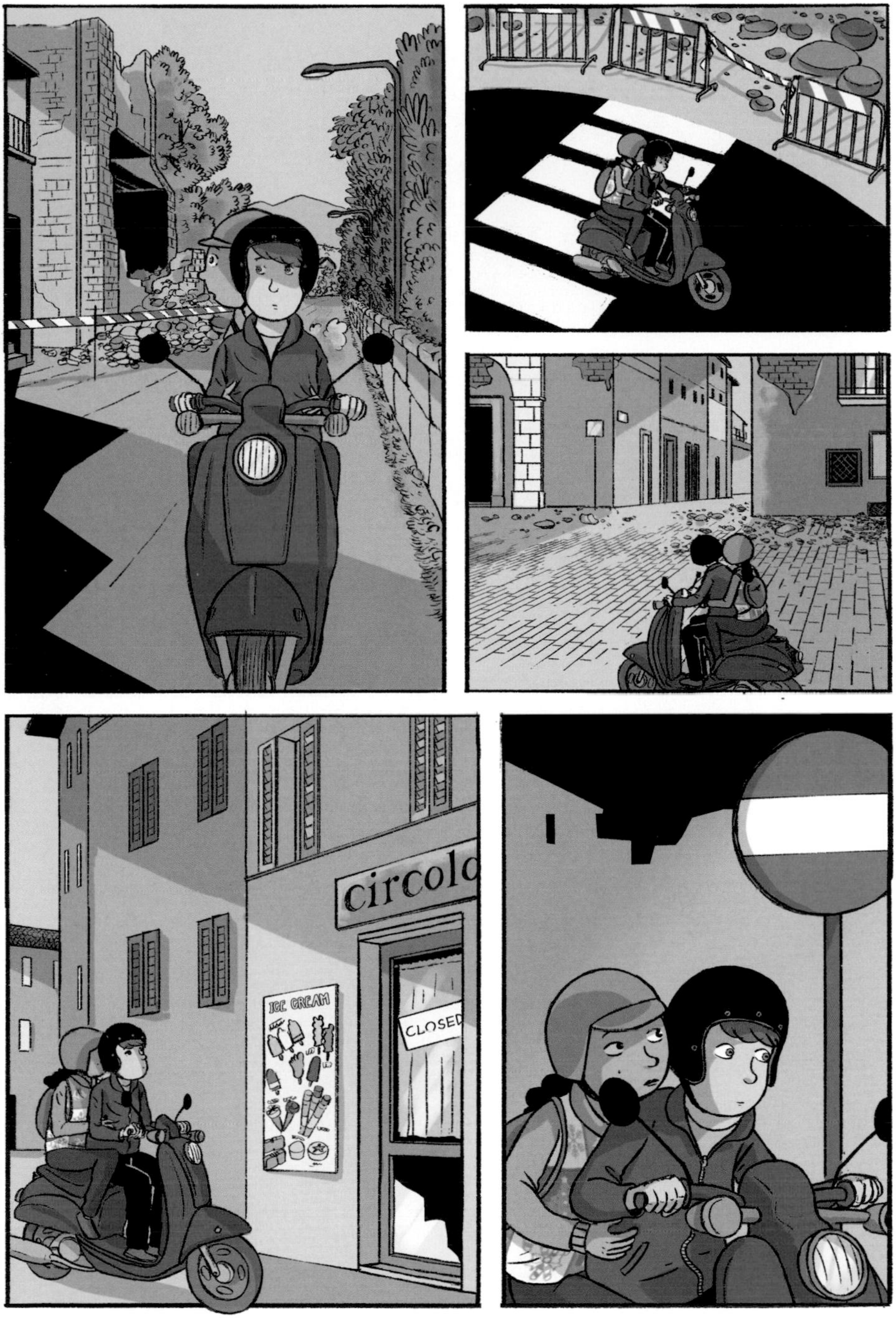
circolo
ICE CREAM
CLOSED

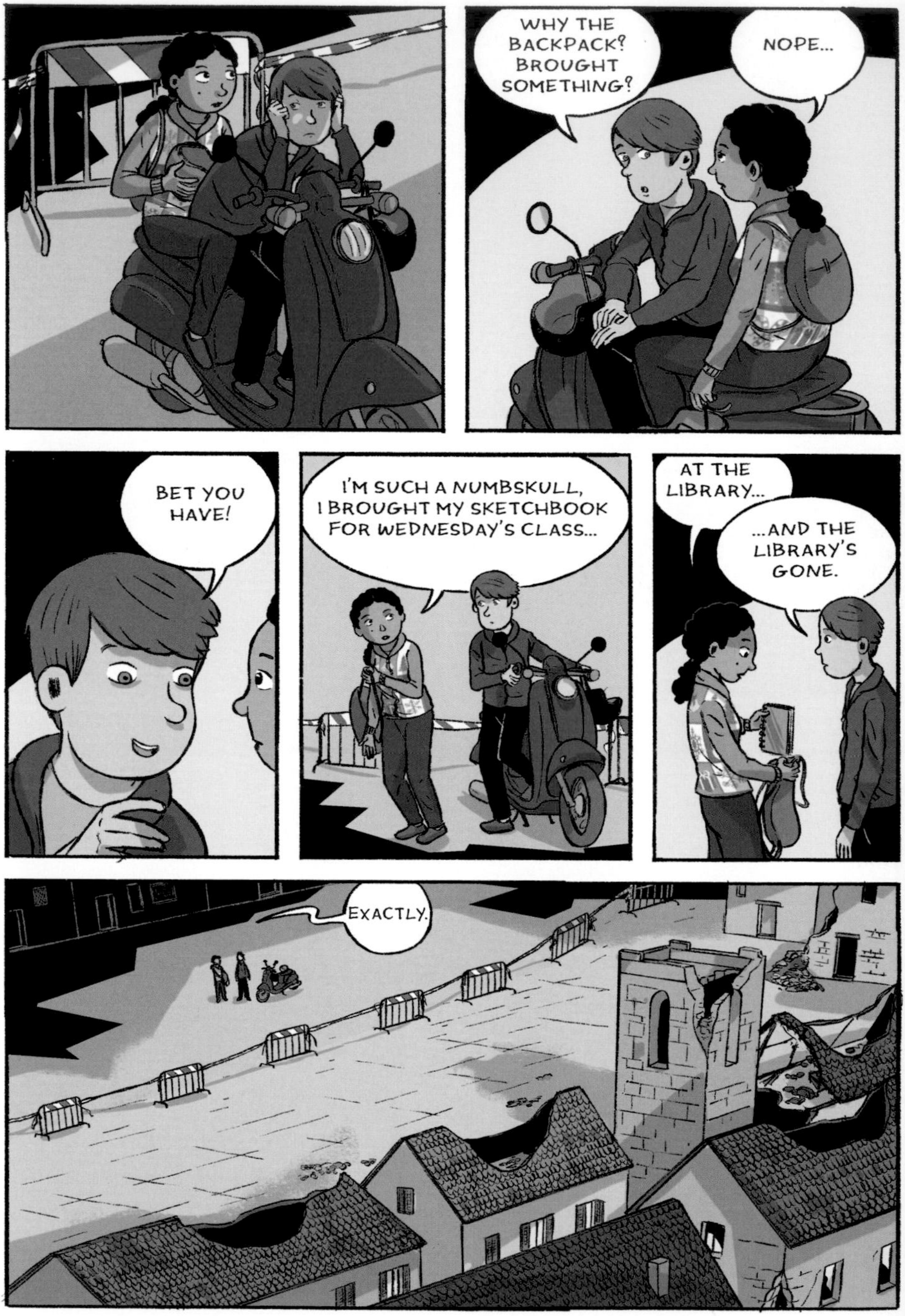
WHY THE BACKPACK? BROUGHT SOMETHING?
NOPE...
BET YOU HAVE!
I'M SUCH A NUMBSKULL, I BROUGHT MY SKETCHBOOK FOR WEDNESDAY'S CLASS...
AT THE LIBRARY...
...AND THE LIBRARY'S GONE.
EXACTLY.

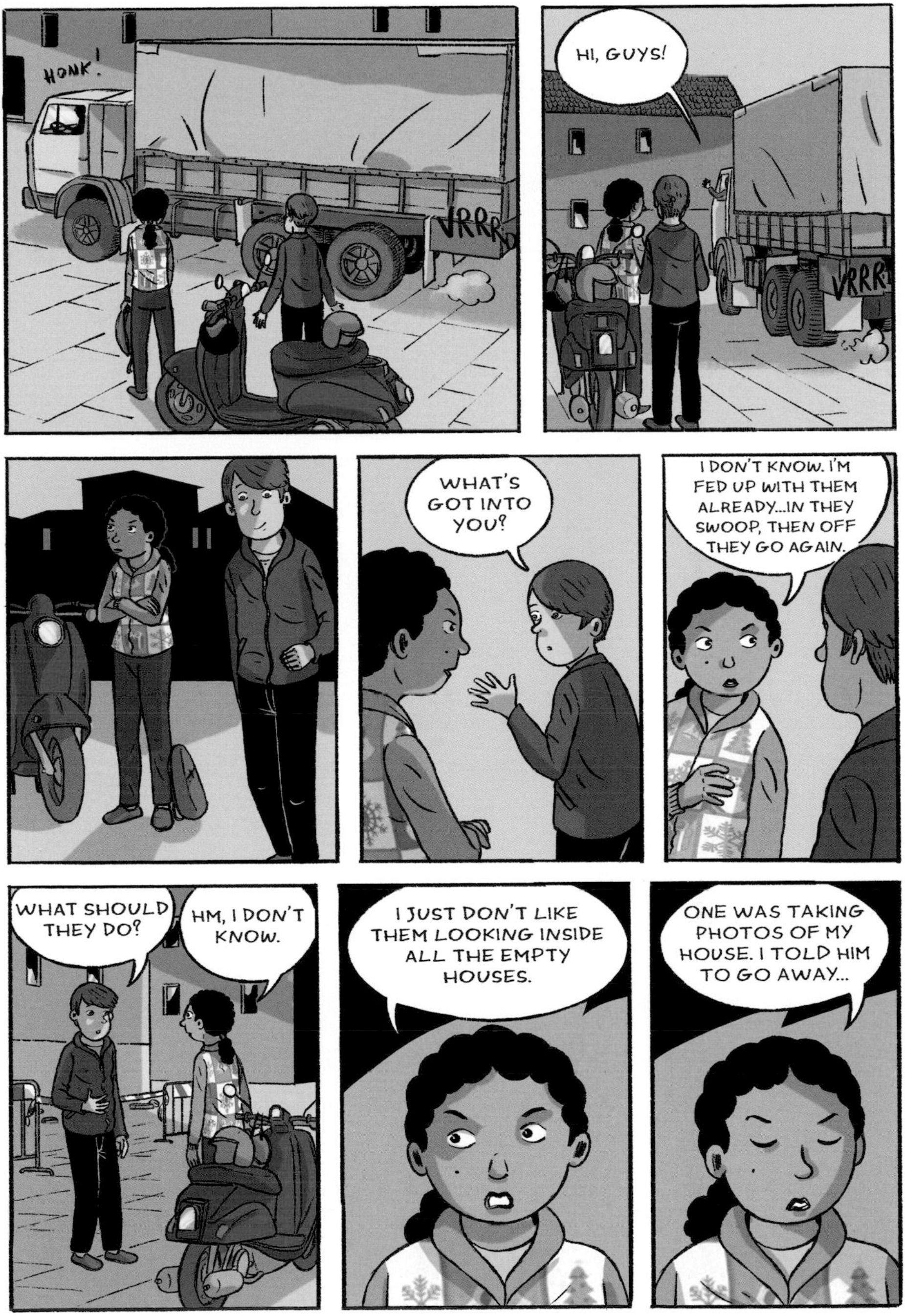
HONK!
VRRR
HI, GUYS!
VRRR
WHAT'S GOT INTO YOU?
I DON'T KNOW. I'M FED UP WITH THEM ALREADY...IN THEY SWOOP, THEN OFF THEY GO AGAIN.
WHAT SHOULD THEY DO?
HM, I DON'T KNOW.
I JUST DON'T LIKE THEM LOOKING INSIDE ALL THE EMPTY HOUSES.
ONE WAS TAKING PHOTOS OF MY HOUSE. I TOLD HIM TO GO AWAY...

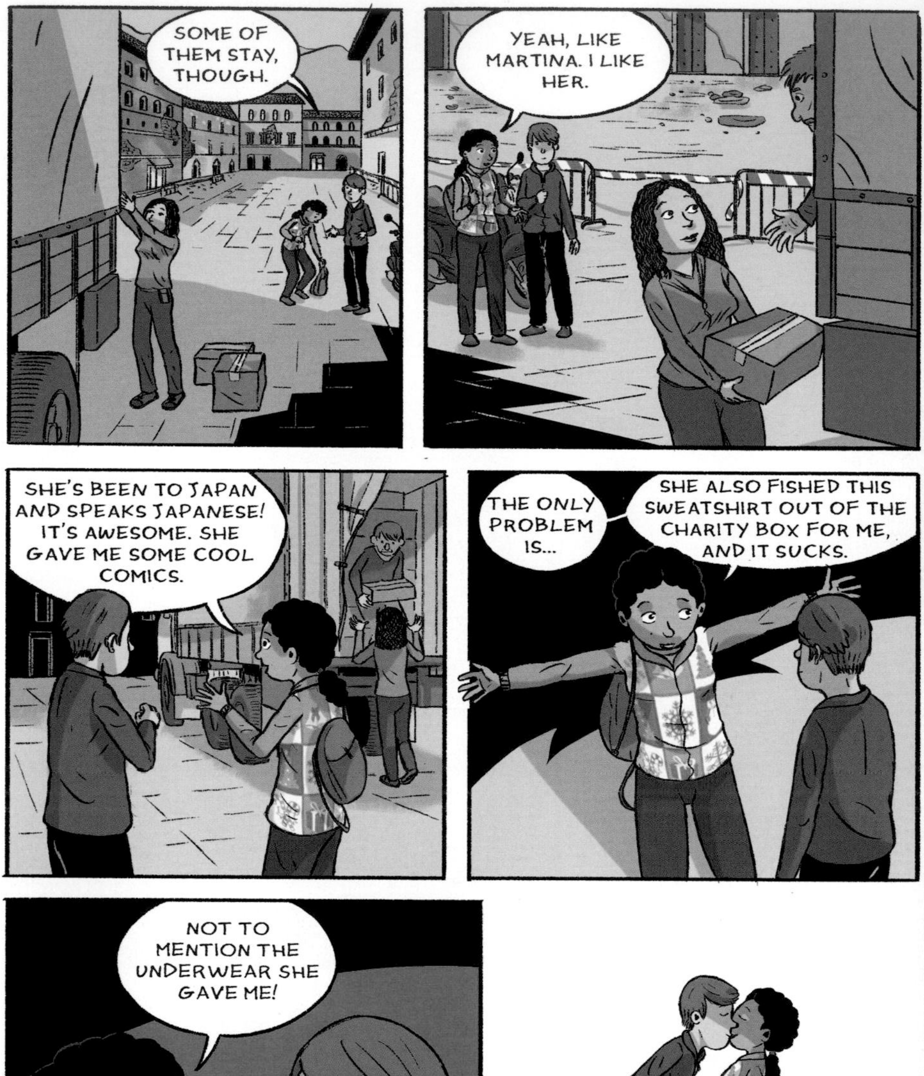
SOME OF THEM STAY, THOUGH.
YEAH, LIKE MARTINA. I LIKE HER.
SHE'S BEEN TO JAPAN AND SPEAKS JAPANESE! IT'S AWESOME. SHE GAVE ME SOME COOL COMICS.
THE ONLY PROBLEM IS...
SHE ALSO FISHED THIS SWEATSHIRT OUT OF THE CHARITY BOX FOR ME, AND IT SUCKS.
NOT TO MENTION THE UNDERWEAR SHE GAVE ME!

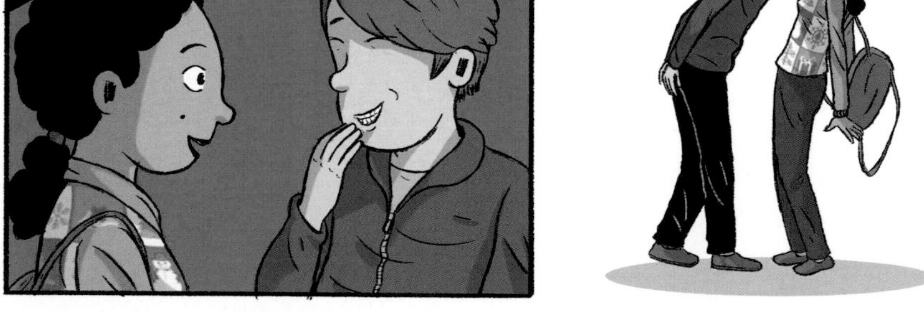

3.
In which the crash comes.

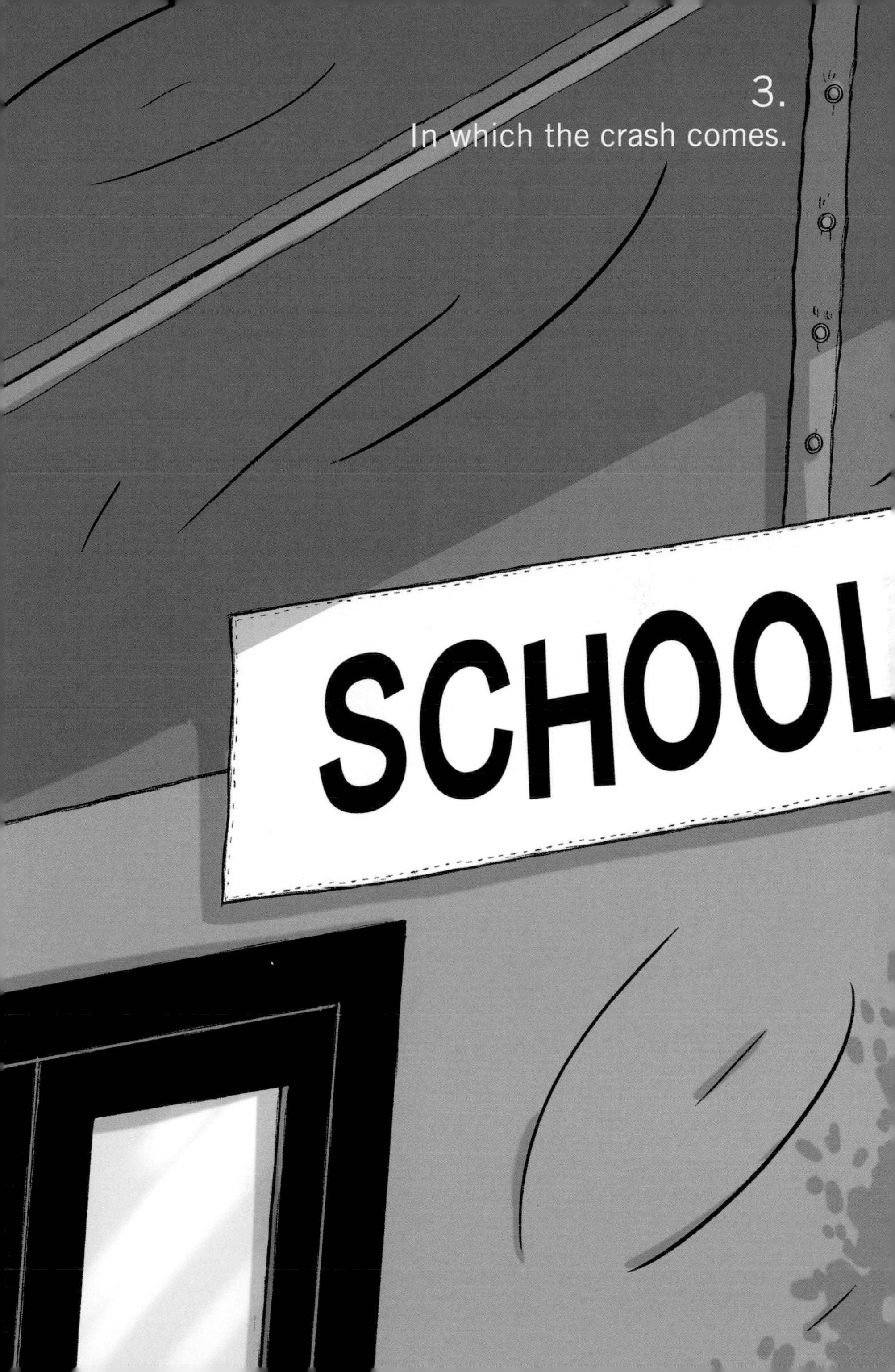
SCHOOL

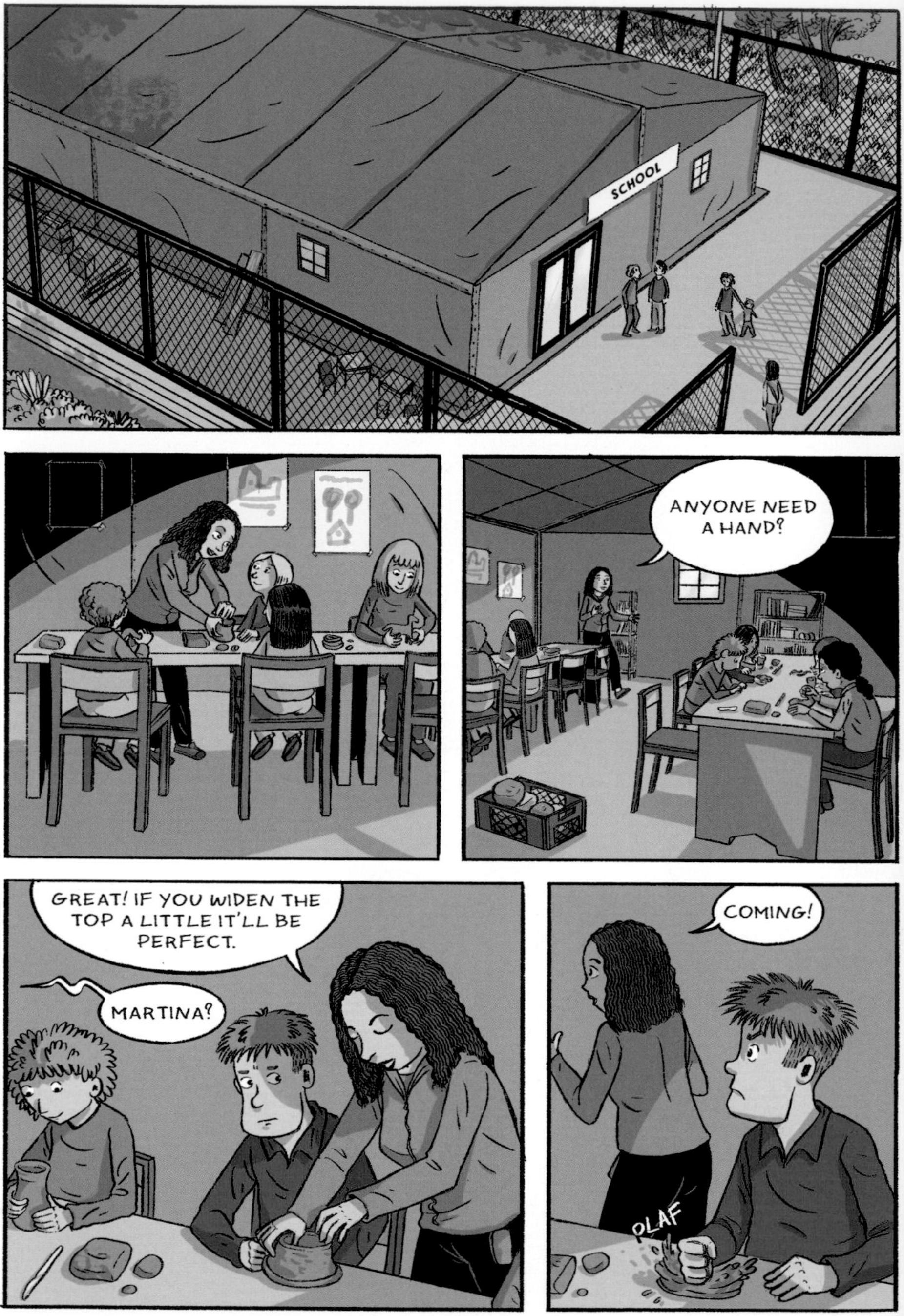
SCHOOL
ANYONE NEED A HAND?
GREAT! IF YOU WIDEN THE TOP A LITTLE IT'LL BE PERFECT.
MARTINA?
COMING!
PLAF

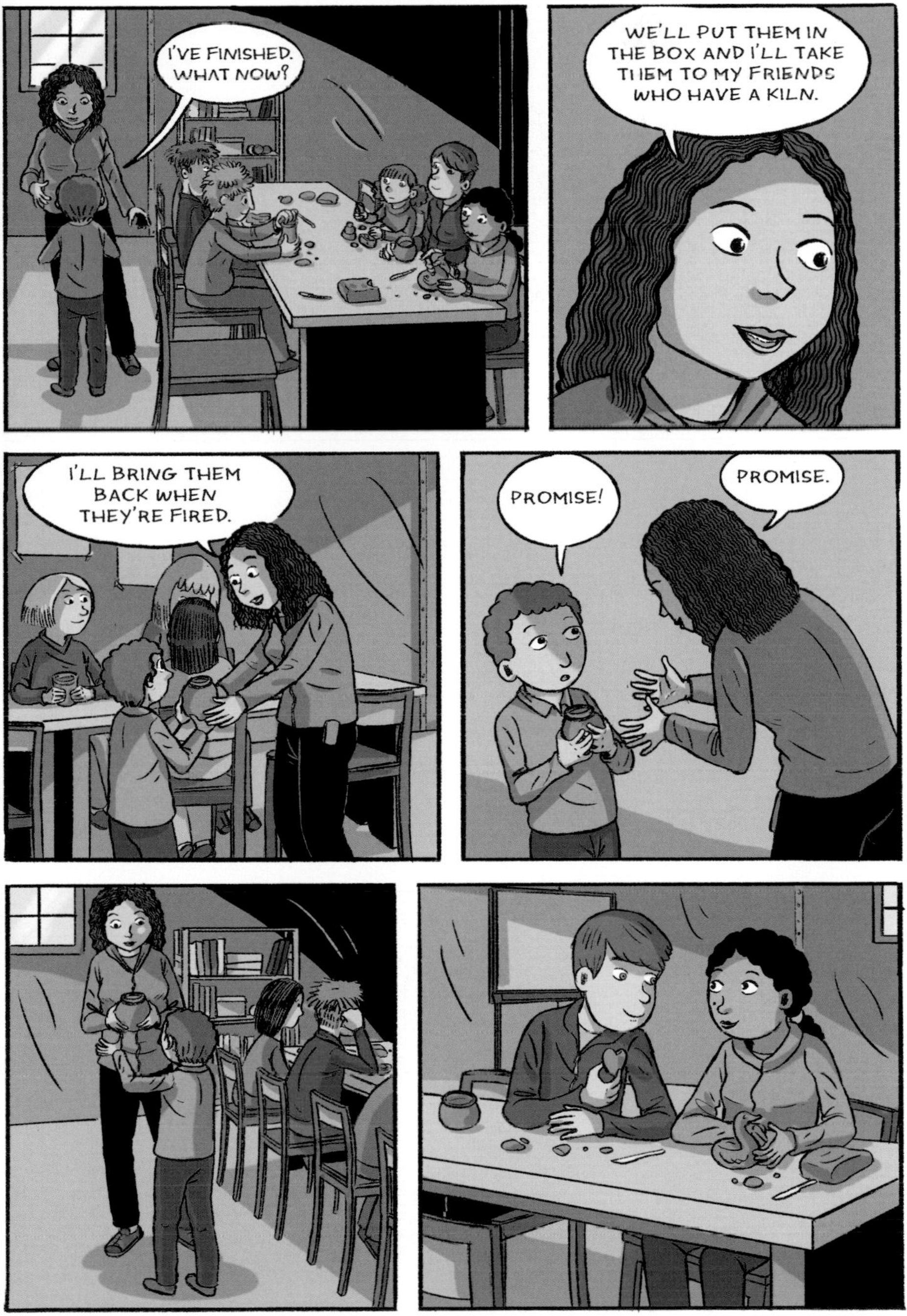
I'VE FINISHED. WHAT NOW?
WE'LL PUT THEM IN THE BOX AND I'LL TAKE THEM TO MY FRIENDS WHO HAVE A KILN.
I'LL BRING THEM BACK WHEN THEY'RE FIRED.
PROMISE!
PROMISE.

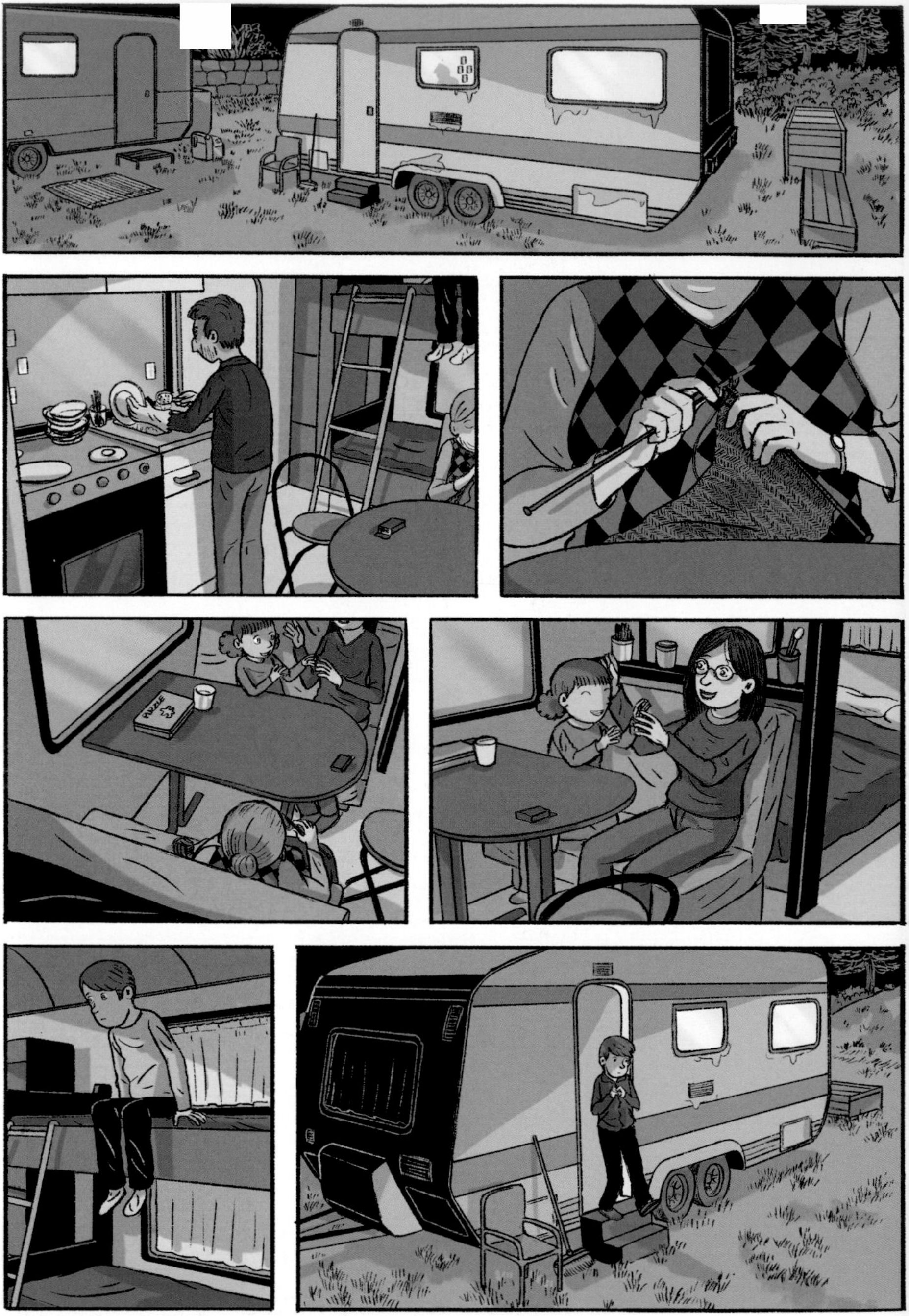
PUZZLE

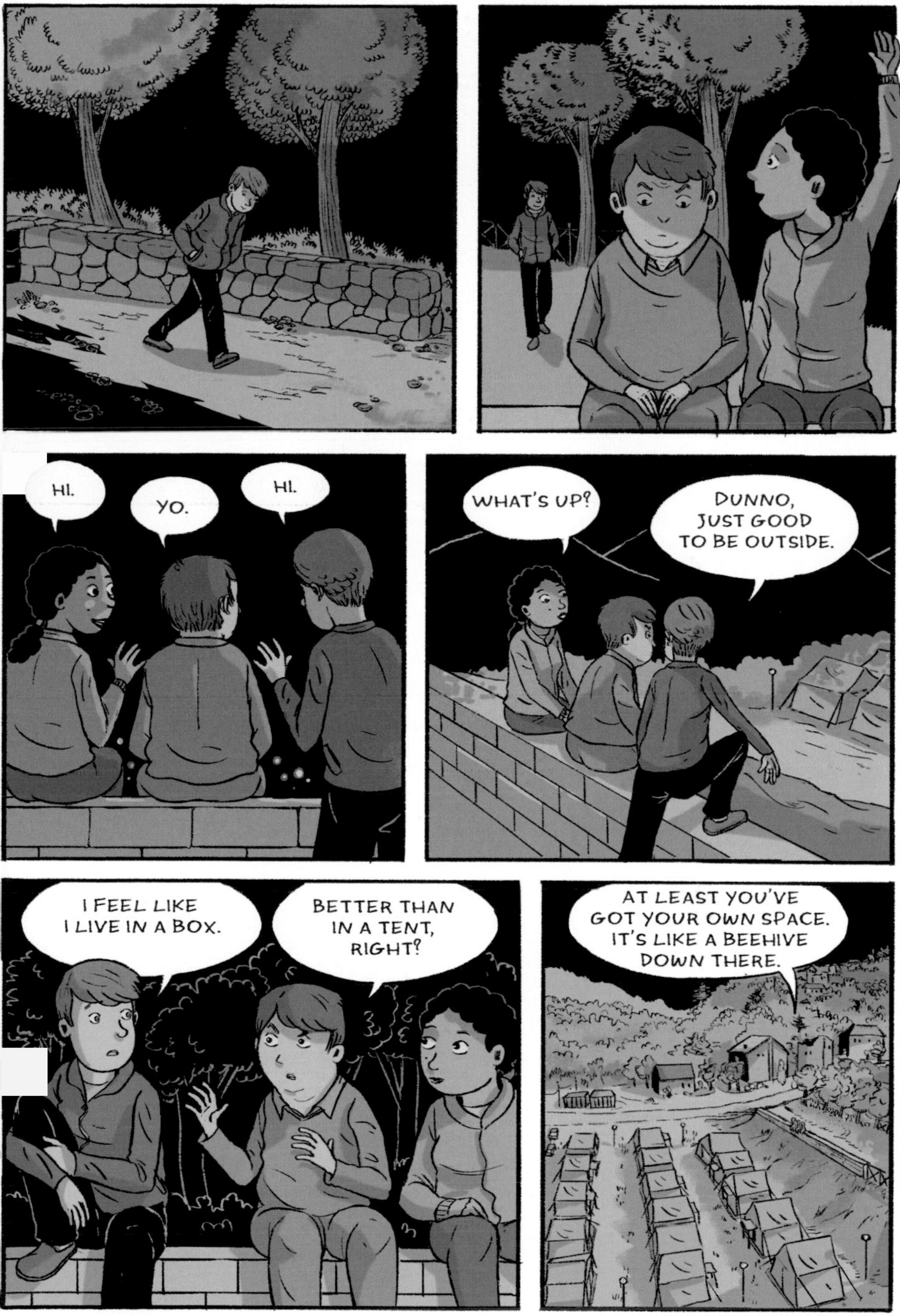
HI.
YO.
HI.
WHAT'S UP?
DUNNO, JUST GOOD TO BE OUTSIDE.
I FEEL LIKE I LIVE IN A BOX.
BETTER THAN IN A TENT, RIGHT?
AT LEAST YOU'VE GOT YOUR OWN SPACE. IT'S LIKE A BEEHIVE DOWN THERE.

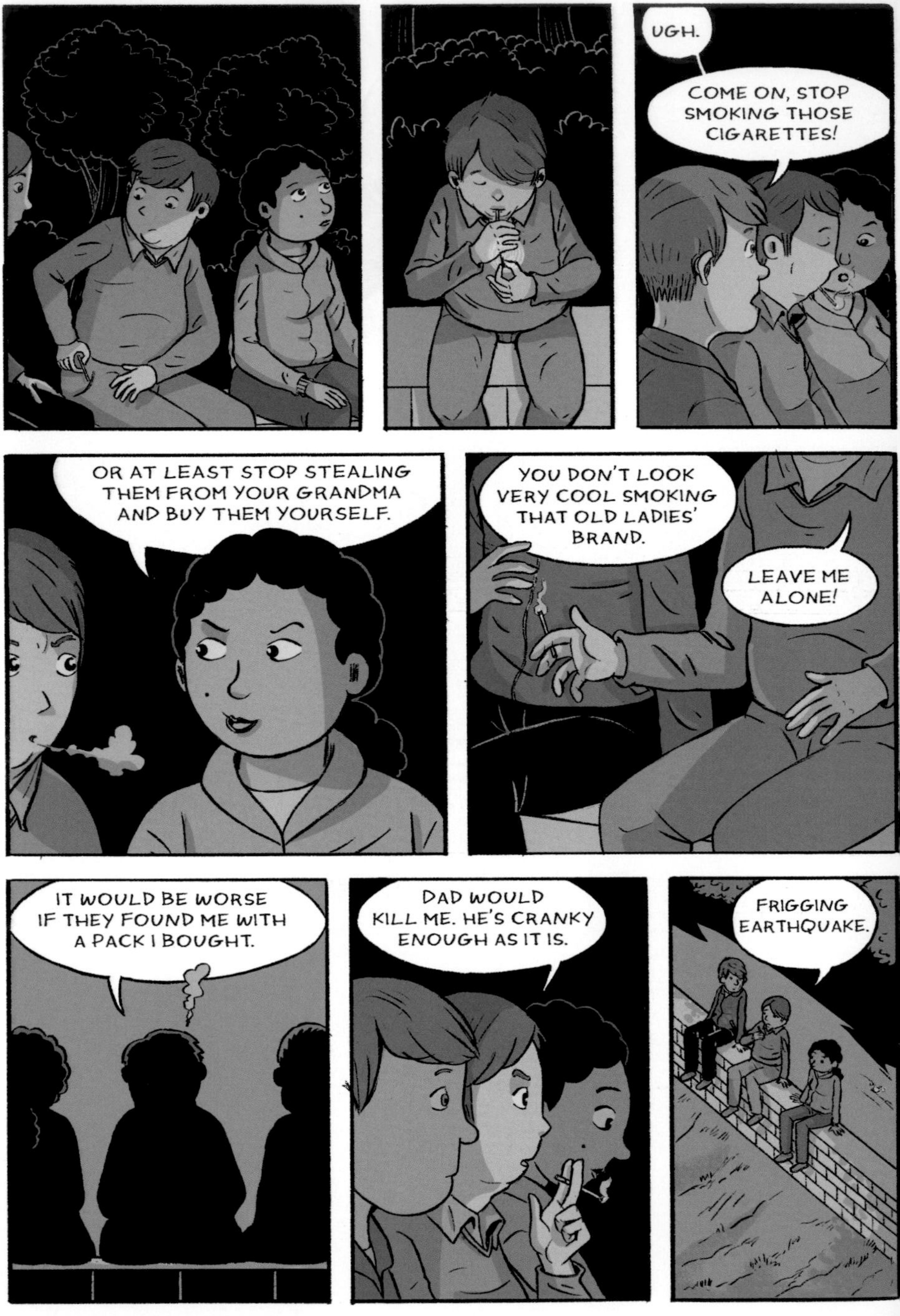
UGH.
COME ON, STOP SMOKING THOSE CIGARETTES!
OR AT LEAST STOP STEALING THEM FROM YOUR GRANDMA AND BUY THEM YOURSELF.
YOU DON'T LOOK VERY COOL SMOKING THAT OLD LADIES' BRAND.
LEAVE ME ALONE!
IT WOULD BE WORSE IF THEY FOUND ME WITH A PACK I BOUGHT.
DAD WOULD KILL ME. HE'S CRANKY ENOUGH AS IT IS.
FRIGGING EARTHQUAKE.

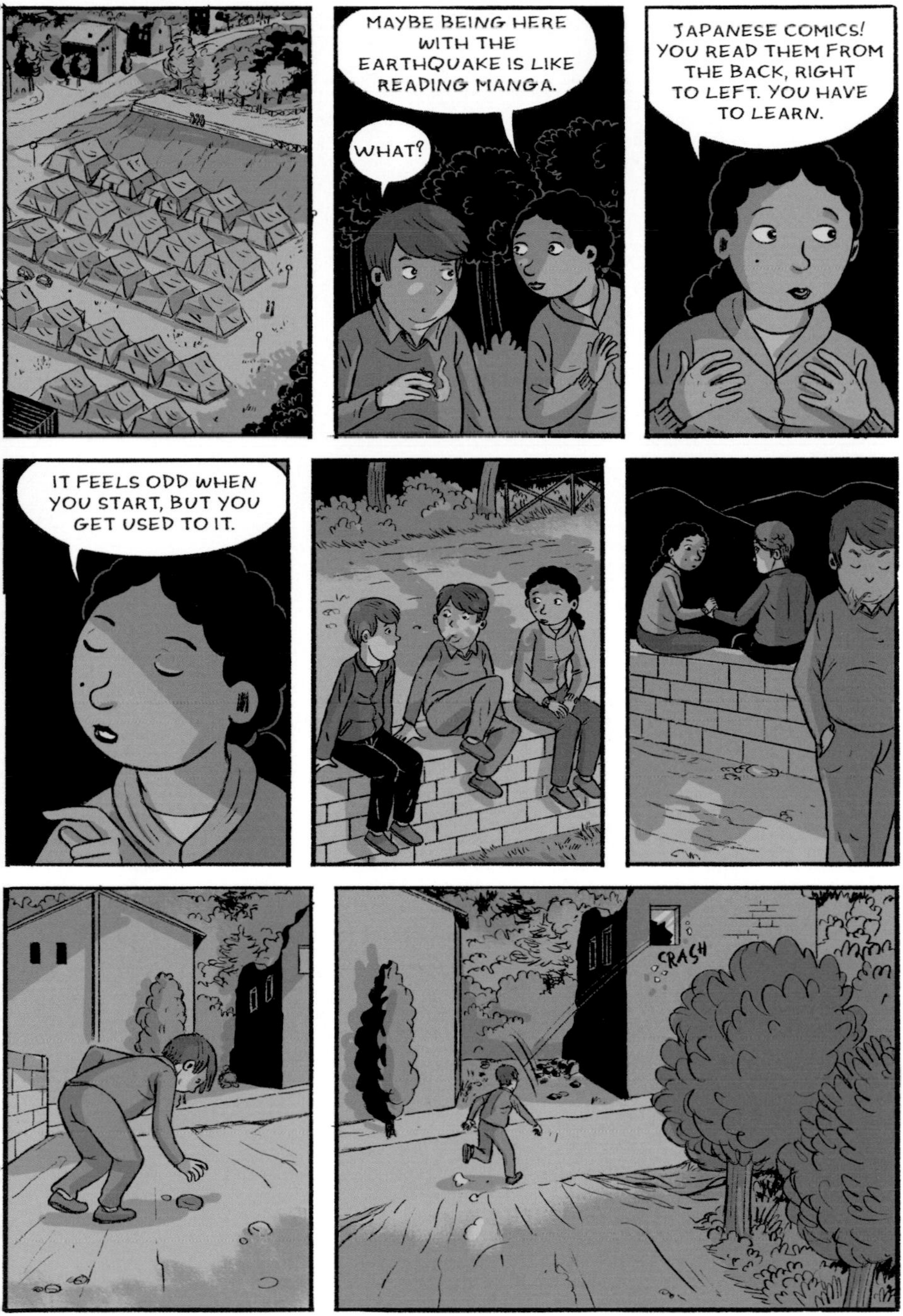
MAYBE BEING HERE WITH THE EARTHQUAKE IS LIKE READING MANGA.
WHAT?
JAPANESE COMICS! YOU READ THEM FROM THE BACK, RIGHT TO LEFT. YOU HAVE TO LEARN.
IT FEELS ODD WHEN YOU START, BUT YOU GET USED TO IT.
CRASH

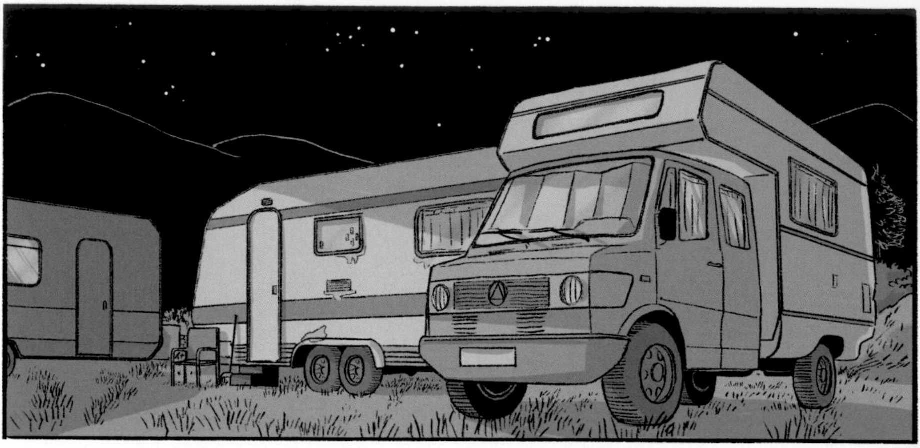

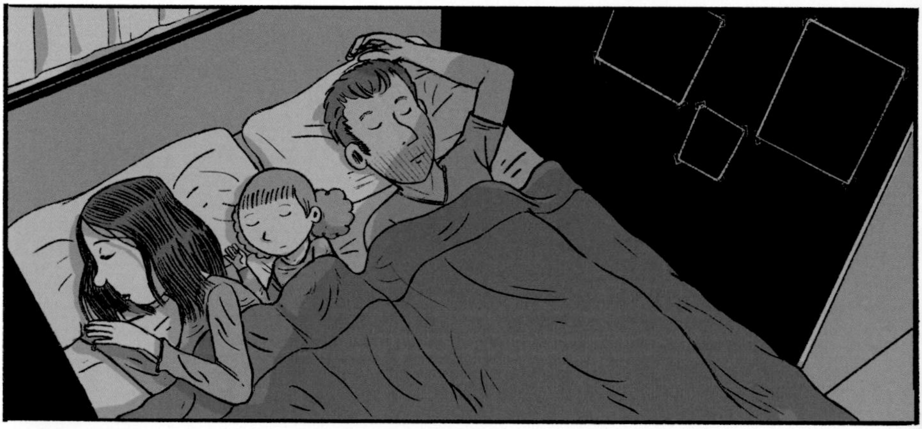

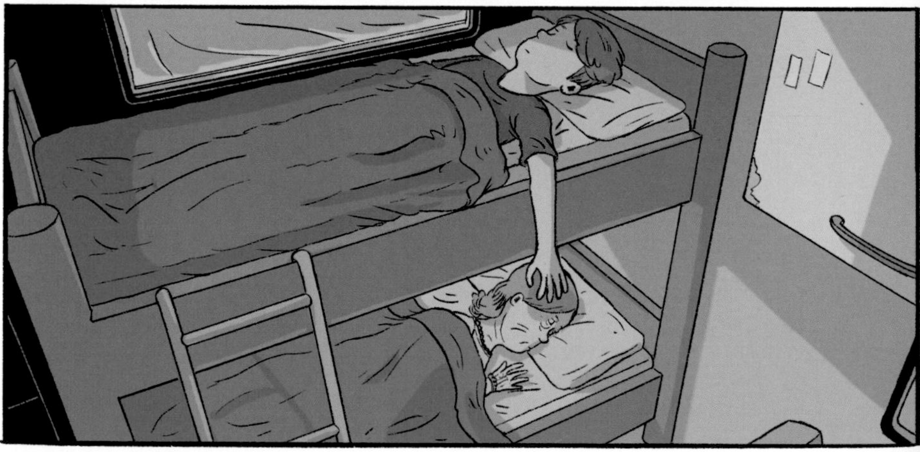

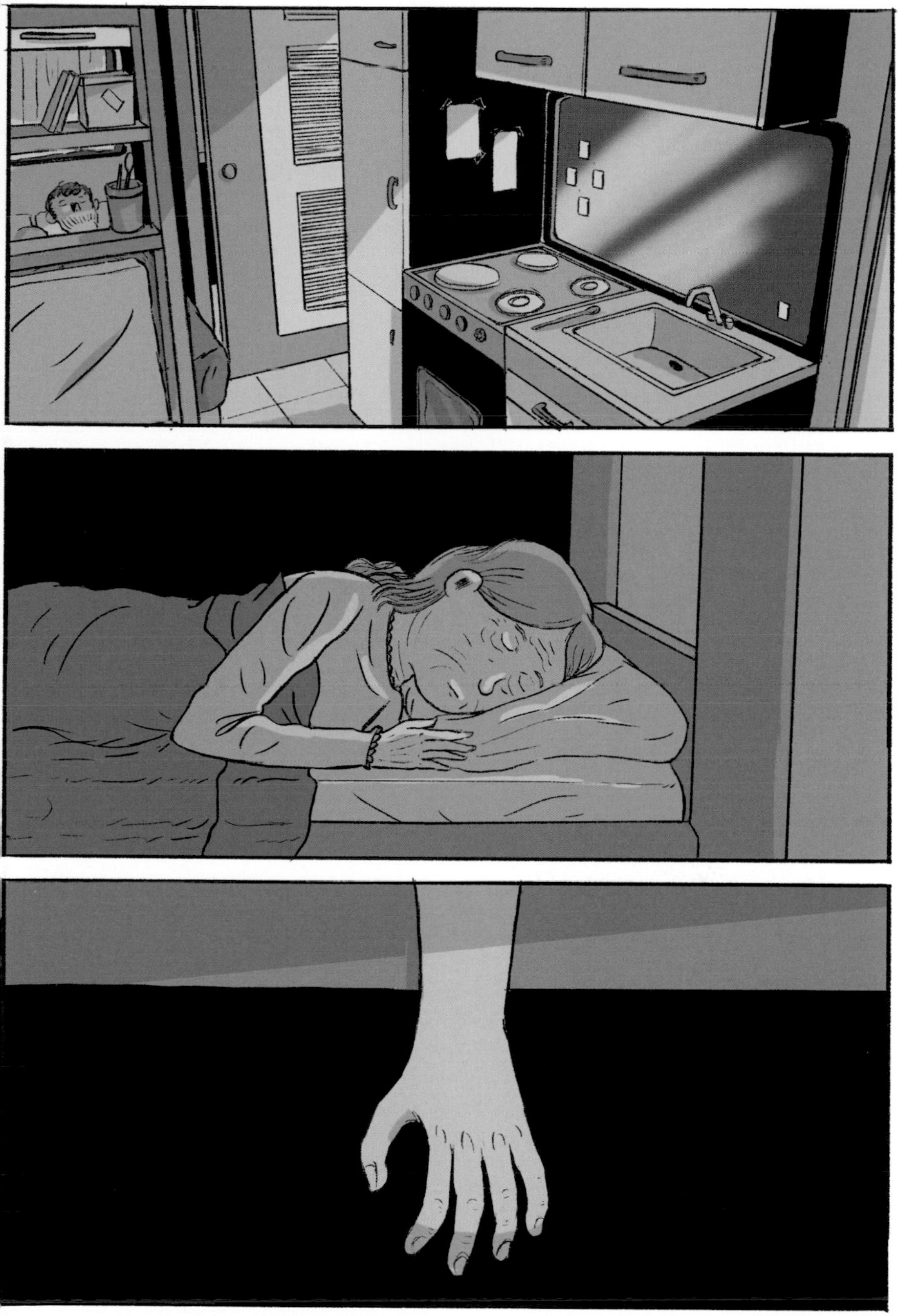

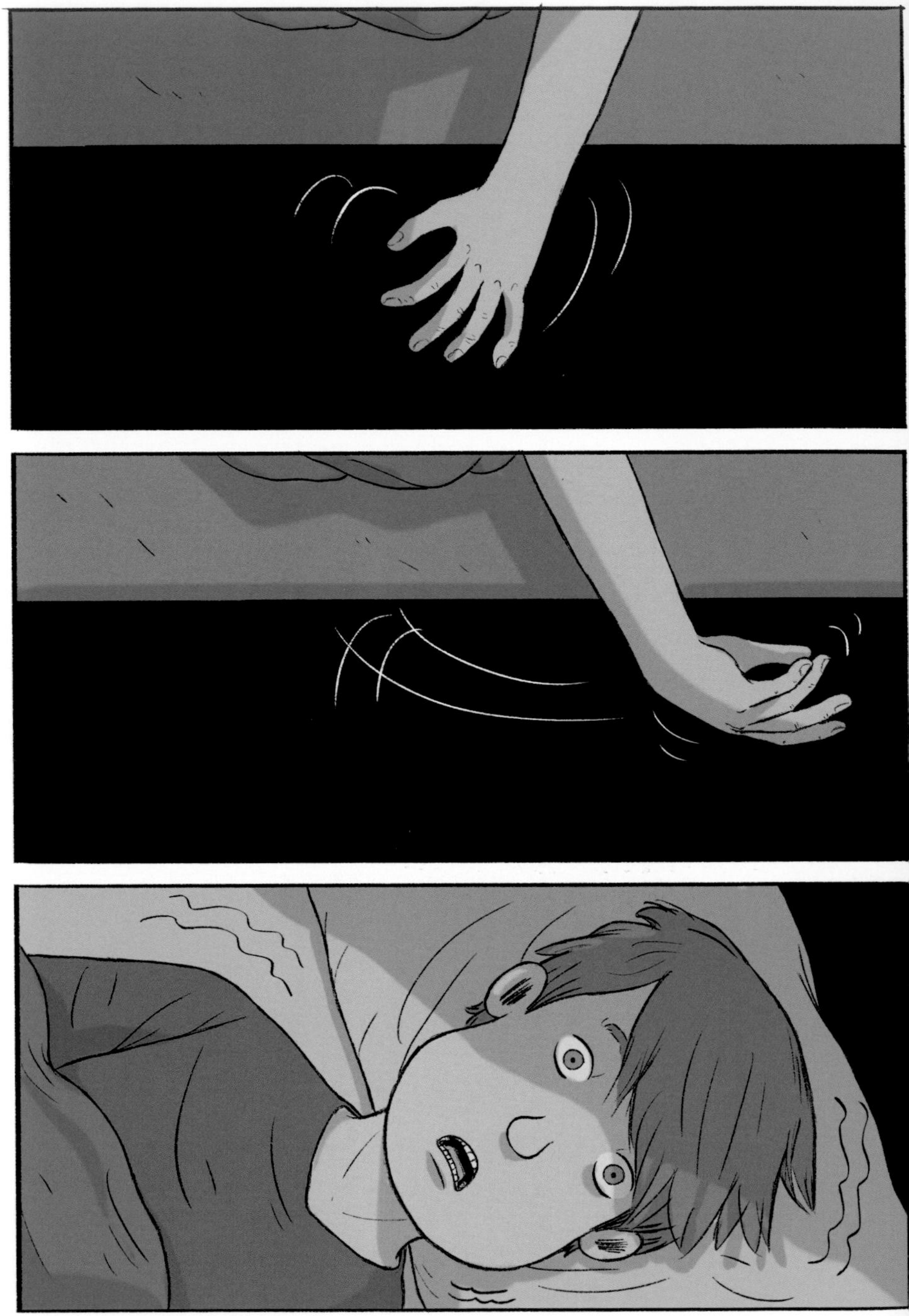

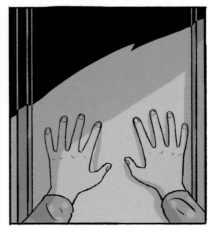

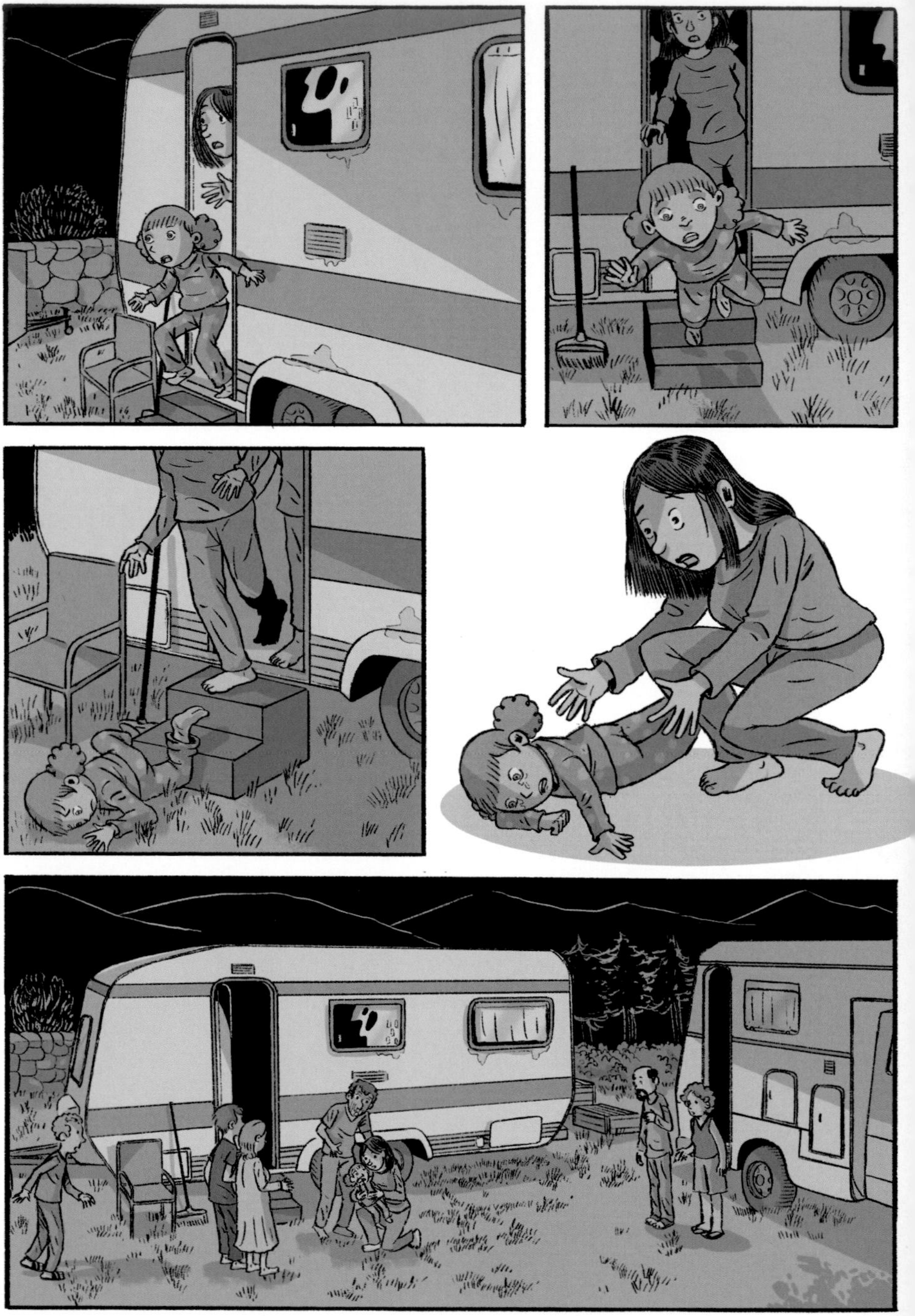

4.
In which we realize we're all on the turtle's back.

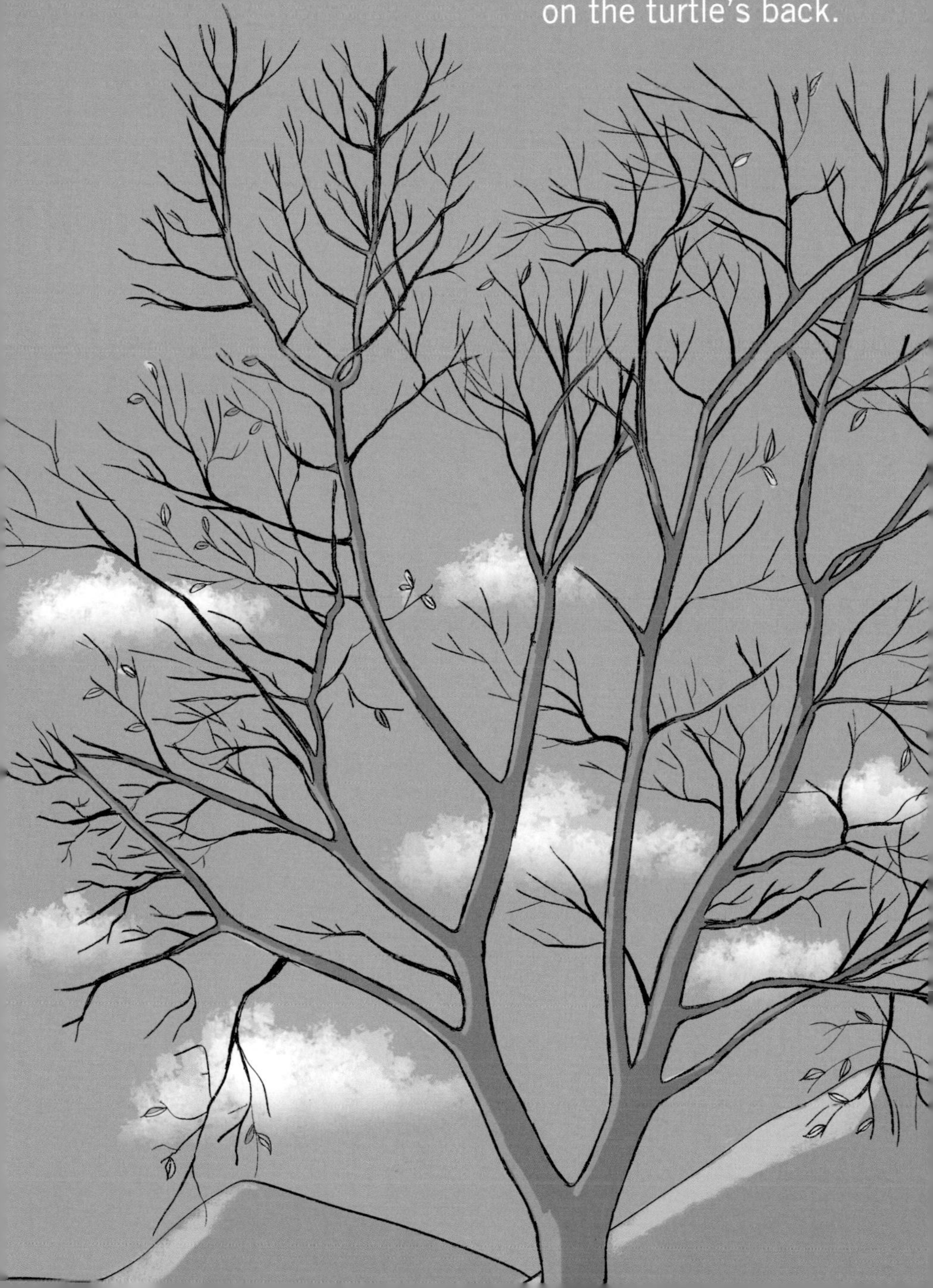

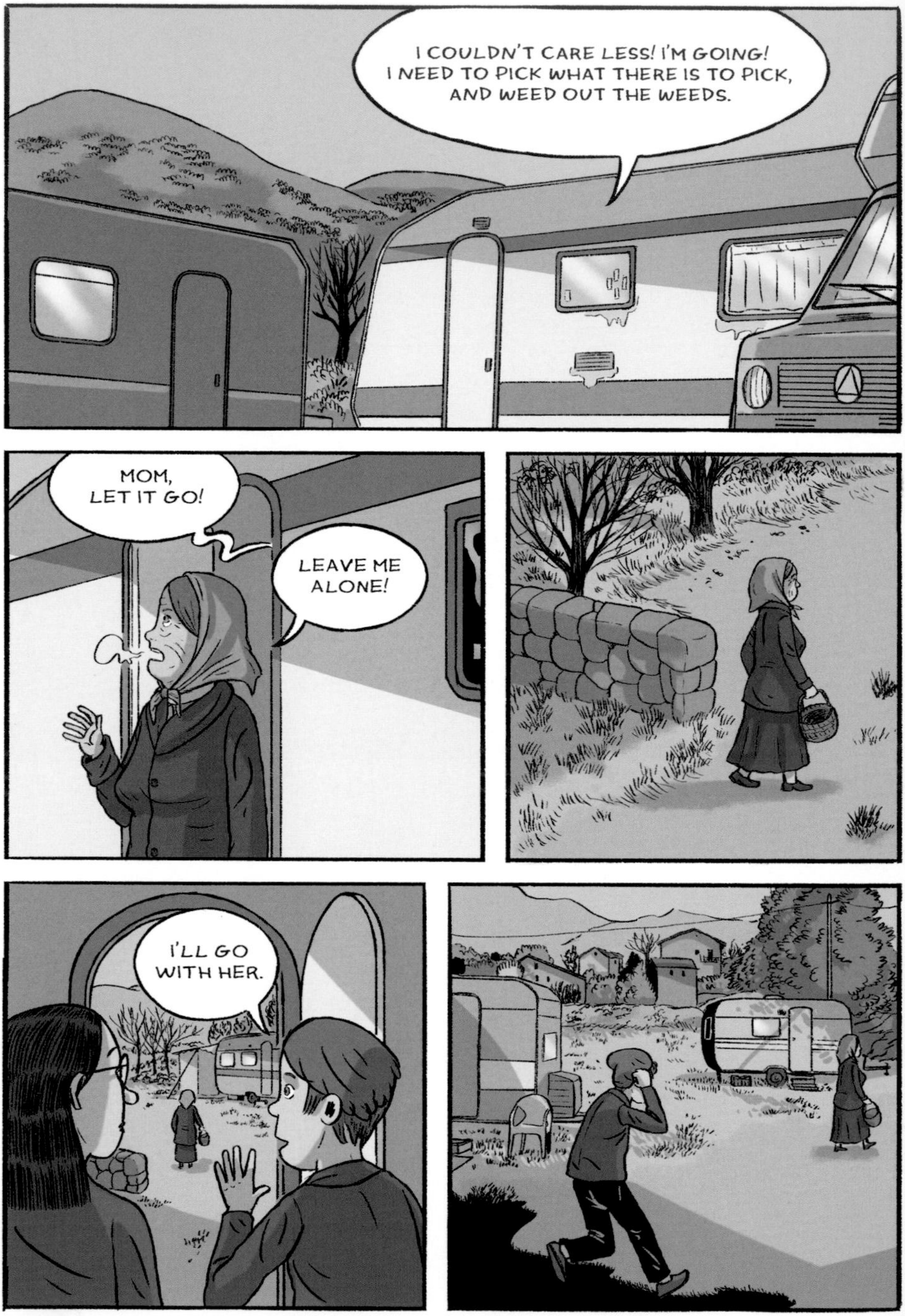
I COULDN'T CARE LESS! I'M GOING! I NEED TO PICK WHAT THERE IS TO PICK, AND WEED OUT THE WEEDS.
MOM, LET IT GO!
LEAVE ME ALONE!
I'LL GO WITH HER.

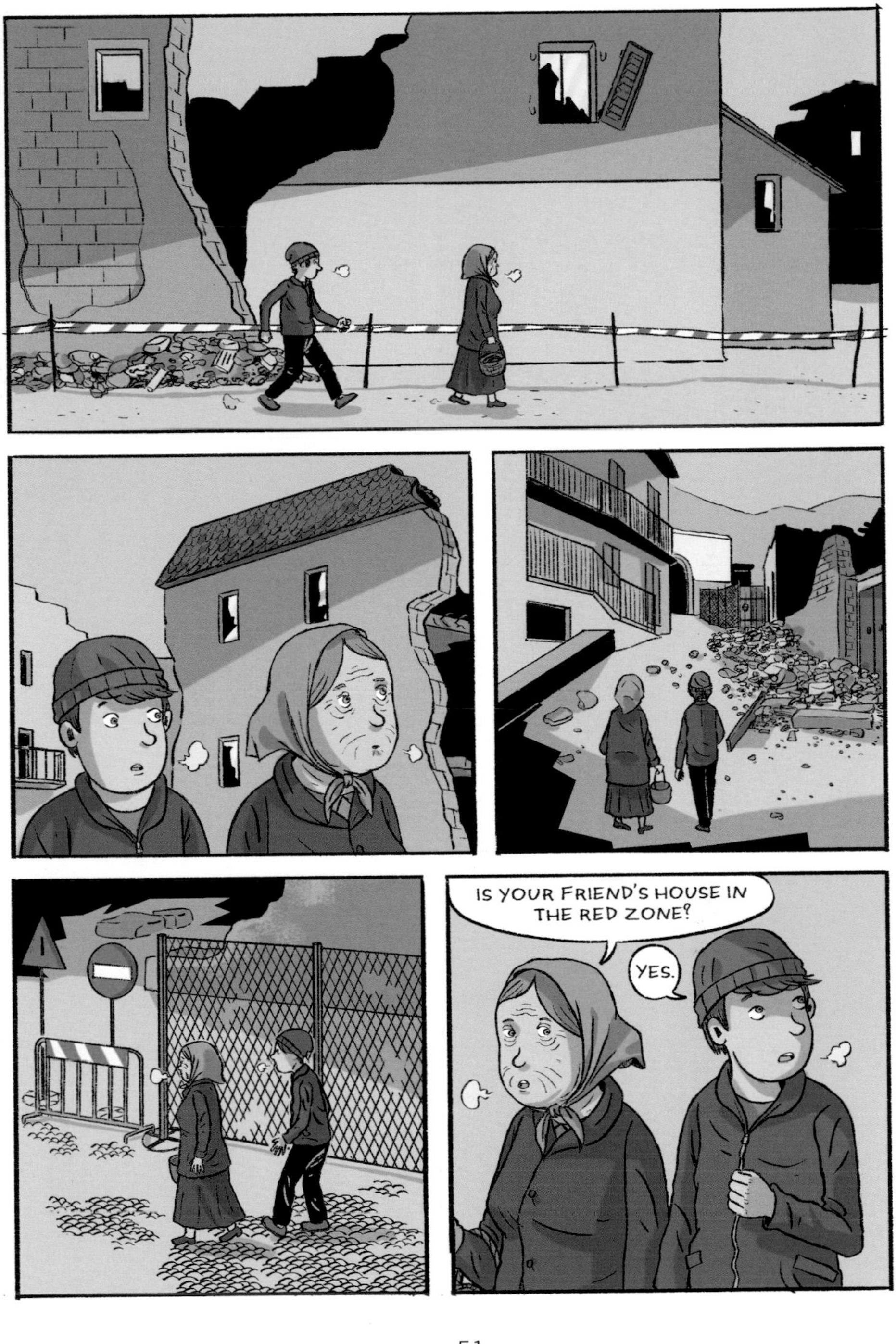
IS YOUR FRIEND'S HOUSE IN THE RED ZONE?
YES.

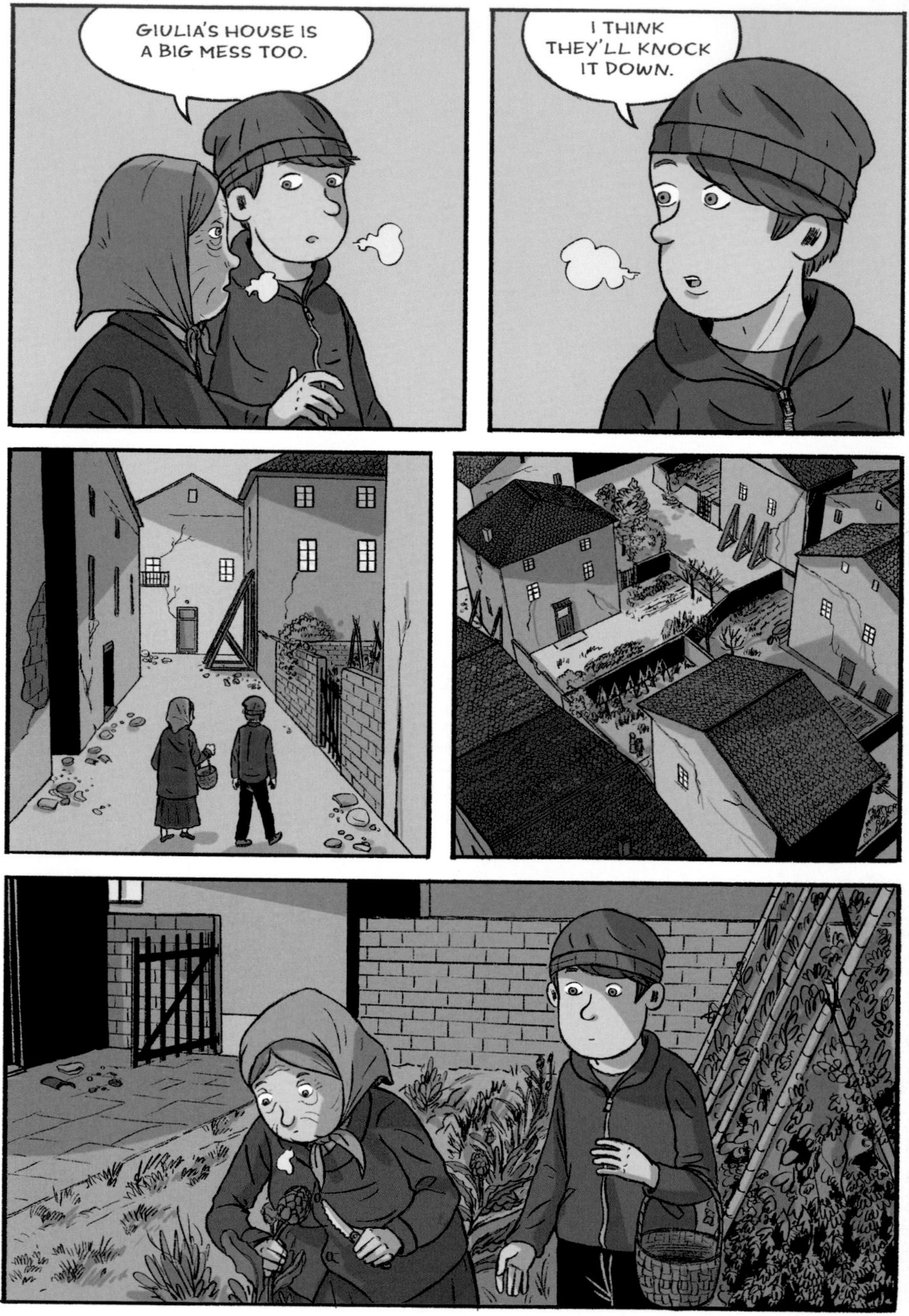
GIULIA'S HOUSE IS A BIG MESS TOO.
I THINK THEY'LL KNOCK IT DOWN.

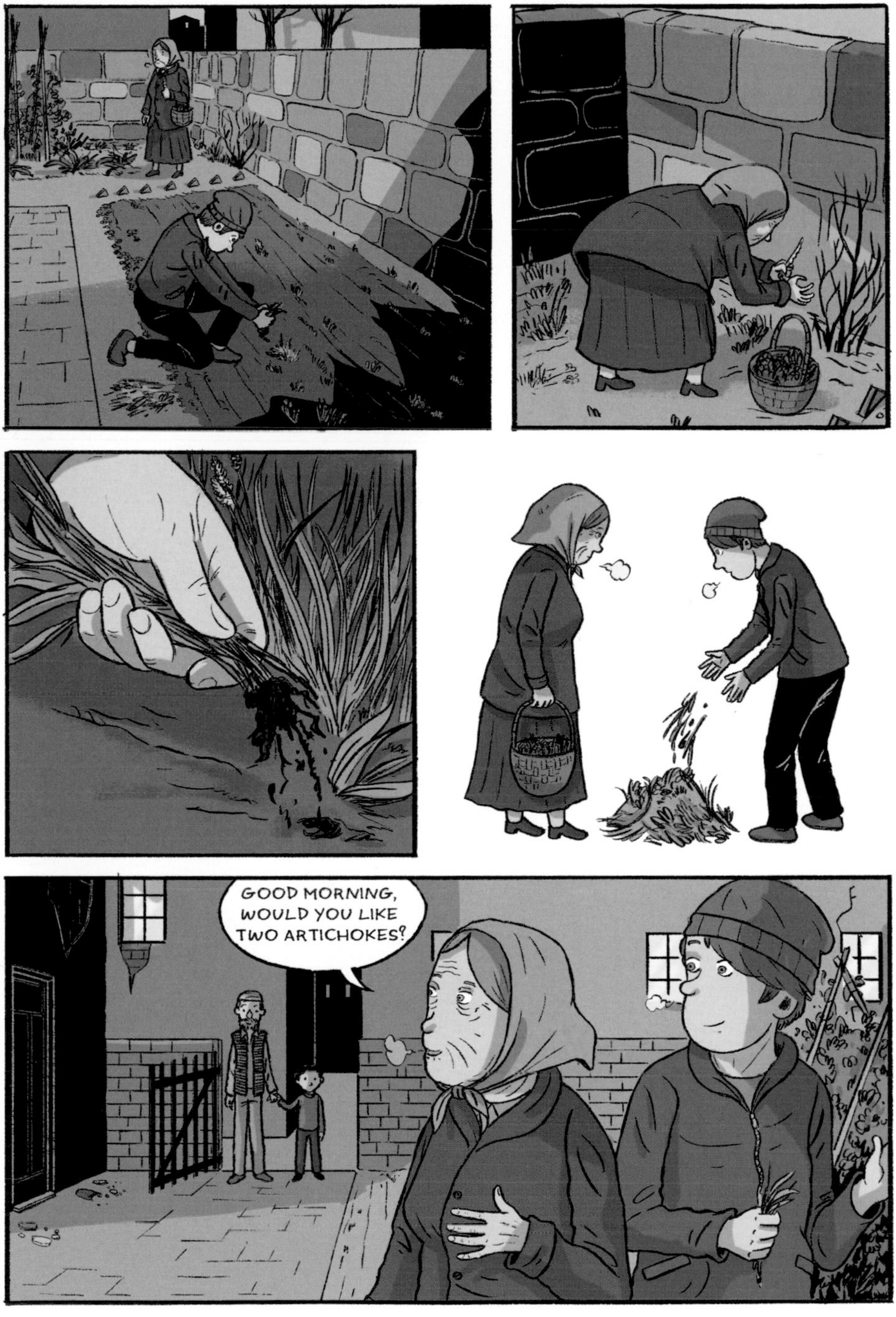
GOOD MORNING, WOULD YOU LIKE TWO ARTICHOKES?

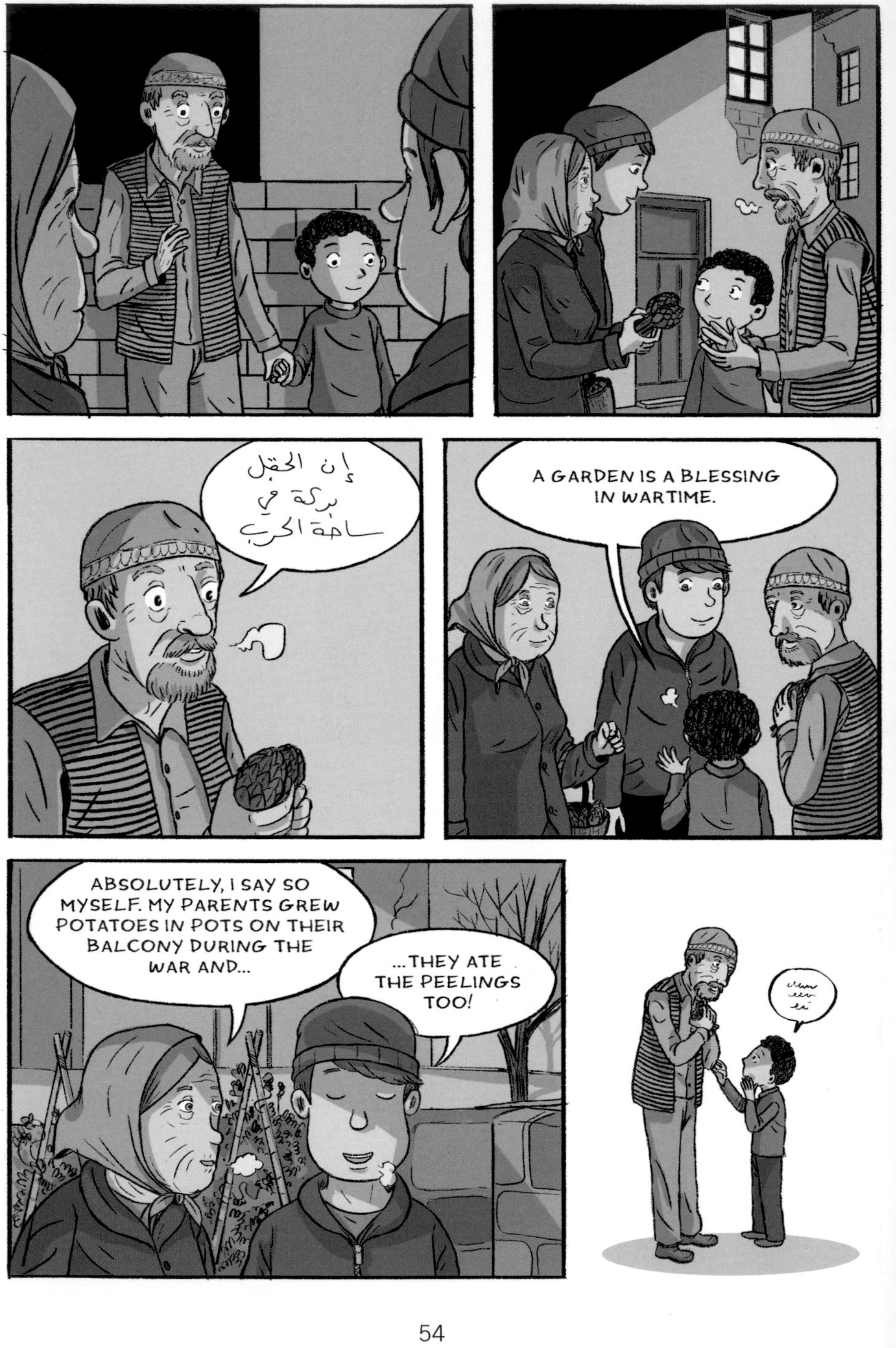
إن الحقل
بركة في
ساحة الحرب
A GARDEN IS A BLESSING IN WARTIME.
ABSOLUTELY, I SAY SO MYSELF. MY PARENTS GREW POTATOES IN POTS ON THEIR BALCONY DURING THE WAR AND...
...THEY ATE THE PEELINGS TOO!

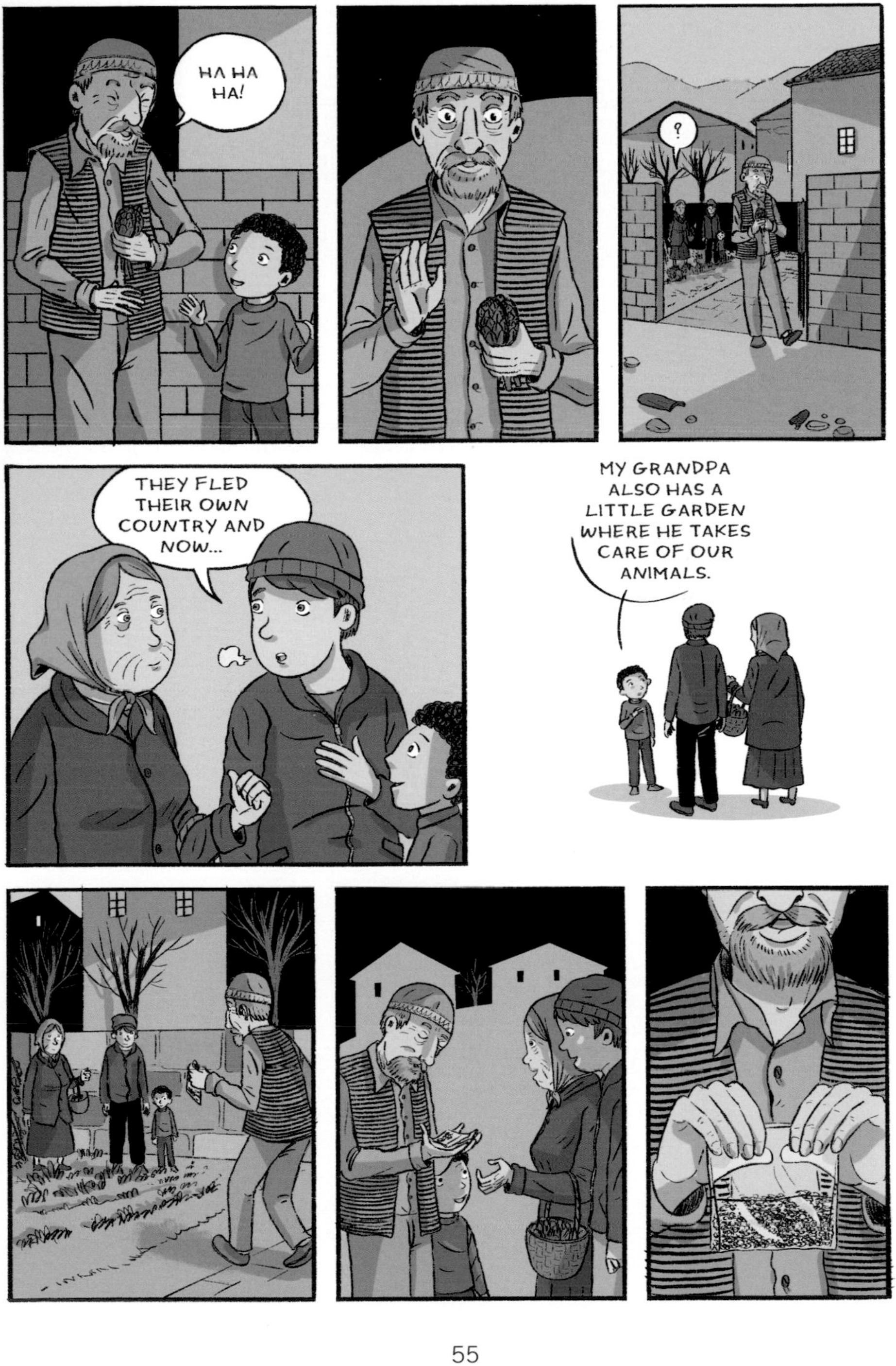
HA HA HA!
?
THEY FLED THEIR OWN COUNTRY AND NOW...
MY GRANDPA ALSO HAS A LITTLE GARDEN WHERE HE TAKES CARE OF OUR ANIMALS.

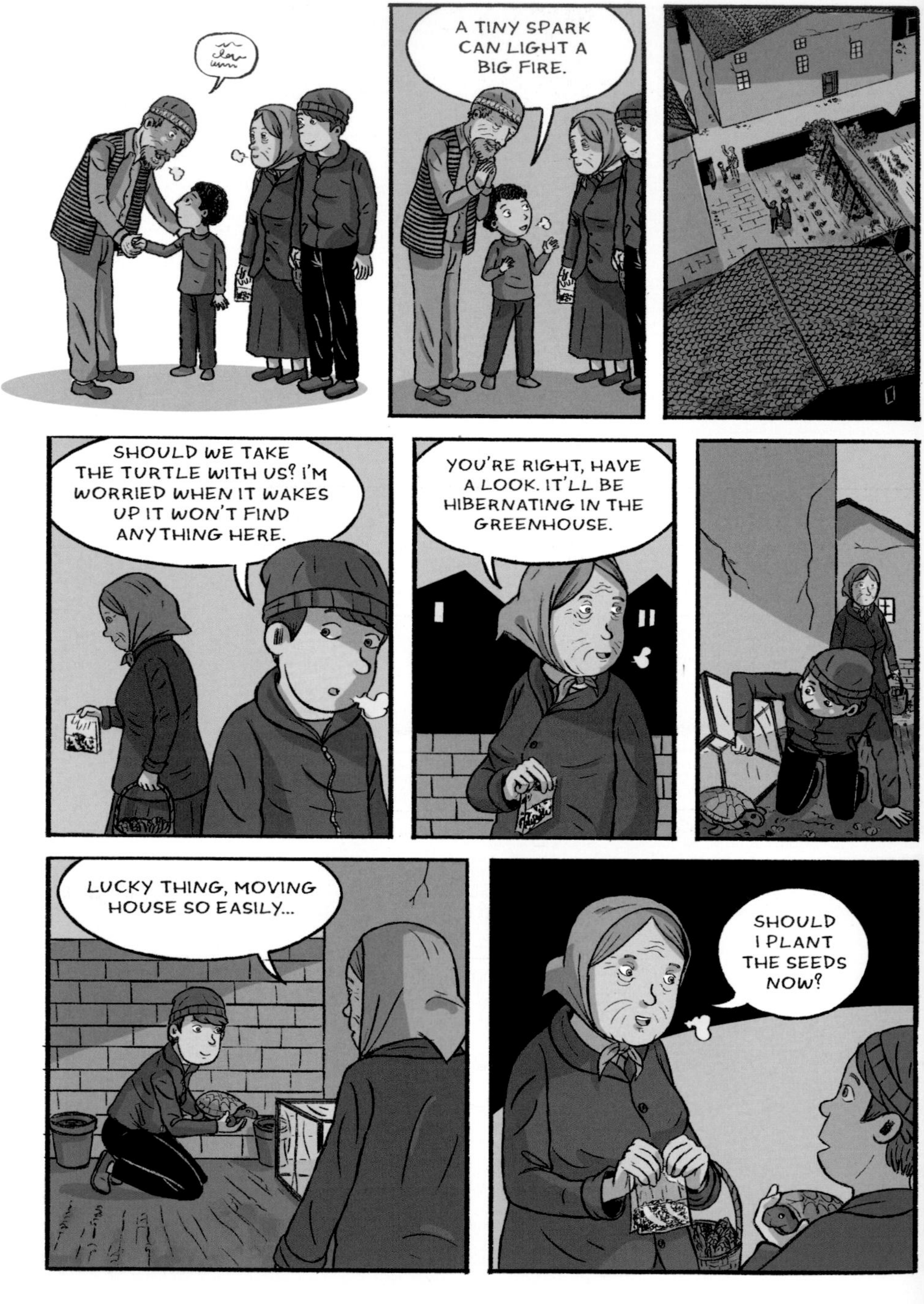
A TINY SPARK CAN LIGHT A BIG FIRE.
SHOULD WE TAKE THE TURTLE WITH US? I'M WORRIED WHEN IT WAKES UP IT WON'T FIND ANYTHING HERE.
YOU'RE RIGHT, HAVE A LOOK. IT'LL BE HIBERNATING IN THE GREENHOUSE.
LUCKY THING, MOVING HOUSE SO EASILY...
SHOULD I PLANT THE SEEDS NOW?

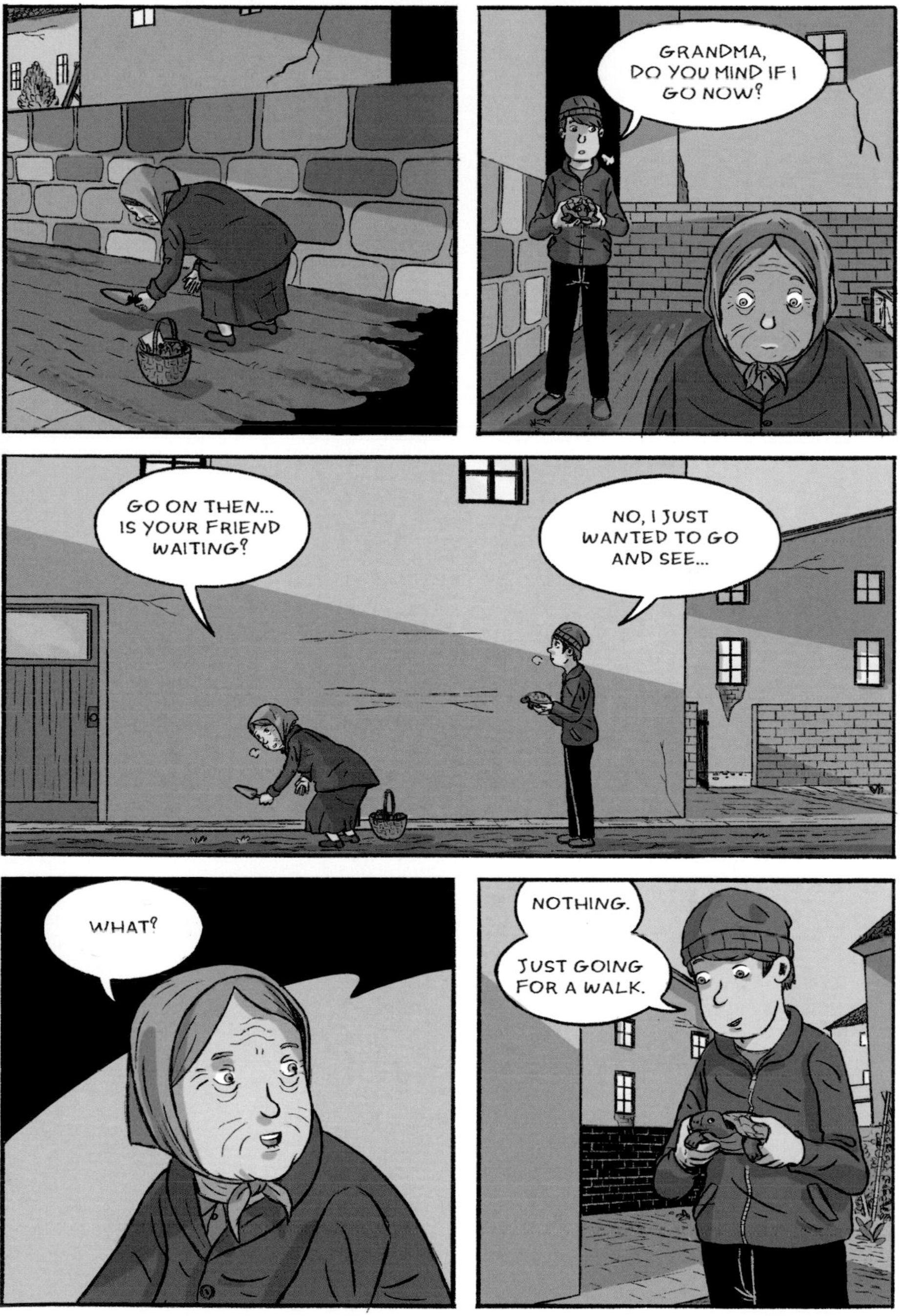
GRANDMA,
DO YOU MIND IF I
GO NOW?
GO ON THEN...
IS YOUR FRIEND
WAITING?
NO, I JUST
WANTED TO GO
AND SEE...
WHAT?
NOTHING.
JUST GOING
FOR A WALK.

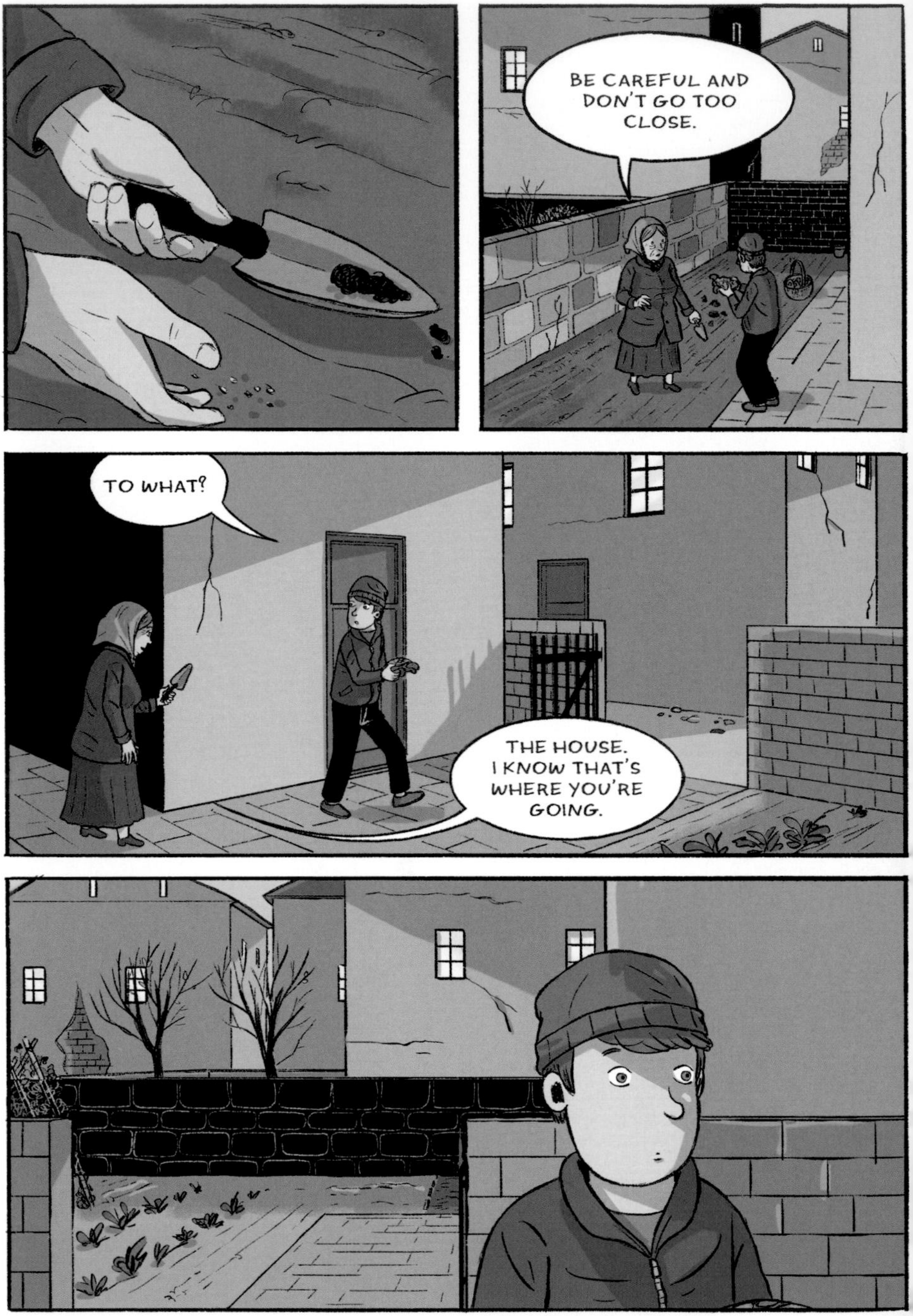

BE CAREFUL AND DON'T GO TOO CLOSE.
TO WHAT?
THE HOUSE. I KNOW THAT'S WHERE YOU'RE GOING.

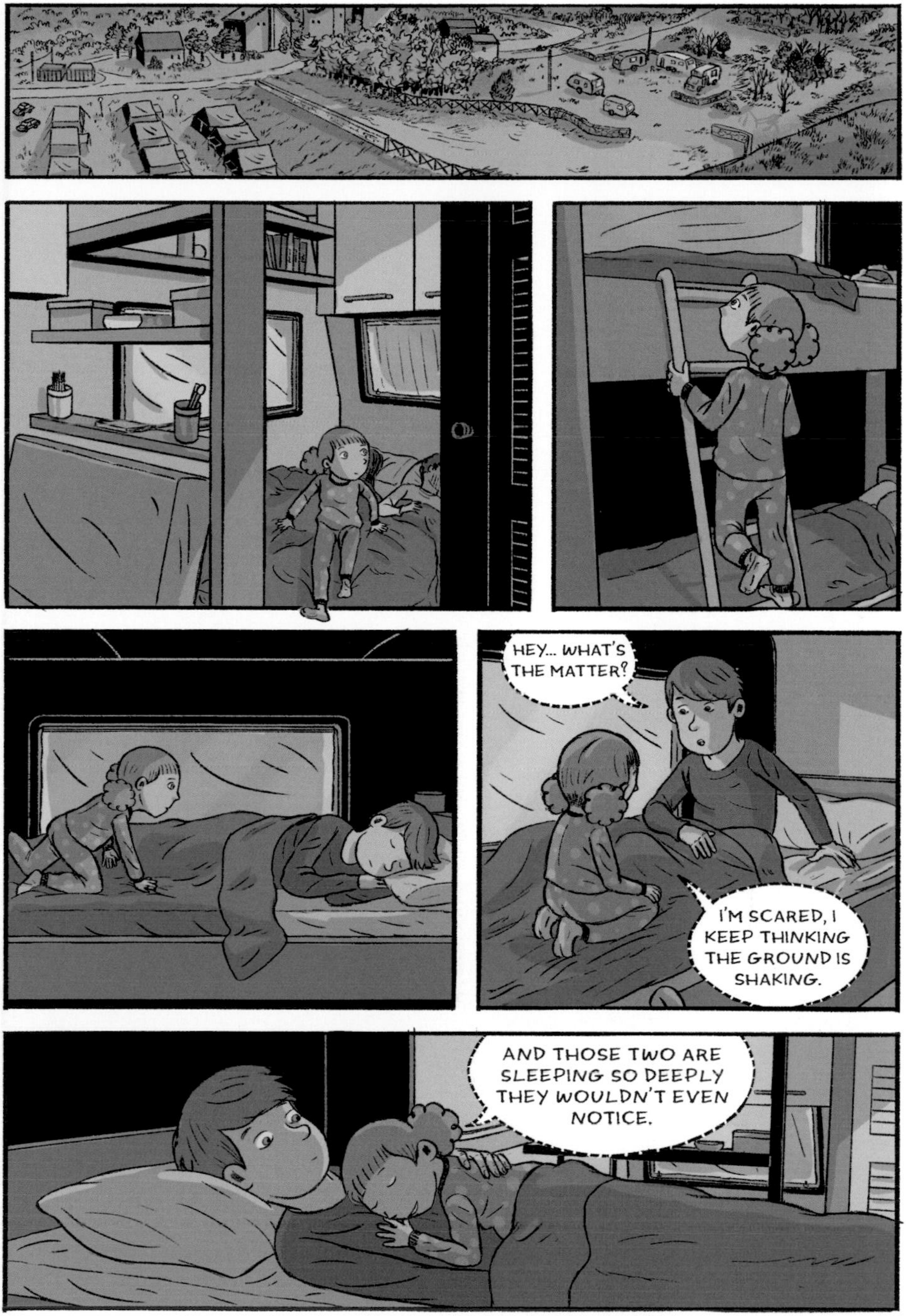
HEY... WHAT'S THE MATTER?
I'M SCARED, I KEEP THINKING THE GROUND IS SHAKING.
AND THOSE TWO ARE SLEEPING SO DEEPLY THEY WOULDN'T EVEN NOTICE.

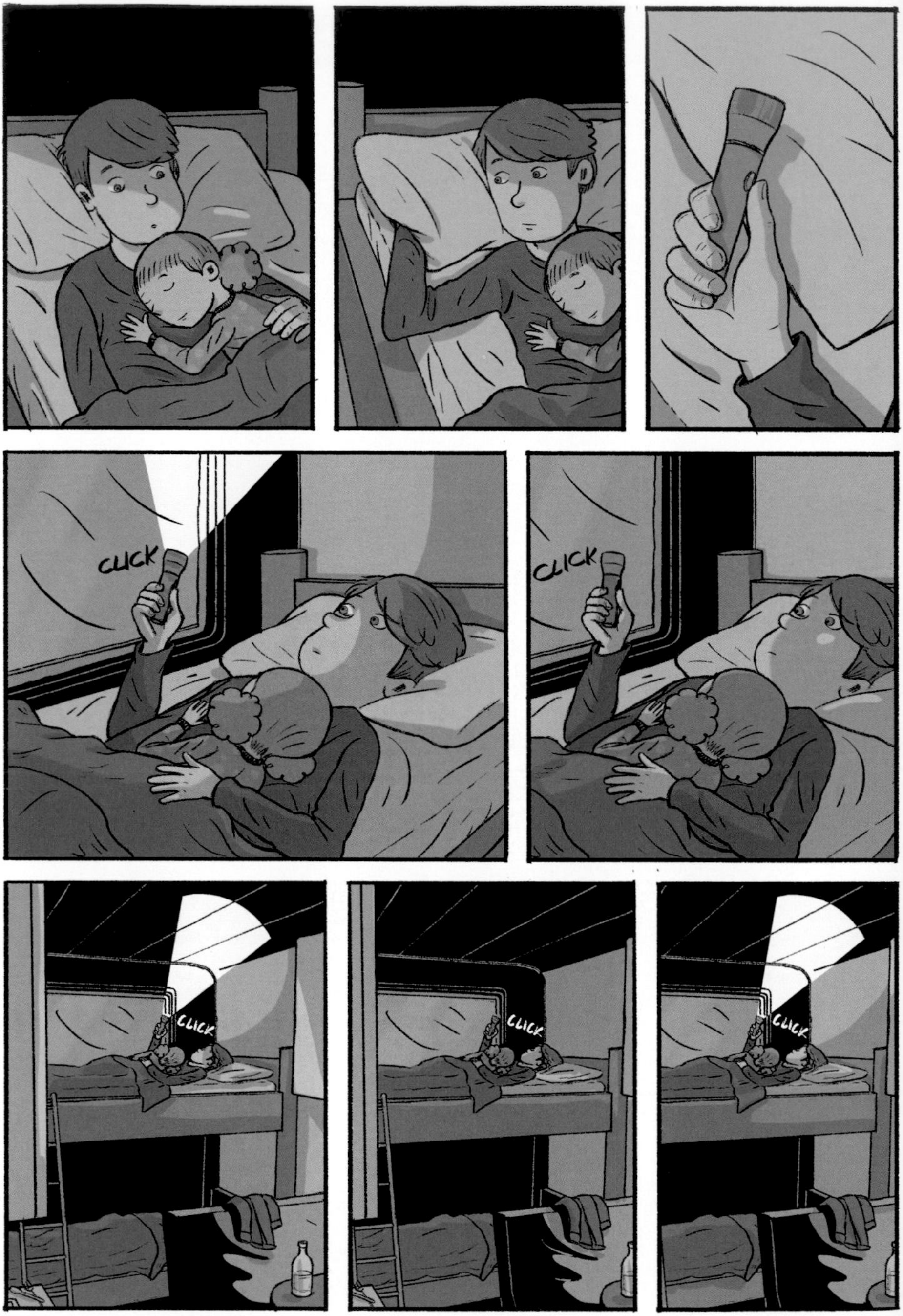
CLICK
CLICK
CLICK
CLICK
CLICK

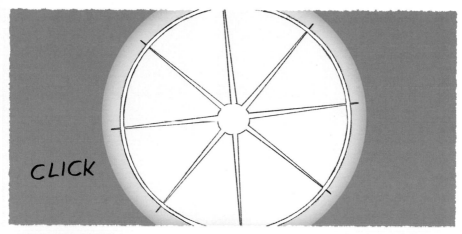

CLICK

THERE HE IS!

ARTHUR!
ARTHUR!

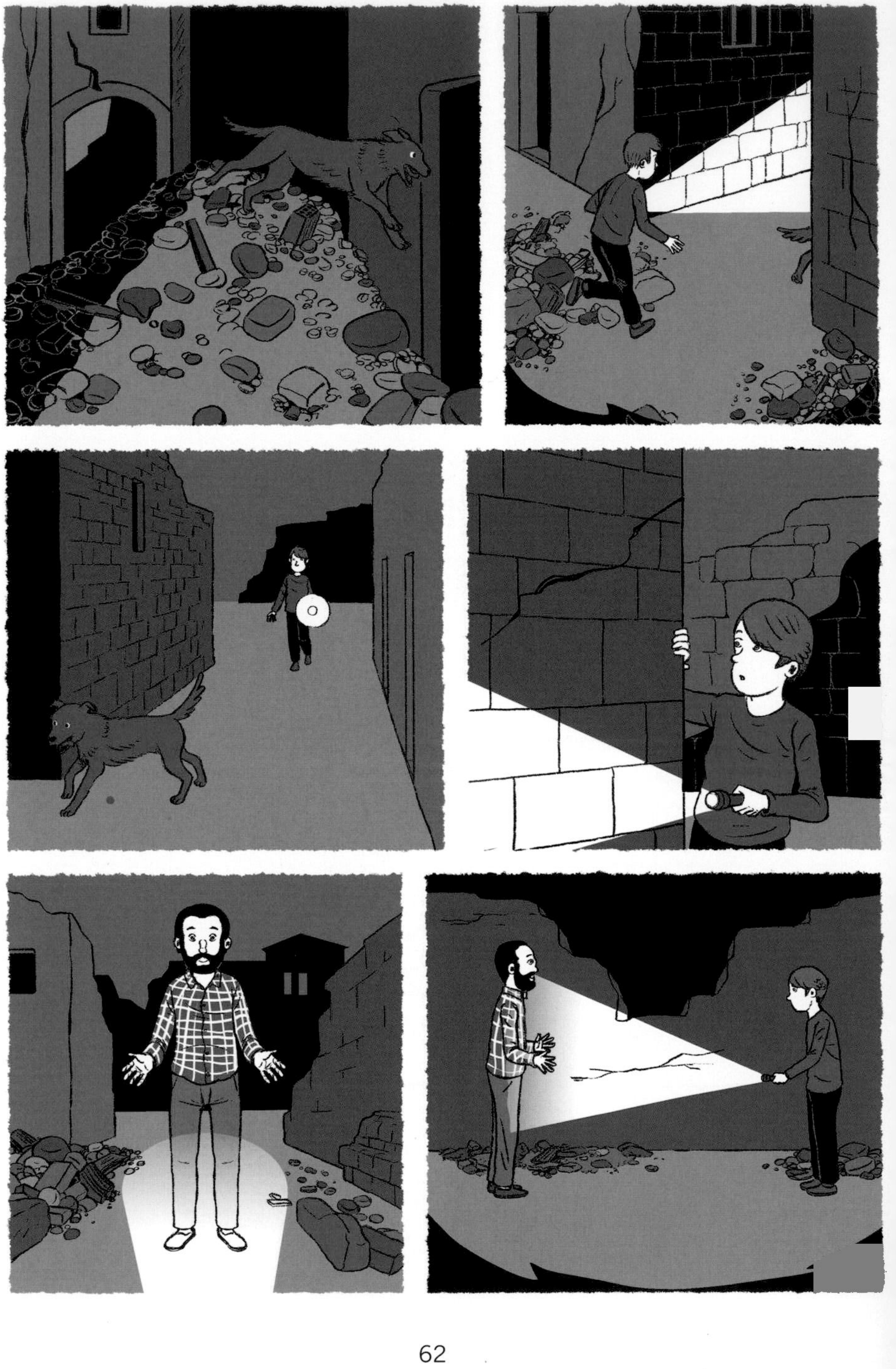

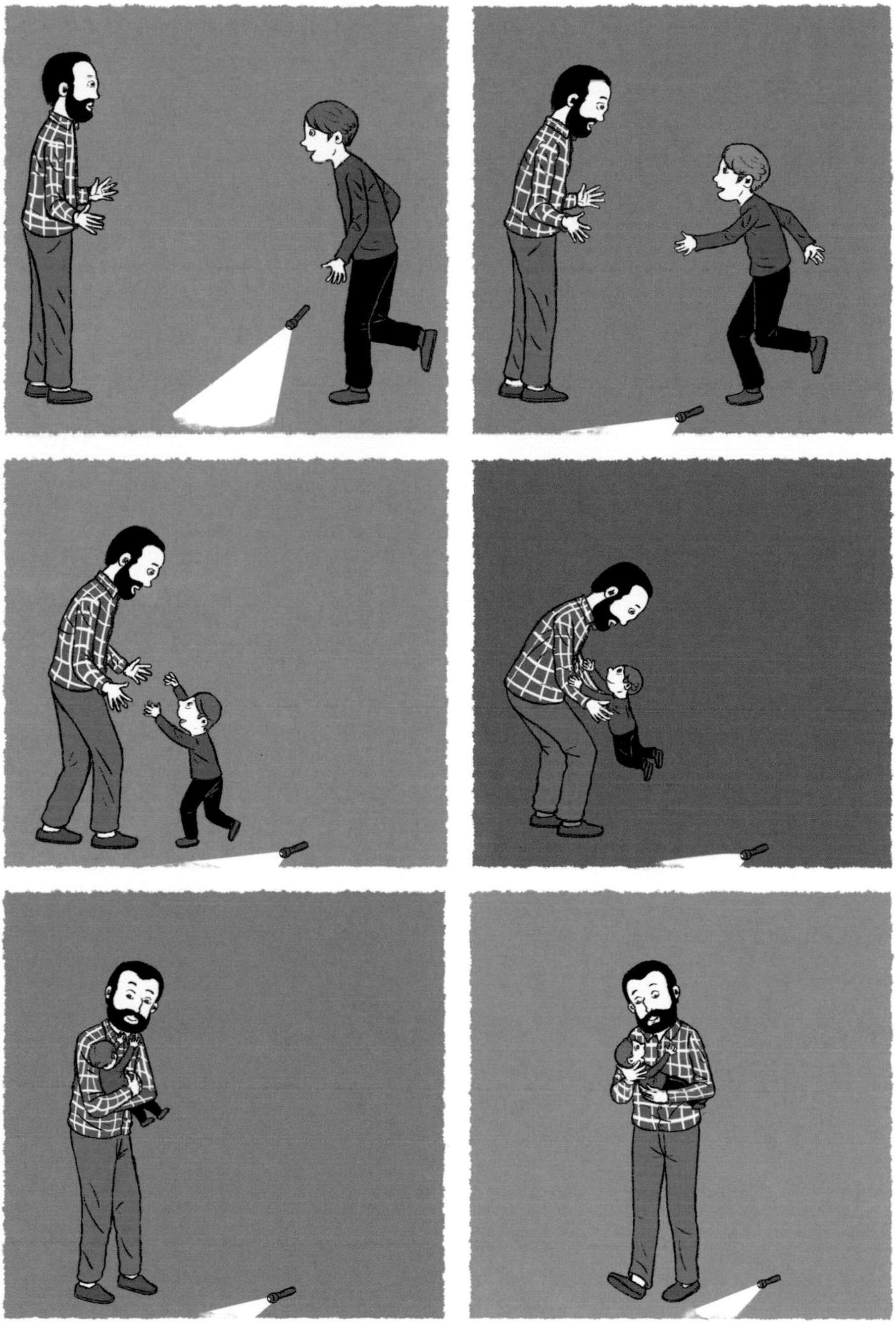

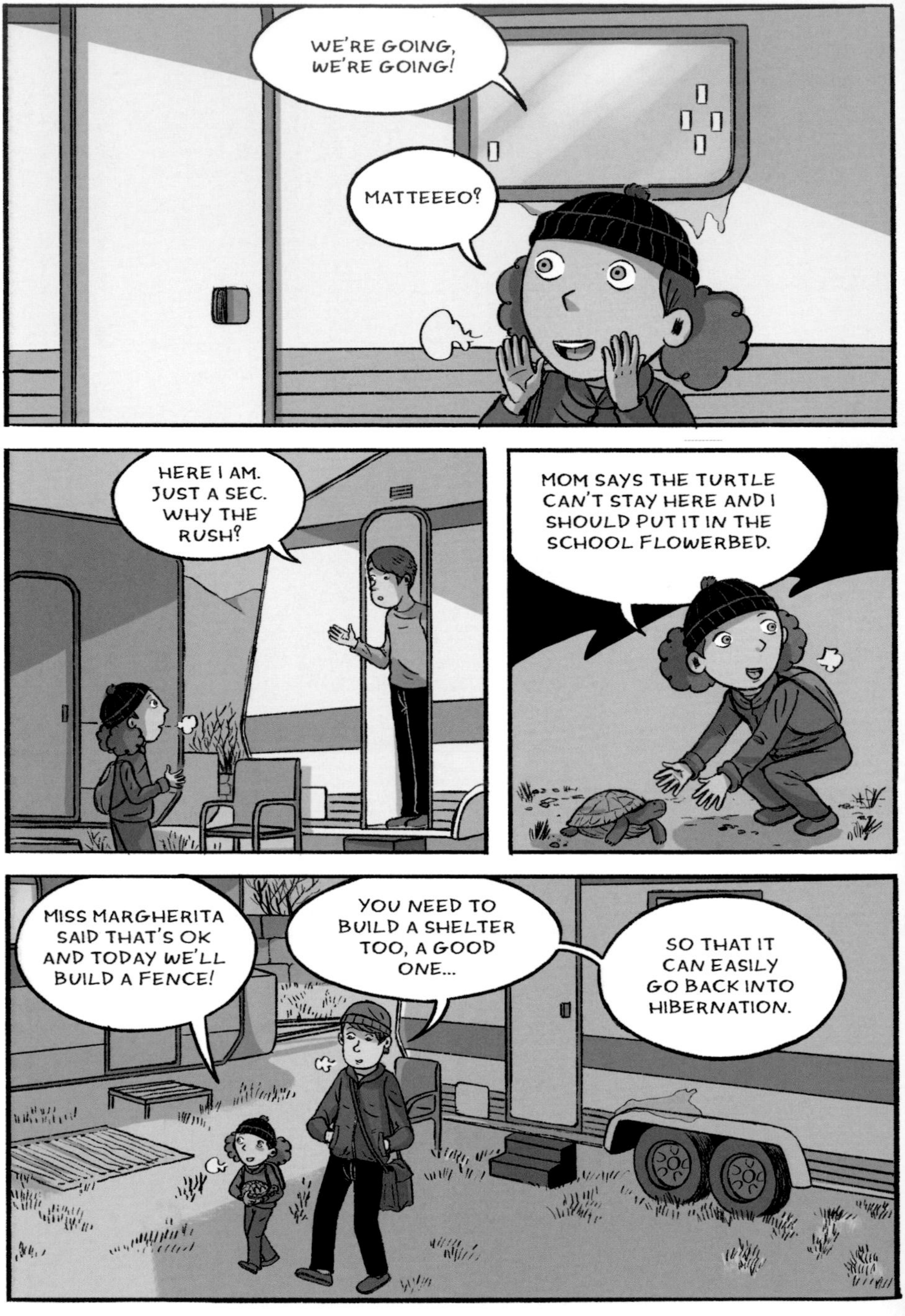
WE'RE GOING, WE'RE GOING!
MATTEEEO?
HERE I AM. JUST A SEC. WHY THE RUSH?
MOM SAYS THE TURTLE CAN'T STAY HERE AND I SHOULD PUT IT IN THE SCHOOL FLOWERBED.
MISS MARGHERITA SAID THAT'S OK AND TODAY WE'LL BUILD A FENCE!
YOU NEED TO BUILD A SHELTER TOO, A GOOD ONE...
SO THAT IT CAN EASILY GO BACK INTO HIBERNATION.

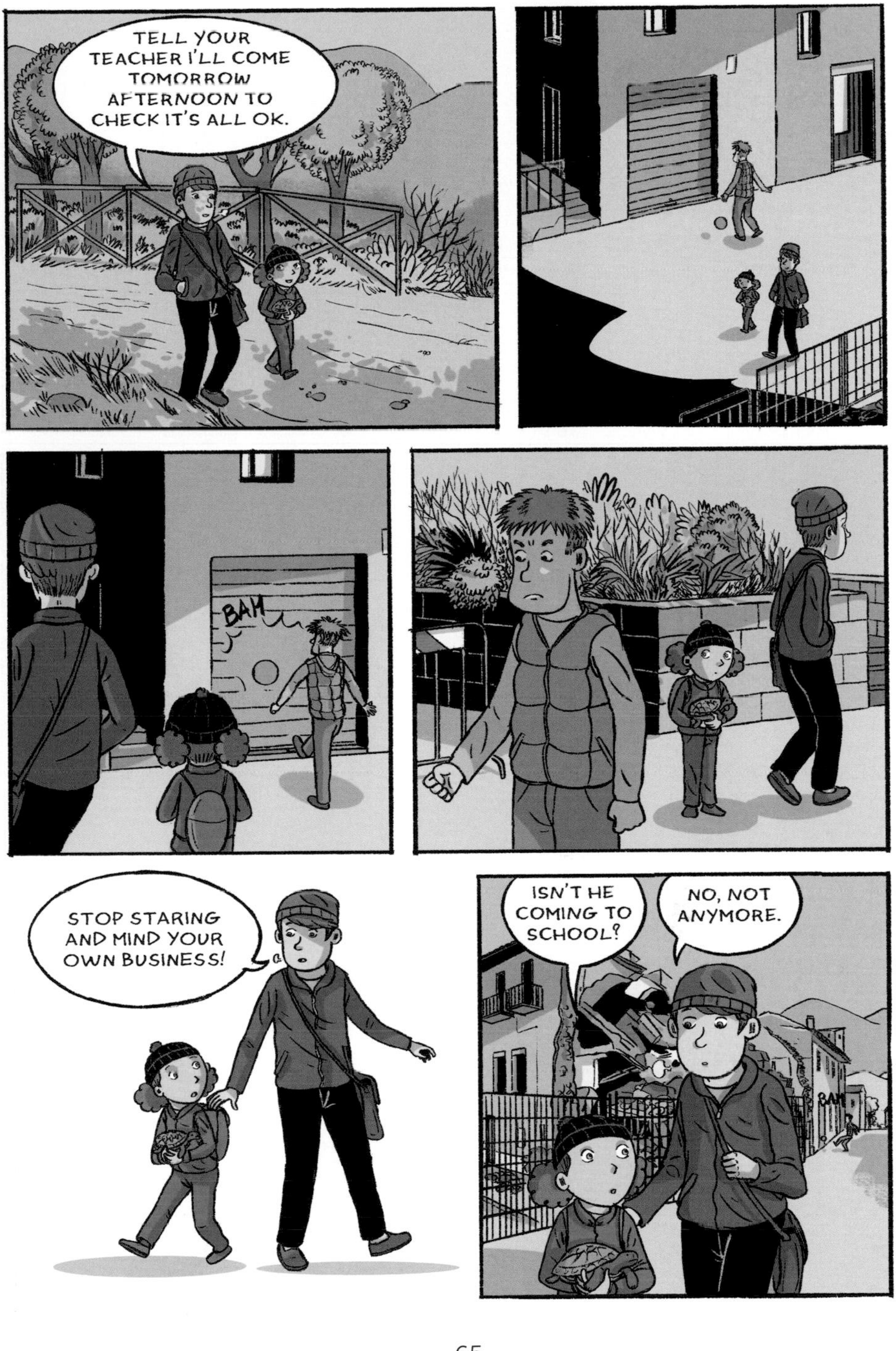
TELL YOUR TEACHER I'LL COME TOMORROW AFTERNOON TO CHECK IT'S ALL OK.
BAM
STOP STARING AND MIND YOUR OWN BUSINESS!
ISN'T HE COMING TO SCHOOL?
NO, NOT ANYMORE.

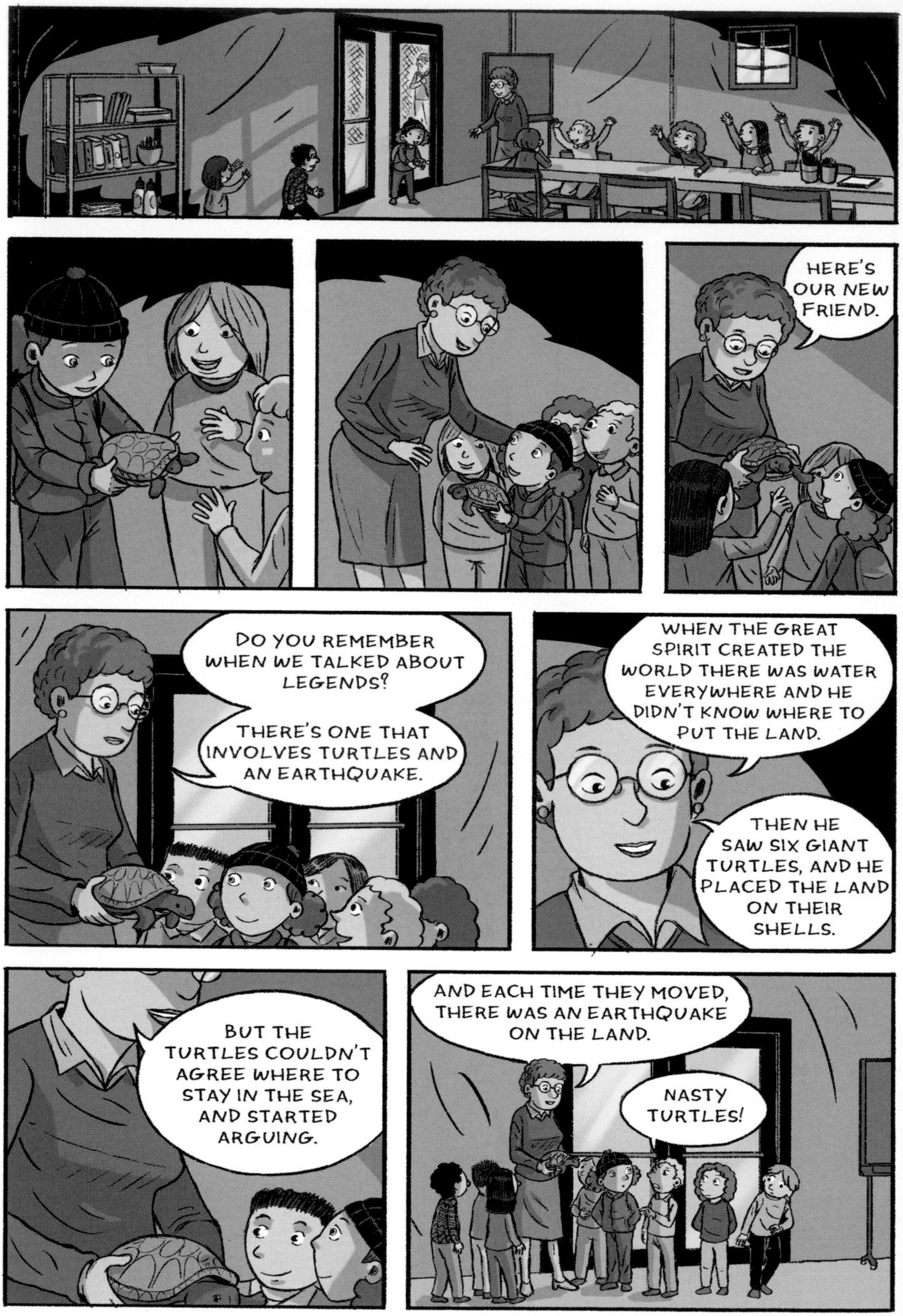
HERE'S OUR NEW FRIEND.
DO YOU REMEMBER WHEN WE TALKED ABOUT LEGENDS?
THERE'S ONE THAT INVOLVES TURTLES AND AN EARTHQUAKE.
WHEN THE GREAT SPIRIT CREATED THE WORLD THERE WAS WATER EVERYWHERE AND HE DIDN'T KNOW WHERE TO PUT THE LAND.
THEN HE SAW SIX GIANT TURTLES, AND HE PLACED THE LAND ON THEIR SHELLS.
BUT THE TURTLES COULDN'T AGREE WHERE TO STAY IN THE SEA, AND STARTED ARGUING.
AND EACH TIME THEY MOVED, THERE WAS AN EARTHQUAKE ON THE LAND.
NASTY TURTLES!

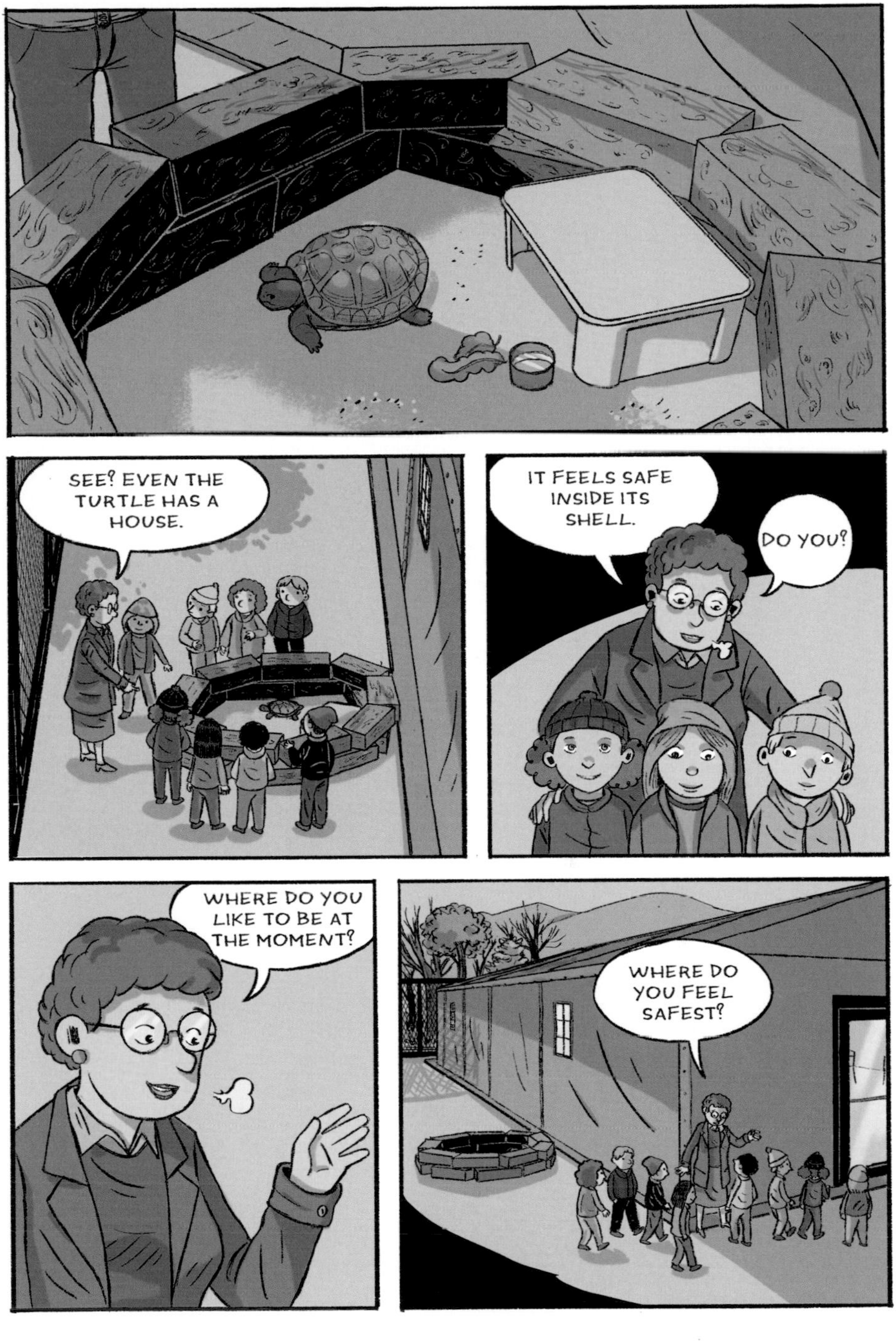
SEE? EVEN THE TURTLE HAS A HOUSE.
IT FEELS SAFE INSIDE ITS SHELL.
DO YOU?
WHERE DO YOU LIKE TO BE AT THE MOMENT?
WHERE DO YOU FEEL SAFEST?

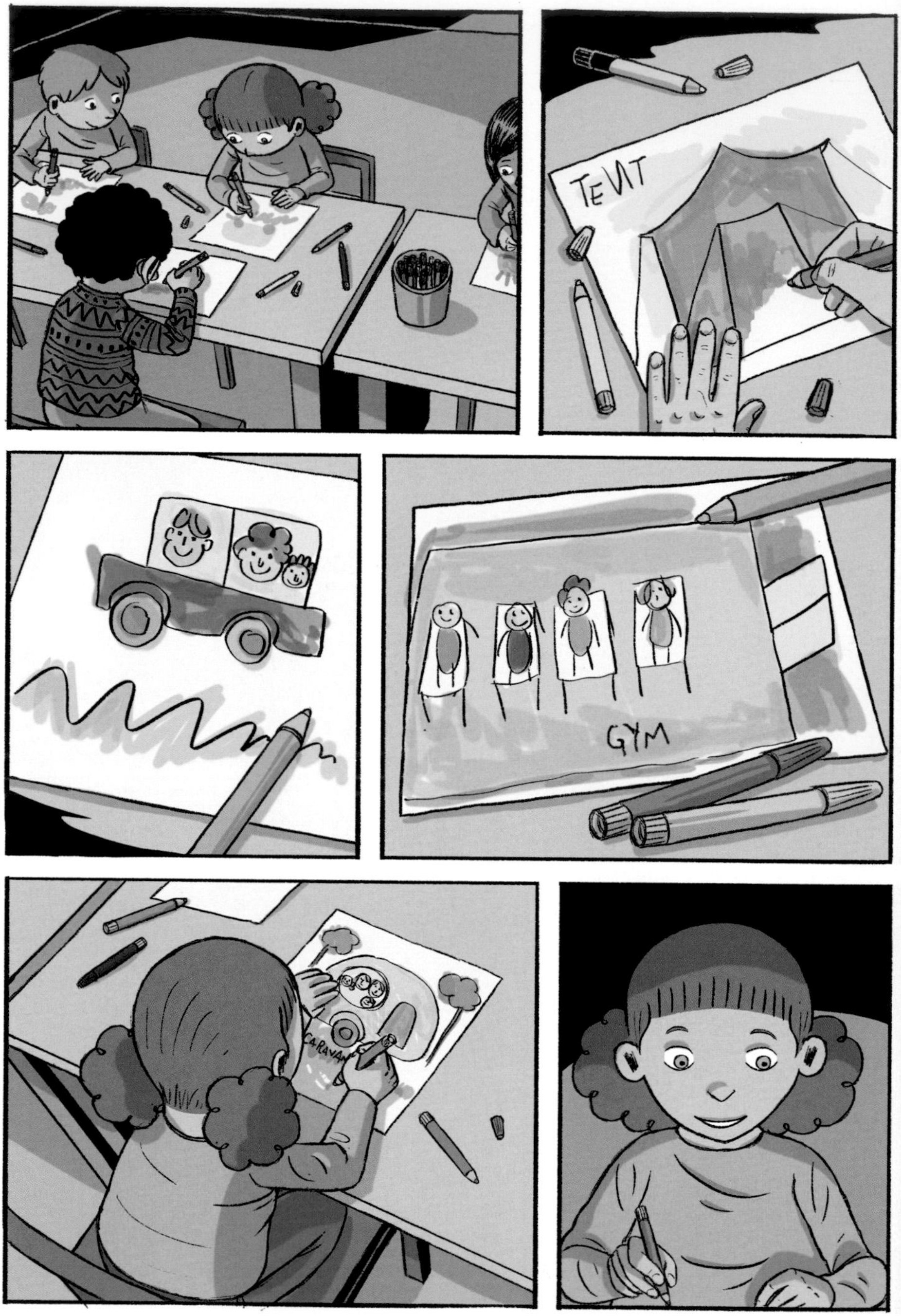
TENT
GYM
CARAVAN

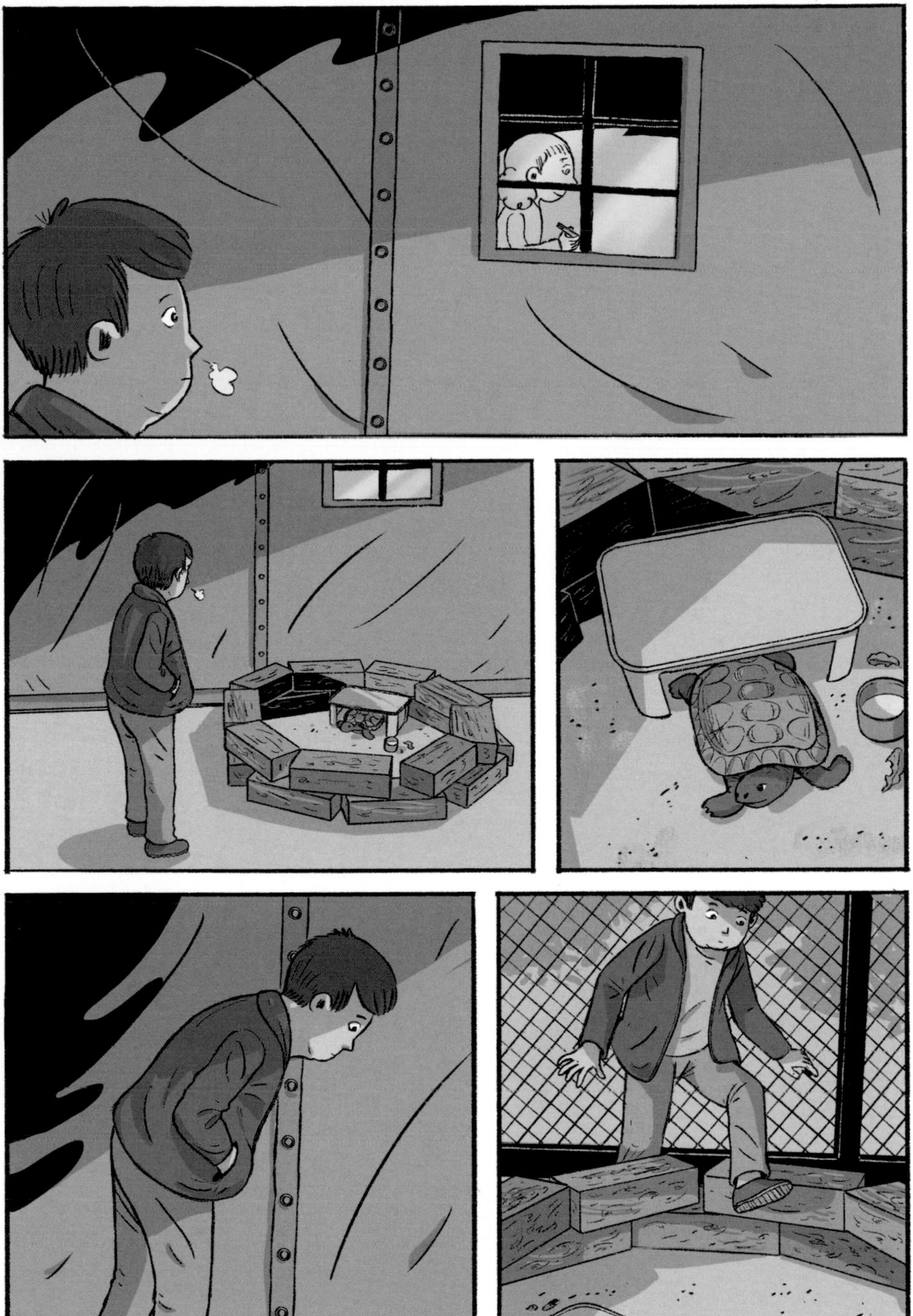

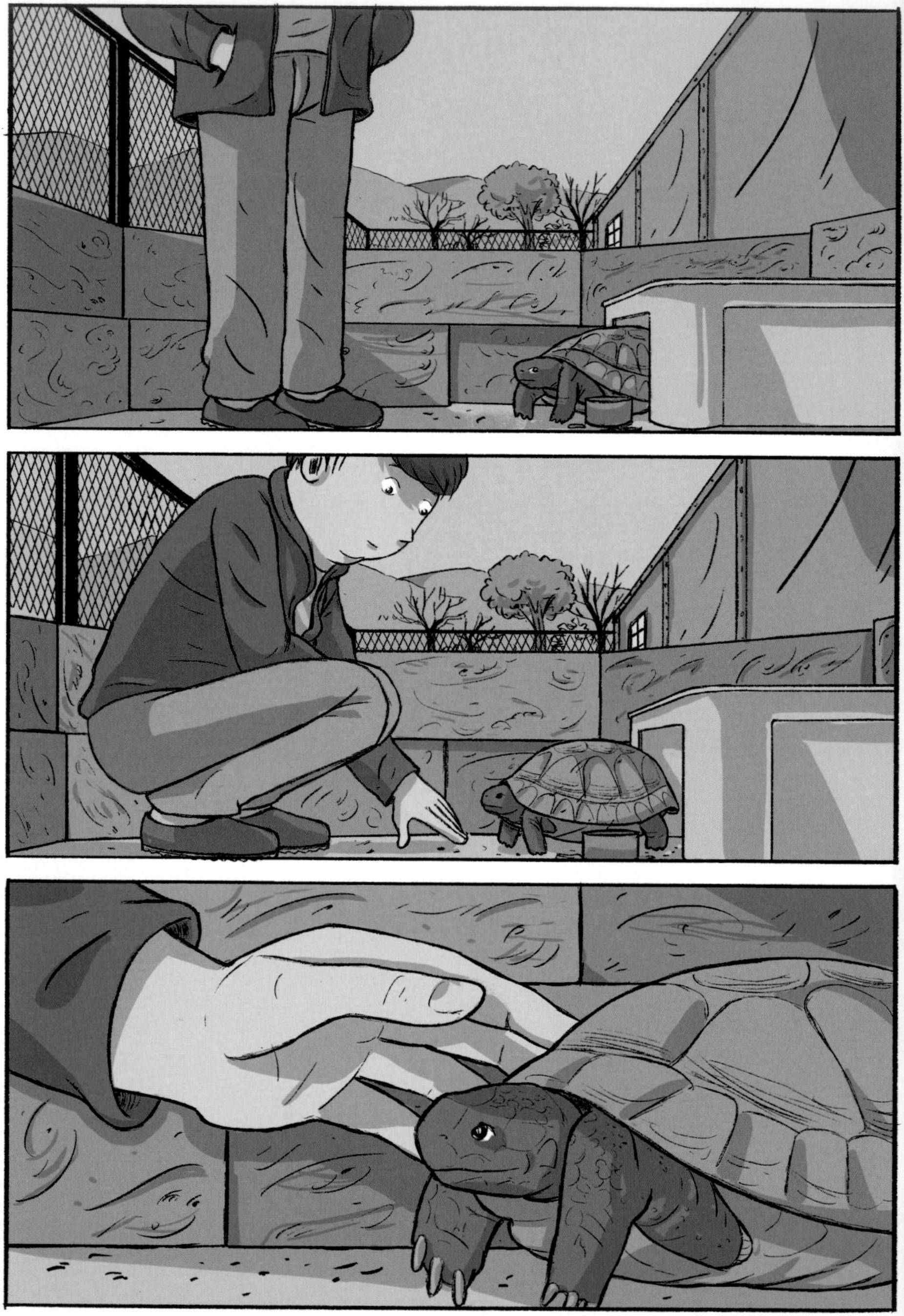

5.

In which it suddenly gets colder.

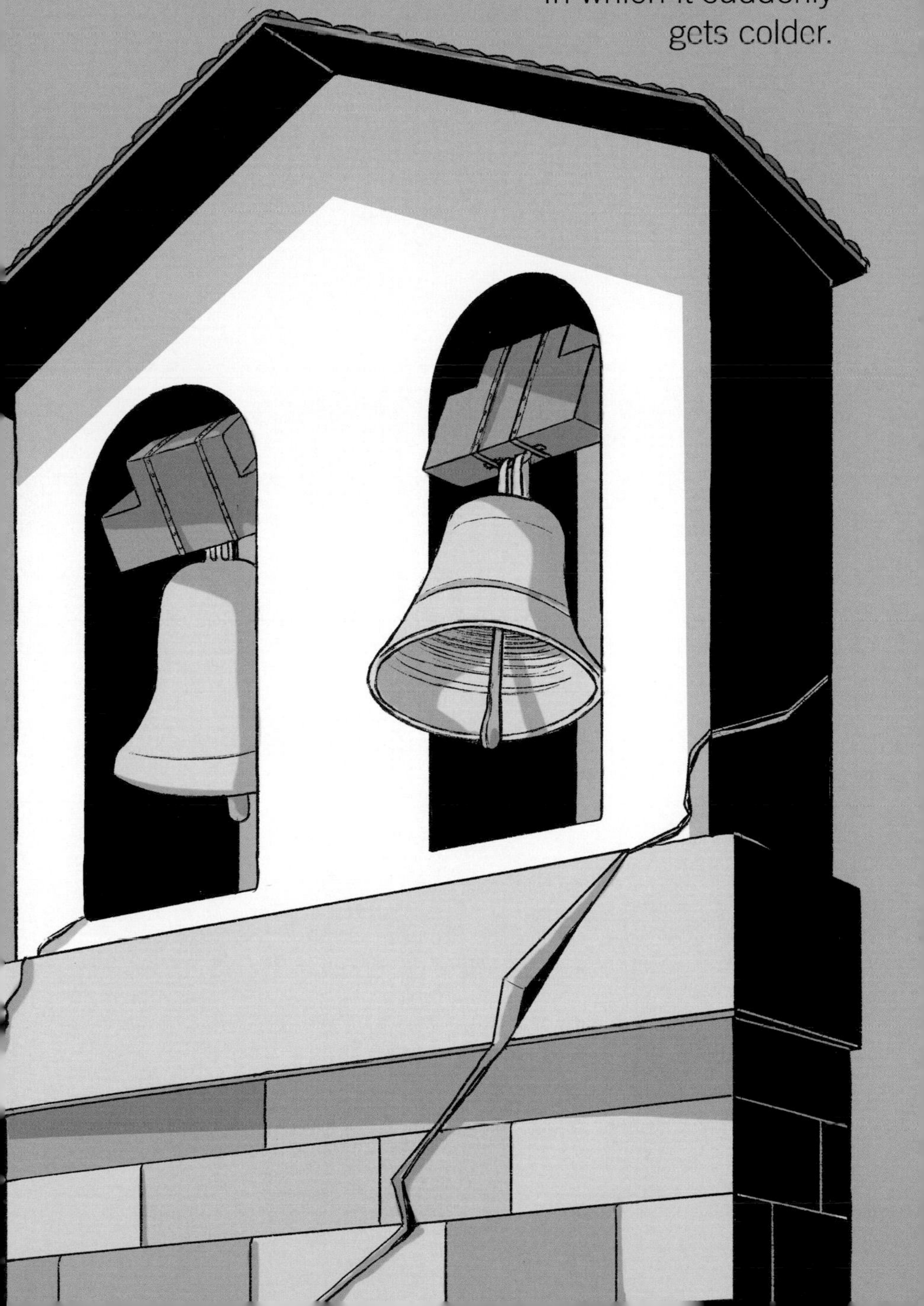

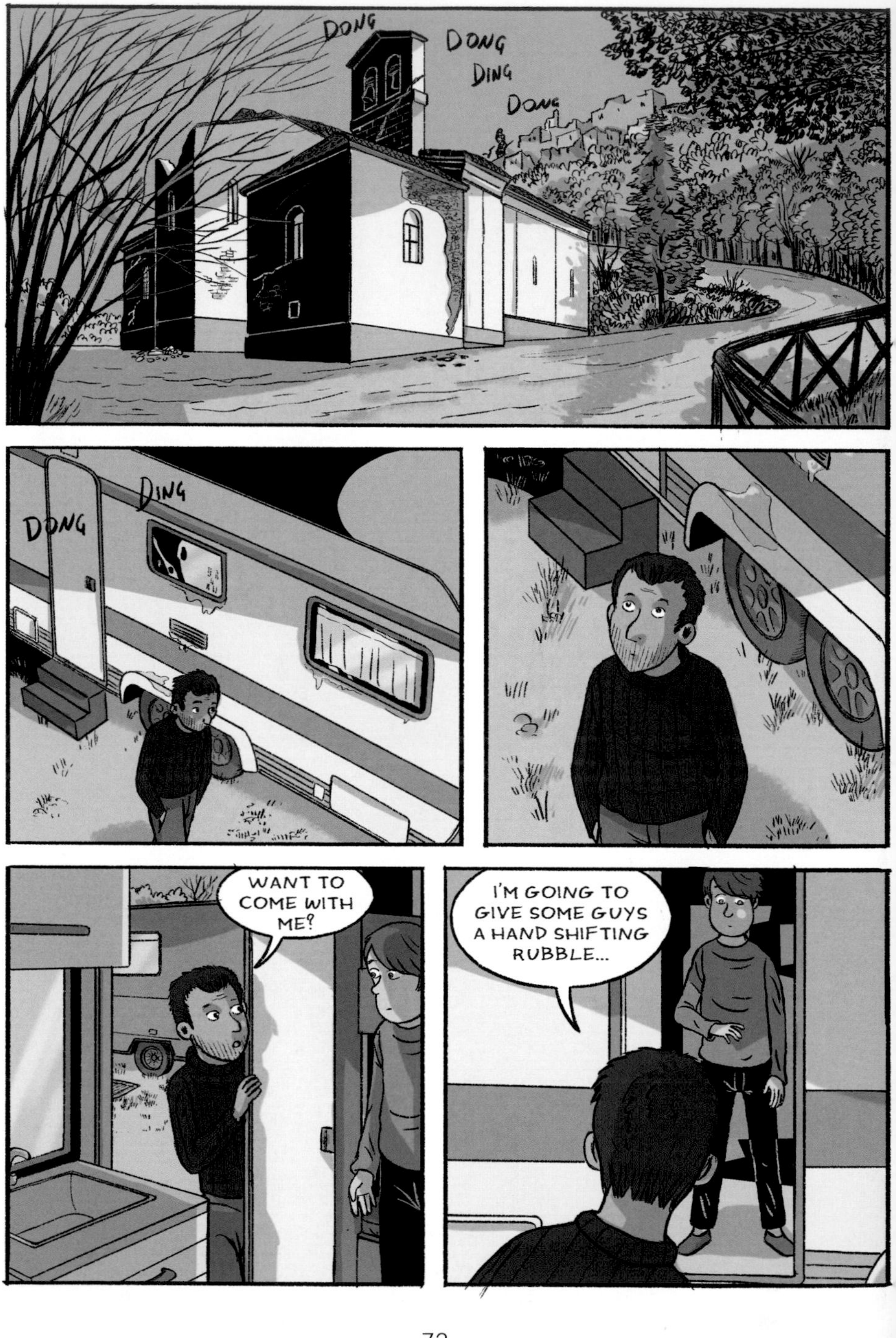
DONG
DONG
DING
DONG
DING
DONG
WANT TO COME WITH ME?
I'M GOING TO GIVE SOME GUYS A HAND SHIFTING RUBBLE...

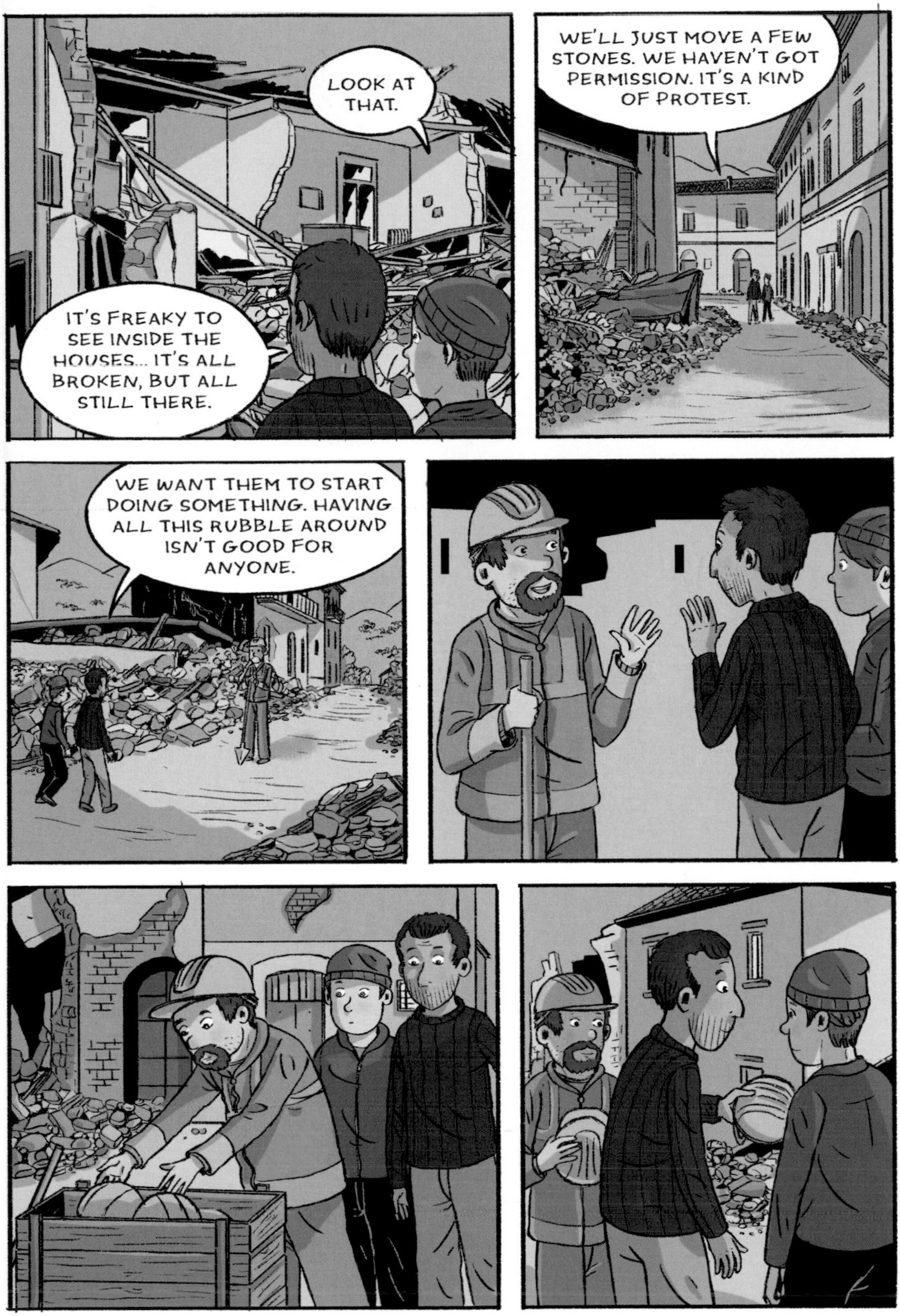
LOOK AT THAT.
IT'S FREAKY TO SEE INSIDE THE HOUSES... IT'S ALL BROKEN, BUT ALL STILL THERE.
WE'LL JUST MOVE A FEW STONES. WE HAVEN'T GOT PERMISSION. IT'S A KIND OF PROTEST.
WE WANT THEM TO START DOING SOMETHING. HAVING ALL THIS RUBBLE AROUND ISN'T GOOD FOR ANYONE.

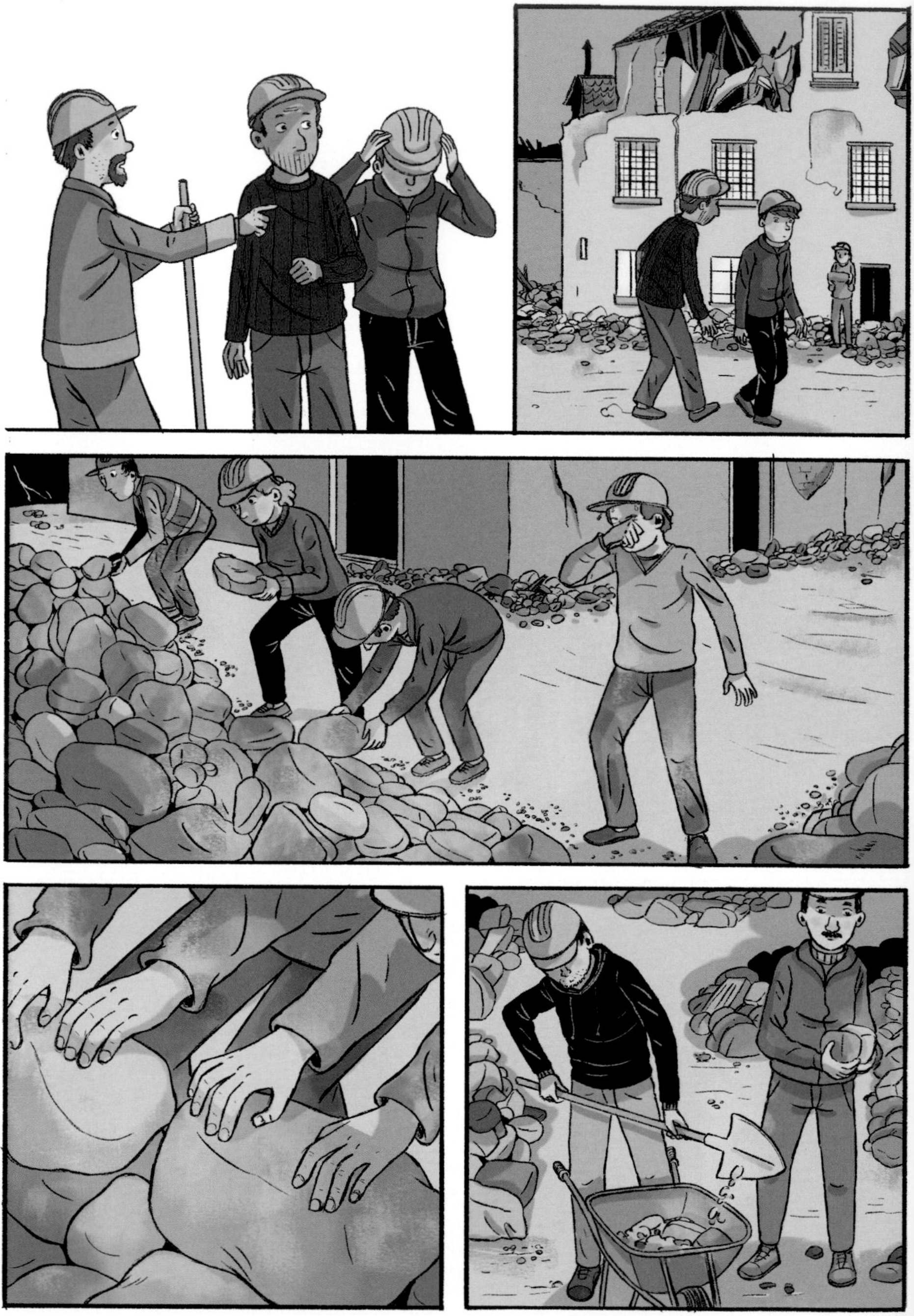

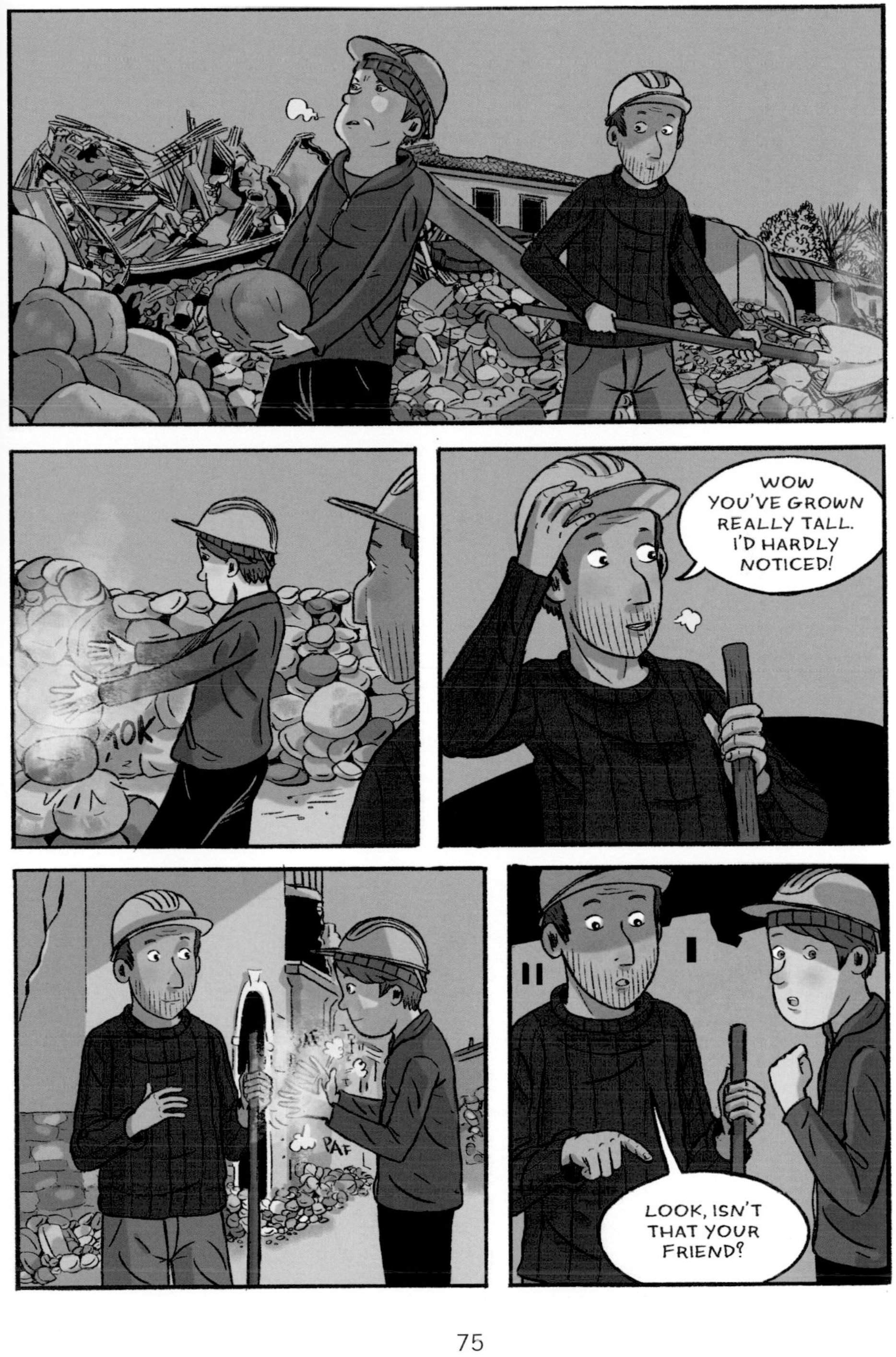

WOW YOU'VE GROWN REALLY TALL. I'D HARDLY NOTICED!
TOK
PAF
LOOK, ISN'T THAT YOUR FRIEND?

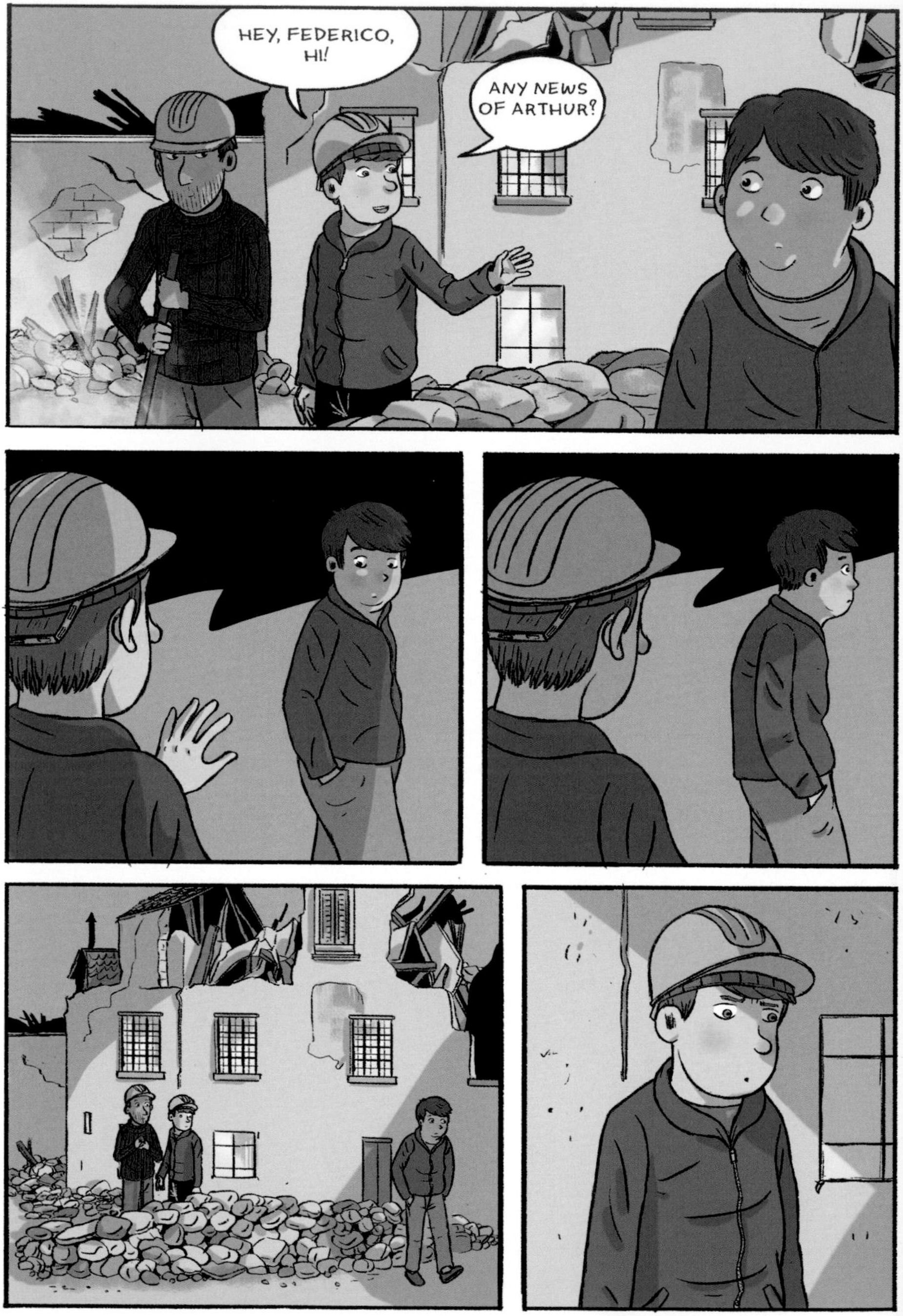
HEY, FEDERICO, HI!
ANY NEWS OF ARTHUR?

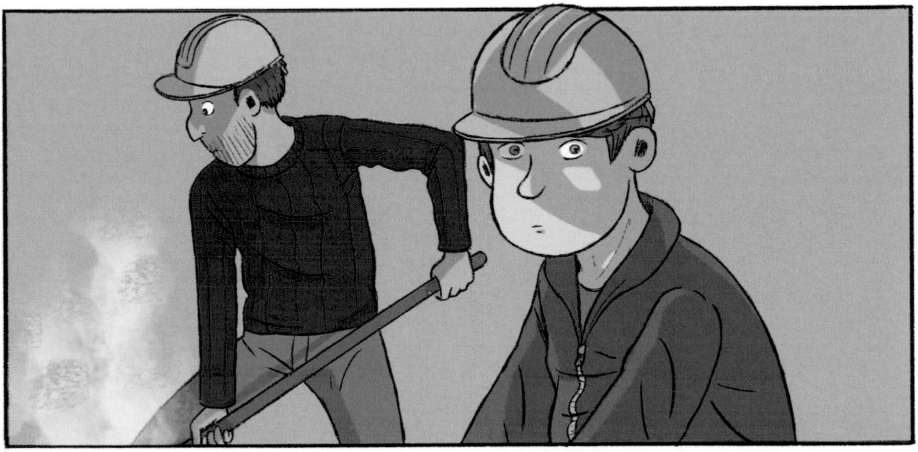

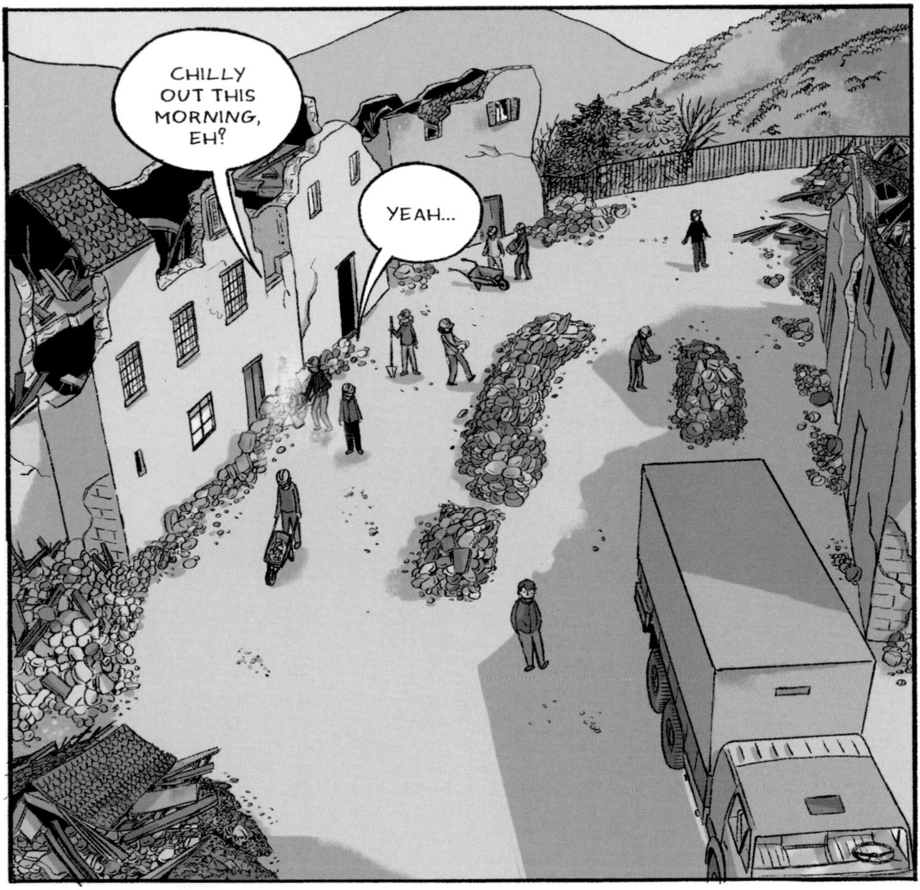
CHILLY OUT THIS MORNING, EH?
YEAH...

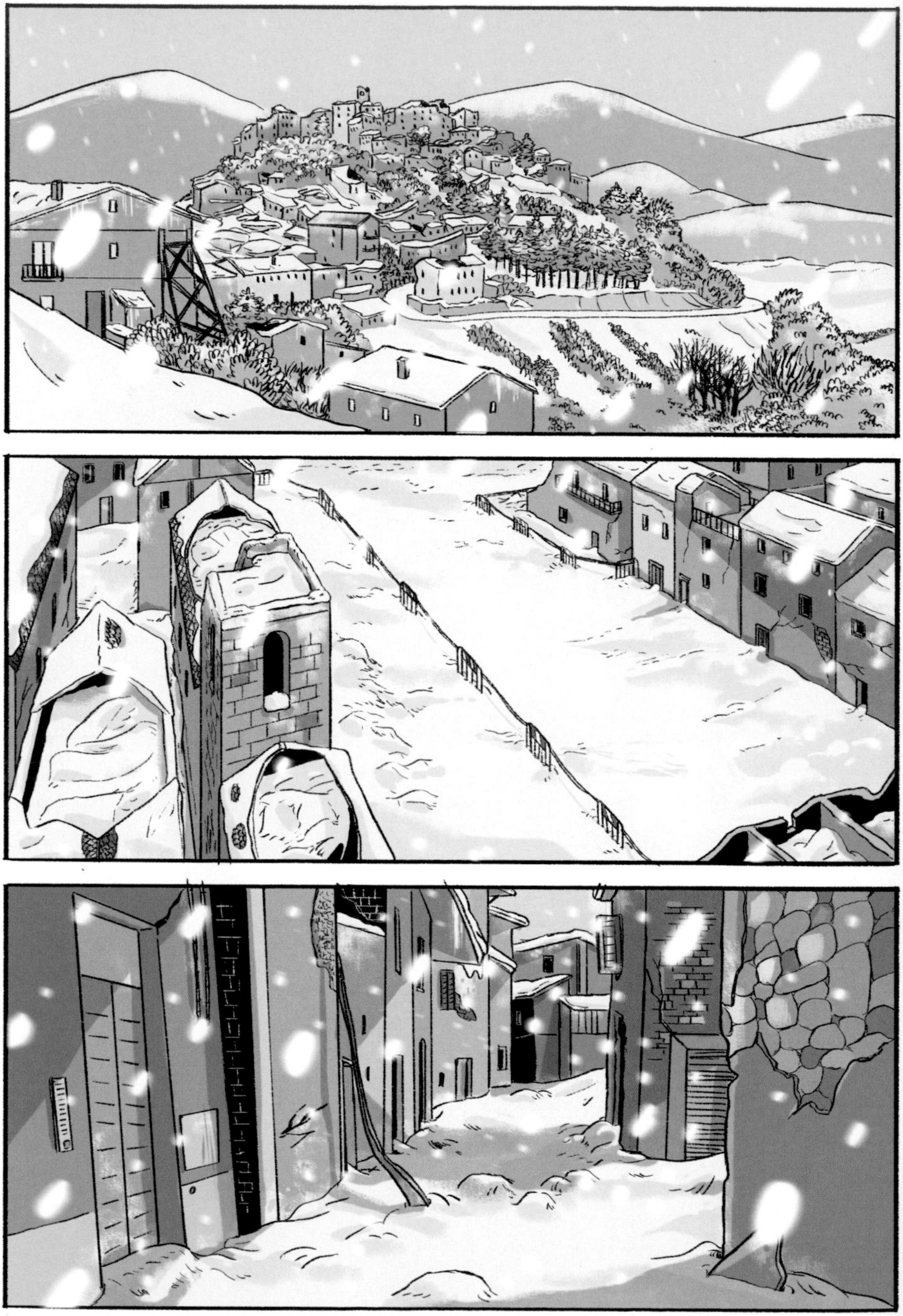

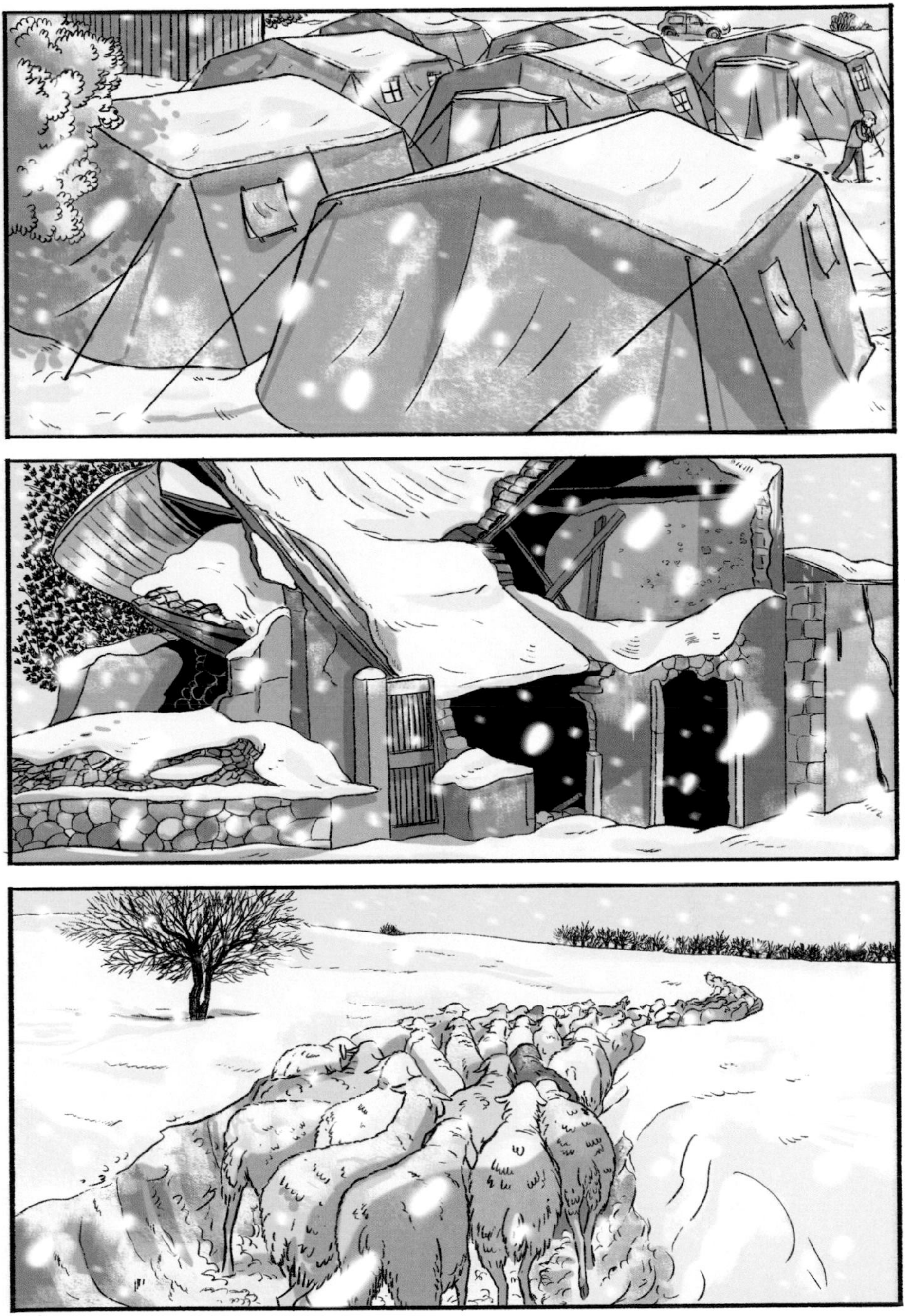

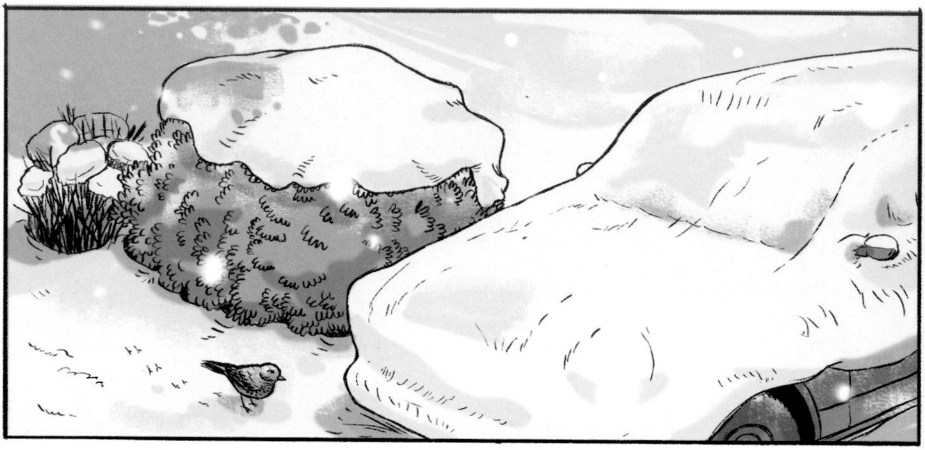

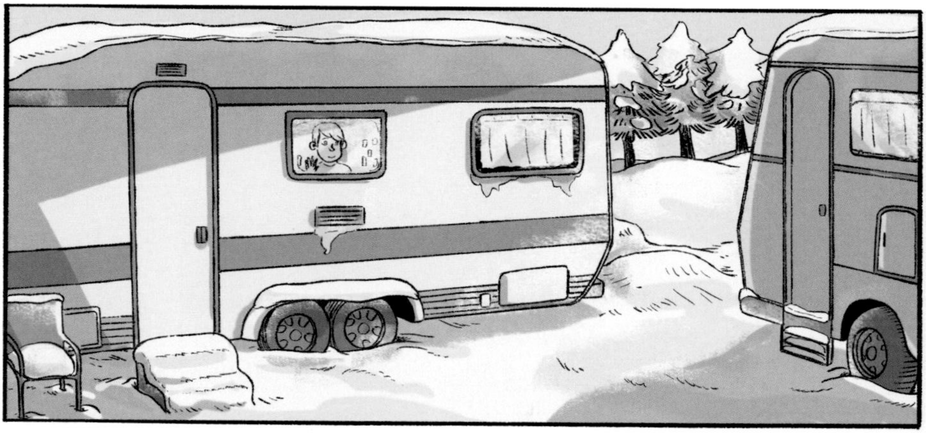

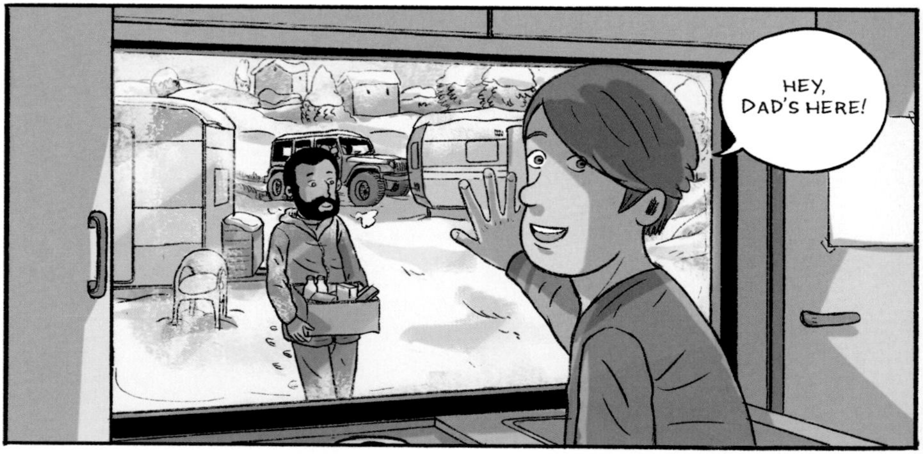
HEY, DAD'S HERE!

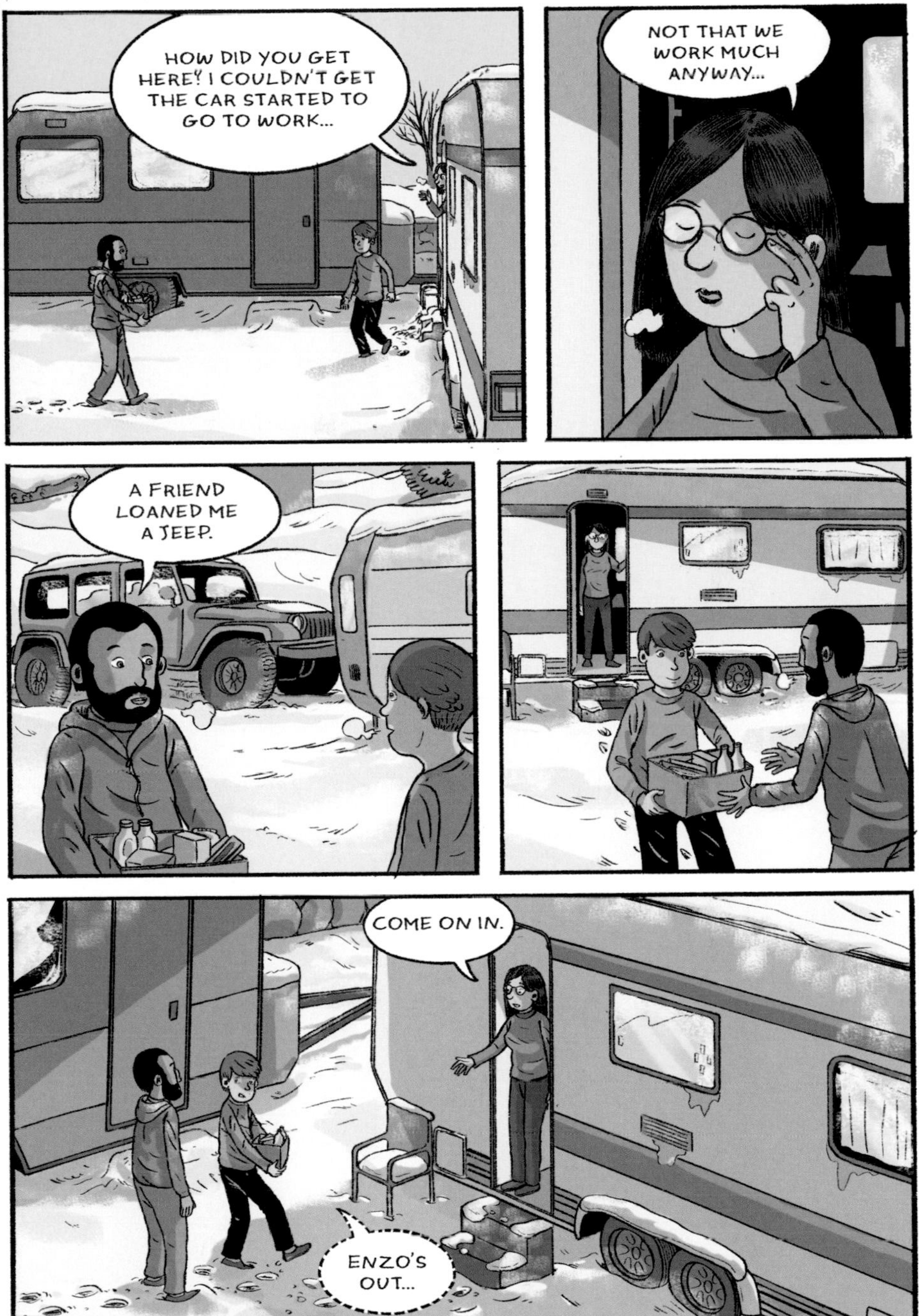
HOW DID YOU GET HERE? I COULDN'T GET THE CAR STARTED TO GO TO WORK...
NOT THAT WE WORK MUCH ANYWAY...
A FRIEND LOANED ME A JEEP.
COME ON IN.
ENZO'S OUT...

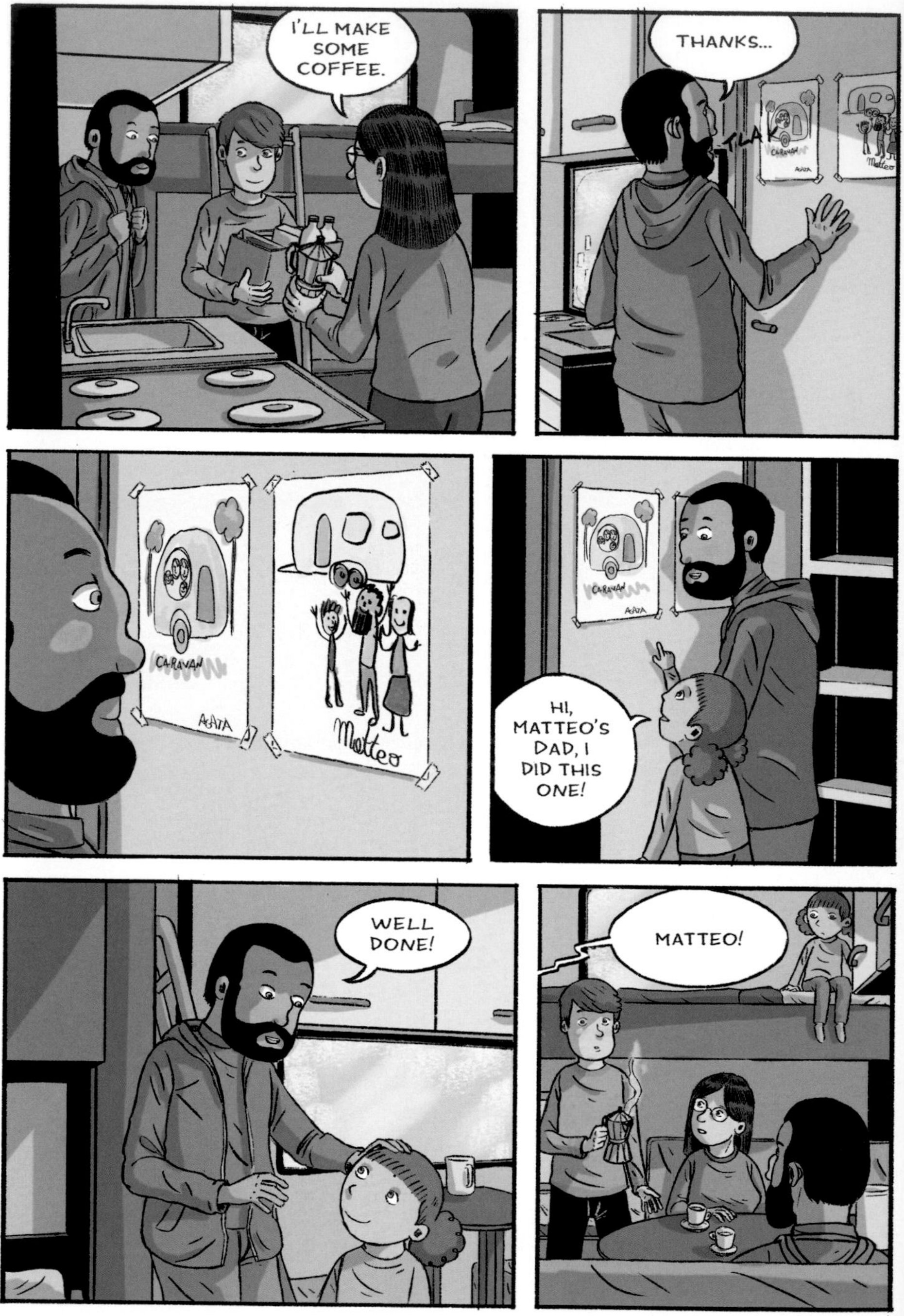
I'LL MAKE SOME COFFEE.
THANKS...
TILAK
CARAVAN
AGATA
Matteo
HI, MATTEO'S DAD, I DID THIS ONE!
WELL DONE!
MATTEO!

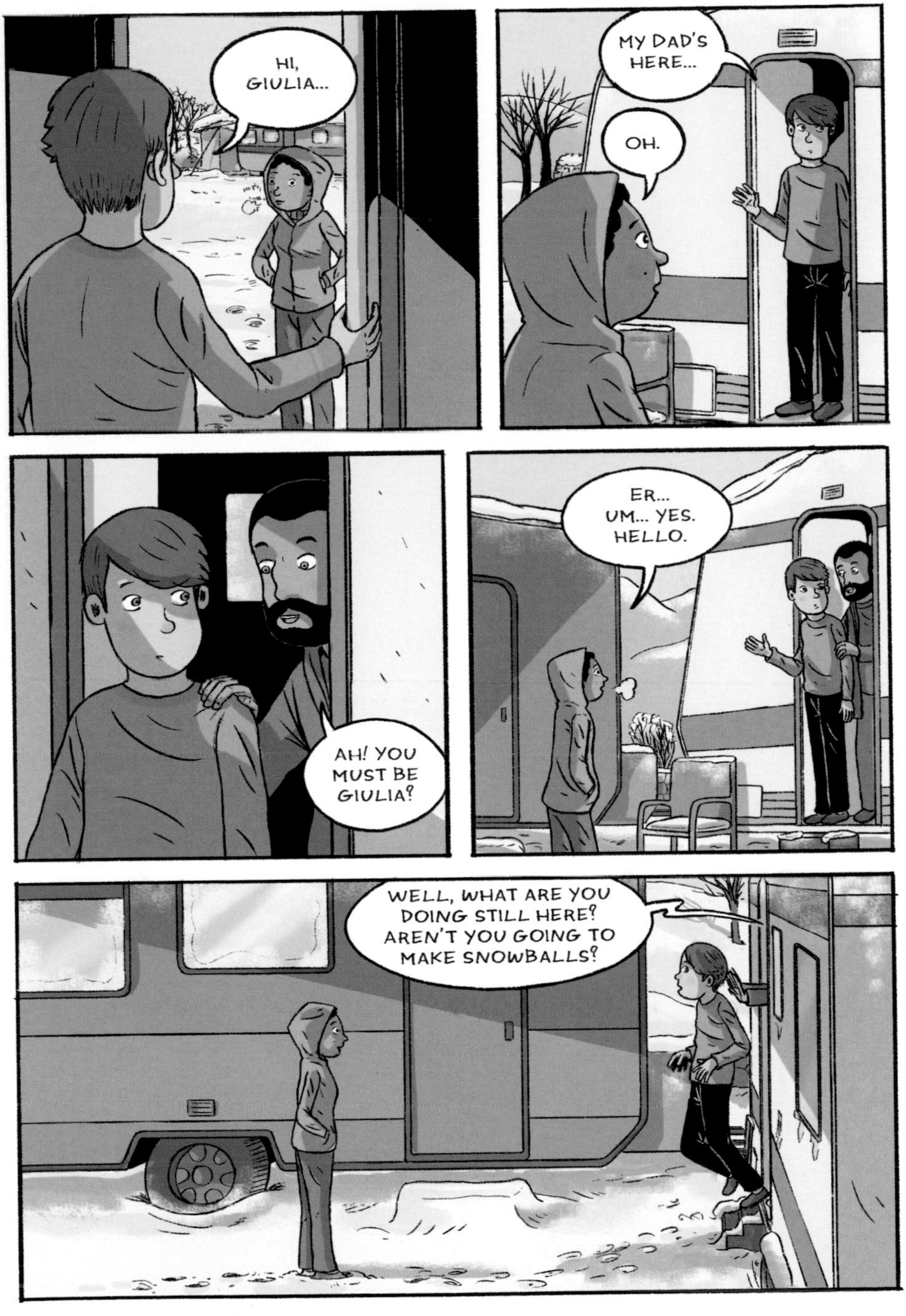
HI, GIULIA...
MY DAD'S HERE...
OH.
AH! YOU MUST BE GIULIA?
ER... UM... YES. HELLO.
WELL, WHAT ARE YOU DOING STILL HERE? AREN'T YOU GOING TO MAKE SNOWBALLS?

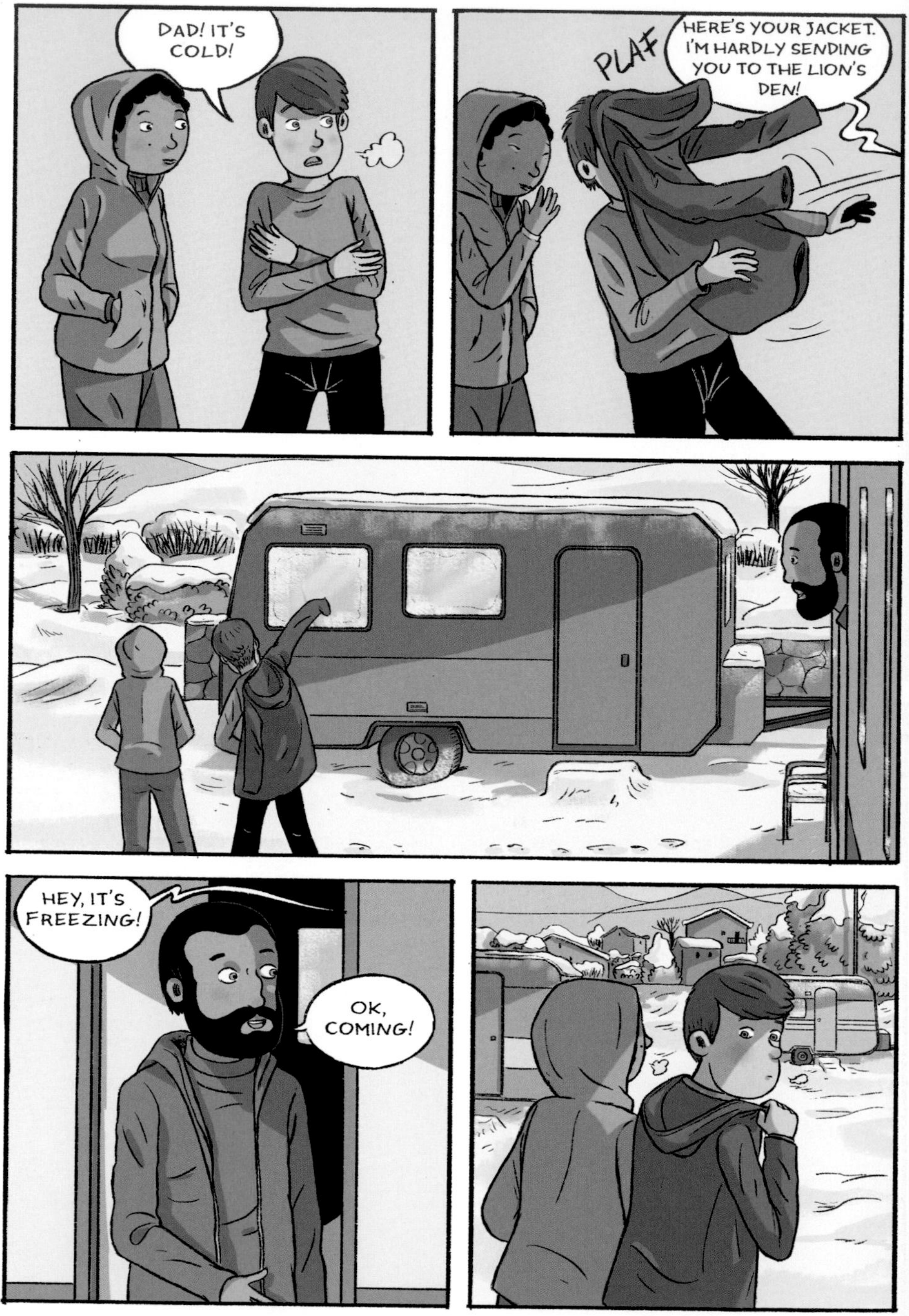
DAD! IT'S COLD!
PLAF
HERE'S YOUR JACKET. I'M HARDLY SENDING YOU TO THE LION'S DEN!
HEY, IT'S FREEZING!
OK, COMING!

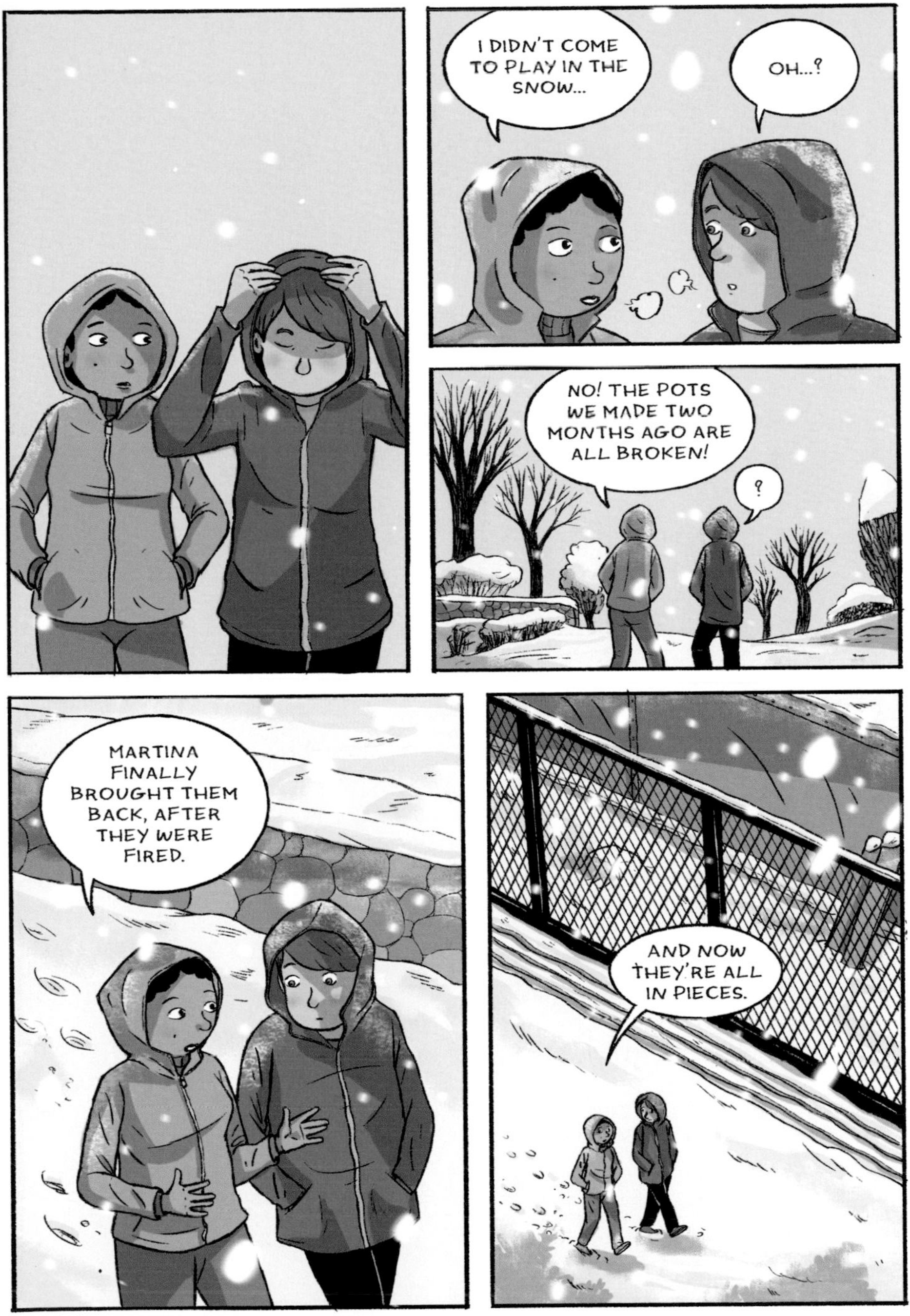
I DIDN'T COME TO PLAY IN THE SNOW...
OH...?
NO! THE POTS WE MADE TWO MONTHS AGO ARE ALL BROKEN!
?
MARTINA FINALLY BROUGHT THEM BACK, AFTER THEY WERE FIRED.
AND NOW THEY'RE ALL IN PIECES.

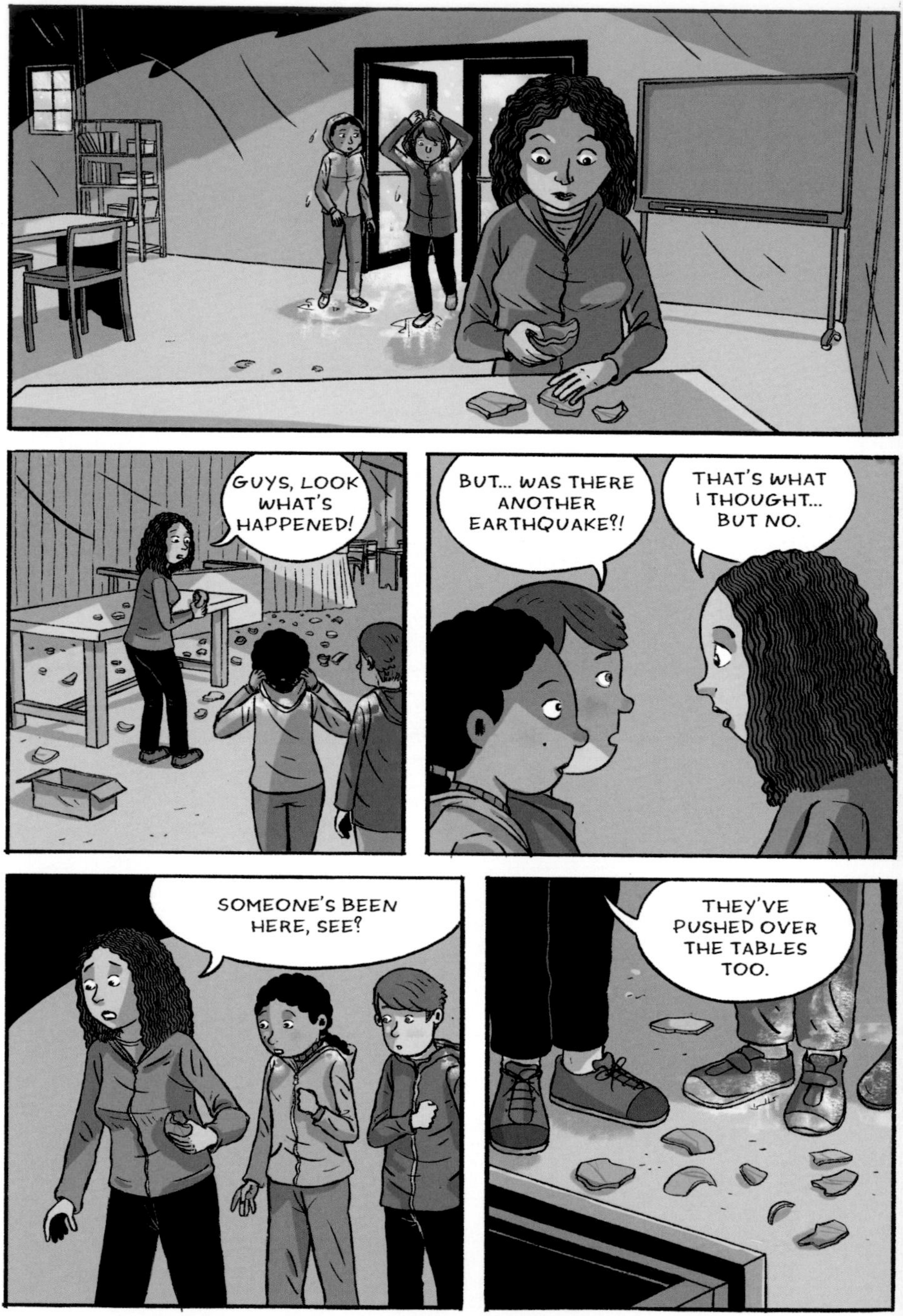
GUYS, LOOK WHAT'S HAPPENED!
BUT... WAS THERE ANOTHER EARTHQUAKE?!
THAT'S WHAT I THOUGHT... BUT NO.
SOMEONE'S BEEN HERE, SEE?
THEY'VE PUSHED OVER THE TABLES TOO.

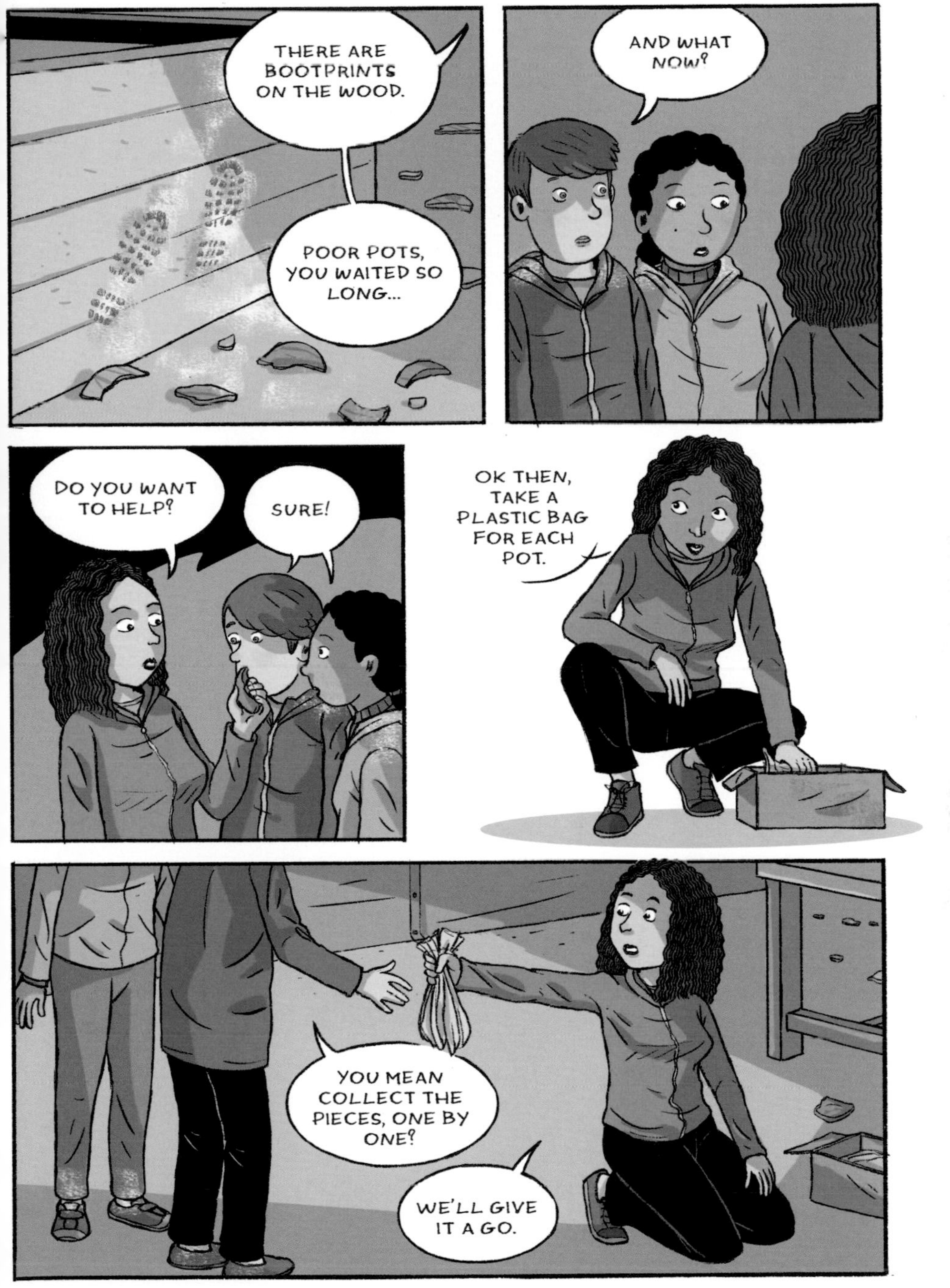
THERE ARE BOOTPRINTS ON THE WOOD.
POOR POTS, YOU WAITED SO LONG...
AND WHAT NOW?
DO YOU WANT TO HELP?
SURE!
OK THEN, TAKE A PLASTIC BAG FOR EACH POT.
YOU MEAN COLLECT THE PIECES, ONE BY ONE?
WE'LL GIVE IT A GO.

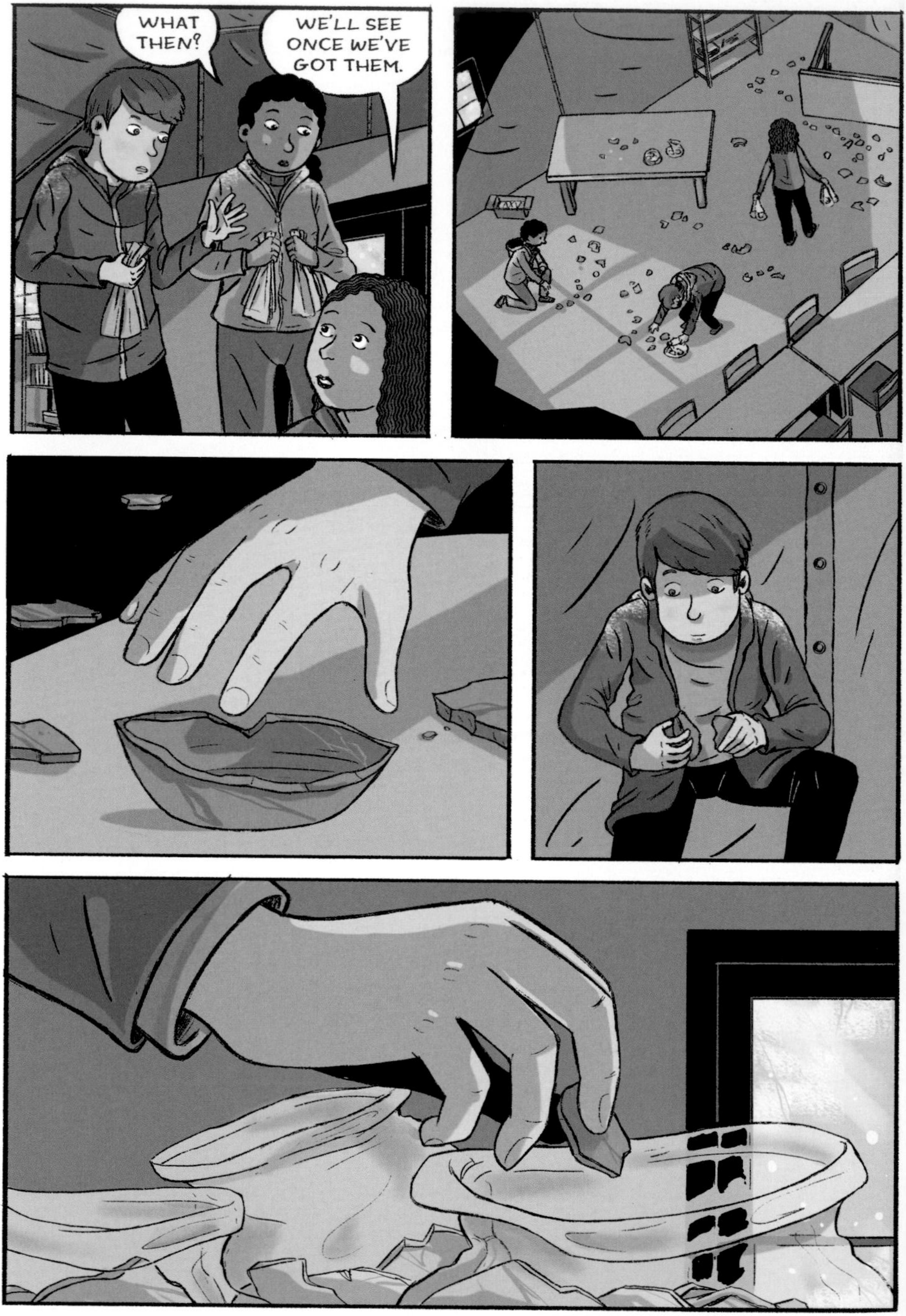
WHAT THEN?
WE'LL SEE ONCE WE'VE GOT THEM.

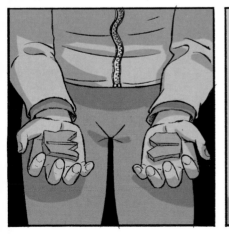

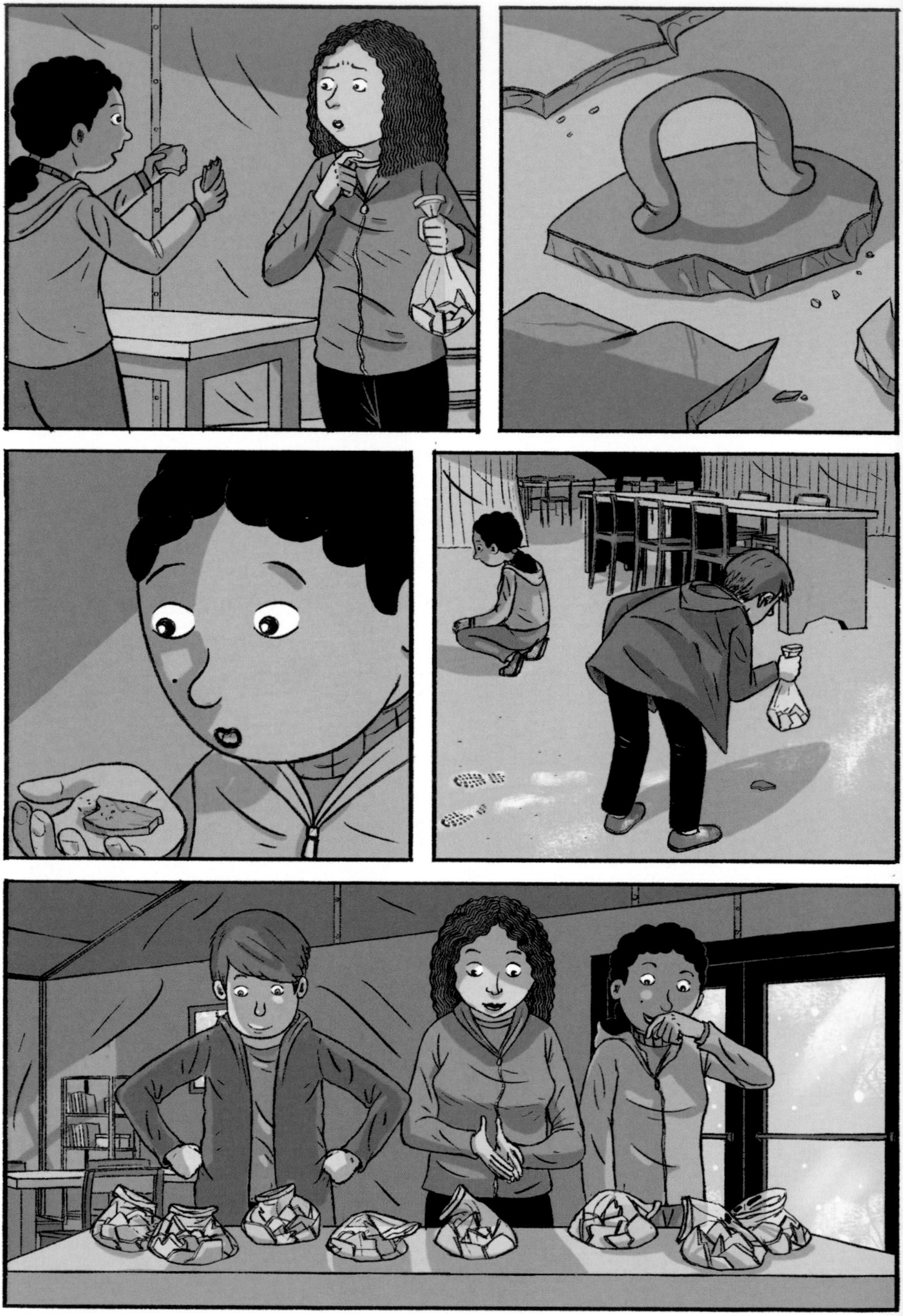

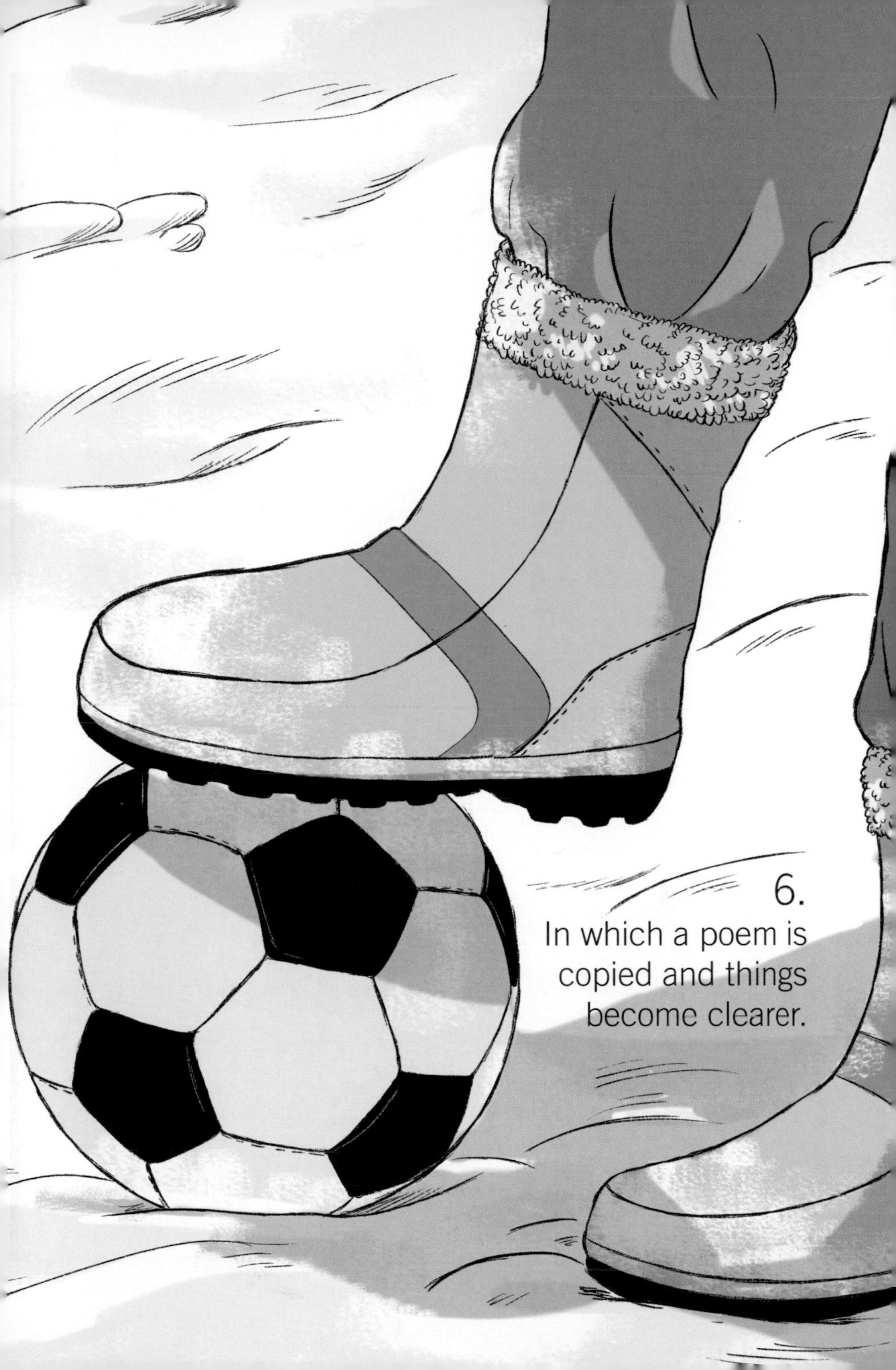

6.

In which a poem is copied and things become clearer.

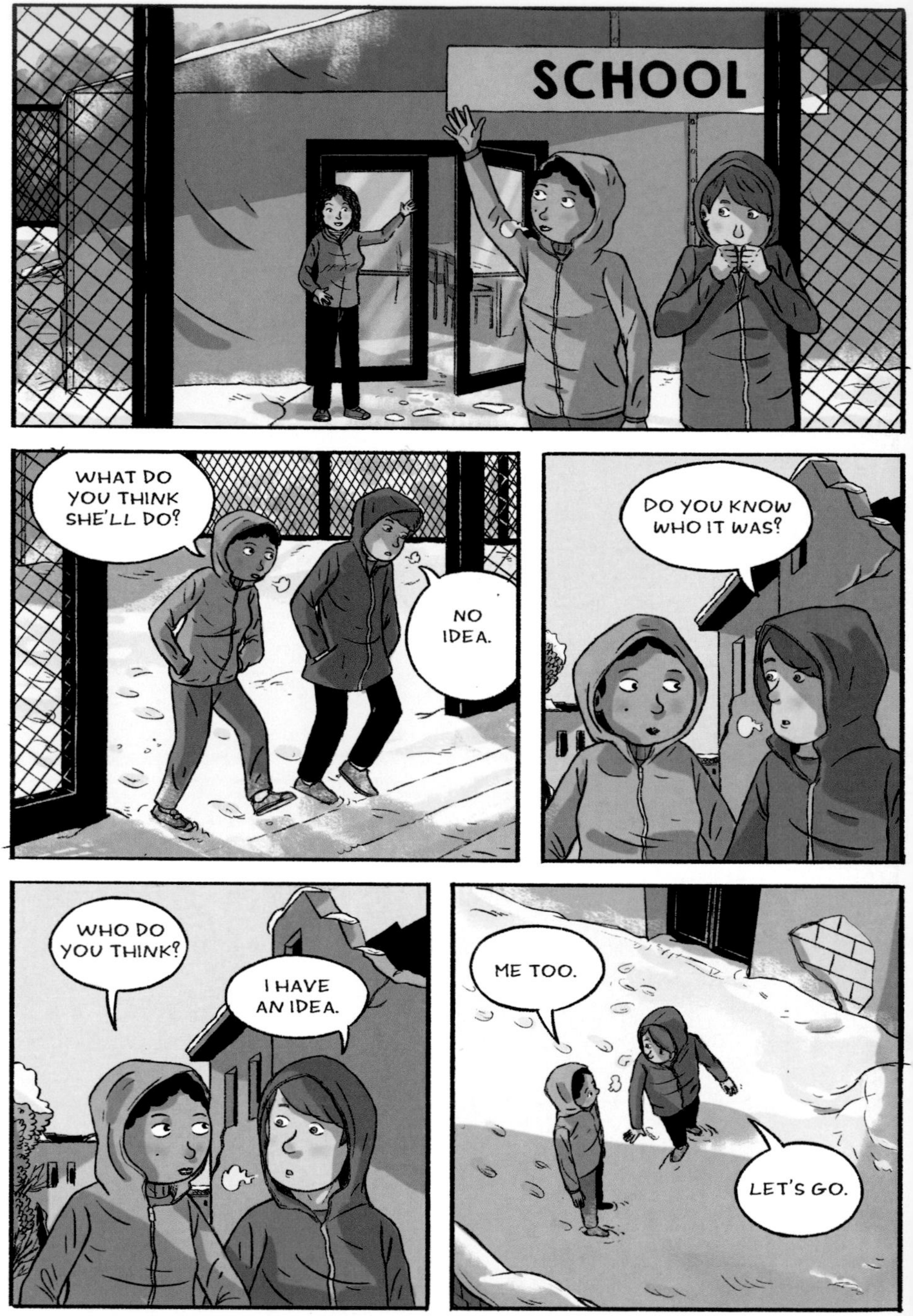
SCHOOL
WHAT DO YOU THINK SHE'LL DO?
NO IDEA.
DO YOU KNOW WHO IT WAS?
WHO DO YOU THINK?
I HAVE AN IDEA.
ME TOO.
LET'S GO.

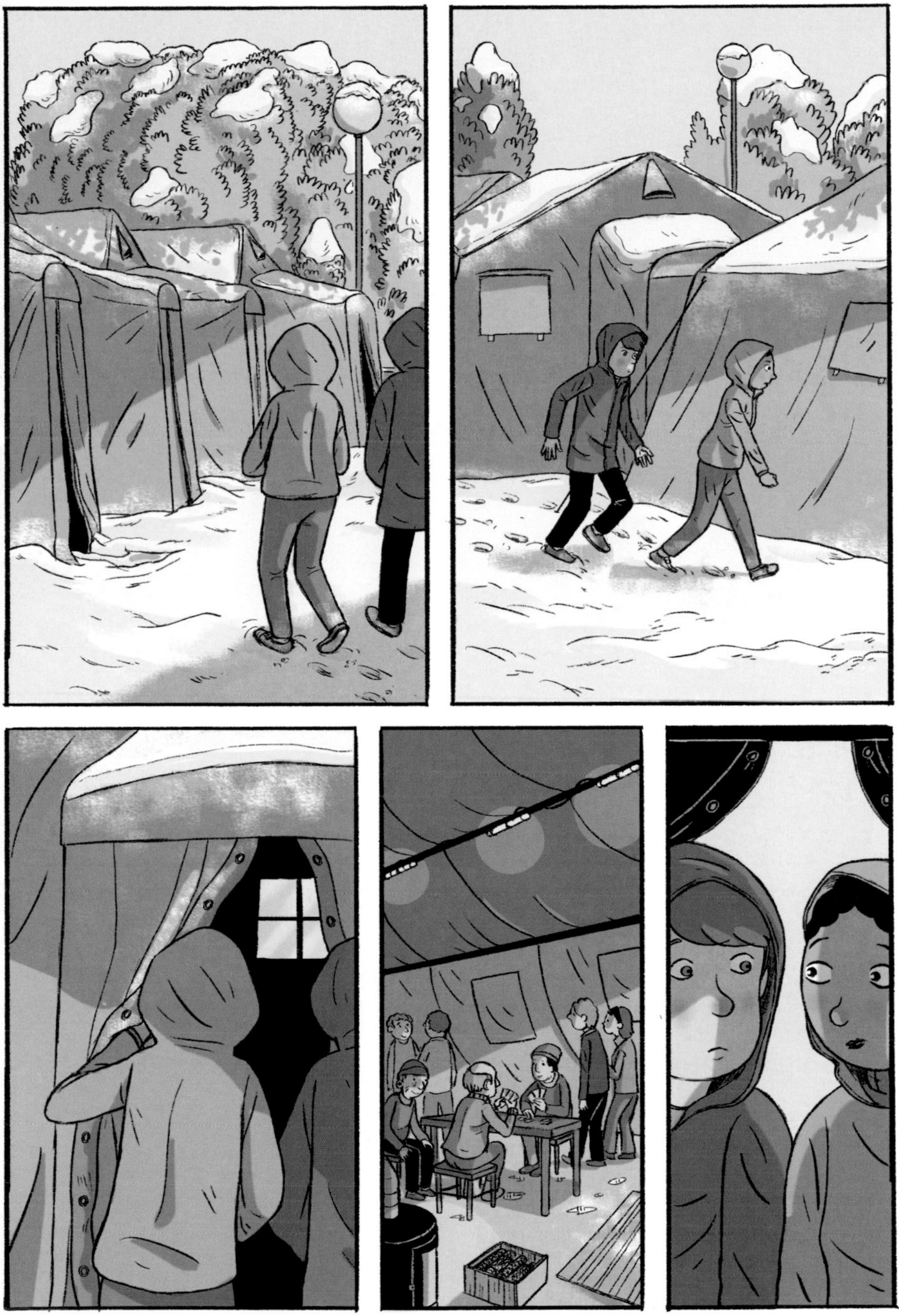

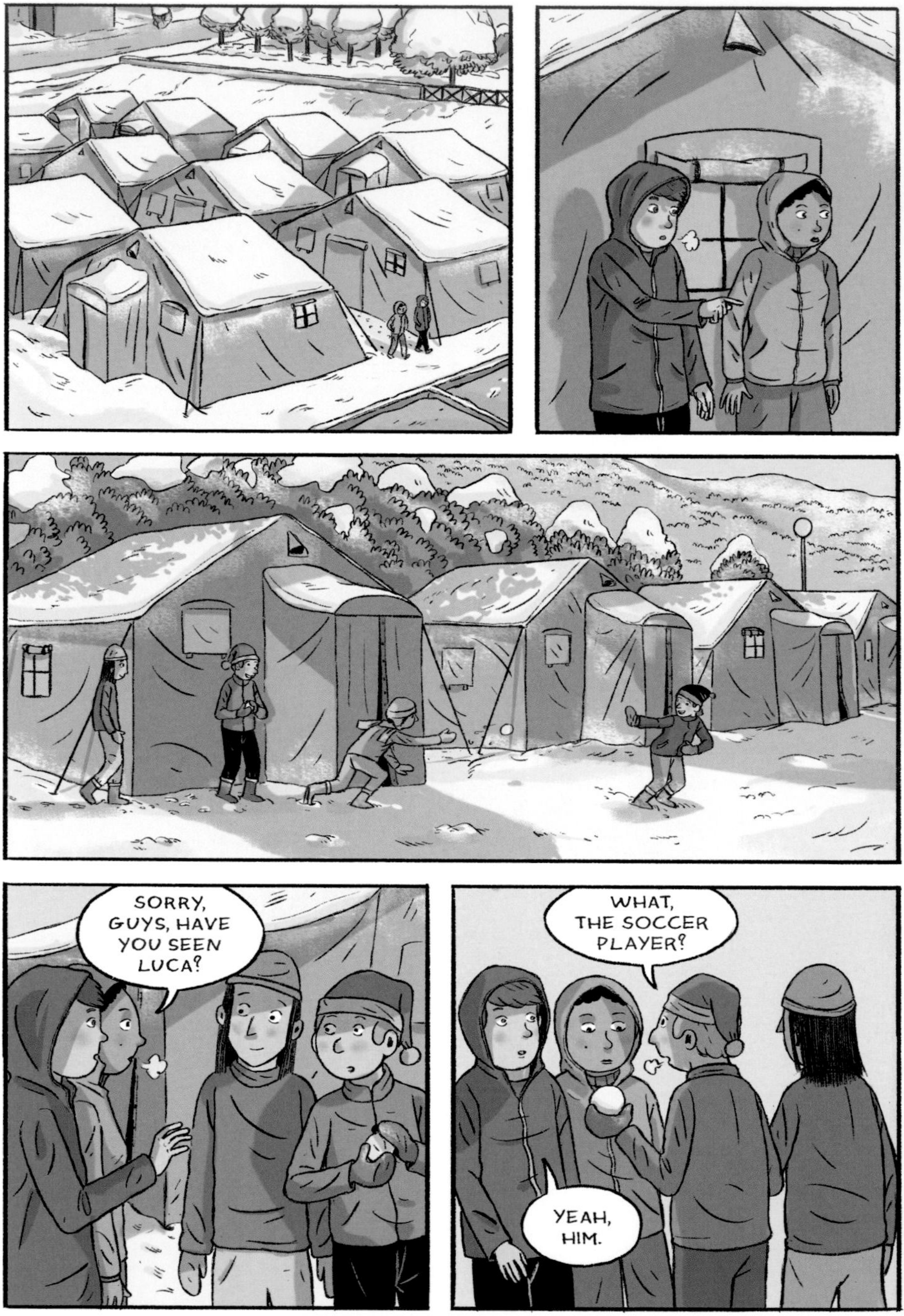
SORRY, GUYS, HAVE YOU SEEN LUCA?
WHAT, THE SOCCER PLAYER?
YEAH, HIM.

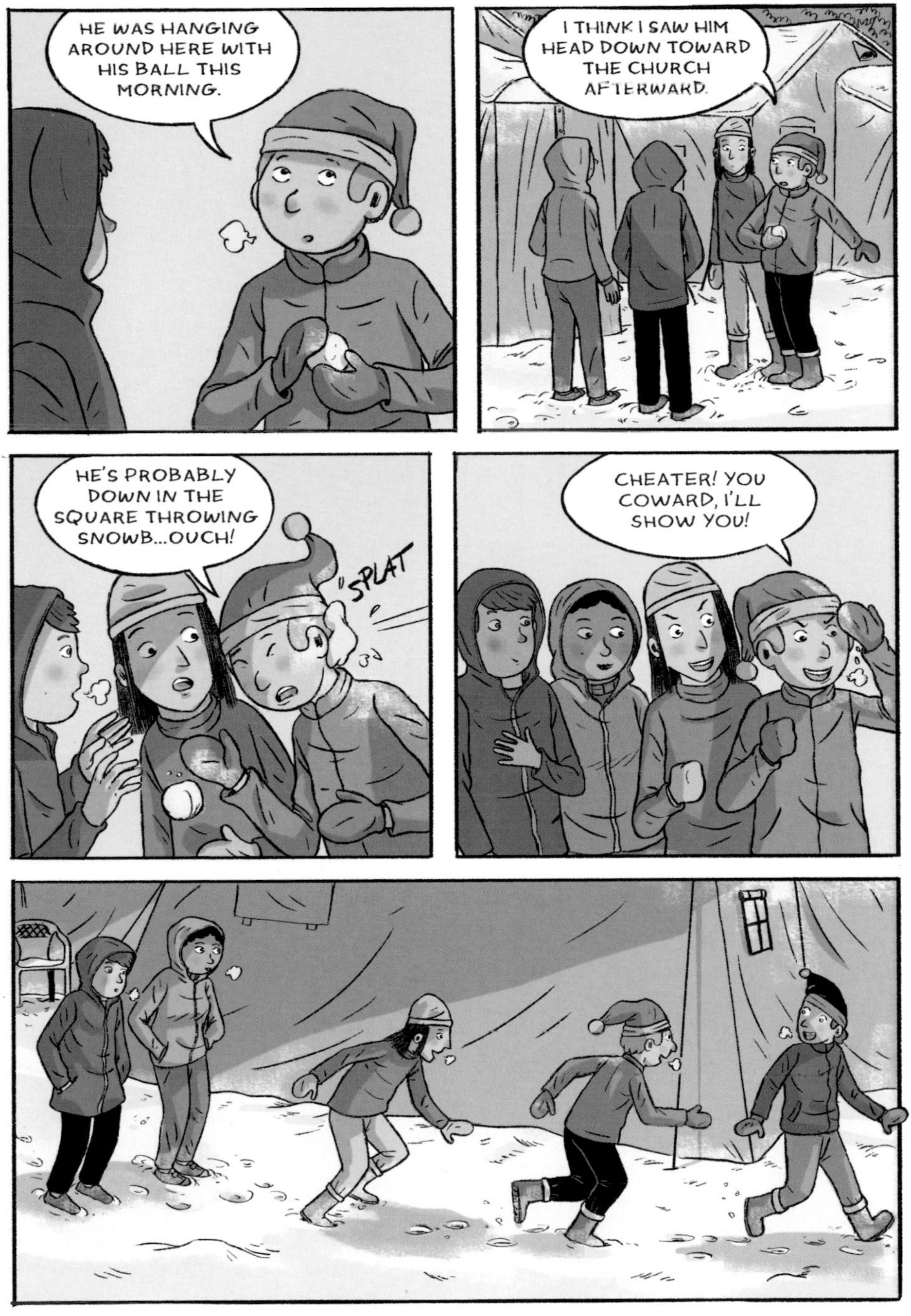
HE WAS HANGING AROUND HERE WITH HIS BALL THIS MORNING.
I THINK I SAW HIM HEAD DOWN TOWARD THE CHURCH AFTERWARD.
HE'S PROBABLY DOWN IN THE SQUARE THROWING SNOWB...OUCH!
SPLAT
CHEATER! YOU COWARD, I'LL SHOW YOU!

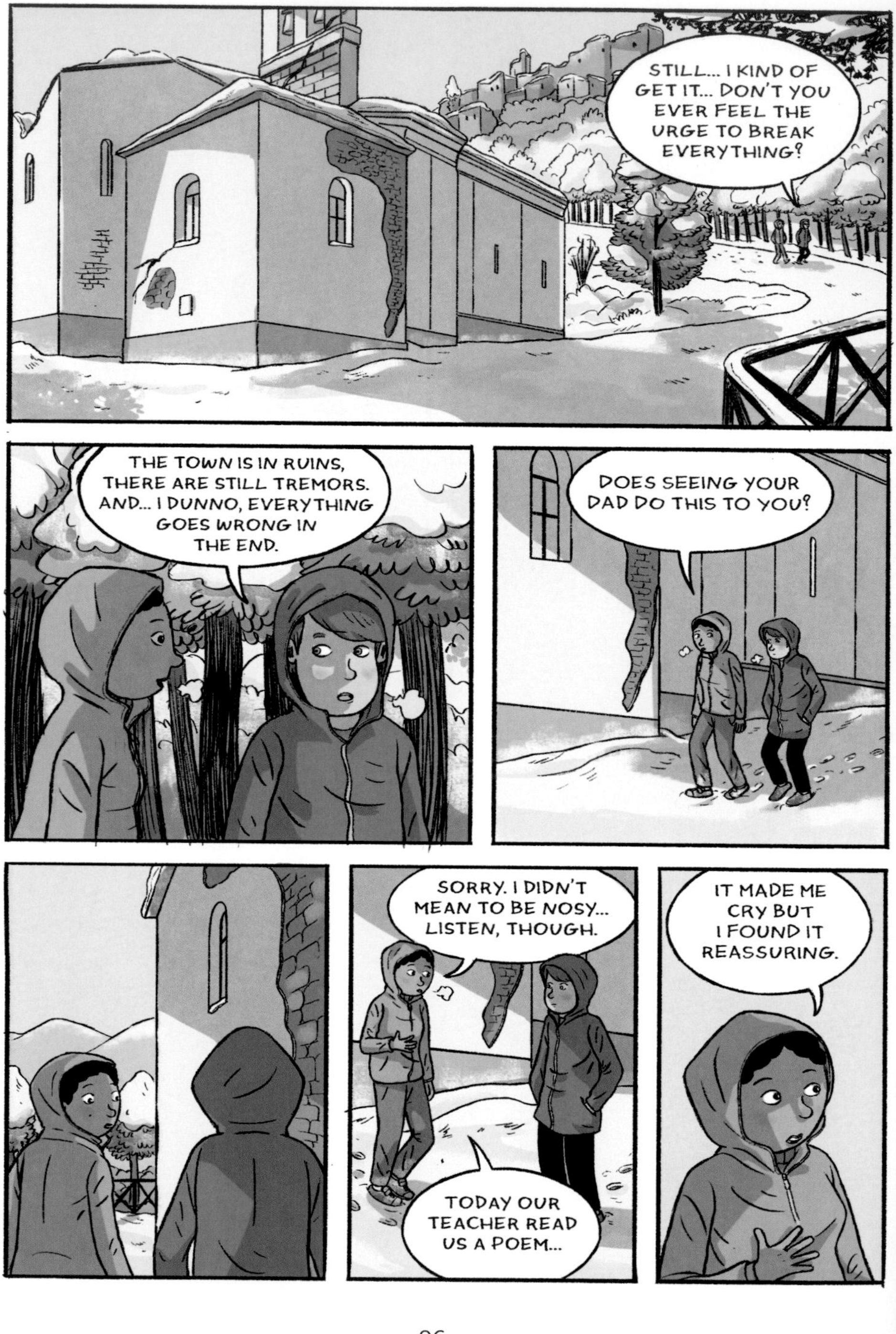
STILL... I KIND OF GET IT... DON'T YOU EVER FEEL THE URGE TO BREAK EVERYTHING?
THE TOWN IS IN RUINS, THERE ARE STILL TREMORS. AND... I DUNNO, EVERYTHING GOES WRONG IN THE END.
DOES SEEING YOUR DAD DO THIS TO YOU?
SORRY. I DIDN'T MEAN TO BE NOSY... LISTEN, THOUGH.
TODAY OUR TEACHER READ US A POEM...
IT MADE ME CRY BUT I FOUND IT REASSURING.

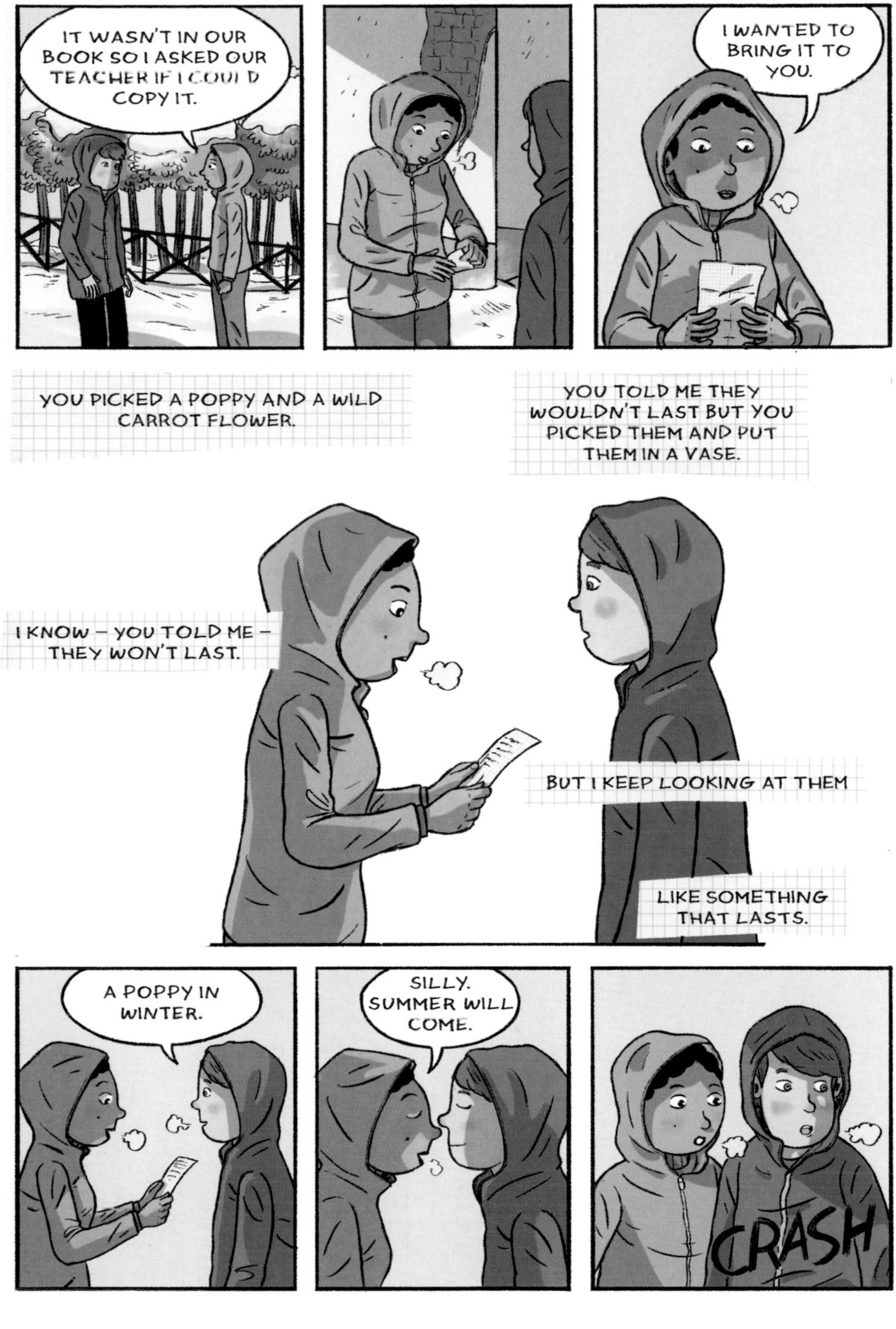
IT WASN'T IN OUR BOOK SO I ASKED OUR TEACHER IF I COULD COPY IT.
I WANTED TO BRING IT TO YOU.
YOU PICKED A POPPY AND A WILD CARROT FLOWER.
YOU TOLD ME THEY WOULDN'T LAST BUT YOU PICKED THEM AND PUT THEM IN A VASE.
I KNOW – YOU TOLD ME – THEY WON'T LAST.
BUT I KEEP LOOKING AT THEM
LIKE SOMETHING THAT LASTS.
A POPPY IN WINTER.
SILLY. SUMMER WILL COME.
CRASH

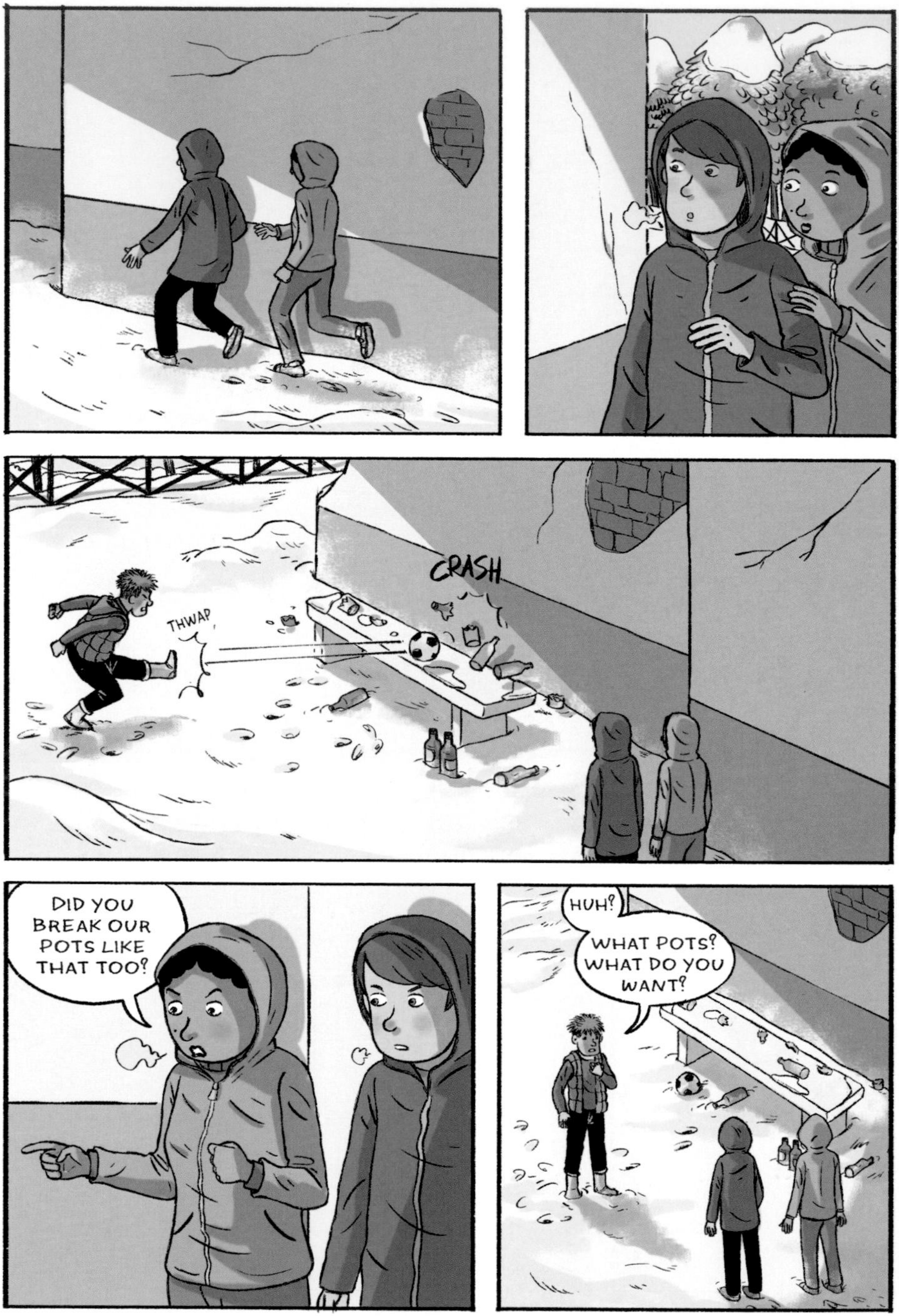
CRASH
THWAP
DID YOU BREAK OUR POTS LIKE THAT TOO?
HUH?
WHAT POTS? WHAT DO YOU WANT?

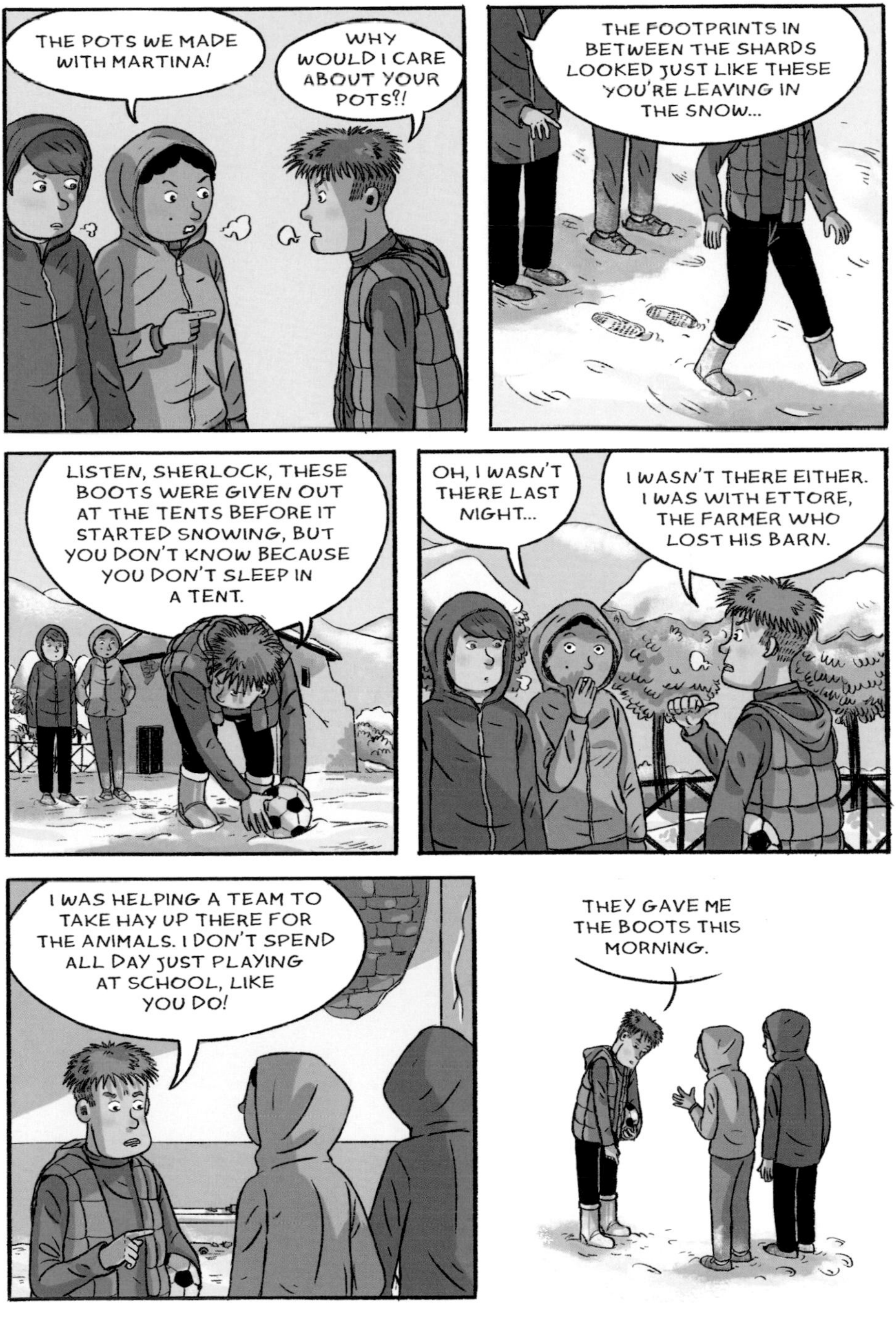
THE POTS WE MADE WITH MARTINA!
WHY WOULD I CARE ABOUT YOUR POTS?!
THE FOOTPRINTS IN BETWEEN THE SHARDS LOOKED JUST LIKE THESE YOU'RE LEAVING IN THE SNOW...
LISTEN, SHERLOCK, THESE BOOTS WERE GIVEN OUT AT THE TENTS BEFORE IT STARTED SNOWING, BUT YOU DON'T KNOW BECAUSE YOU DON'T SLEEP IN A TENT.
OH, I WASN'T THERE LAST NIGHT...
I WASN'T THERE EITHER. I WAS WITH ETTORE, THE FARMER WHO LOST HIS BARN.
I WAS HELPING A TEAM TO TAKE HAY UP THERE FOR THE ANIMALS. I DON'T SPEND ALL DAY JUST PLAYING AT SCHOOL, LIKE YOU DO!
THEY GAVE ME THE BOOTS THIS MORNING.

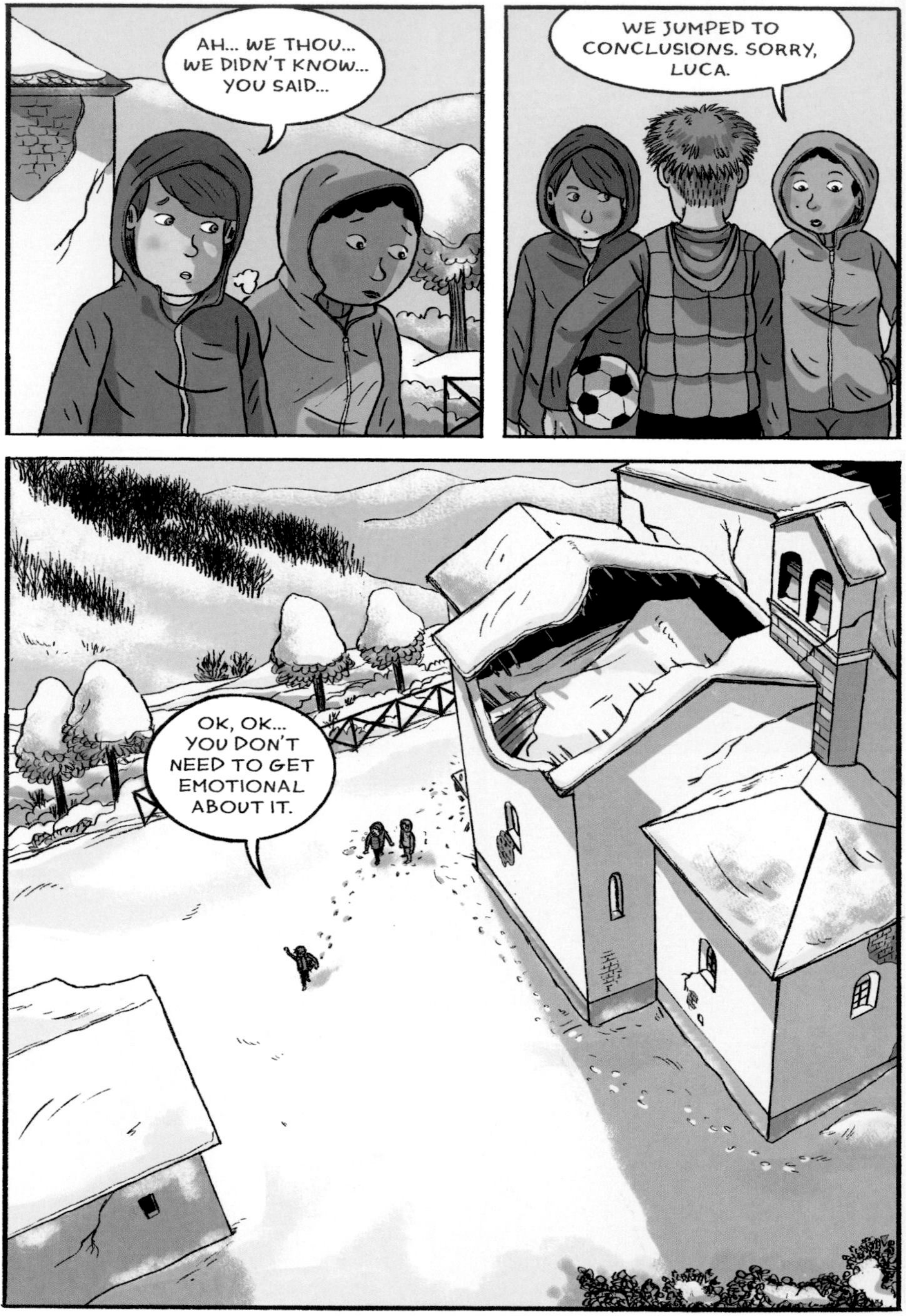
AH... WE THOU... WE DIDN'T KNOW... YOU SAID...
WE JUMPED TO CONCLUSIONS. SORRY, LUCA.
OK, OK... YOU DON'T NEED TO GET EMOTIONAL ABOUT IT.

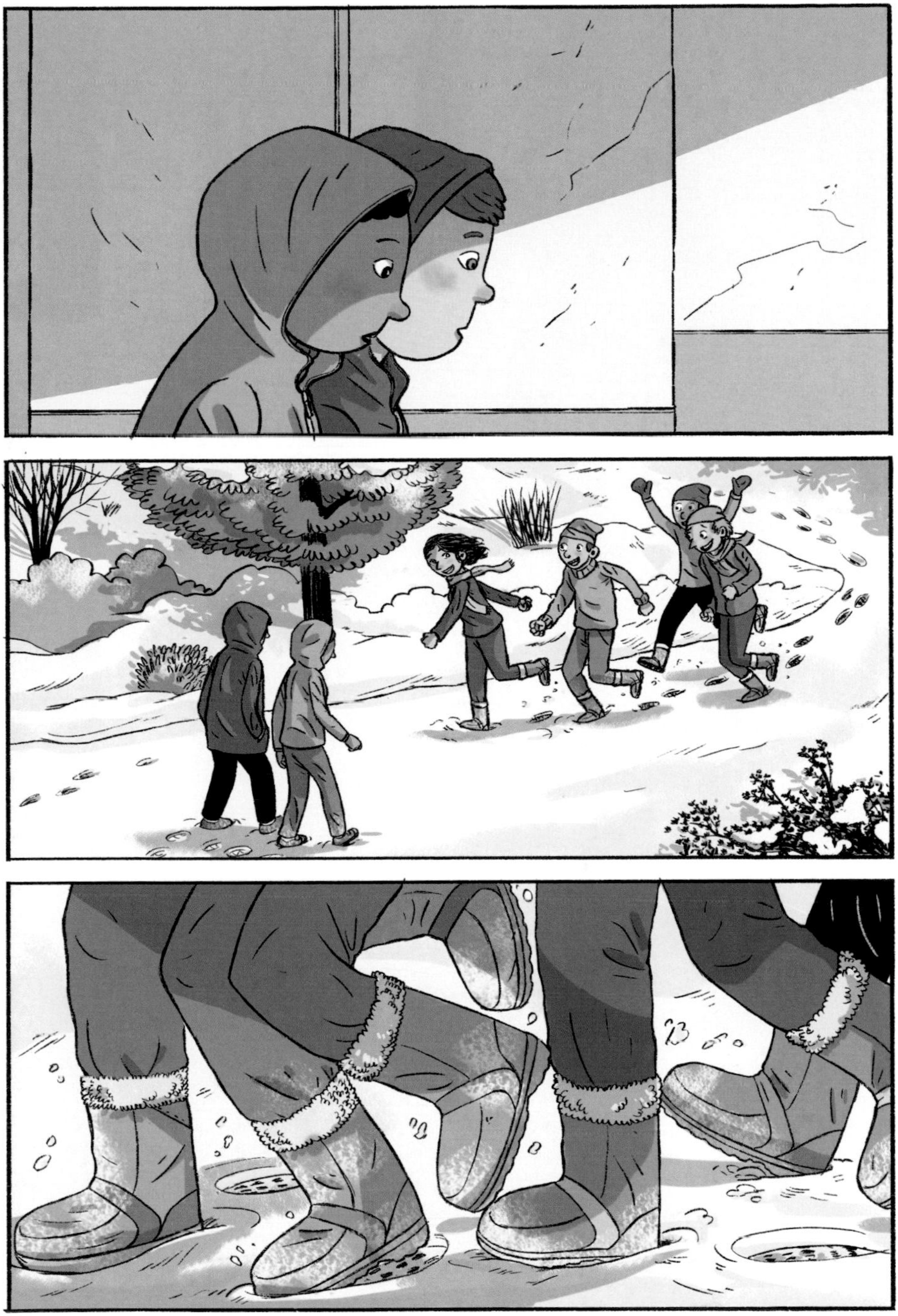

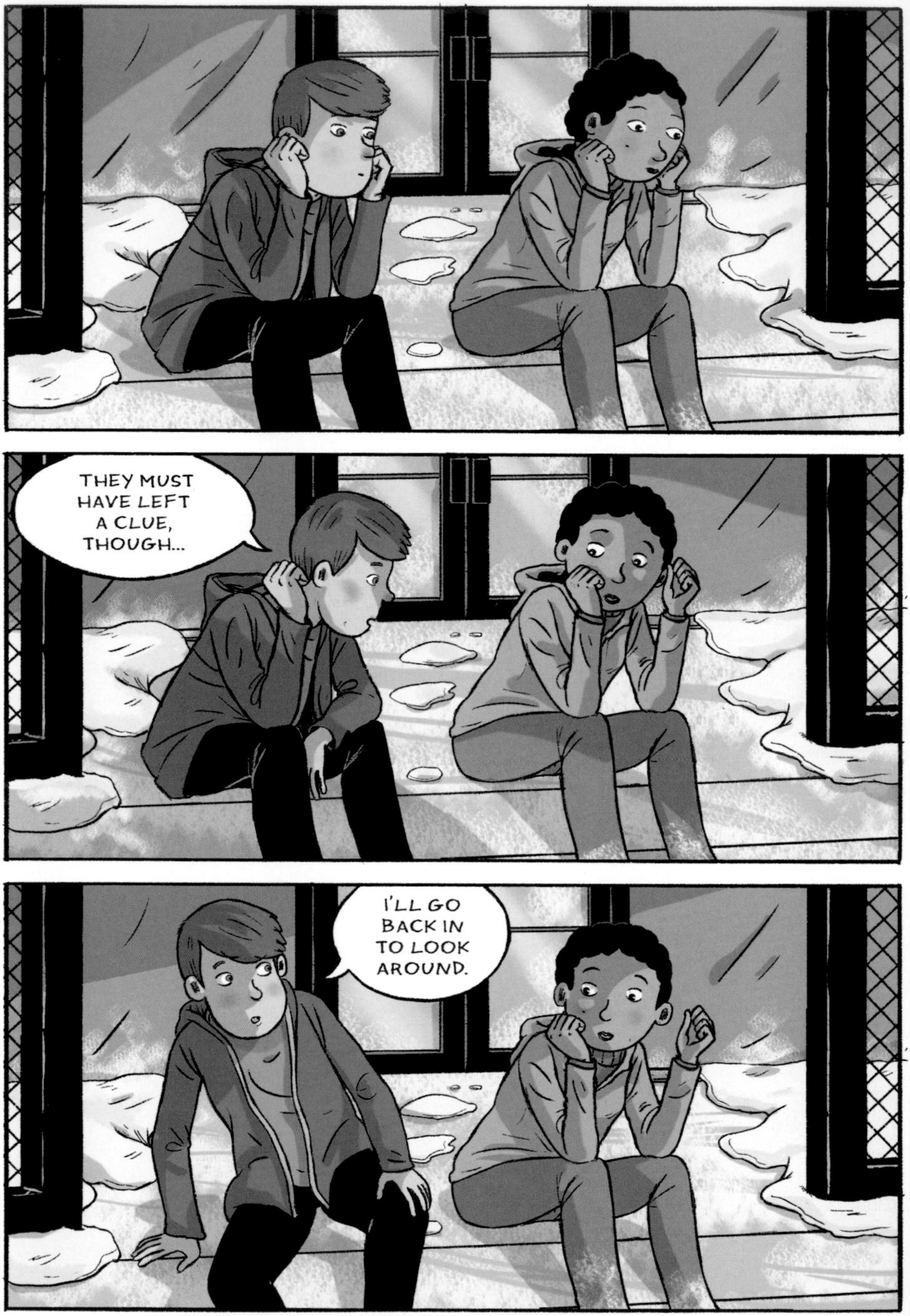
THEY MUST HAVE LEFT A CLUE, THOUGH...
I'LL GO BACK IN TO LOOK AROUND.

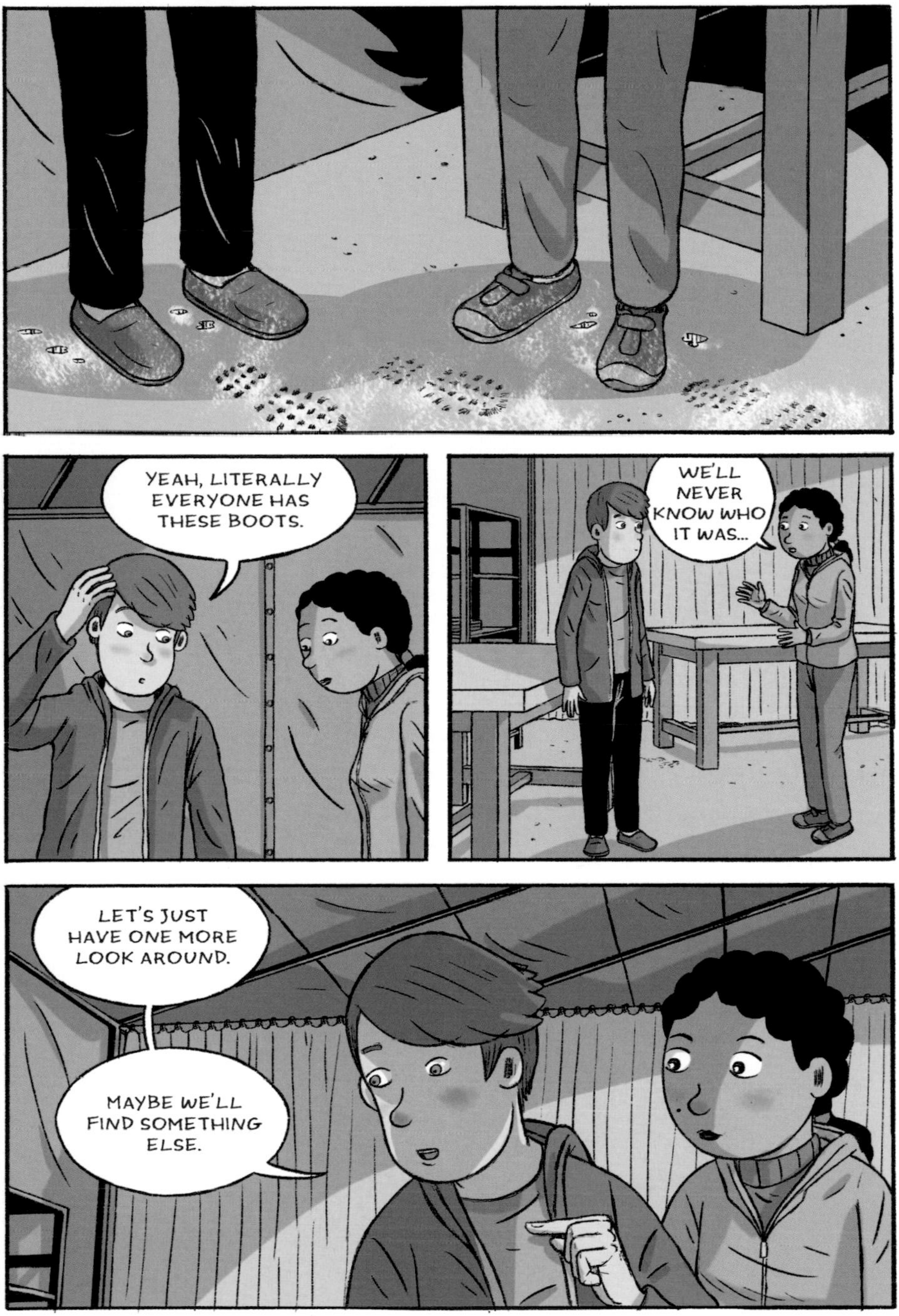
YEAH, LITERALLY EVERYONE HAS THESE BOOTS.
WE'LL NEVER KNOW WHO IT WAS...
LET'S JUST HAVE ONE MORE LOOK AROUND.
MAYBE WE'LL FIND SOMETHING ELSE.

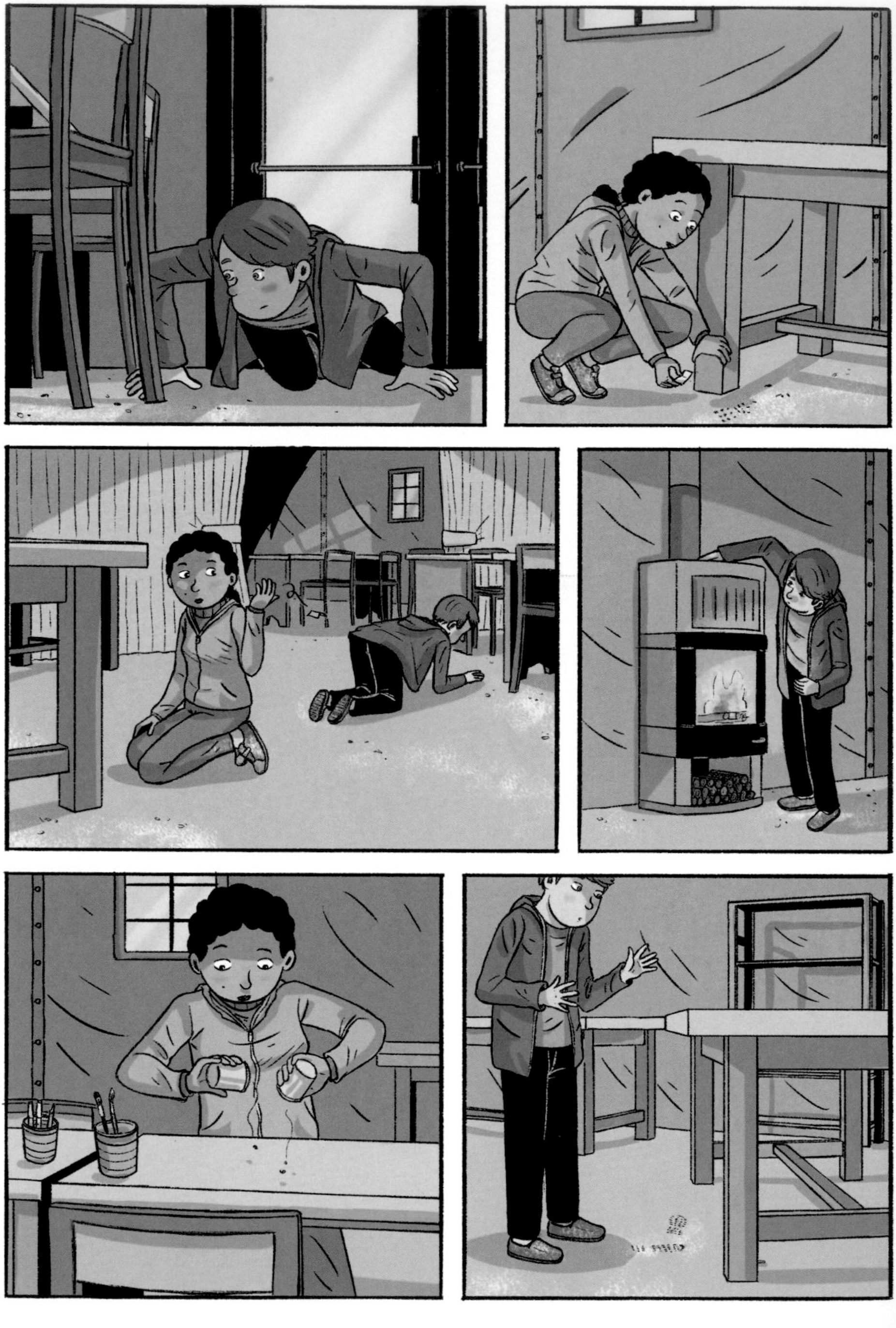

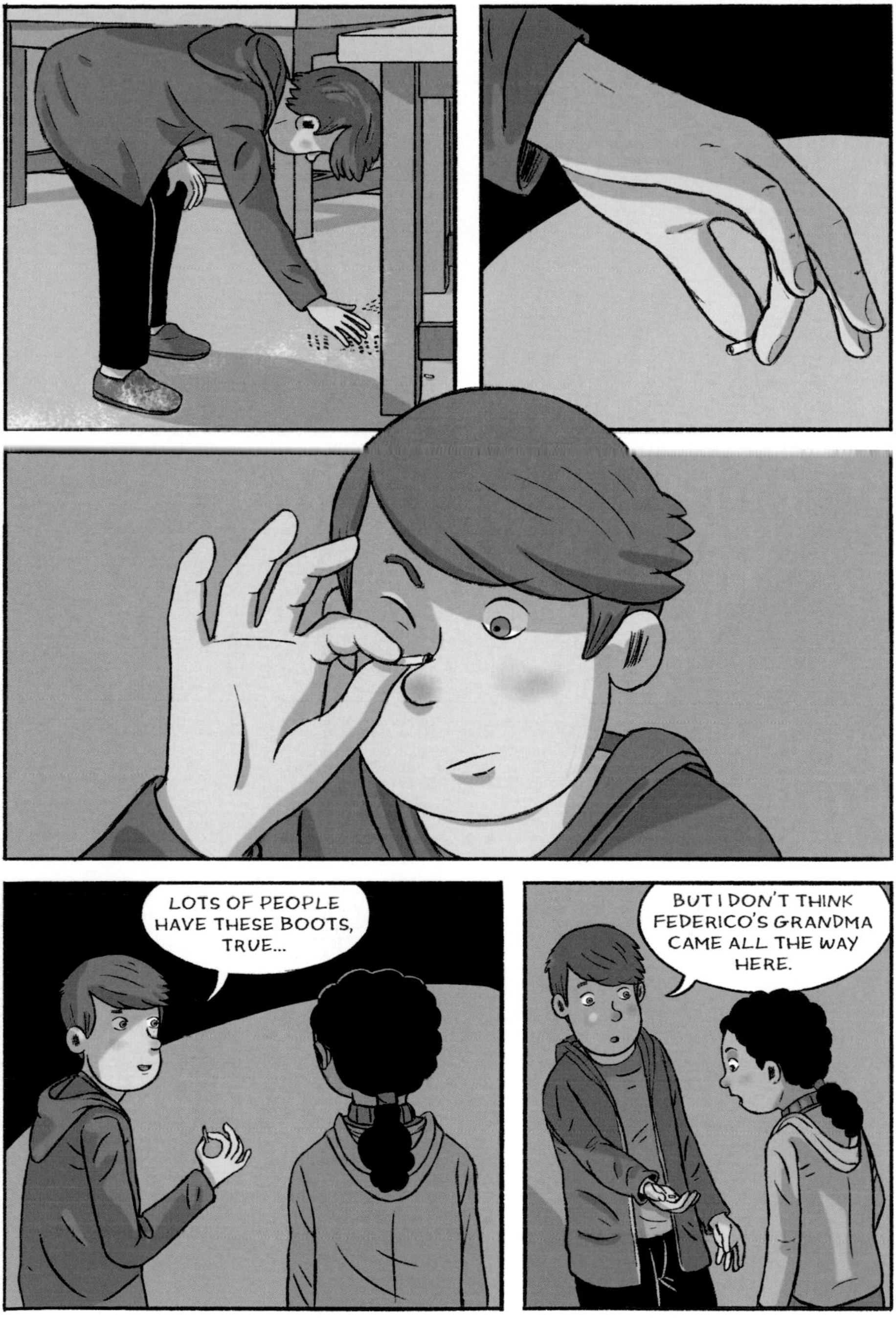
LOTS OF PEOPLE HAVE THESE BOOTS, TRUE...
BUT I DON'T THINK FEDERICO'S GRANDMA CAME ALL THE WAY HERE.

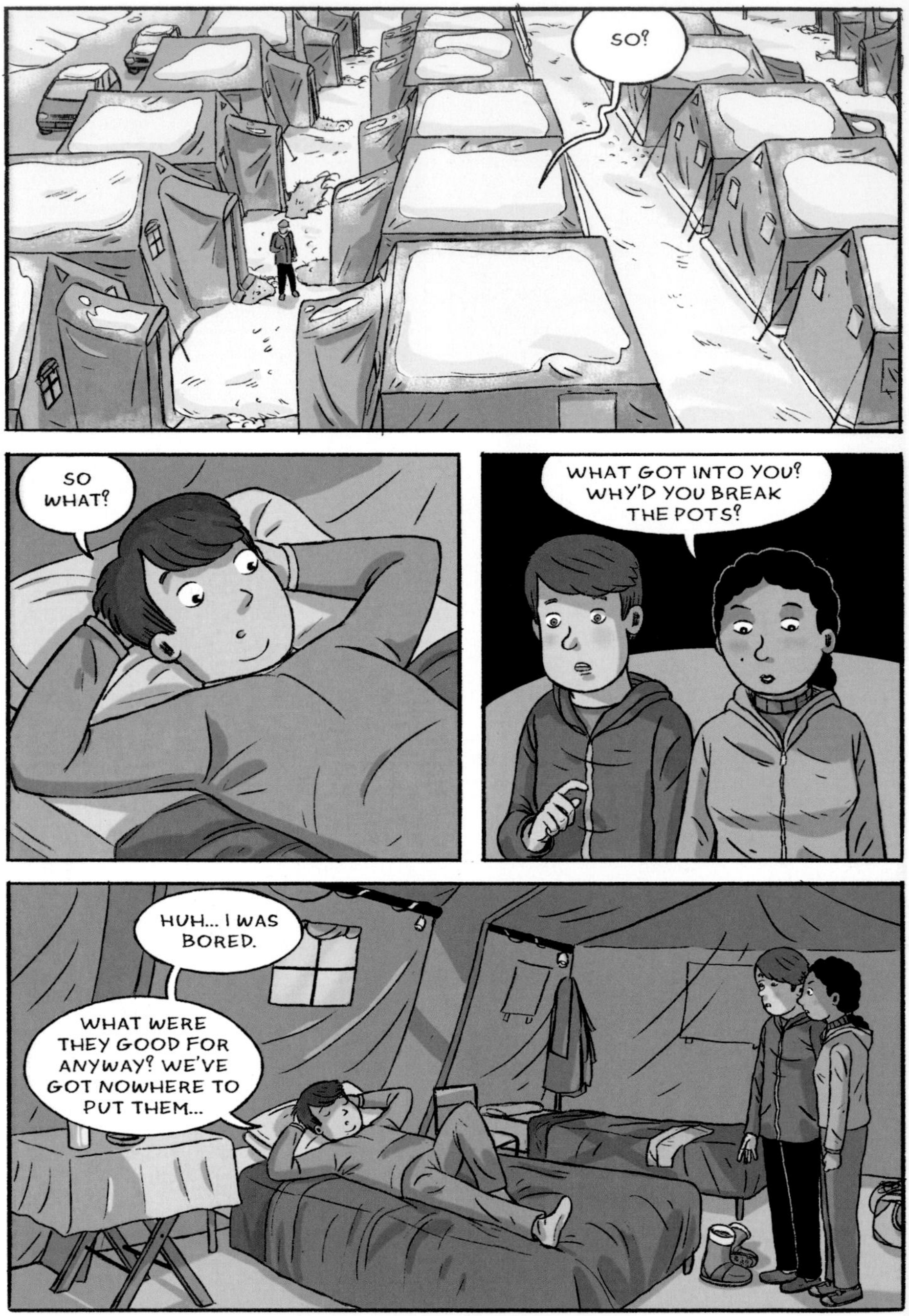
SO?
SO WHAT?
WHAT GOT INTO YOU? WHY'D YOU BREAK THE POTS?
HUH... I WAS BORED.
WHAT WERE THEY GOOD FOR ANYWAY? WE'VE GOT NOWHERE TO PUT THEM...

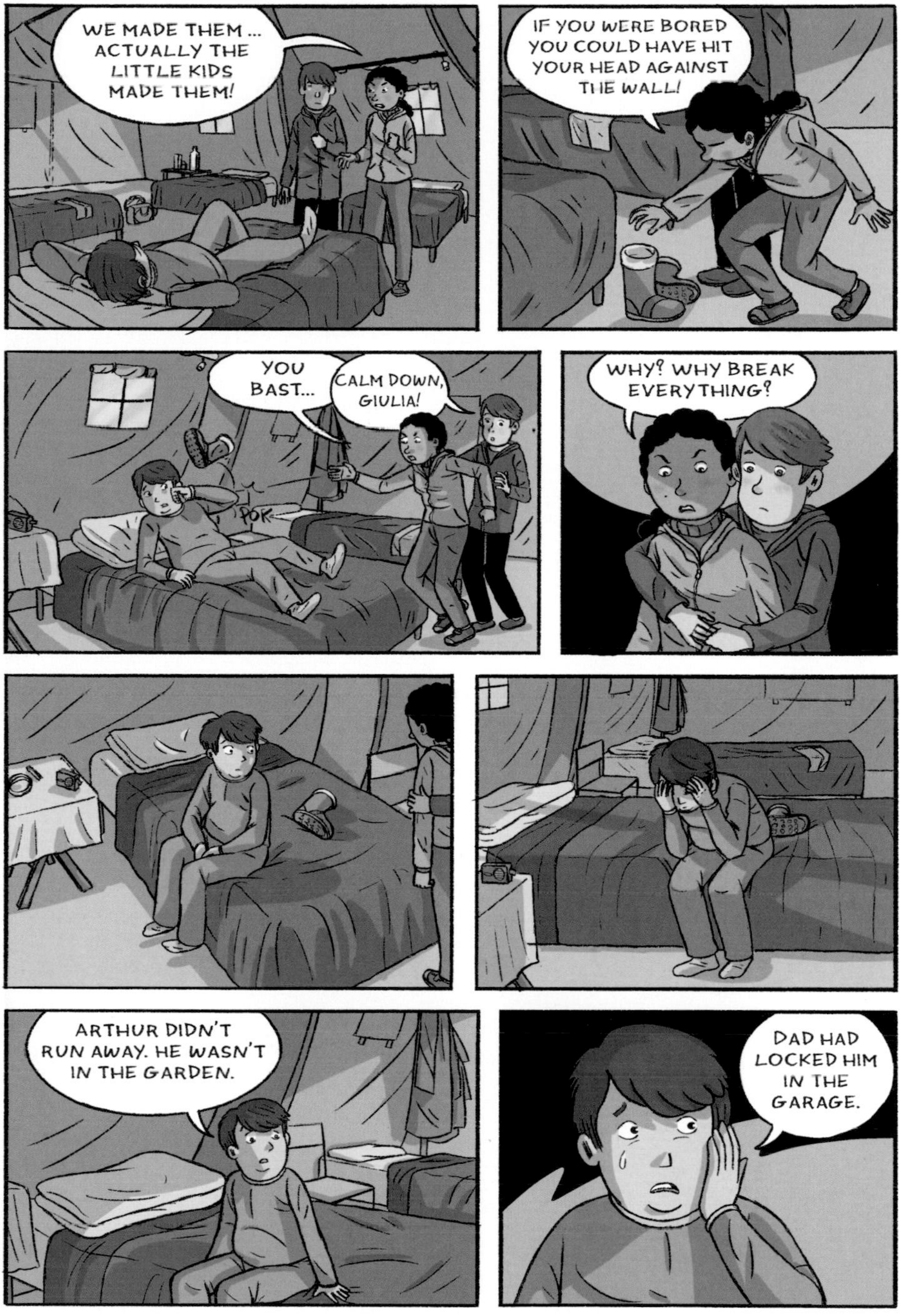
WE MADE THEM ... ACTUALLY THE LITTLE KIDS MADE THEM!
IF YOU WERE BORED YOU COULD HAVE HIT YOUR HEAD AGAINST THE WALL!
YOU BAST...
CALM DOWN, GIULIA!
POK
WHY? WHY BREAK EVERYTHING?
ARTHUR DIDN'T RUN AWAY. HE WASN'T IN THE GARDEN.
DAD HAD LOCKED HIM IN THE GARAGE.

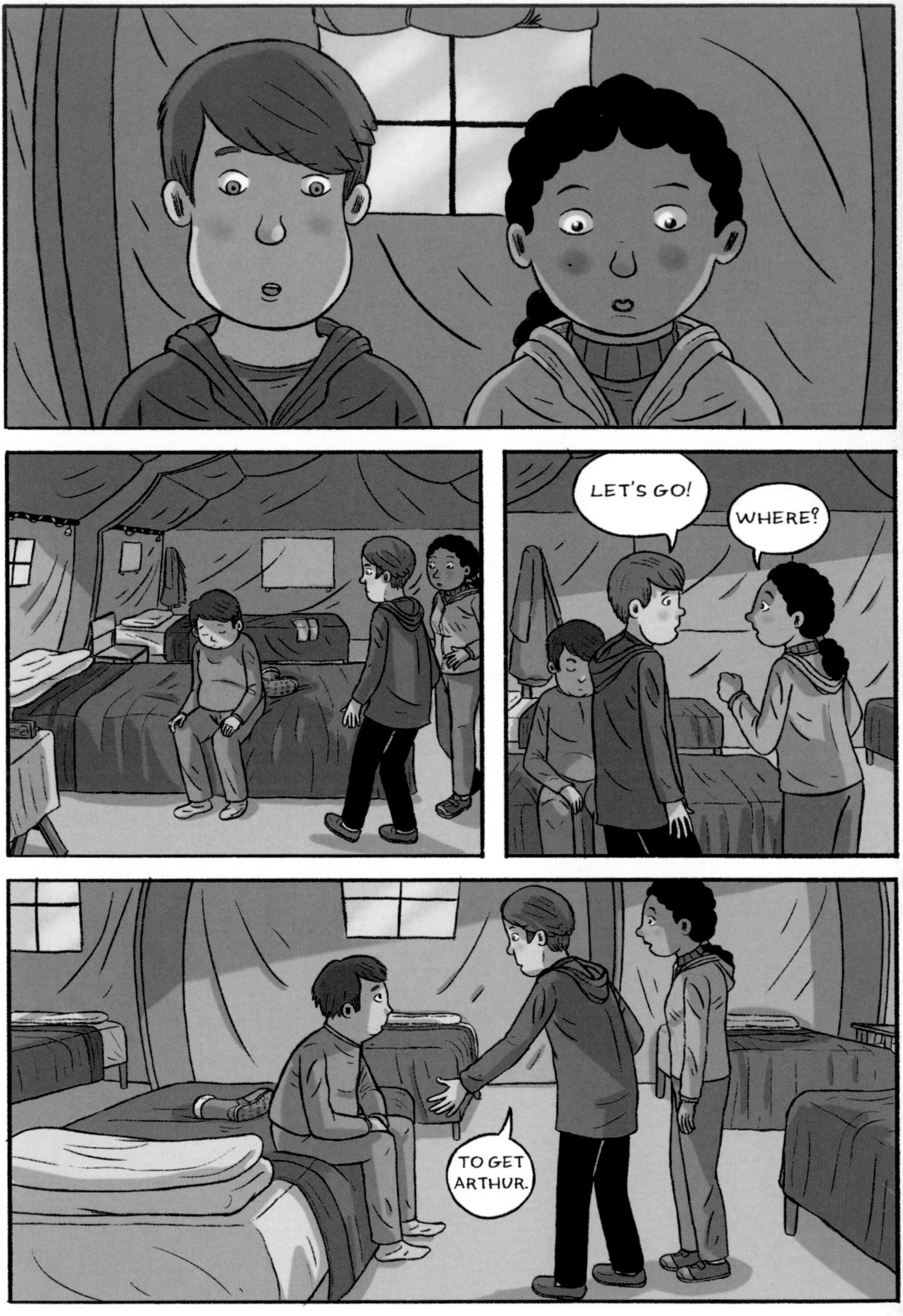
LET'S GO!
WHERE?
TO GET ARTHUR.

7.
In which we do what needs to be done.

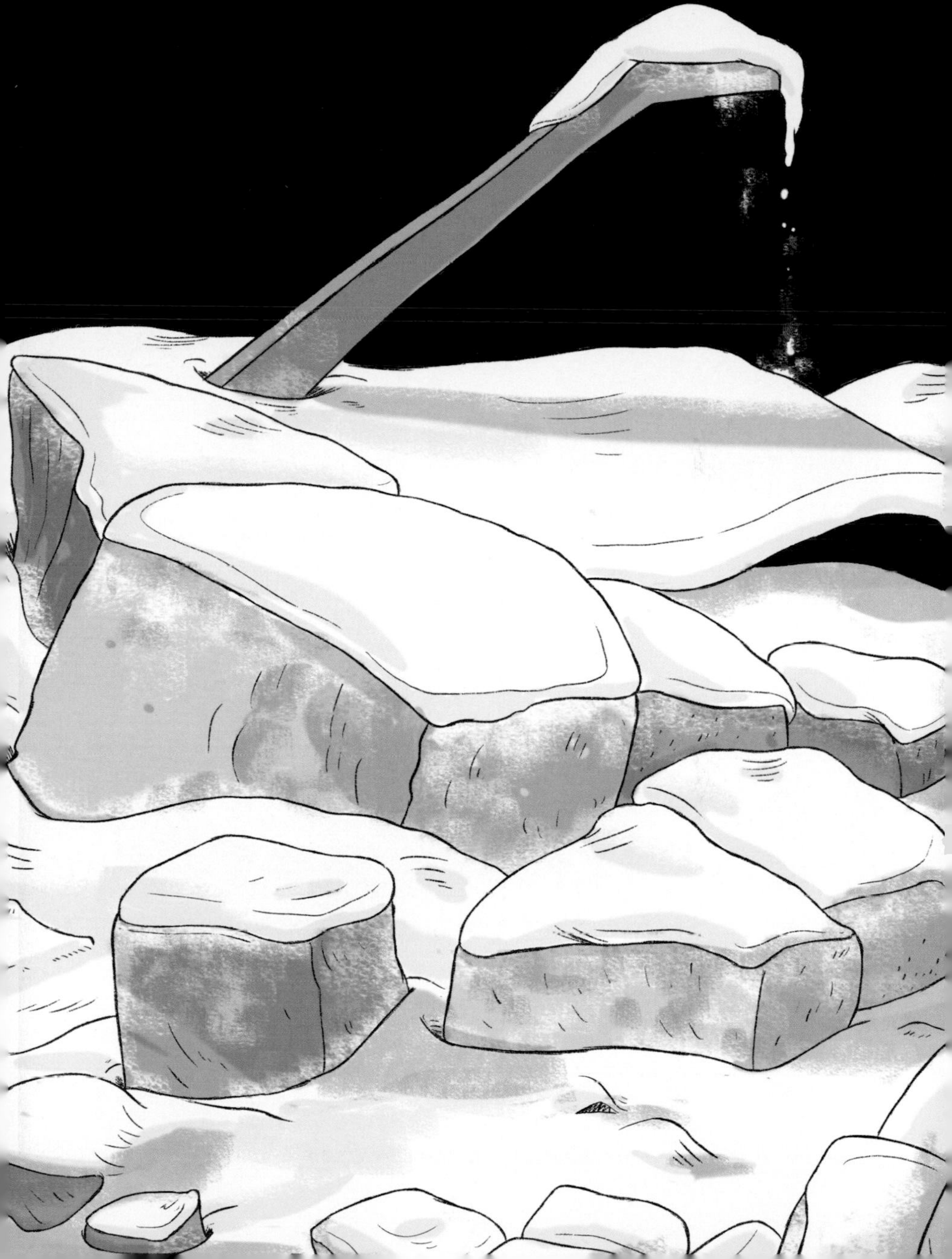

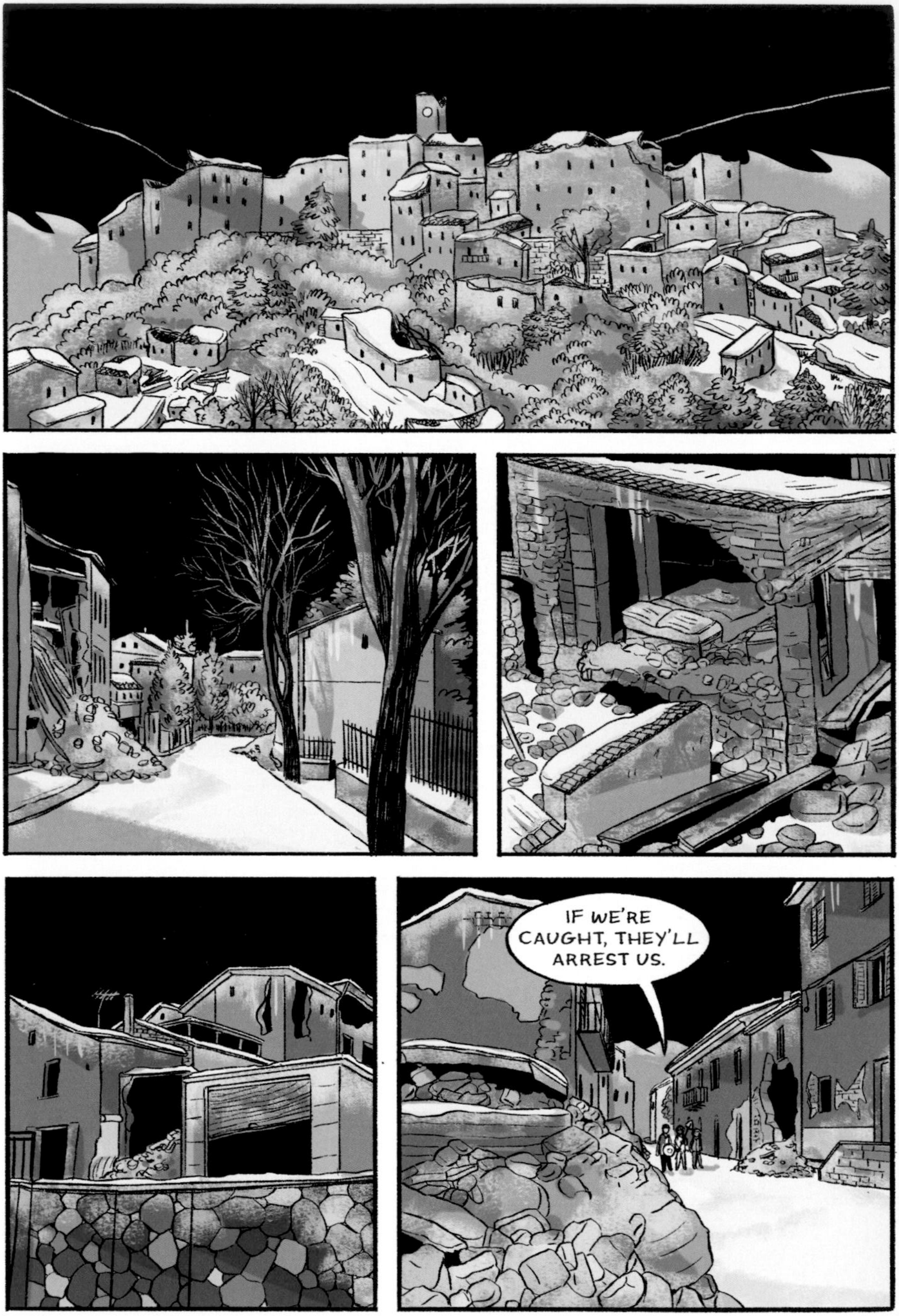
IF WE'RE CAUGHT, THEY'LL ARREST US.

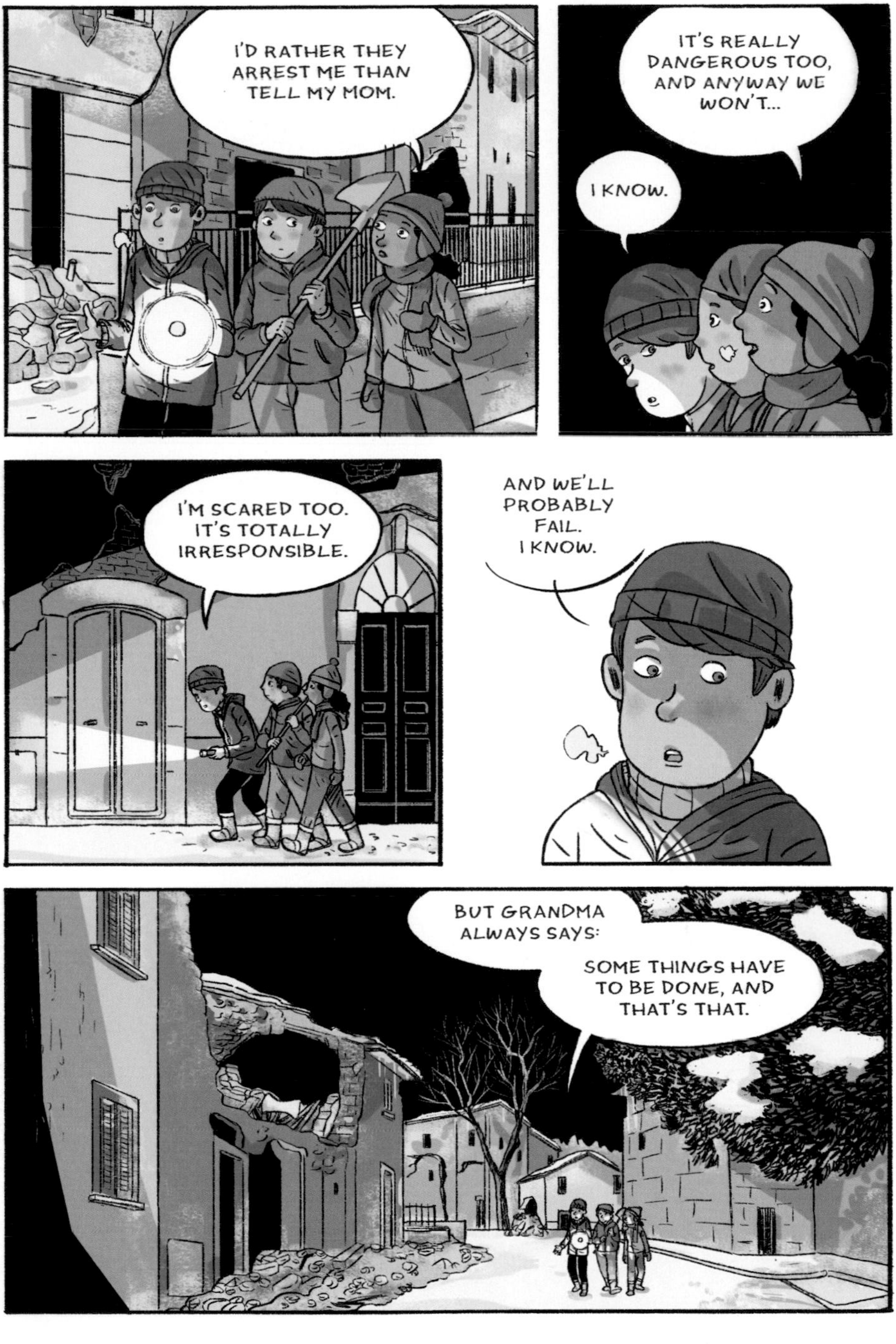

I'D RATHER THEY ARREST ME THAN TELL MY MOM.
IT'S REALLY DANGEROUS TOO, AND ANYWAY WE WON'T...
I KNOW.
I'M SCARED TOO. IT'S TOTALLY IRRESPONSIBLE.
AND WE'LL PROBABLY FAIL. I KNOW.
BUT GRANDMA ALWAYS SAYS:
SOME THINGS HAVE TO BE DONE, AND THAT'S THAT.

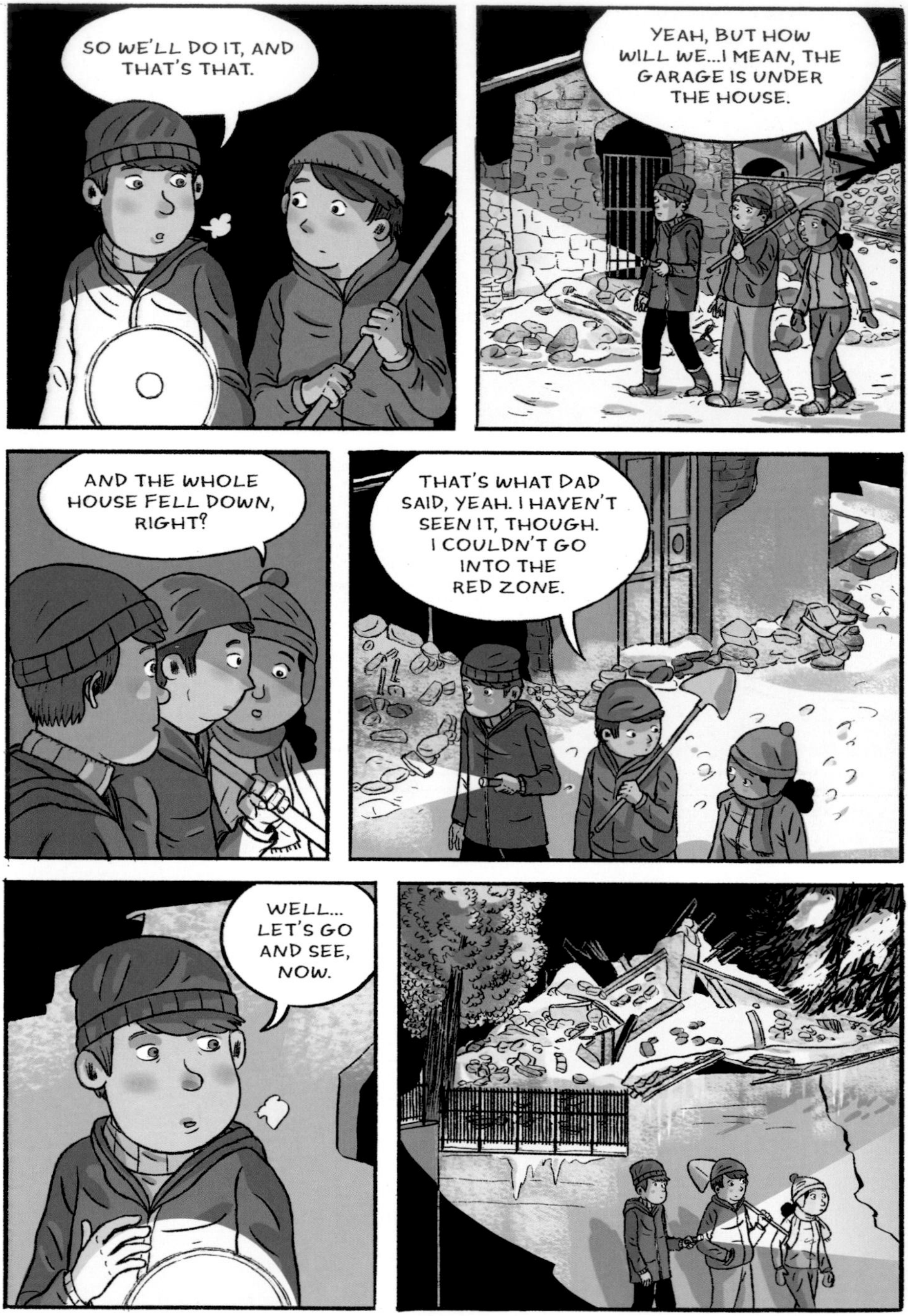
SO WE'LL DO IT, AND THAT'S THAT.
YEAH, BUT HOW WILL WE...I MEAN, THE GARAGE IS UNDER THE HOUSE.
AND THE WHOLE HOUSE FELL DOWN, RIGHT?
THAT'S WHAT DAD SAID, YEAH. I HAVEN'T SEEN IT, THOUGH. I COULDN'T GO INTO THE RED ZONE.
WELL... LET'S GO AND SEE, NOW.

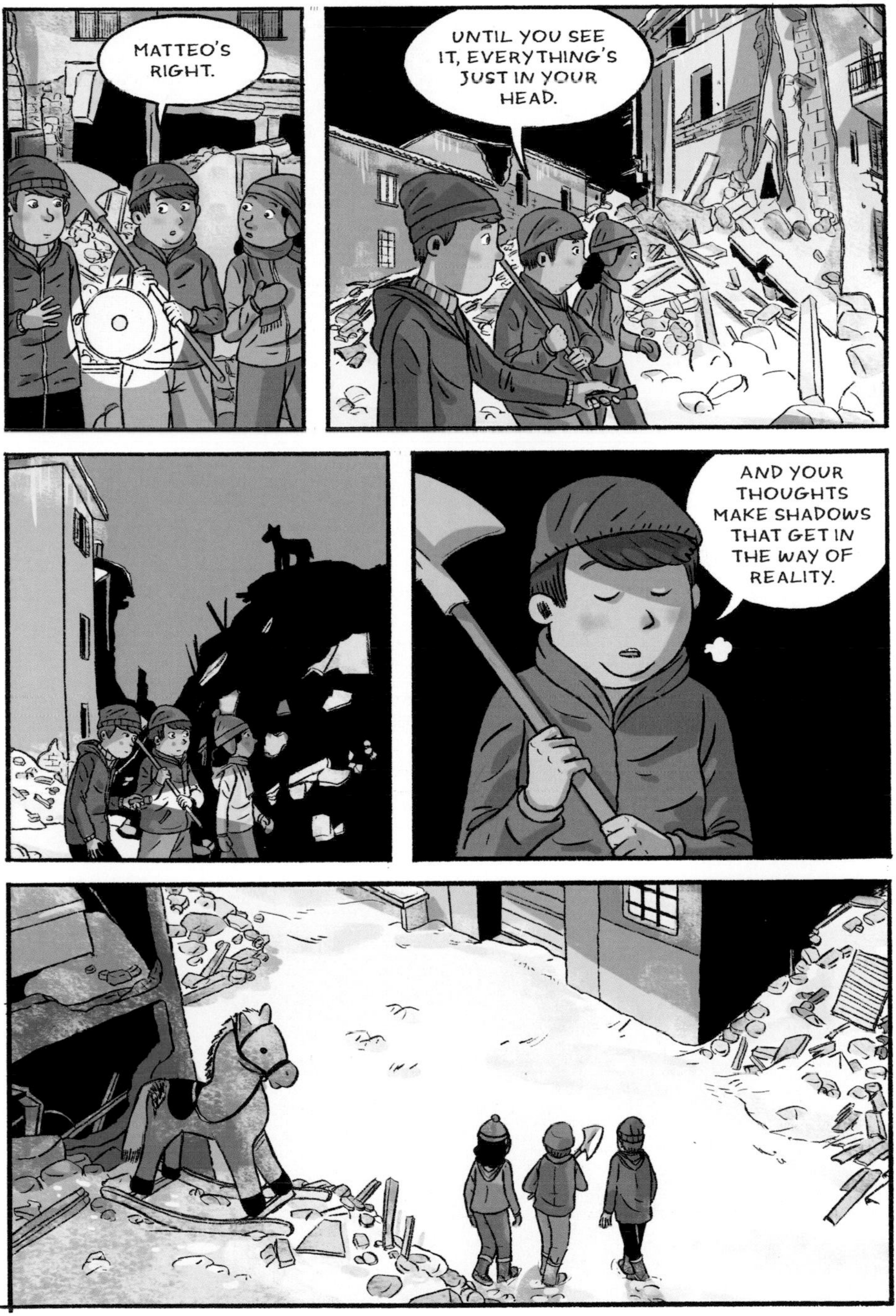
MATTEO'S RIGHT.
UNTIL YOU SEE IT, EVERYTHING'S JUST IN YOUR HEAD.
AND YOUR THOUGHTS MAKE SHADOWS THAT GET IN THE WAY OF REALITY.

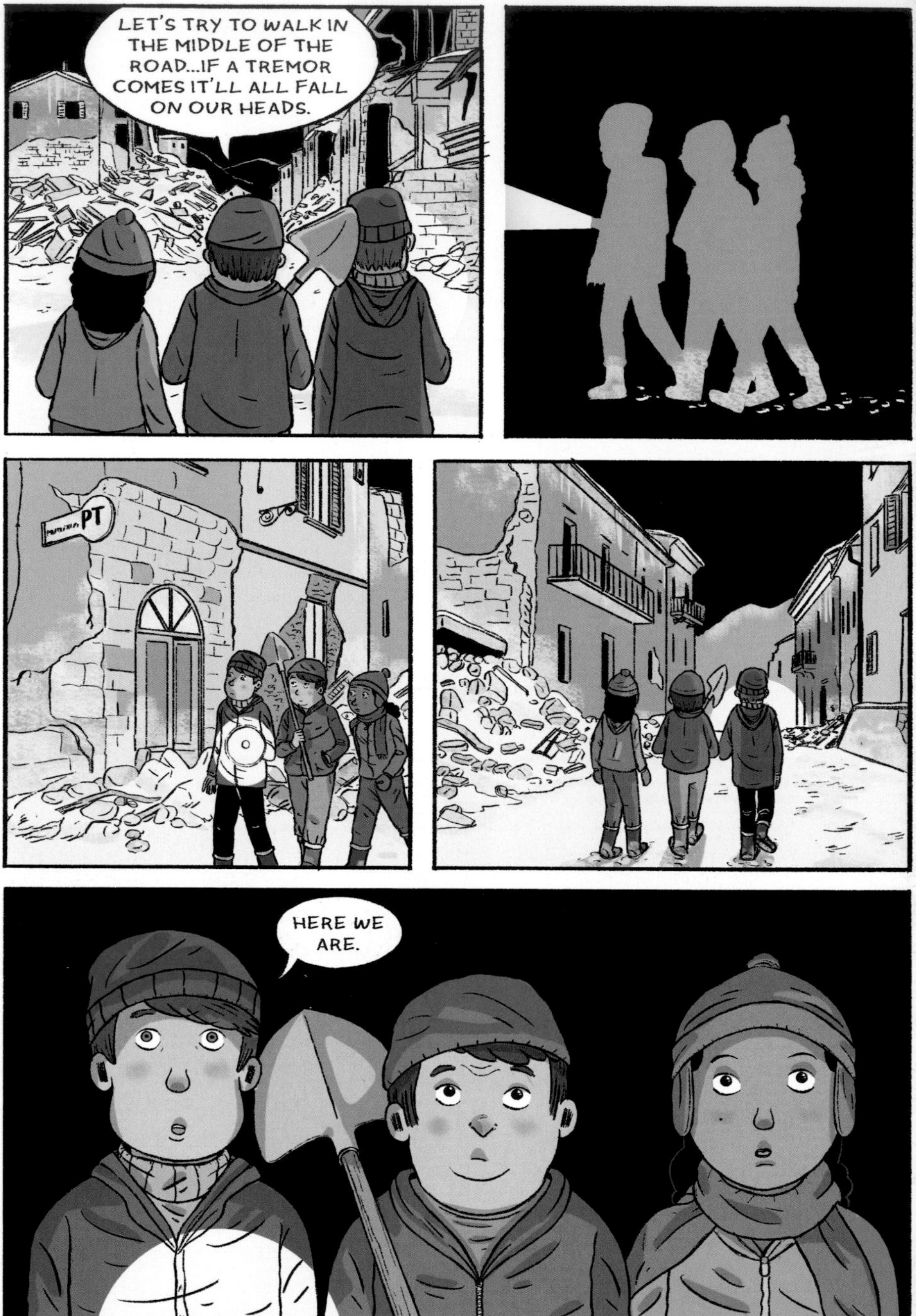
LET'S TRY TO WALK IN THE MIDDLE OF THE ROAD...IF A TREMOR COMES IT'LL ALL FALL ON OUR HEADS.
PT
HERE WE ARE.

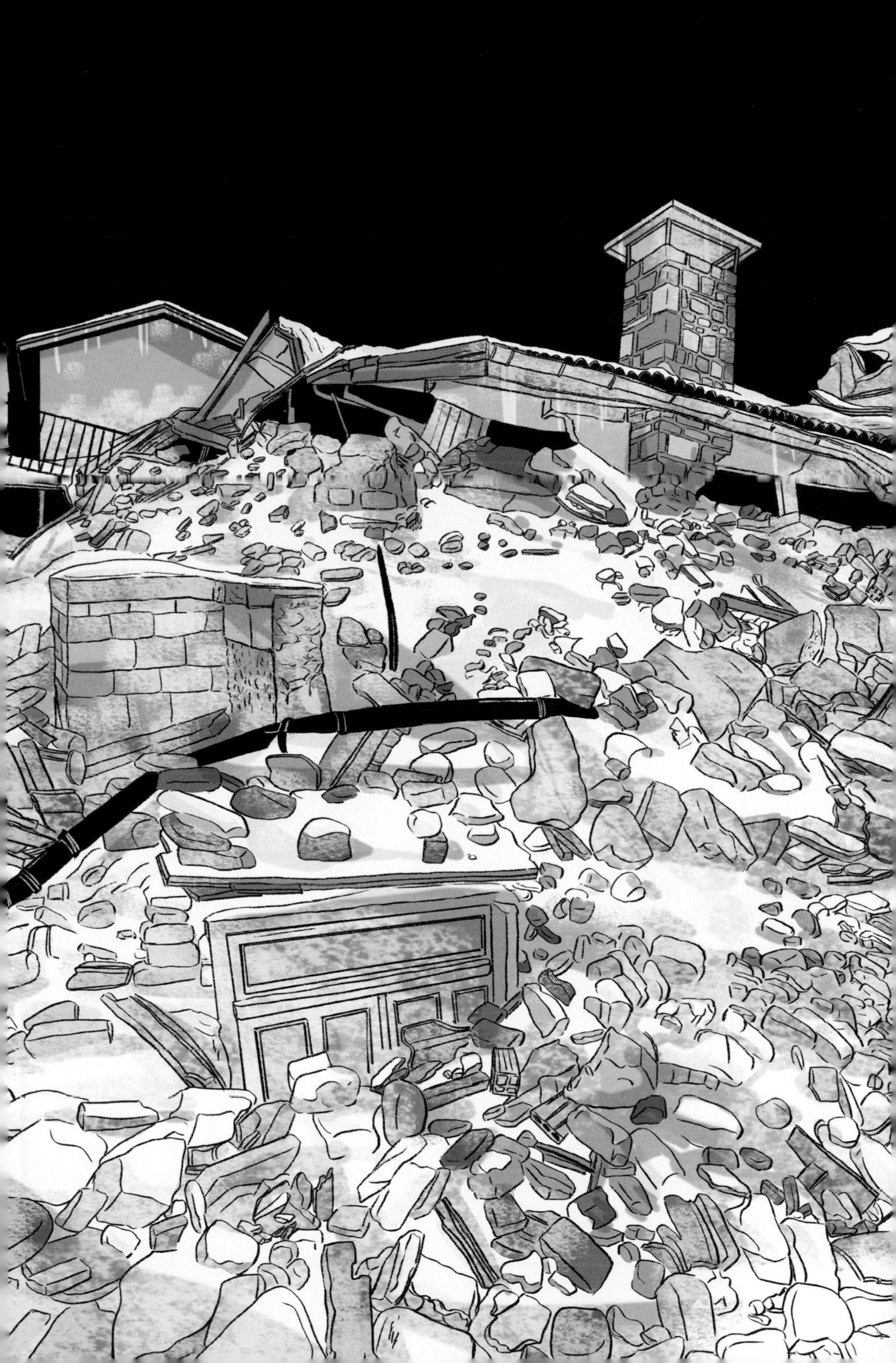

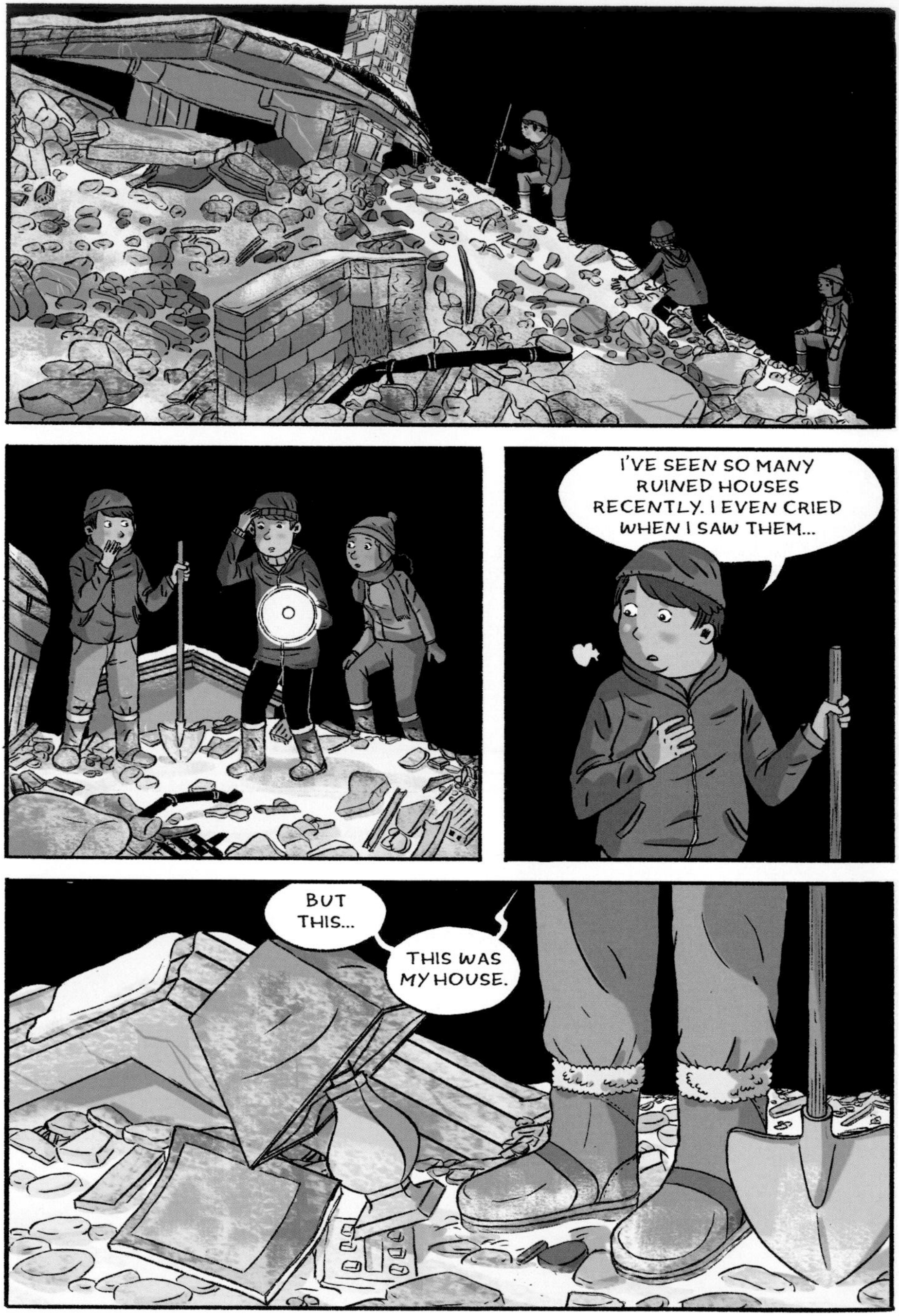
I'VE SEEN SO MANY RUINED HOUSES RECENTLY. I EVEN CRIED WHEN I SAW THEM...
BUT THIS...
THIS WAS MY HOUSE.

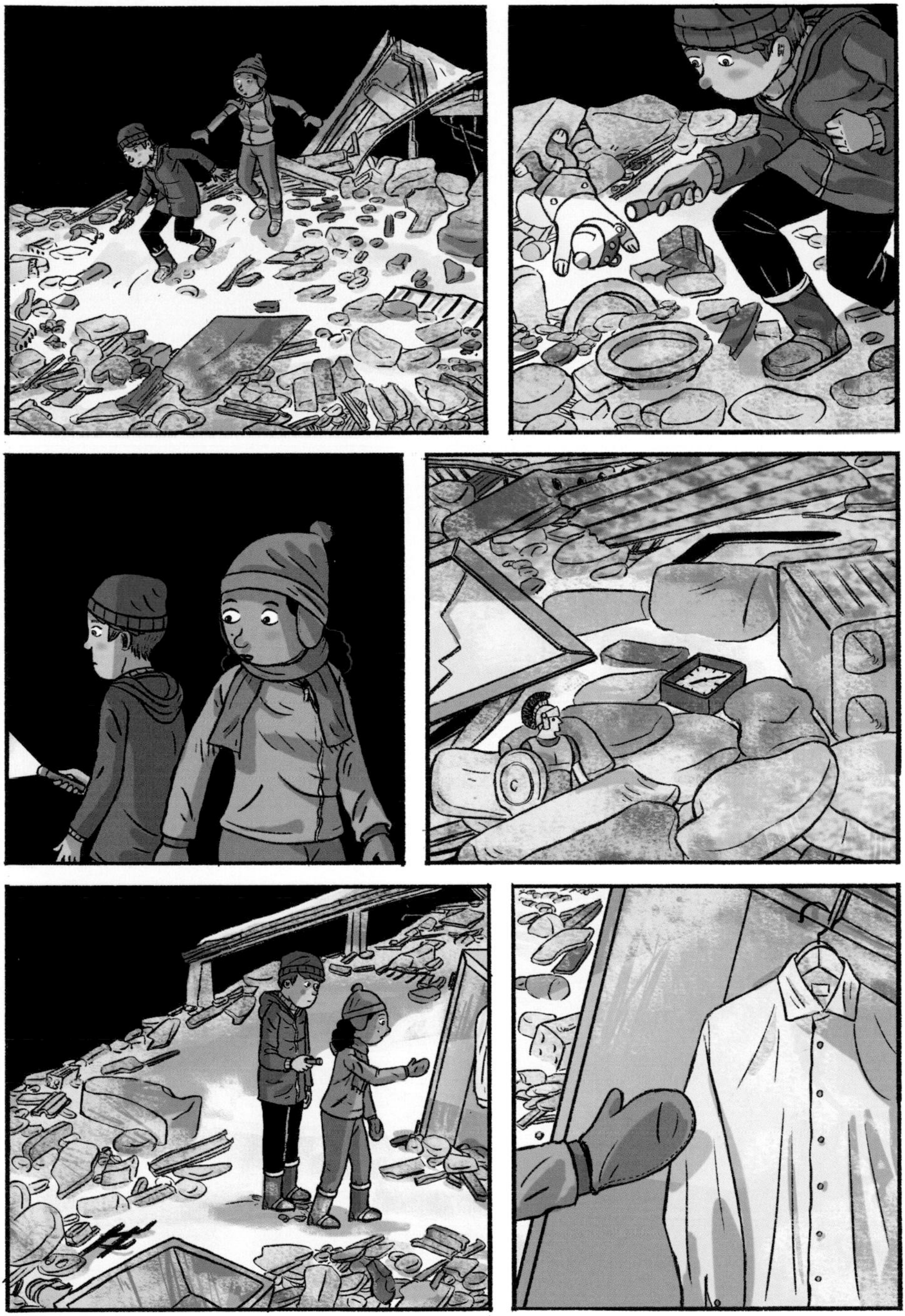

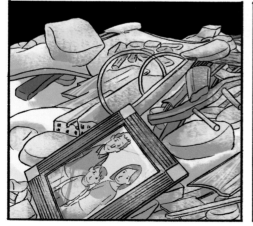

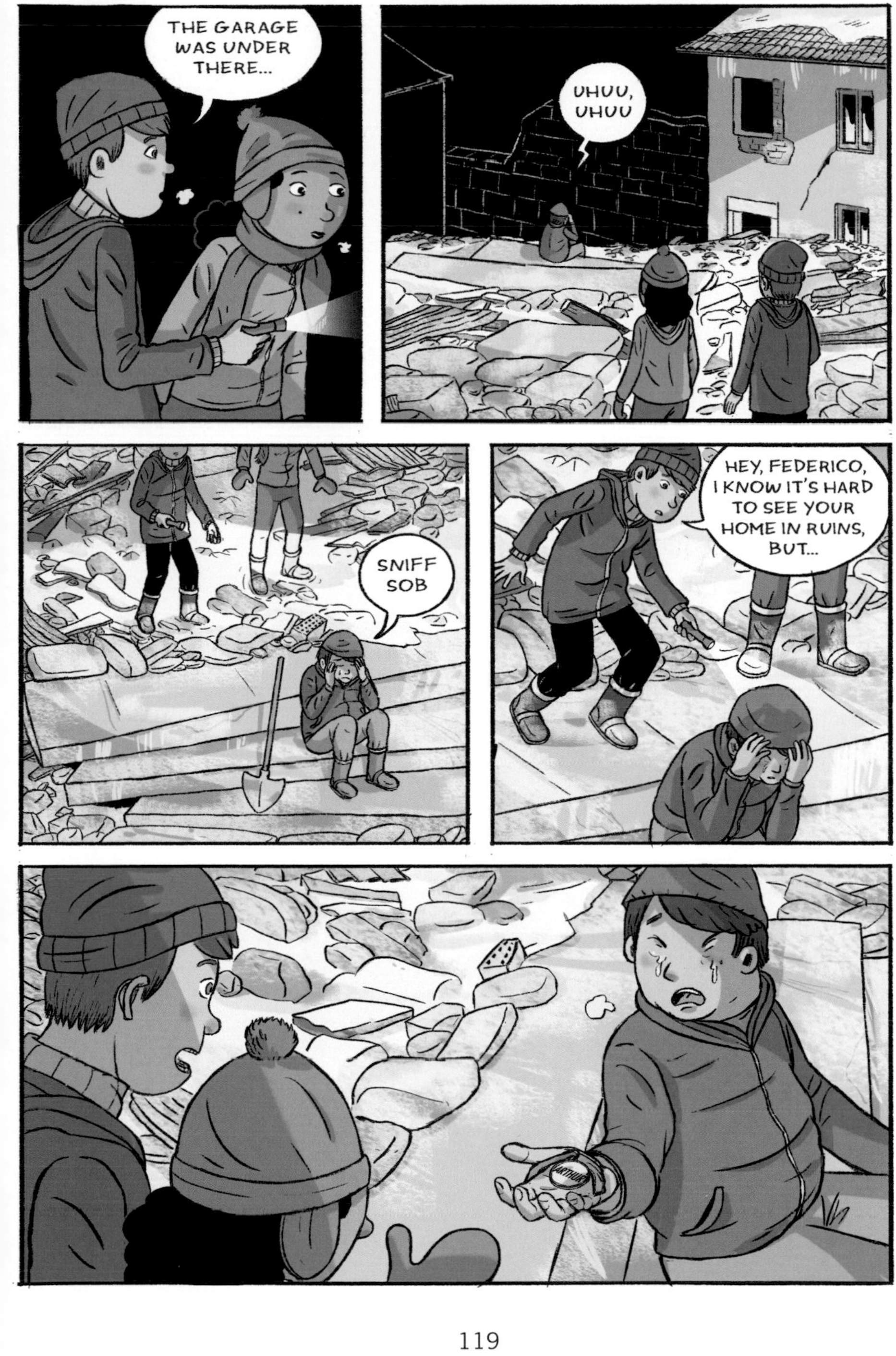
THE GARAGE WAS UNDER THERE...
UHUU, UHUU
SNIFF SOB
HEY, FEDERICO, I KNOW IT'S HARD TO SEE YOUR HOME IN RUINS, BUT...

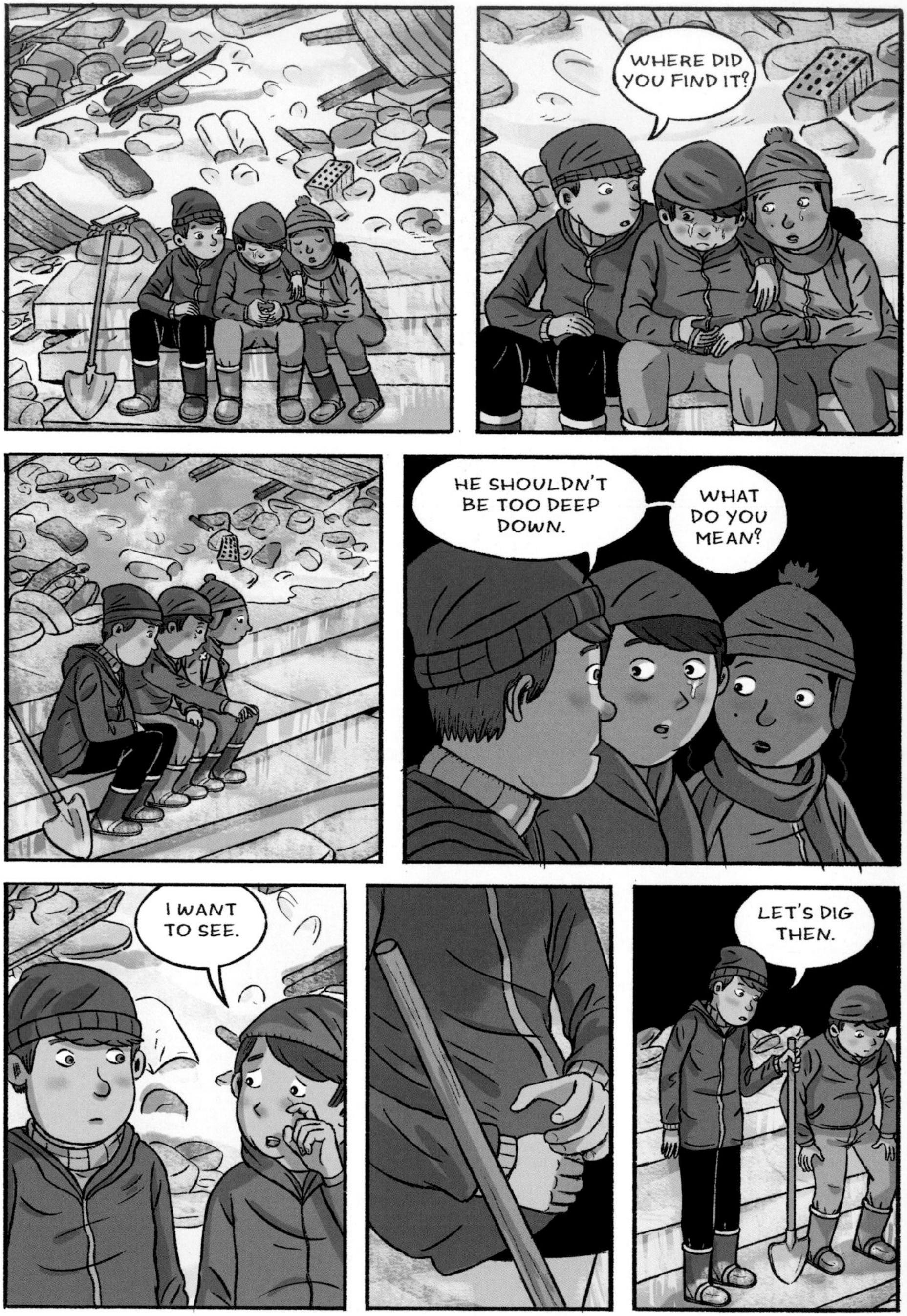
WHERE DID YOU FIND IT?
HE SHOULDN'T BE TOO DEEP DOWN.
WHAT DO YOU MEAN?
I WANT TO SEE.
LET'S DIG THEN.

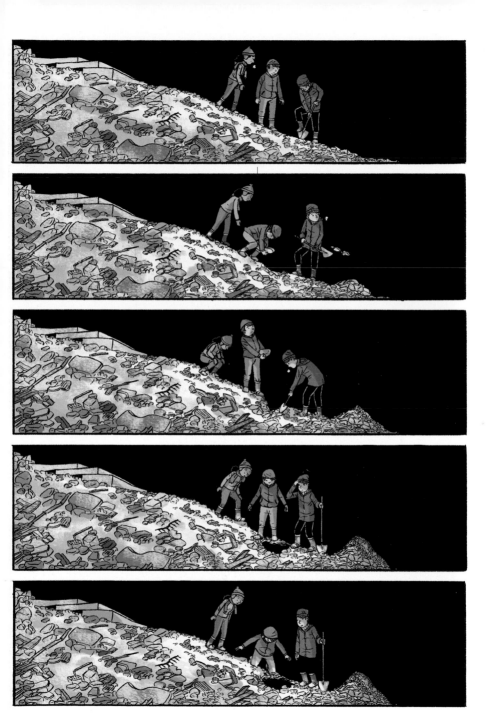

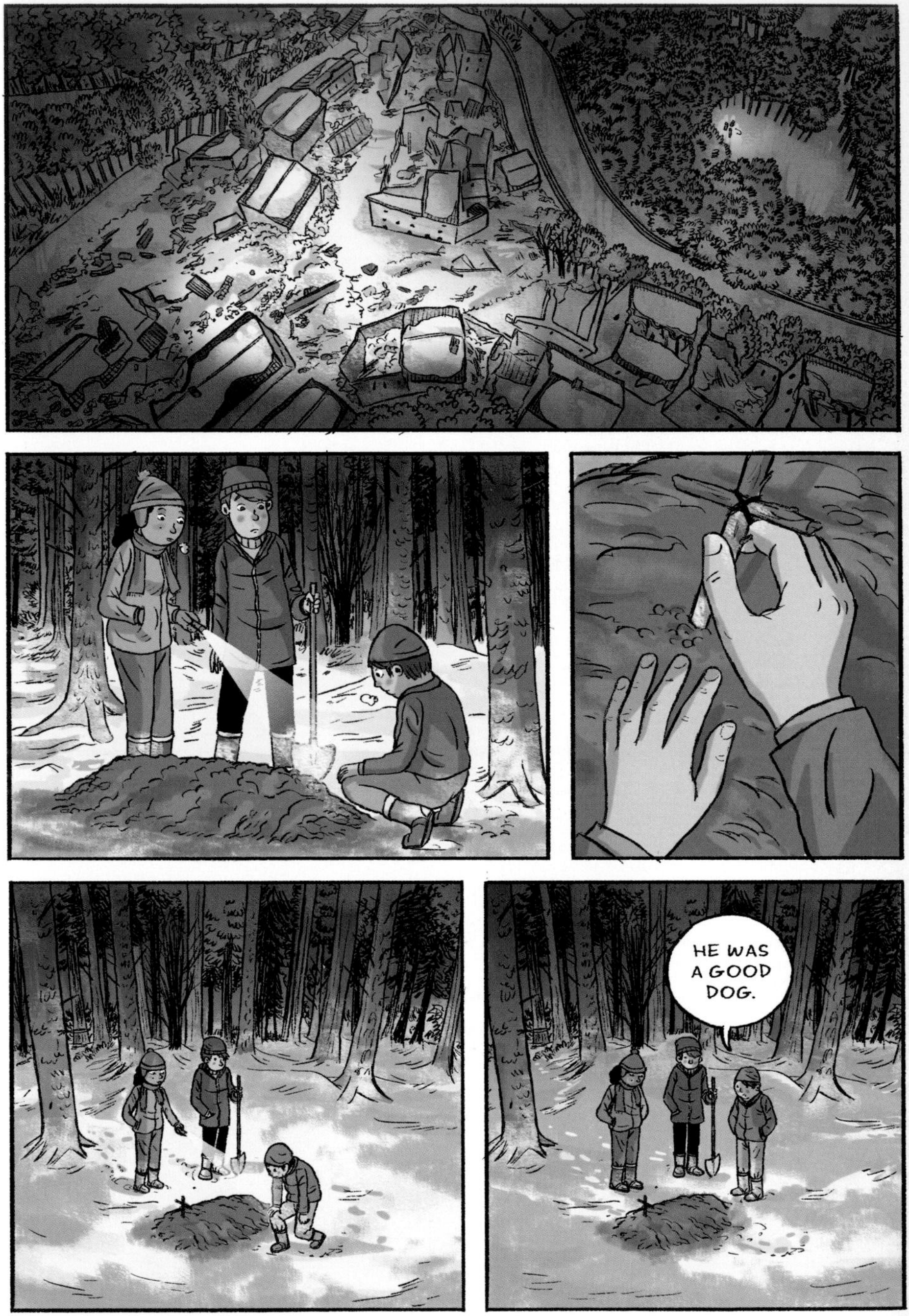
HE WAS A GOOD DOG.

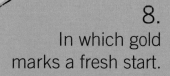

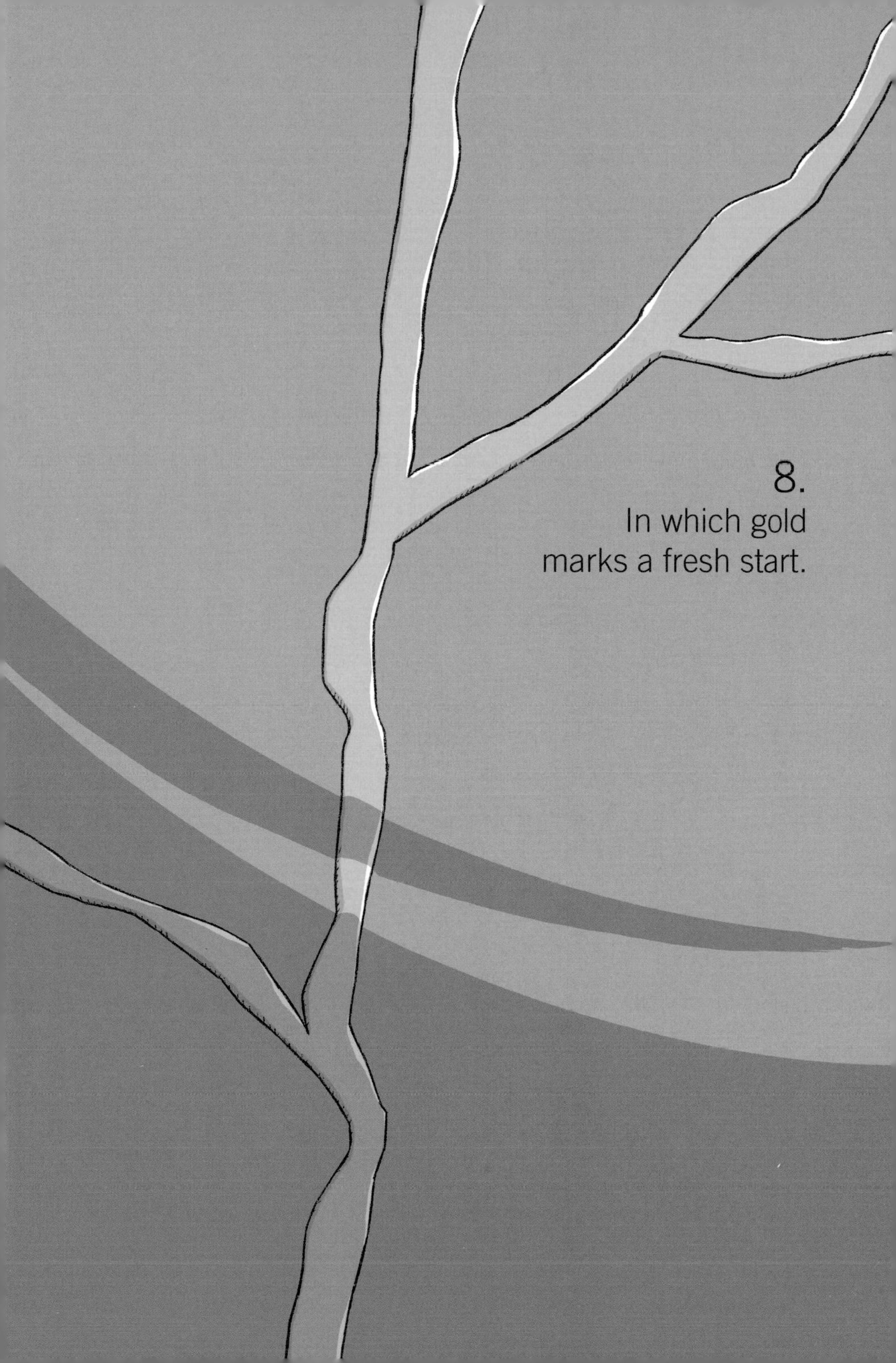

8.
In which gold
marks a fresh start.

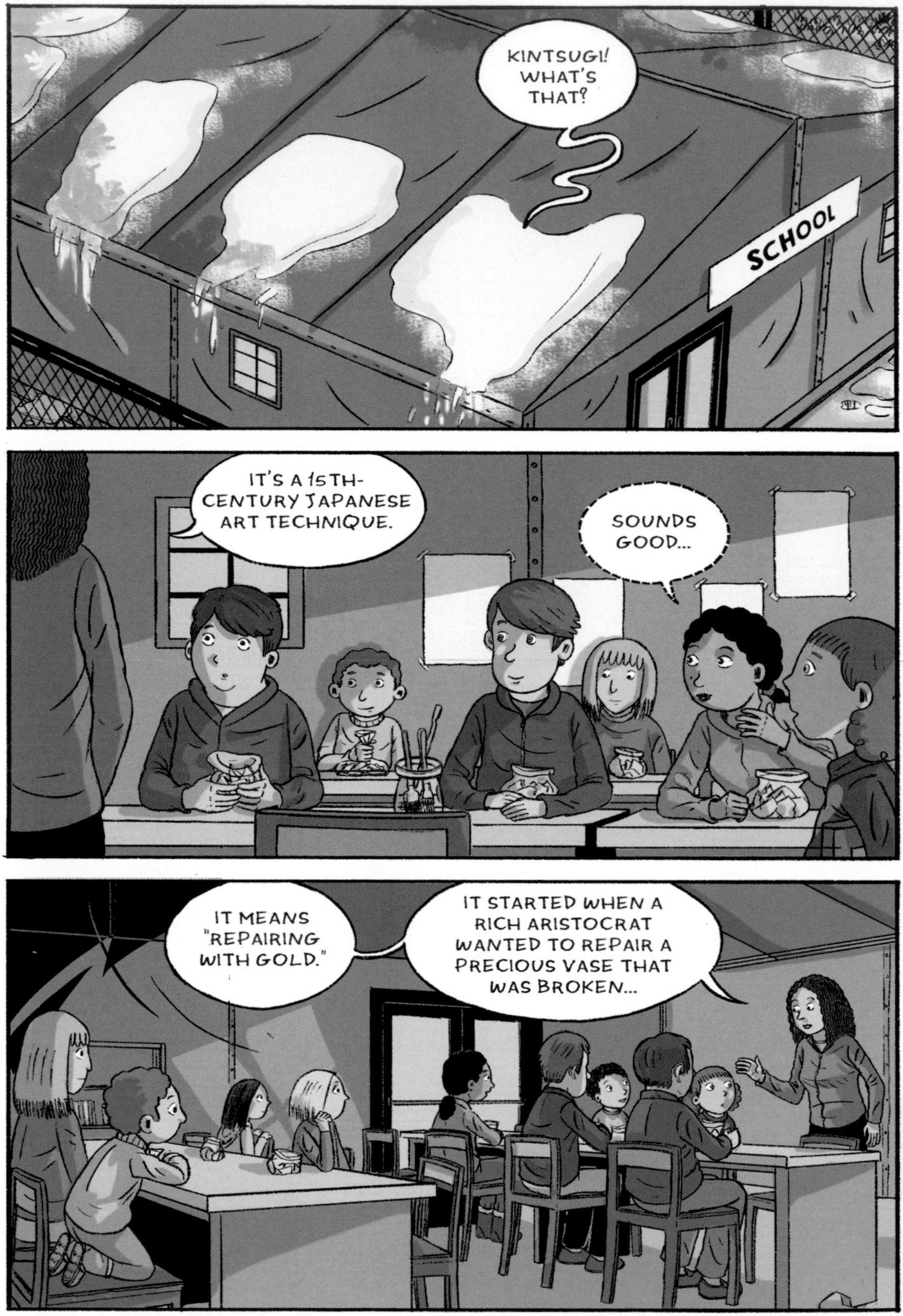
KINTSUGI! WHAT'S THAT?
SCHOOL
IT'S A 15TH-CENTURY JAPANESE ART TECHNIQUE.
SOUNDS GOOD...
IT MEANS "REPAIRING WITH GOLD."
IT STARTED WHEN A RICH ARISTOCRAT WANTED TO REPAIR A PRECIOUS VASE THAT WAS BROKEN...

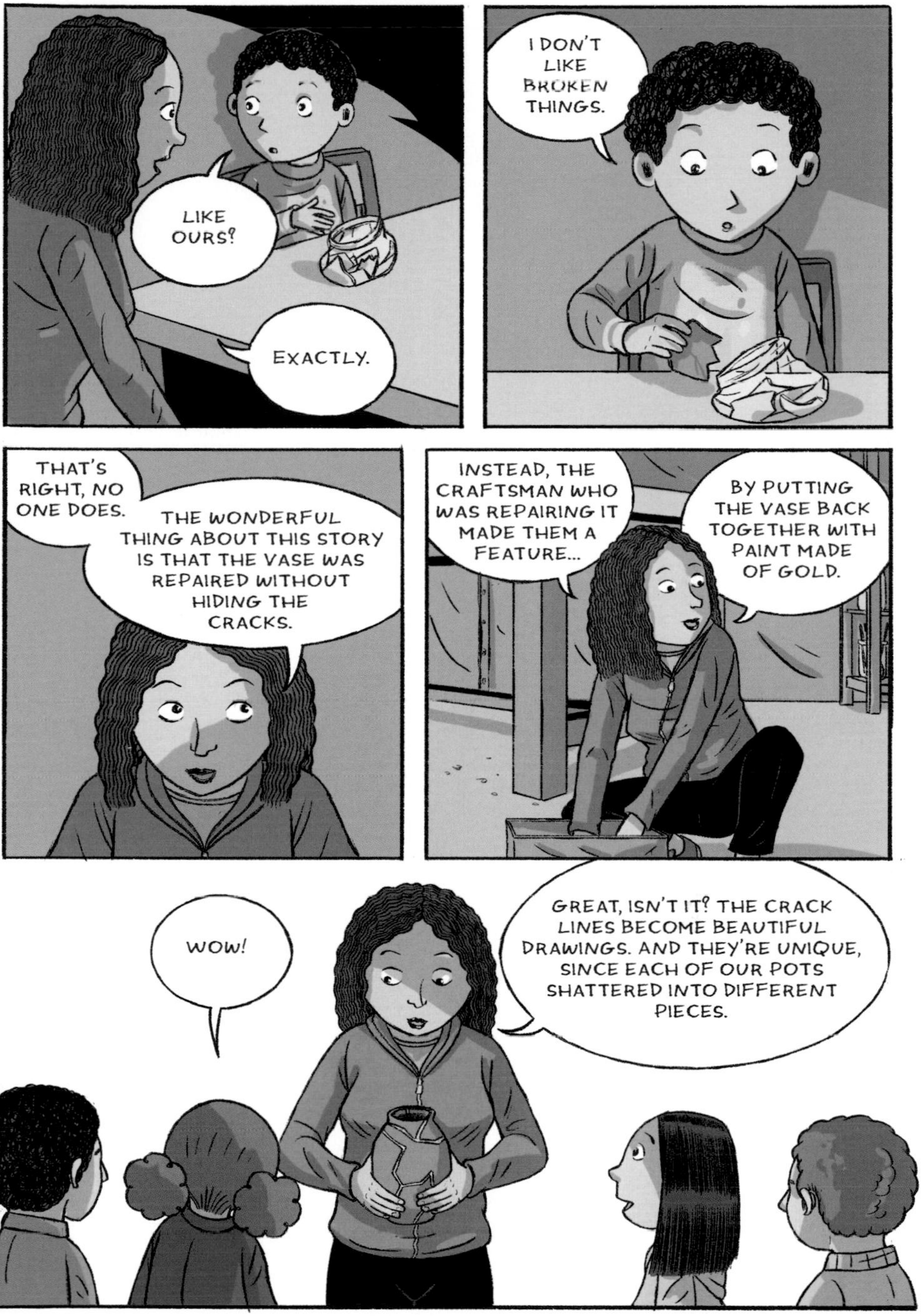

LIKE OURS?
EXACTLY.
I DON'T LIKE BROKEN THINGS.
THAT'S RIGHT, NO ONE DOES.
THE WONDERFUL THING ABOUT THIS STORY IS THAT THE VASE WAS REPAIRED WITHOUT HIDING THE CRACKS.
INSTEAD, THE CRAFTSMAN WHO WAS REPAIRING IT MADE THEM A FEATURE...
BY PUTTING THE VASE BACK TOGETHER WITH PAINT MADE OF GOLD.
WOW!
GREAT, ISN'T IT? THE CRACK LINES BECOME BEAUTIFUL DRAWINGS. AND THEY'RE UNIQUE, SINCE EACH OF OUR POTS SHATTERED INTO DIFFERENT PIECES.

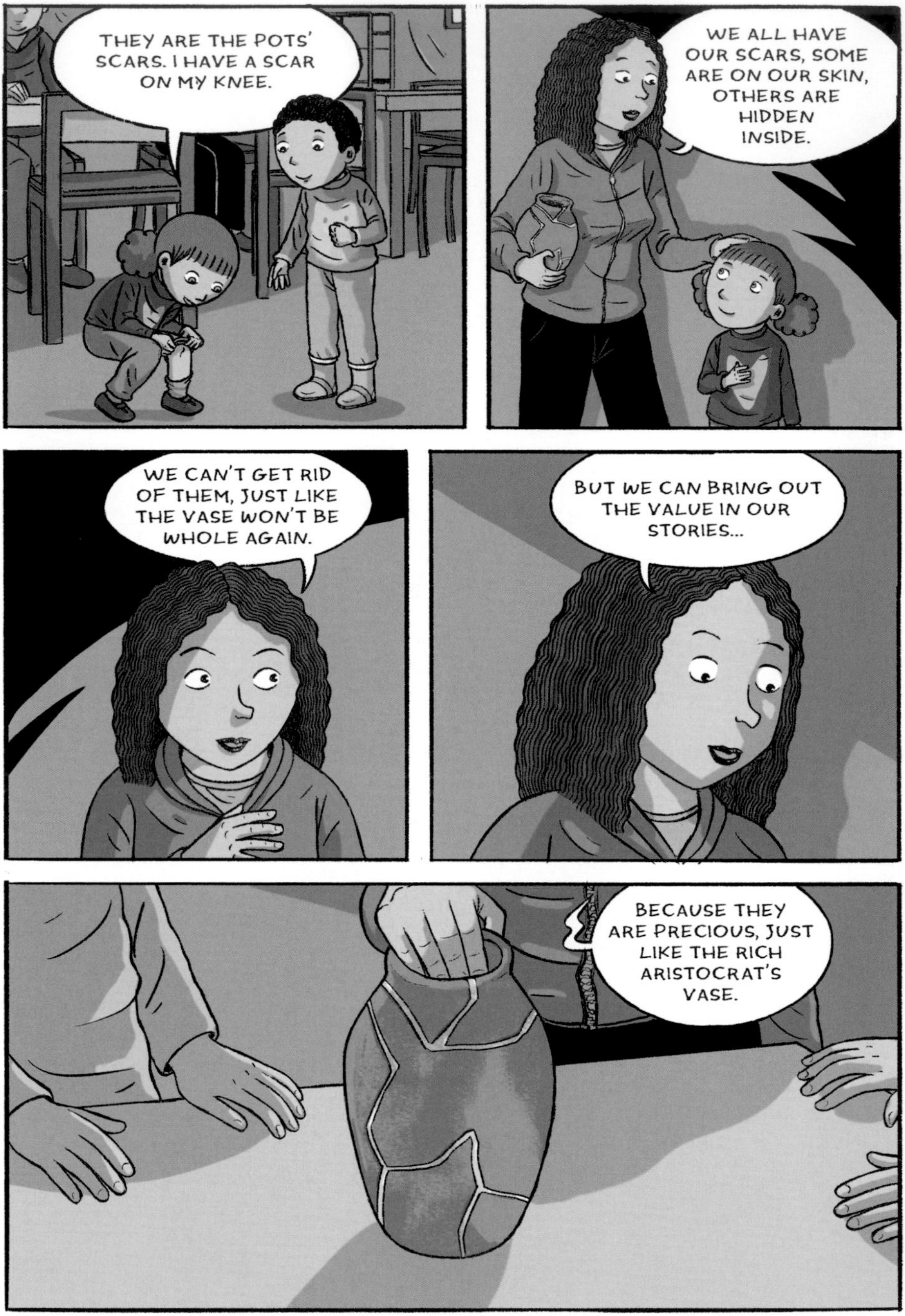
THEY ARE THE POTS' SCARS. I HAVE A SCAR ON MY KNEE.
WE ALL HAVE OUR SCARS, SOME ARE ON OUR SKIN, OTHERS ARE HIDDEN INSIDE.
WE CAN'T GET RID OF THEM, JUST LIKE THE VASE WON'T BE WHOLE AGAIN.
BUT WE CAN BRING OUT THE VALUE IN OUR STORIES...
BECAUSE THEY ARE PRECIOUS, JUST LIKE THE RICH ARISTOCRAT'S VASE.

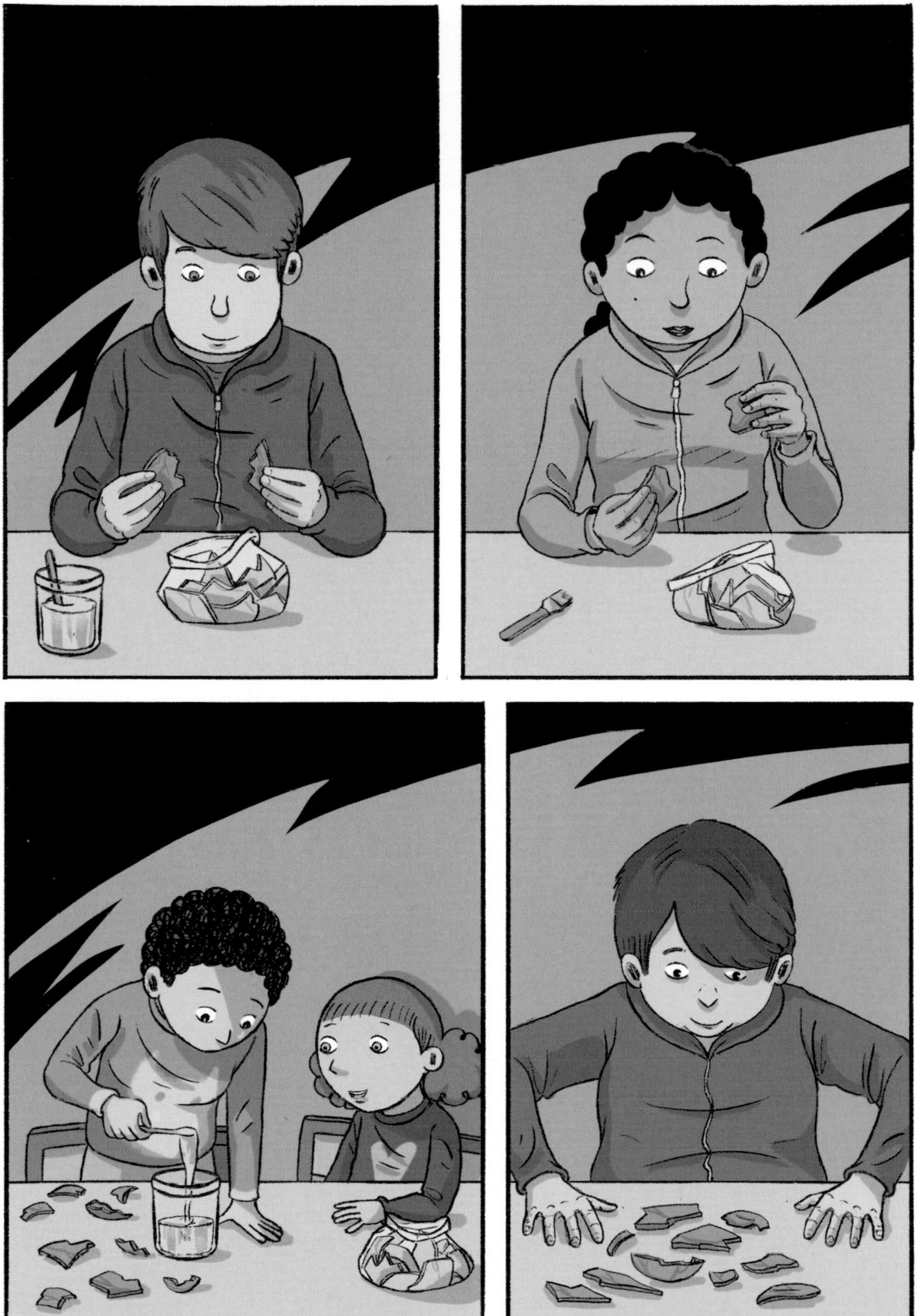

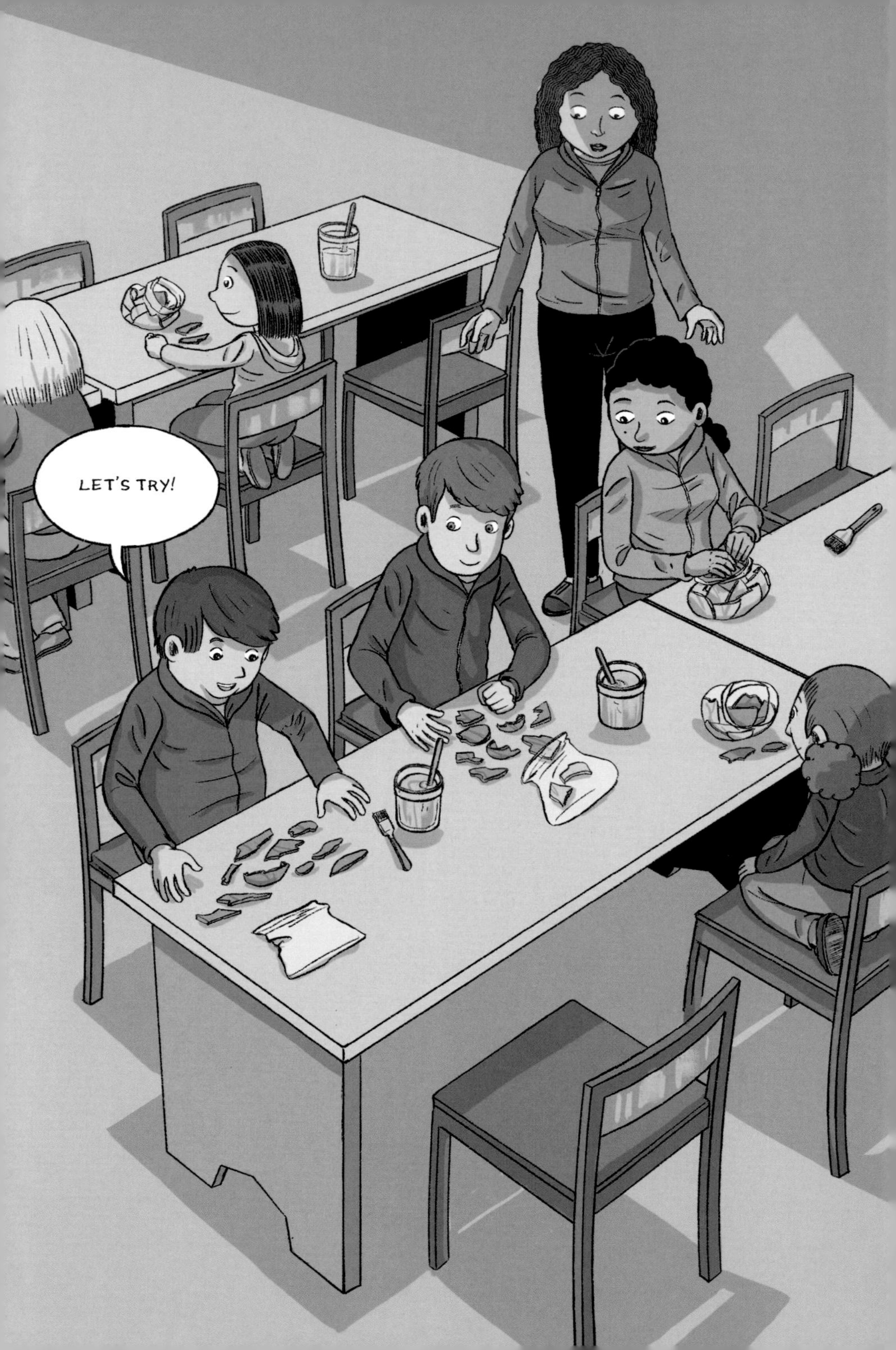
LET'S TRY!

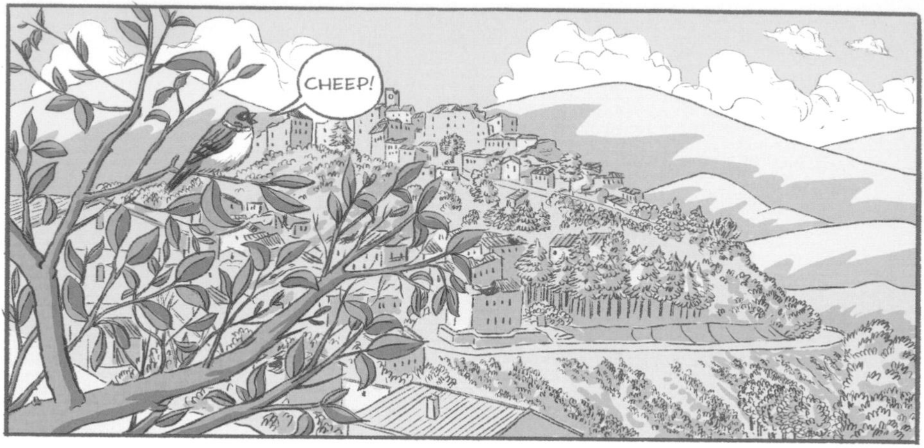
CHEEP!

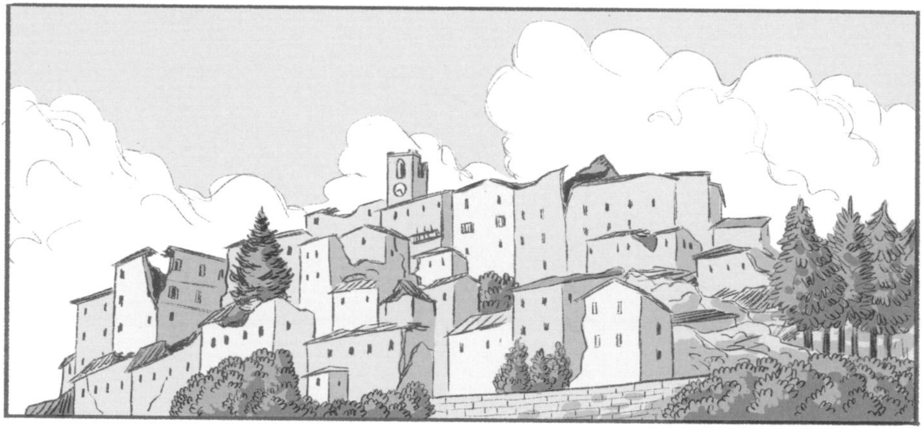

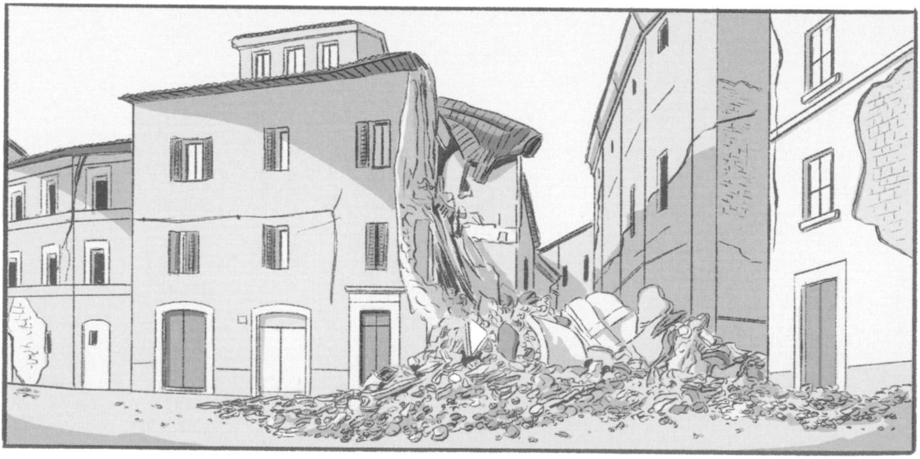

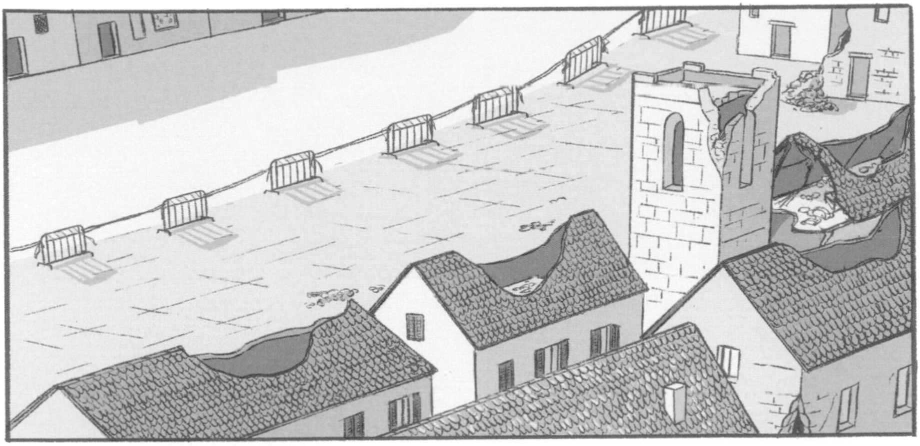

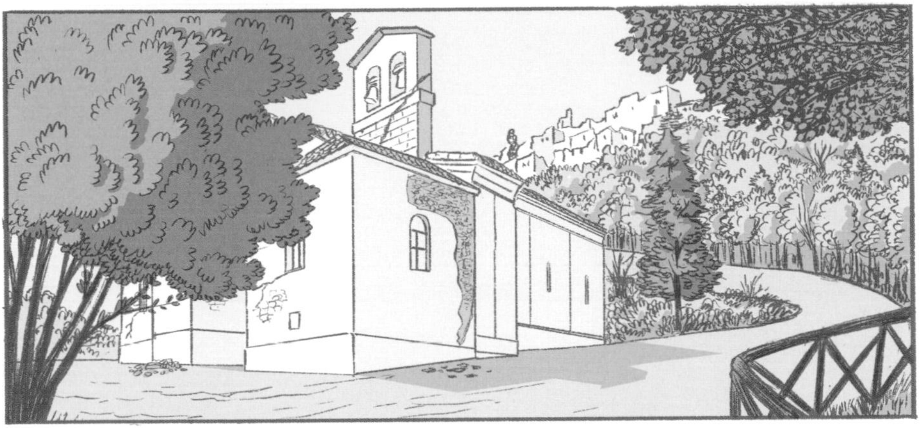

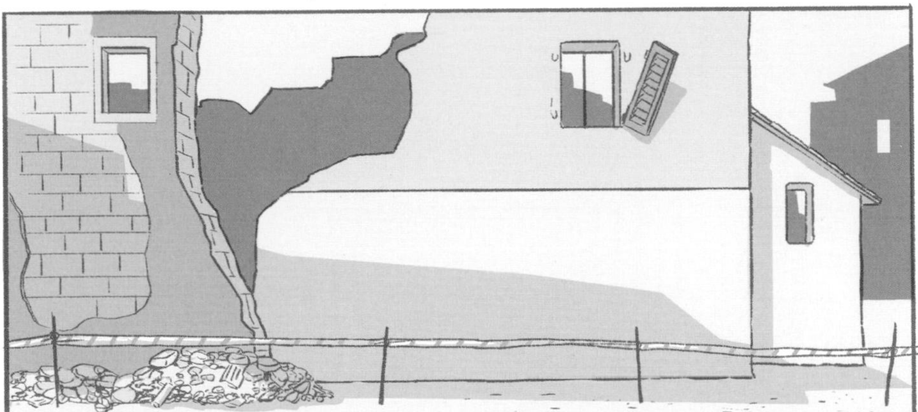

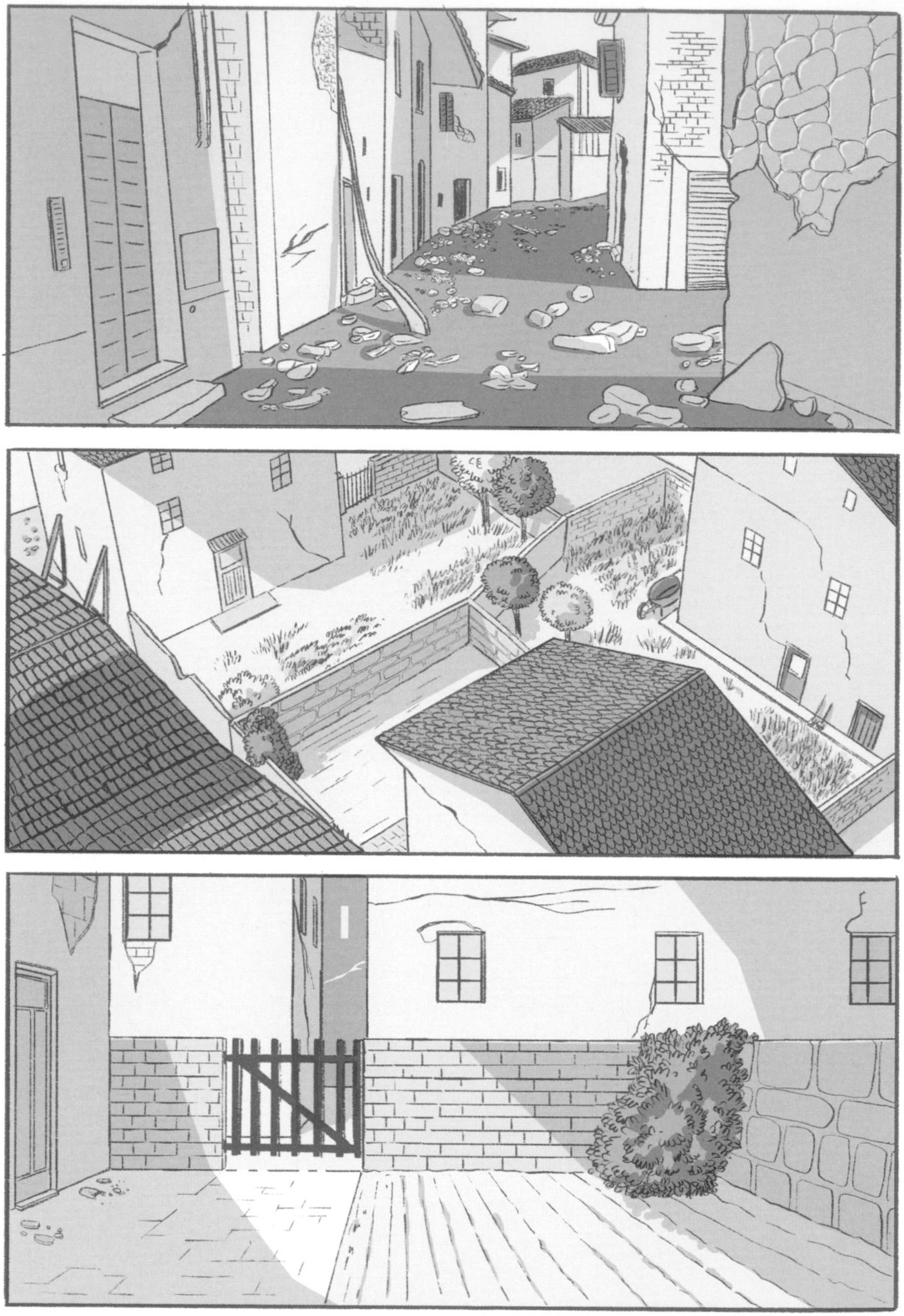

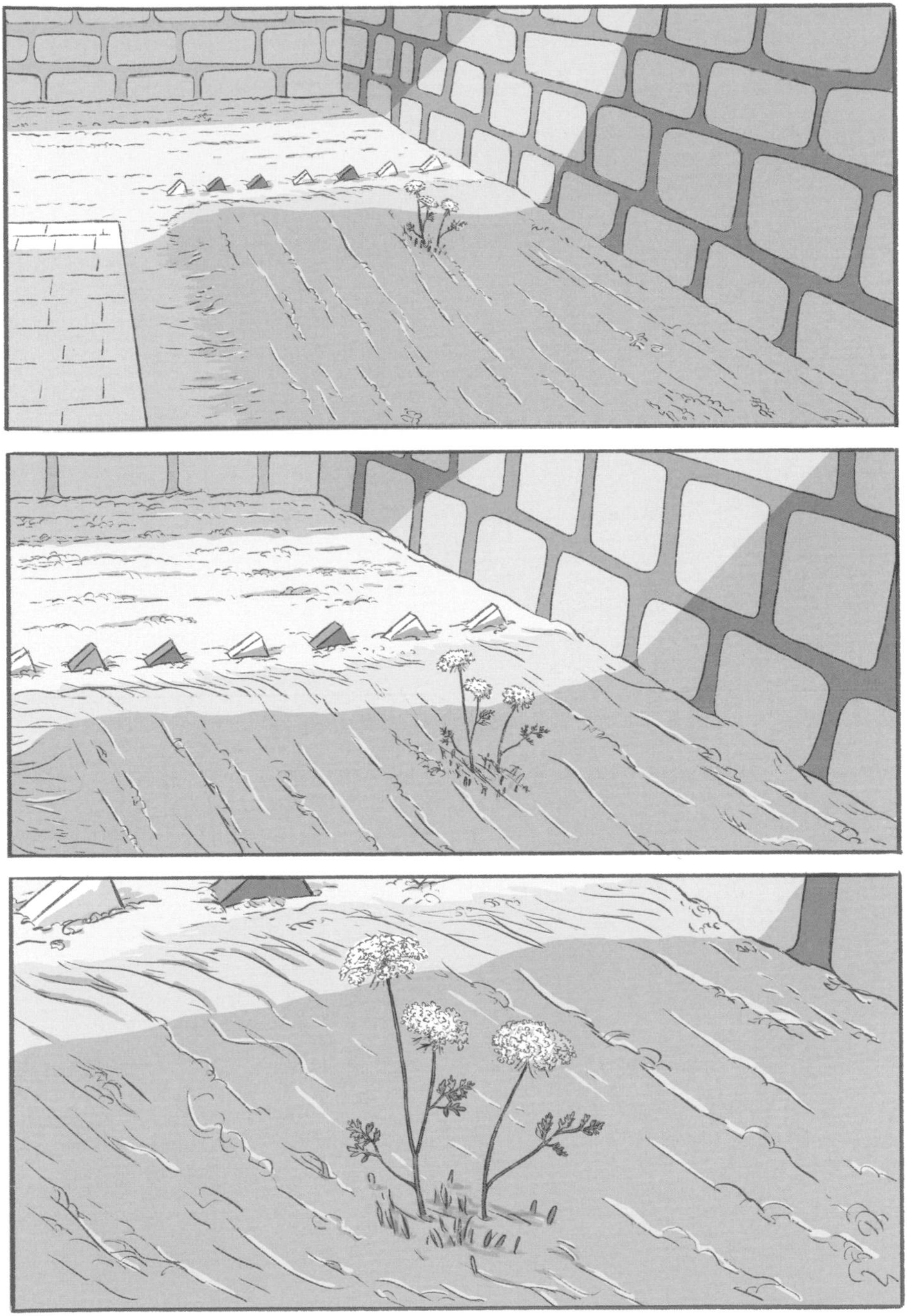

Dear reader,

The story you just read is very special to me. I wrote it after the earthquakes that hit the central regions of Italy in 2016. The village where I live wasn't affected by the earthquake, but we welcomed many evacuees from the regions that were devastated by the calamity. Overnight, hundreds of people—men, women, and children—found themselves homeless, jobless, or without a school, far away from the places where they lived and had friends. The earthquake was a violent change that ended the lives they knew and forced them to start again. After spending time with the survivors and getting to know them, I decided I wanted to tell their stories in a graphic novel. My goal was to create something that could help kids from all over the world who have had to face similar sudden and difficult changes. *The Red Zone* is a story that shows how easily the balance of our lives can be interrupted. However, we can help each other, we can stand up, and together we can rebuild our "red zone."

Silvia Vecchini
October 2018

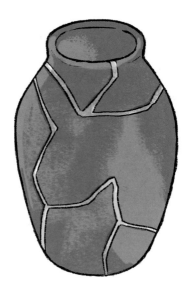

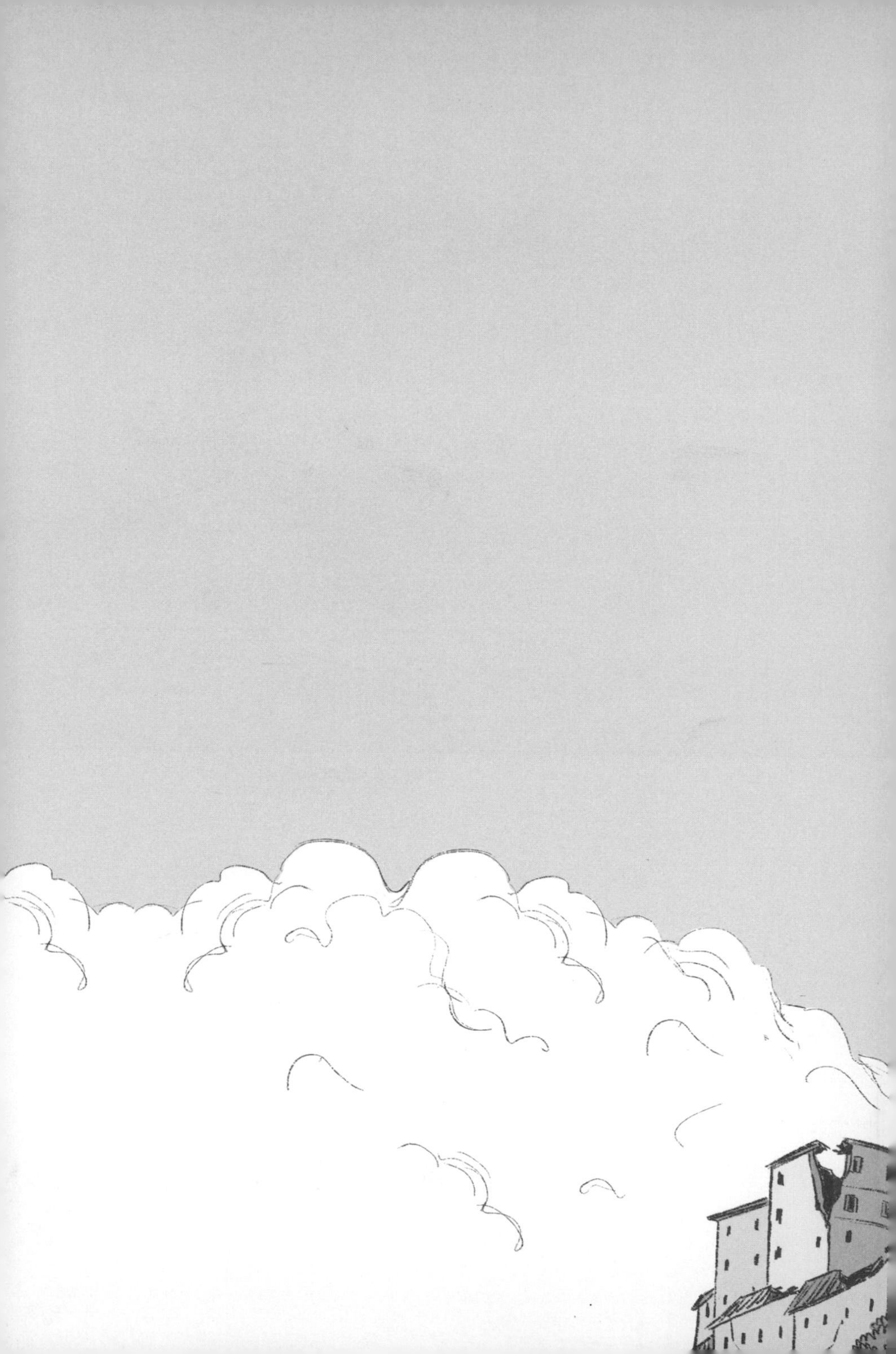